*A Saint City Novel*

*A Saint City Novel*

# LILITH SAINTCROW

www.lilithsaintcrow.com

# TABLE OF CONTENTS

# BROTHER'S KEEPER

# ONE

A SHRILL SCREAM jerked her out of the deep well of sleep.

Selene fumbled for the phone, pushed her hair back, pressed the talk button. "Mrph." She managed the trick of rolling over and blinking at the alarm clock. *Oh, God, what now?* "This had better be good."

"Lena?" A familiar voice wheezed into the other end of the phone. He gasped again. "Lena, it's me."

*Oh no. Not another panic attack.* "Danny?" Selene sat straight up, her heart pounding. "Danny, what's wrong? Are you okay?" Sweat began to prickle under her arms, the covers turned to strangling fingers before she realized she was awake.

"Cold," he whispered, breath coming in staccato gasps. "Selene. Help. *Help* you—"

Selene swung her feet to the cold floor, switching the phone to her right ear, trapping it on her shoulder. "Where are you? Danny? Talk to me." She grabbed her canvas bag the moment her feet hit the floor, craning her neck to read the Ident display. *Daniel Thompson*, his familiar number. He was at home.

*Where else would he be?* Danny hadn't left his apartment for nearly five years. "Keep breathing. Deep breaths, down into your tummy. I'll be right there."

"No," Danny pleaded. His asthmatic wheeze was getting worse. "Cold...*Lena*. Don't. Danger—" The line went dead.

Selene slammed the phone back into the cradle, her breath hissing in. Her fingers tingled—a sure sign of something awful. *What was I dreaming? Something about the sea, again.* She raced for the bathroom, grabbing a handful of clothes from the dirty-laundry hamper by the door. *Just keep breathing, Danny. Don't let the panic get too big for you. I'm on my way.* She tripped, nearly fell face-first, banging her forehead on the door. "Shit!"

She yanked her jeans up with one hand and turned on the faucet with the other, splashed her face with cold water. Tossed her thick blonde mane into a sloppy ponytail and raced for the door, ripping her sweater at the neck as she forced it over her head. She had to hop on one foot to yank her socks on, she jammed her feet into her boots and flung her bag over her head, catching the strap in her hair. *Just keep him calm enough to remember not to hurt himself, God. Please.*

She slowed down at the end of her block, searching for a cab. *One down, nine to go.* Rain kissed her cheeks and made the sidewalk slick and slightly gritty under the orange wash of city light as she sprinted across the street. Deep heaving gasps of chill air made her lungs burn.

Selene crossed Cliff Street, slowing down, pacing herself. *Can't run myself out on the first blocks or I'll be useless before I get halfway there. If this is another one of his practical jokes I am just going to* kill *him.*

It wouldn't be, though. It was far more likely he'd been injured while out of his body—or he was having trouble staying *in* his body even inside the wards she'd built for him.

*Three down, seven to go.* Selene's boots pounded the sidewalk. Rain whispered on the deserted streets and along the length of her messy ponytail, dripped down her neck as she reached Martin Street and cut across the intersection. There were more streetlamps here, she checked her watch as she ran.

Two-thirty. Santiago City held its breath under the mantle of chill night.

The back of Selene's neck prickled, uneasiness rippling just under her skin.

*Why can't these things happen in the daylight? Or when I don't have lecture in the morning? This had better be something good, Danny, I swear to God if you're just throwing another snit-fit I will* never *forgive you. Never, ever, ever.*

Something chill and panicked began to revolve under her breastbone. *Getting a premonition.* Her breath came in miserable harsh sobs of effort. *Either that or I'm just spooked. Who wouldn't be at two AM in this busted-down part of town?* She set her teeth, grimly ignoring the stitch in her side. *Danny. Just breathe, please God, let him remember to breathe. Don't let him be in the kitchen, there's knives in there. This sounds like a doozy, he hasn't had a bad panic attack in at least six months, Christ don't let him hurt himself.* Sometimes pain was all he could use to nail himself into his flesh, and—

"Hey, Selene."

Selene whirled. "Bruce!" she choked, her hand leaping instinctively to her throat. The silver medallion was still under her sweater, warm against her skin. She hadn't taken it off. "Good God, don't *do* that!" She clenched her hands at her side. *If only he was human, I could punch him.*

Bruce grinned down at her, canines glittering in the pallid orange light, his eyes glowing just like a small nocturnal animal's. Beneath his loud polyester sport jacket and eye-searing yellow tie, his narrow spotted chest was pale and hairless. "Don't worry so much, Lena. I wouldn't *dream* of taking a taste. His Highness wouldn't like that one little bit." His lips curled back even more, exposing more gleaming teeth.

Selene's heart slammed once against her ribs. Taking a long deep breath, she willed her pulse to slow. *Focus, goddammit! Danny needs you, you can't fight if you're busy screaming.*

"I don't have time for your bullshit, Bruce. Danny's in trouble."

"I'll go with you." Bruce shrugged and peeled his lanky frame away from the streetlamp. He'd just been Turned, and still looked almost human.

Almost. The feral glow in his eyes and the quick jerking of his movements screamed "not-quite-normal."

Still, for a Nichtvren, Bruce was as close to human as possible. He didn't have the scary immobility of older suckheads. Small blessing, but she'd take it. "That's not necessary—" she began.

Bruce folded his arms, the smile gone. "Danny's under Nikolai's protection too, Selene. And if I let you go over there and get hurt, His Highness will peel off my skin in strips and salt me down." Bruce shivered, his long pink tongue wetting his lips. "Trust me. I'll go with you."

"Oh, for Christ's sweet sake." Selene wasn't about to argue with an undead sucklizard. He fell into step beside her, long legs easily keeping pace as she trotted up the sidewalk. She glanced down. Black loafers and no socks. *All you're missing is a clutch of gold chains and chest hair.* "I don't know what Nikolai's thinking." She sped up. "I'm perfectly safe."

Bruce managed a high thin giggle. "Oh, no you're not, chickadee. You should be glad His Highness took an interest in you." He didn't even sound winded.

*I don't need Nikolai's protection. I did just fine on my own.*

Okay, so she didn't *want* Nikolai's protection. She'd rather tap dance naked through a minefield singing *Petticoat Junction.* Just because Nikolai was the prime paranormal Power in the city, responsible for keeping the peace among all the other factions of paranormal citizenry, didn't mean anything, right? His Highness Nikolai indeed. Just another suckhead come out from the shadows under the protection of the Paranormal Species Act.

Only this one had an interest in her. A deep, abiding, and *personal* interest. A not-entirely-unpleasant shiver traced down Selene's back.

*Danny, please be okay. Don't bite your tongue or cut yourself.*

Her bag shifted, clinking when it banged against her shoulder. Steel and salt, the tools she needed to banish anything evil or unwanted; it didn't pay as well as teaching but God knew there was a need for her Talents. She'd been so tired when she got home she hadn't unpacked, poltergeist infestations were like that. Not very difficult, but messy and draining. She pushed the strap higher. "I don't need his...protection or...yours, suckhead."

"That's what *you* think." Bruce grinned down at her, his words soft and even. "Want me to carry your bag?"

"Of...course...not." Selene broke into a jog again. *To hell with pacing myself. Danny needs me.*

The medallion warmed against her skin, reacting to Bruce's presence—at least, she *hoped* that was what it was reacting to. By the time they reached Danny's building, the metal thrummed with Power. Gooseflesh raced down her body; she choked back a final gasp as she rounded the final corner and saw the slim, tall black shape in front of the doors.

Bruce smirked, letting out a soft little snort of laughter. Selene curled her hands into fists, resisting the urge to claw the smile from his face. *Jumping the Nichtvren won't get you anywhere, Selene. Just ignore him, and concentrate on what matters. Danny, my God, please be okay. Remember the visualizations I taught you.*

The tall black-clad shape half-turned, halfway up the concrete steps. *Oh, no. Could this possibly get any worse?*

Of course not. Of course Nikolai would show up now. He always seemed to know when there was trouble.

Bruce dropped back. *At least I won't have to see that fucking smirk on his face. Danny, please be okay, don't be banging your head on the wall again. I'm on my way, I'm almost there.*

Her heart slammed once against the cage of her ribs and her fingers curled into fists. Heat flamed in her cheeks, spread down her neck, and merged with the growing heat of the medallion between her breasts. She fought for control, ribs flaring as she struggled against hyperventilation.

Hands in his coat pockets, chin tilted toward her, Nikolai's dark eyes catalogued her tangled blonde hair, camel coat, scuffed boots. Her fingers itched to straighten her clothes, brush back her hair, check for loose threads. As usual, he was so contained she longed to see him roughed up a little.

*I suppose you learn a little self-control when you're a Master powerful enough to rule Saint City. He's the Prime, after all. We all live our little lives in his long dark shadow.*

A few strands of crow-black hair fell over his eyes as Selene, impelled by the medallion's growing heat and the pull of Nikolai's eyes, skidded to a stop inches from him. Her ponytail swung heavily, but he didn't reach out to grab her arm and "protect" her from falling headlong on the steps. Her heart actually *leapt*, to see him again.

*He's not human, you know that, stop STARING at him!*

Nikolai said nothing, the light stroking his high cheekbones. His mouth, usually curled into a half-smile, was compressed into a thin line. His dark, electric eyes flicked over Bruce, who cringed another three steps back.

13

Selene suppressed a burst of nasty satisfaction. *Serves you right.* She started up the stairs, pressing her left hand against the sudden stitch gripping her side. Her toe caught on the second step.

She fetched up short when Nikolai closed his hand around her left arm, steadied her before she could fall over, and let her go, all in the space of a moment. "Selene." The chill rain-soaked air shivered under the word, his voice soft and irresistible. At least he didn't have the scary gold-green sheen on his eyes tonight, Selene hated that. "Stirling."

"I was on watch." Bruce didn't sound half so smug now. Of course, he was an accident, Turned as a joke or mistake; Nichtvren didn't Turn ugly humans. It was an unwritten rule: only the pretty or the ruthless were given the gift of immortality, and Bruce was neither. Why Nikolai kept him around was anyone's guess, and Selene didn't want to ask. Bruce's doglike attachment and gratefulness for any crumb Nikolai threw his way was telling enough.

Besides, if she asked she had a sneaking suspicion Bruce might answer, and she wouldn't like the answer at all. Not to mention what she might have to pay for it.

*Story of my life. Always calculating what it'll cost me to know something. Danny, please be okay.*

Selene brushed past Nikolai. Her boots smacked against cold, wet concrete. She reached the glassed-in front door and stopped short, digging in her coat pocket for her keys. *So Nikolai's having me watched. Good to know.*

Her fingers rooted fruitlessly around in her pocket and found nothing but an empty gum wrapper. "Oh, no." Her keys were on the table by the door at her apartment, she had *not* scooped them up on her way out. Just run right past them in her frantic dash. "Bloody *fucking* hell on a cheese-coated *stick.*"

"You need to go in?" Nikolai's breath brushed her cheek, the faint smell of aftershave and male closing around her. He was *right* behind her, so far into her personal space it wasn't even funny.

Her violent start nearly toppled her into the firmly shut door. She hadn't heard or *sensed* him, he'd just appeared out of thin air. *Dammit, does he have to do that all the time?* The only place she could escape was through the glass itself. Selene stared at the door, taking in deep harsh breaths and willing it to open. There was a quick, light patter of footsteps—Bruce, making off into the night. "I left my keys at home. Danny called. I think it's a panic attack, and when he gets them he sometimes hurts himself. There's an intercom—"

Nikolai reached around her, his body molded to hers, and touched the lock. The gold and carnelian signet ring gleamed wetly in the uncertain light as his pale fingers brushed the metal. He went absolutely still. The medallion's metal cooled abruptly between Selene's breasts, responding to the controlled flare of energy. She could almost See what he was doing, despite the stealthy camouflage of a Master Nichtvren's aura. The only thing scarier than their power was their creepy invisibility.

*I really wish he'd quit crowding me.* Her worry returned, sharp and acrid. Her lungs burned, the stitch knotting her left side again. *Please, Danny. Please be okay. I don't even care anymore if it's one of your midnight games, I hope you're all right.*

The lock clicked open with a muffled *thunk* and Selene grabbed the handle before it could close again. Nikolai's hand brushed hers, slid over the handle, and he stepped aside and pulled the door open. She yanked her hand away, her skin burning from the brief touch. *He did that on purpose.*

"Thanks," she managed around the dry lump in her throat. *Stop it,* she thought desperately, biting the inside of her cheek. The pain helped her focus. *It's only Nikolai. You know what he is, and why he's doing this. You're here for Danny, remember?*

"My pleasure." His eyes dropped to the medallion safely hidden under her sweater. The metal flushed with icy heat now.

*He's looking at my chest like he sees dinner there.* Heat sizzled along Selene's nerves. "Oh, stop that." She stepped through the door, sliding past him, suddenly grateful for someone else's presence. Her heart hammered thinly, the taste of burning in her mouth. *Danny. Just remember to breathe, kiddo. Little sister's almost there to take care of you.* "I suppose Bruce called you. And that you want to come up."

"Of course." His voice stroked her cheek, slid down her neck. He leaned back against the open door, his dark eyes now fixed on her face. Selene gulped down another breath, her heartbeat evening out. The familiar bank of mailbox doors was on her right, and the peeling linoleum floor glared back at the dirty ceiling. "It is pleasant to see you, Selene."

Nikolai cat-stepped into the foyer, gracefully avoiding the closing door. Little droplets of rain glittered in his hair, sparked by the fluorescent lights. Under his coat, he wore a dark-blue silk T-shirt and a pair of designer jeans. The shirt moved slightly as muscle tensed underneath.

Selene dropped her eyes, turned away from him. Oddly enough, he wore a high-end pair of black Nikos trainers. *Vampire fashion just ain't what it used to be. Where's the fangs and the black cape, not to mention the evening wear?* Her heart sped up, thundered in her ears. *God love me, I'm going to have a fucking cardiac arrest right here in the foyer.*

"Well, come on, then." She started up the orange-carpeted stairs, sidling away from him. Nikolai followed closely behind, but not too close, letting Selene take the lead. For once.

*Given how he's always going on about how I need "protecting," it's a wonder he's letting me in the building at all. But dammit, if he showed up at the door he'd just scare Danny more. He's being tactful for once. Lucky me.*

Her legs trembled and she rubbed at her eyes as she trooped up the stairs. Nikolai made no sound. "Would you make a little noise?" She immediately regretted asking. The silence behind her intensified. "God. I just hope he's okay." *He will be, it's probably nothing. He just stayed out of his body for too long and had trouble when he came back, another panic attack and the numbness. He's okay. Be okay, Danny, please?*

Nikolai's footsteps echoed as he climbed behind her. That was a relief, but Selene still felt the weight of his black eyes as they reached the fourth floor. Her thighs and ass burned. Climbing stairs after almost-running ten blocks without rest was a workout she could do without.

Nikolai's arm came over her shoulder again and held the heavy fire door open. The hall was dingy, most of the light fixtures missing bulbs, and a drift of fast food wrappers curled up at the far end. Selene's nose dripped from the chill. She rubbed at it with the back of her hand, tried not to sniff too loudly. Threadbare orange carpet whispered under her boots. The entire hall was so familiar she barely paid any attention. Down the hall a wedge of light speared through the gloom.

Danny's door was open.

# TWO

LONG JAGGED SPLINTERS popped out from the frame, the door broken into pieces loosely hanging from hinges. Lighter, unpainted wood peered through ragged vertical cracks. *Oh, Jesus. Oh no.*

"*Danny!*" Selene leapt forward just as Nikolai's hand closed around her arm and pulled her back, jerking her arm almost out of its socket. "Let *go* of me!"

"No," he said, quietly. "Let me."

"He's *my* brother." She struggled frantically, achieved exactly nothing.

Nikolai's fingers tightened, digging into her softer, human flesh. He pushed her back against the wall. "Stay here." He looked down at her, his lips a thin line and his dark eyes fathomless. No cat-shine in them now, either. *He must be worried.*

Selene's lungs labored to catch even a small breath. Her back and arms prickled. "Nikolai—" she began, but he laid a finger on her lips. The contact was electric. Her entire body went liquid, a moan starting in her chest. Selene strangled it before it reached her lips, making a thin dry sound instead. *Stop it, stop it, no time for this, stop it, God, what kind of a Talent did you give me if it makes me feel like this? Goddammit, please, don't.*

Nikolai's skin was fever-warm. He must have fed, he was metabolizing whatever he'd taken that night—blood, or death, or pain, or sex. Was it wrong to be grateful it hadn't been her? Though God knew she'd done her share of feeding him. Being *fed* by him.

*Danny.* Selene tried to slip along the wall away from Nikolai, but he pinned her in place without even trying. He was being gentle, he could have broken her arm or put her *through* the wall if he'd wanted to. With hardly any effort.

He wasn't human, after all.

"Move again and I will force your compliance." Nikolai leaned closer, his lips a breath away from Selene's, inhaling. Tasting her breath. *Well, the dead do breathe, when they want to. Just like the first night I met him.* She hastily shoved the thought away, freezing in place. It was a mark of *possession*, smelling her breath like that; a Nichtvren didn't get that close unless he or she intended to feed or mark you. If she struggled, his predatory instinct might come into play and he might well decide to sink his fangs in her throat right here.

So instead of looking at him, she stared over his shoulder. There was a spot of discolored, peeling paint on the opposite wall. Selene looked intently at it, her eyes hot and dry. His gaze was a heavy weight, waiting for her to speak, argue, something. Selene bit the inside of her cheek. *I'm not going to give you the fucking satisfaction. Something hacked his door down, oh God, oh God. Oh, Danny.*

The weight of Nikolai's will slowly lessened when she didn't struggle. It took everything Selene had not to move, to stay still and passive. *I will not give you the excuse. Danny, please be okay. Come on, Nikolai, you're so blasted interested in both of us, help him!* "Danny." The whisper escaped despite her. Nikolai took another long breath, leaning close. Her knees went weak.

"Stay here." He disappeared. Selene felt the shimmer of Power in the close still air of the hallway. To a sensitive human it would feel like a chill walking up the spine, a tightness under the lungs. Someone without psychic sensitivity might feel a momentary breeze, a cold draft, a sudden flash of fear that would quickly be disregarded.

Even after the Awakening and the war, people preferred to be oblivious.

The shimmer slipped through the space between the door and the shattered frame. *God, please. Please, God.*

Always begging. They called paranormals like her— *tantraiiken*—the "beggars." Always moaning and pleasing. It was hard not to, when you had a Talent that made your body betray you over and over again.

*Think about something useful.* Why was Nikolai here? Or Bruce? Bruce's hunting ground wasn't around Selene's apartment building, at least, it hadn't been three weeks ago, when he'd turned up...well, Turned.

Nikolai must have set Bruce to watch her. Why *now* when she'd known Nikolai for all this time?

*Known might be too strong a word. You can't know a Nichtvren. They're not human, no matter how charming they can occasionally be. You're food to them.* Hadn't she cautioned her classes on this one particular point? That series of lectures was always well-attended, until Selene started the slides. Seeing the bodies they left drained or eviscerated in some places sort of put a damper on the aura of glamour and mystery.

Selene's back prickled, her breath coming in shallow adrenaline-laden sips. *Danny, be okay. God, please, let him just be panicked. Let him just be upset but okay. Or even just a little hurt. Let him be alive.*

Caught between fear and anticipation, Selene let out a slow sharp breath. Her knees shook slightly, the outer edges of her shields thickening reflexively. The jeans she'd thrown on were damp at the ankles from the rain, and would be damp between her legs soon.

A sexwitch didn't feel fear the way other people did. No, being afraid just turned into a different sensation entirely. One below the belt, thick and warm enough to make her heartbeat pound in her ears, a trickle of heat beginning way down low.

*I hate this.* The thought was so familiar it was gone almost as soon as it started.

Agonized dread spiraled, kick-started a wave of desire that tipped her head back against the wall, forced her breath into another jagged half-gasp. Any more of this and she'd be a quivering ball of need and nerves by the time Nikolai reappeared.

*Goddammit, focus!* She shook out her trembling hands; if she had to throw Power she would need her fingers. Her heartbeat thundered in her ears. She repeated the mantra, as if it would help. *Please, God. Please let my brother be safe.*

Begging, again. Loathing crawled up her spine, mixed with the desire, and turned her stomach into a sudsing, bubbling washing cauldron.

Her apartment had a tiny washer and dryer now. Back in the camps it had been the cauldrons, if you were lucky enough to get your hands on some soap. Endless rounds of scrubbing.

The shimmer returned. Nikolai solidified right in front of her, a faint breeze blowing stray strands of hair back, her forehead cold as the moisture evaporated. Wisps of hair stirred at her nape. Her ponytail was loose.

He looked absolutely solid, *real.* Did his victims ever see him coming? It was like swimming with a shark and suddenly wondering if you'd cut yourself shaving that morning.

Selene met his gaze, tipping her head back. Nothing. She blinked, and then looked at the shattered door again.

Nikolai caught her shoulders, pushed her back against the wall. "We will call the police."

Her body, traitor that it was, understood before she did. Her heart plummeted into her belly with a splash, and the stew of desire and horror faded under a wave of stark chemical adrenaline. "What's this *we*? What's wrong with Danny? What's *happened?*"

He smiled, and Selene would've backed up if she wasn't already pressed against the wall. There were few things worse than Nikolai's lazy, genuinely good-humored grin. Especially his eyeteeth—*fangs,* she corrected herself, *the word is fangs, let's call it what it is, you're old enough to call things what they are.* She could all too well imagine what those teeth could do to her jugular.

*It's not his teeth, though. It's the rest of him I have trouble with.*

"You will disturb the evidence. The police prefer to observe the formalities." Nikolai was calm, too calm, and that grin...

*Danny...* A despairing moan.

Nikolai continued, softly and pitilessly. "We will go downstairs and call the police. *Verscht za?*"

She slid away toward the door, blindly. Nikolai pinned her to the wall again, his body curving into hers. Heat slammed through her; she tasted copper adrenaline. Selene drew in a sharp breath and kicked, missing him somehow. He smiled, caught her wrists. He could hold her all night and struggling would only excite him—and her.

"Stop it." Her voice broke, helplessly.

"You are being unwise." His tone was a mere murmur, so reasonable. "Do as I say, Selene. Help me."

"Help *you?* What the hell for?" She tried to pull free again. The steel vise of his fingers strangled her wrists. A twisting wire of pain lanced up both arms. Jerking backward, she smacked her head against the wall, brief starry pain twinkling in front of her eyes. "Tell me what happened."

"Your brother is dead, Selene. Now we must call the police. Will you be come with me or shall I drag you?" Nikolai smiled, absently, his expression suddenly remote. "I would enjoy carrying you. Particularly if you struggle."

"Let go of me. I'll go downstairs and call the police." *Like a good little girl.* Her teeth clenched together, her jaw aching. She'd have a goose-egg on the back of her head for sure. *Danny. Ohgod.*

"Very good," he breathed, and released her, finger by finger. Selene stared up into the lightless pools of his eyes. A kind of stunned calm slipped down over her body. So *dark.* So endlessly dark.

When he spoke next, it was in something approximating a normal tone. "I am sorry, Selene. I will help you, however I can."

*Christ, does he have to sound like he means it? Any help from you is help I can do without.* "Leave me alone." Her lips were too numb to work properly. "If you won't let me see, just leave me alone."

"You do not want to see. It is...disturbing. Now come."

THE METAL BOX of the pay phone gleamed dully under the fluorescents. A phone book, four years out of date and scarred with a tangle of permacolor spray graffiti, dangled from a rust-pitted chain. Someone had tagged the plastic hood at the top of the box—an out-of-date gang sign, a phone number, a caricature of a donkey, other symbols much less pleasant. There were even a couple of bullet holes, whether from mop-up after the war or a more recent turf battle, who could tell?

Selene picked up the receiver in nerveless fingers, staring at the graffiti-covered plastic.

"I suspect you will want to call your police friend first." Nikolai produced two quarter-credit coins with a flick of his fingers, dropped them in. Selene's eyes burned dryly, the numbers on the square silver buttons blurring. Nikolai even dialed the number, his signet ring flashing dully, blood on gold. Somewhere in the numbness a thought surfaced. *How does Nikolai know Jack's number?*

The phone rang four times. "Urmph."

Selene couldn't get the words past the dust in her throat. Nikolai bumped against her, sending a rush of fire through her veins, kick-starting her brain. "Maureen?" she whispered, her voice coming from a deep screaming well of panic. "It's Selene Thompson. I need to talk to Jack. Now."

"What the..." Maureen's tone changed suddenly. Mother to the world, that was Maureen. She'd cooked Selene dinner more than once, during the cases Jack needed paranormal help on. "Sweetheart, are you okay? Jack, wake up."

Selene's knees nearly buckled, a moan bubbling up. The vision of the hacked and shattered door rose up in front of her. *Dear God what happened to his door...Danny...*

Nikolai's fingers slid under her ponytail, fever-hot. Fire spread from her nape, a deluge of sensation pooling in her belly. She hated the feeling, hated *him*, but the Power would help her. She was going into shock. Years of training kicked in, turning the desire into Power, shocking her back in control, her mind adding, subtracting, calculating. *What happened? He hasn't left here in five years. What went wrong?*

Danny was a Journeyman, an adept at etheric and astral travel. He didn't need to leave his apartment, and anyway couldn't bear to be away from the safety of the wards and defenses Selene erected around his three-room world. Nothing touched him inside his magickal cocoon, no thoughts or emotions that might compromise his body when he projected. Time had strengthened Danny's gifts, making him more sensitive to random buffetings, but also more sensitive to Selene's defenses and powers. He couldn't be with her all the time, so an apartment of his own with heavy shielding was the best—

She stiffened. *The wards!* They were a part of Danny now; he had taken over maintaining them since Selene had other problems. But they were originally *her* wards and would answer her call.

They would have recorded what went on inside Danny's walls.

"Jack here." Detective Jack Pepper's cigarette-rough voice came over the line. "What the *hell?*"

Her voice almost refused to work. "It's Selene. Something's killed Danny. Jack, Nikolai's here." *I sound like I'm twelve years old again. And scared. I sound so scared.*

Selene heard Jack breathing. "Jesus, why is he there? Forget it; I don't want to know. Hang up and call 911. You got it?" The sound of cloth against cloth filtered through the phone. Jack was sitting up. Maureen's whispered questions, then...silence.

"I... He c-c-called me. Said he was c-c-cold and something about danger." Autopilot pushed the words out, she listened to her own ragged gasping breath. *Danny, oh God. Danny. Jesus Christ...*

"Selene, put Nikolai on the phone, honey. Now." Jack was fully awake. A click and a flare of a lighter, deep indrawn breath. *It must be bad if he's smoking in bed, Maureen won't like that.*

She handed the phone to Nikolai. He slid closer, pressing her into the phone booth, his fingers kneading heat into her neck.

*I wonder what a gun would do to him?* The thought surfaced, she pushed it hastily away. She wasn't sure if he could hear it; Nichtvren were psychic as well as physical predators. If he heard her, what would he do?

"Yes?" Nikolai paused. "Bad enough... No, not human... I did not. Nor did she. The door is shattered. She will of course not enter the apartment." Selene strained to listen. "Of course. I will stay out of sight. I would not want to cause trouble for my Selene."

Her neck muscles burned. *"My Selene"? Oh, boy. We're going to have to have a talk about that, suckhead.*

Selene's mind skittered sideways. *The door. What happened?* Nikolai brushed his thumb over her nape. Lightning shot down her spine and burst in the pit of her stomach. *Oh, God.*

"I will." Nikolai reached over her shoulder again, hung up. His hands slipped down over her shoulders. He gently turned her to face him, Selene didn't resist. Her head was full of a rushing, roaring noise, his voice came from very far away. "You must call the emergency services, Selene. You received a call from your brother. It was interrupted and you came to see if he was well. You noticed the door had been forced and decided to call 711. Do you understand?"

She stared up at him, his face suddenly oddly foreign. He looked more like a stranger than ever. Selene took a deep shuddering breath, fury crystallizing under the surface of her mind. "Why are you doing this, Nikolai? One dead human, more or less."

His fingers tightened. "One dead human under *my* protection, dear one. Whatever killed him is very dangerous. Now you will call the emergency services and you will be a very good girl for me." He touched his lips to her forehead, a gentle kiss that made her body burn, fire spilling through her veins. *How can I even think about that when Danny's upstairs?*

It was her goddamn curse. Hot acid guilt rose in the back of her throat. *I should have gone in there, I should have seen.*

Her eyes filled with tears. "I hate you," she whispered, looking up into Nikolai's dark eyes. "I *hate* you."

"Call them." The corner of his mouth quirked up, as if he found her amusing.

She turned back to the phone and blindly picked up the receiver. Punched the seven, the one, the one. A deep breath. Nikolai moved away suddenly, and she swayed, grabbing the metal edge of the booth to steady herself. One ring. Two. Three. Four. Five.

"711, what are you reporting?" A passionless, professional voice, possibly female.

For one awful moment Selene couldn't remember who she was or what she was doing. The metal bit into her fingers. Blood pounded in her ears and the hallway swirled beneath her. "My-my brother. He c-c-called me. I c-c-came to his apartment and the d-d-door is b-b-roken and I'm afraid t-t-to go inside."

*How strange.* Inside the glass ball of hysterical calm descending upon her, she listened to her own disconnected words. *I sound like I'm scared to death.* It was her voice giving information, stammering out the story to the operator. Danny never left his apartment. The door was broken. She was afraid. Tiny diamond mice fleeing the huge black wolf running around in her brain made her voice jittery, made her hands tremble.

She glanced over her shoulder. The empty foyer glared under the fluorescents. There was no sign of Bruce or of Nikolai, though the medallion throbbed a heated beat between her breasts.

The urge to tear it off and throw it away made her shake. *Danny. Oh, Danny, please. Please, God.*

She slumped, trembling, against the phone box. Her nails drove into her palm. The terrified mice spun round and round inside her brain.

"Miss, please try to be calm. We have dispatched a unit to your location."

*Try to be calm? Danny. Oh, God. How can I be calm if you're dead?*

# THREE

THE FOURTH TIME the operator told her to be calm, Selene jammed the phone back down. She looked at the closed-tight, judgemental mailboxes, and then at the stairs again; the medallion tingled harshly. A warning. Her throat was full of something hard and slick, she swallowed several times, resting her forehead against cool cheap metal.

*Don't go back,* the operator had said. *Stay outside the building. Stay and wait for the police. It's safest to wait for the police, ma'am.*

Selene's hoarse inarticulate moan bounced off the stairwell walls. The stairs squeaked under her slow feet. Her legs burned numbly.

She only got halfway up to the first floor before Nikolai's hand closed over her elbow. She gave a startled, wounded little cry and found herself facing him, looking at his chest. He was somehow on the step above her, and his mouth moved, fangs flashing in something less than a good-natured grin. It was more like a smirk, or a warning.

"No," he said. Selene stared at him, and he gave her a little shake. Her head wobbled, the entire stairwell reeling. "Outside. This is not for you."

"He's my—" Her mouth was so dry the words were a croak.

"Your brother. Yes." He used his grip on her arm to pull her down the stairs. Selene went limp, resisting him, but he slid his arm around her shoulders and simply dragged her as if she weighed nothing. Her boots dropped from stair to stair as if they weren't attached to the rest of her. "You cannot help him now. And I would not have you see this, *milaya.*"

"I hate you." The fluorescents seared her wet eyes. "I wish I'd never met you."

He gave a gracious nod, as if she'd complimented him. "Thank you." They reached the bottom of the stairs. He half-carried her across the peeling linoleum. He shouldered the door to the building open, dragged her out and let the door go. The lock engaged.

Selene looked up at him. He set her down on the cold, wet sidewalk and brushed her hair back, settled her camel coat on her shoulders, stroked her sore damp forehead; she'd be lucky to escape a bruise from cracking her head against the wall.

His fingers were still warm. Too warm to be human, feverish, but oddly soothing.

She hated that comfort. Just like she hated the thin thread of desire that curled through her, her curse waking up, Power scraping against raw nerves.

Distant sirens cracked the still air. *Breathe. In through the nose, out through the mouth. Breathe.*

The mantra didn't help. "I mean it." Her voice shook. "I *hate* you."

"And yet you need me." He smiled, an almost-tender expression that made her entire body go cold. Selene might have stumbled backward, but his fingers closed around her wrist, a loose bracelet. Sirens hammered at the roof of the night. "Selene, you do not wish to see what lies in that room. Remember your brother the way he was."

"I don't *need* you." Selene tore her wrist away. His fingers tightened slightly, just to let her know he could hold her, before he let her go and she swayed. There was something hard and small and spiny in her hand, cold metal.

A police cruiser materialized around the corner, whooping and braying. She opened her hand to find her key ring. *He must have had Bruce sneak into my house and get my keys. The little thief. Always creeping around, peeping in windows and doing Nikolai's bidding. No wonder His Highness keeps him around.*

She looked up. Except for the police car—siren, flashing lights—the street was deserted. Nikolai had vanished. She saw the blurring in the air, the shimmer that might have been him or just the tears filling her eyes. She fumbled on the ring for the key to the front of Danny's building.

Numb, her cheeks wet with rain and tears, she raised her hand to flag the cops down. Thankfully, they cut the siren as soon as they pulled to a stop. Selene waved, her bag bumping at her hip. *No poltergeist here, no curse to be broken, no client looking down their nose at me. No, this time the person needing help is me.*

Two cops, a rookie and a graying veteran who looked at her as if he recognized her. Selene hoped he didn't. If he recognized her, he might ask questions. *Hey, aren't you that freak who hangs around with Jack Pepper?*

"My brother." Her teeth chattered. "He's a shut-in. He doesn't leave the apartment. He called me—his doorjamb's all busted up—it's not normal—"

They barked questions at her, who was her brother, what apartment, who was she, was anyone armed, what did she see? The mice scurrying in Selene's head supplied answers. "4C, apartment 4C, Danny Thompson, I'm Selene, I'm his sister— no, nothing, just the door, that's all I saw, it's busted all to hell—"

Before she unlocked the building door for them, the medallion scorched against her skin. Warning her.

*Fuck you, Nikolai.*

She followed the cops up the stairs, sliding the medallion's chain up over her head. She pulled it out of her sweater. Light flared sharply from the silver disc before she tossed it into a dark corner of the second-floor landing. The cops didn't notice— they were too busy looking up the stairs and speaking back and forth in cryptic cop-talk. Both had their guns out. "Fourth floor. Apartment 4C," she repeated, and took a deep breath, choking on tears.

"Go back downstairs," the older cop told her. "Go back downstairs!"

Fourth floor. They saw the shattered door, the wedge of light slicing through the dim hall. The older cop radioed for backup.

They edged forward and cautiously pushed the splintered door open. Told her again to go downstairs. Selene told them she would and stood where she was, hot tears spilling down her cheeks.

Now that she wasn't standing next to Nikolai, the wards vibrated with Selene's nearness, lines of light bleeding out from the hole torn where the door used to be. Something had blasted right through the careful layers of defense she'd painstakingly applied to the walls. What could do that?

She took two steps, and the rookie backed up out of the apartment. He was paper-white and trembling, freckles standing out on his fair face, his blond mustache quivering

After glancing past him once, Selene could see why.

She clamped her right hand over her mouth, staring past the rookie, who stumbled to the side and vomited onto the hall rug. Selene didn't blame him. She could only see a short distance down the entry hall and into the studio room. The kitchen was to the left, bathroom to the right, and she had a clear view almost to the night-dark window, with the orange streetlamps glowing outside.

A moment later her eyes tracked a shimmer up over the streetlamp, a shimmer that resolved into a dark shape balancing atop the streetlamp's arm. A tall shape, crouched down, hands wrapped around the bar, eyes reflecting the light with the green-gold sheen of a cat's eyes at night.

Perched. Just like a vulture.

Selene looked down again, and her hand tightened over her mouth. Her throat burned with bile. The shapes she was seeing refused to snap into a coherent picture. Blood painted the white-painted walls, soaked into the thin beige carpeting, and the...the *pieces*...

Footsteps echoed in the hall, shouts, radios squawking. Four more cops. Selene stepped back against the wall, her hand still clamped over her mouth, fingernails digging into her cheek. She struggled to swallow the hot acid bile instead of puking like the rookie.

Detective Jack Pepper, his graying buzz-cut and familiar rumpled gray wool coat steaming in the hall's heat, came striding from the other end. She stumbled back, hitting her head against the wall.

Jack gave her a look that could have peeled paint. "Aw, Christ. Get her downstairs," he snapped, as one of the cops took a look past Selene and into the apartment, swearing viciously.

Selene couldn't help herself. She began to sob into her hand, her eyes streaming. The shrill sound echoed under the crackle of radio talk and more sirens outside.

After wiping his mouth, the blond rookie was finally delegated to take her downstairs. Selene had to steady him, her fingers against the creaking leather of his jacket. The queasy flickers of fear coming off the young man were enough to make her flush, her stomach tightening. Her mental shields were as transparent and brittle as crystal, he was hyped enough to broadcast all over the mental spectrum.

*Lawrence, his name is Lawrence. He's an open door right now, and I don't have enough control to shut him out.* Knowledge burned through her, the fear turning into a wash of heat that made her nipples peak and her entire body tighten. Her jeans were definitely damp between her legs.

*I wish I'd stopped to put my panties on.* The sanity of that thought saved her, slapped her back into herself. *Focus, Selene.*

She filled her lungs and tapped in, the rush of Power sparking along her nerves. *I hope he puts me in a car, I can use this and yank the wards off the apartment. A killing like that leaves a mark on the air, the wards will be vibrating with it. I'll be able to track whoever did this to him.* Selene made a slight crooning noise, patted the rookie's shoulder when they reached the foyer. He was looking a little green again, his cheeks pooching out and his lips wet. Selene smelled fear, the sharp tang of human vomit, and her own smell, rich floral musk. *Tantraiiken* musk, the smell of a sexwitch.

*Put me in a police car.* She patted the rookie's back as he heaved near the stairs. A loose ring of cop cars sat in the wet street. More sirens cut the distant darkness. *I don't want to work magick right here on the street. God alone knows what sort of notice it will attract if I pass out, too.*

"It's okay, Lawrence." She looked up in time to see another cop come flying out of the door—some thoughtful soul had braced it open with a chunk of pavement. This man—tall, stocky, brown hair combed over a bald head Selene could see because he'd lost his hat—made it to the bottom of the stairs before he puked, too, vomit spraying out onto the street.

Selene's gorge rose. She swallowed against it. "Nice boy," she said softly, stroking Lawrence's back. "It's okay. You okay?" *Quit retching and put me somewhere quiet where I can Work, you waste.* The coldness of the thought almost surprised her. He was just the type of ordinary civilian to come running to Selene for her help in dealing with something extraordinary—and then decide she was less than a used Kleenex when everything was said and done.

They were all alike, every one of them. Except Danny, and Danny was gone. Selene's jaw clenched, her teeth grinding together.

*Come on. Quit it, so I can Work.*

HE DID PUT her in a police car, mumbling something about her safety and a report, and she closed her eyes, settling back into the cracked vinyl seat. *Finally. What did you eat for dinner, anyway, it certainly stank...oh, God, what am I going to do now? Danny.*

Tears pricked behind Selene's eyes. She pictured the hallway leading into Danny's living space, the foldout bed and salvaged wooden shelves of books and curios and the bloody pieces of—

Her concentration guttered, came back; her ability to visualize under stress had plenty of practice. *Don't fail me now.* She dropped through the floor of her own consciousness, into the place where she truly lived. Her breathing stilled, her heartbeat paused. An onlooker would have thought she was sleeping, or just sitting with her eyes closed, head tilted back, mouth slackly open. In shock.

She dove into a black blood-warm sea, her concentration narrowing to a single point. Pulled on the threads of the Power she'd spent warding Danny's apartment. The defenses recognized her, left the place in the world where they had been bleeding free, and leapt for her.

Selene "caught" the energy, folded it deftly. The resultant mass shrank, a small bright star to her mental vision, taking on more psychic mass as she compressed it. Selene's body arched upward, gasping for air. The energy she'd taken from the hyped-up rookie drained away. Her skin was prickling and her lips wet, her hips rocking forward slightly, tensing, tighter, tighter, aching for release.

The curse was alive and well.

She couldn't afford to let the energy spend. She had to find something physical to hold the Power until she could take a closer look. Her fingers dipped into her black canvas shoulderbag and found smooth wood.

*My athame. Christ. Here I am in the back of a police car with an illegal-to-carry eight-inch ritual knife.*

Years of harsh training brought her focus back; the star of Power drained into the knife, leaving her sick and shaking, her entire body aching for completion. The pain was low between her legs, and it would torture her all night unless she found some way to bleed off the pressure.

The whole event had taken less than three minutes. The rookie was gesturing to an ambulance crew. Lurid light from the cop cars and stuttering flashes from the ambulance painted the street in gaudy flickers. The entire street was now swarming with cops and emergency personnel. Selene slumped down against the cracked vinyl and peered out the window, her senses dilated, looking for a dark blot or a breath of anything that didn't belong. Nothing. Not even a shimmer in the air.

Was Nikolai gone? She couldn't be that lucky.

*Danny.* The numbness was still there. Whatever was locked inside her athame would give her a direction, somewhere to go...hopefully. At the very least, she would see how her brother died.

The *how* might tell her *who*, and once she knew she could start planning. There weren't many things she could take on as a *tantraiiken*, she was worse than useless in a fight since pain and fear turned to desire and swallowed her whole.

But she could give it a try, couldn't she? Nikolai might not help, he might be too interested in getting leverage on her. One more dead human wouldn't matter, even if it was the brother of his semi-pet sexwitch.

The hate was a bright red slash across the middle of her mind, giving her strength. She closed her eyes, set her jaw. Her fingers itched to unzip her jeans, slide down, touch the slick heat between her legs. *Hate myself. Hate you.* She felt her face contort into a screaming mask, tears spilling down her cheeks.

The door creaked open, letting in a burst of chill rainy air. "Hi, princess," Jack said. "Get your ass out. We got a hot date with some paperwork."

Selene blinked, her fists curled at her sides. She let out the breath she'd been holding. Her cheeks hurt, so did her lower belly; her eyes felt hot and scraped.

Jack didn't mean to be cruel, he was just used to treating her like one of the boys. If she had been waiting to join another investigation, he would have acted the same way. Selene would have had an equally brisk response for him. She searched for something sharp and hard as a shield to say.

Instead, her throat swelled with grief. "Danny?" she whispered. It was stupid, she knew it, Nikolai would not have lied and her own eyes had told her the truth. But still. Hope, that great human drug.

Another wave of hatred at her own goddamn weakness spilled through her, gave her another jolt of much-needed strength. She had the wards, safely trapped in her athame.

*Have to find out.* Almost incoherent, she grabbed for the thought. It spilled away like water.

Jack's face turned milk-pale. He was thin and stooped, except for the potbelly straining at his dingy white shirt. His lean hound-dog face under its gray buzzcut was almost always mournful. Now it was actively sad. "Lena... Jesus, I'm sorry. Nikolai was supposed to keep you from seeing...any of that."

*I have a right to see what happened to my brother, Jack.* Selene slid her legs out of the car. She had to catch her breath as the material of her jeans rasped against swollen tissues. She *needed*, and there was no way to fill that need tonight.

She had work to do.

"Nikolai can go to hell," she rasped around the obstruction in her throat. That helped—it sounded like the old Selene, the tough Selene. "I'm sure it's where he's bound sooner or later."

Her palms slid against each other as she twisted her sweat-damp hands. The image of Danny's apartment, framed by a shattered blood-painted doorway, rose up again. Numb disbelief rose with it.

Her jeans were uncomfortably wet, and she was starting to sweat under her arms. Her neck prickled, and she was suddenly aware of empty hunger. She was starving.

*How can I think of food at a time like this? Jesus.*

"I'll do your report up for you. Come by, sign it in the morning. Look, Selene—" He offered her his hand and she took it, nervous sweat slicking her palm. He pulled her to her feet. The car's windows were frosted with vapor. *How long was I in there?*

He then firmly took his hand away from her, tearing her fingers free.

Selene would have kept his hand, run her thumb along the crease on the inside of his wrist, wet her lips with her tongue. Her eyes met his. She *needed*, and he was male. Women were also good for what she needed, but there weren't any around.

*God. Look at what I almost did. I'm a camp whore, and my brother is dead.* The familiar loathing rose up, directed at her own useless self.

"I'm sorry," Jack continued awkwardly. He was starting to sweat now, too, looking down until he realized he was looking at her chest, then staring up over her shoulder at the circus of lights and people in uniforms milling around. "Christ, I'm sorry. Lena...I'm so sorry."

Selene crossed her arms, cupped her elbows in her hands. Jack took her upper arm, kicked the cruiser's door shut, and steered her away from the hive of activity the street had become. People were starting to peek through their windows, lights were coming on. The cops were too busy to pay much attention to one lone woman being led away by Detective Pepper— especially when some of them recognized her as his tame spook, the woman that had broken the Bowan case last month. Just how she did it nobody knew—but then again, nobody wanted to know. The girl was just too weird, maybe even one of those paranormals who had to be registered with the State. And Pepper was starting to look a little weird himself. The joke was that he'd apply for the new Spook Squad soon, just as soon as he could get his head out of a bottle and quit working hopeless freezer-cold homicide cases.

Selene shivered, hugging herself, their easy dismissal of her roaring through the open wound she was becoming. *I've got to get home before I start to scream.*

"You're pretty worn out," Jack said, diffidently. "Look, go home. I'm sorry, Lena. I'm glad you called me. I wish you wouldn't have gone up there." He stopped near a pool of convenient shadow, and Selene looked up.

*Of course.*

Nikolai was there. Part of the darkness itself, his long black coat melding with the gloom that filled an alley's entrance.

Jack faced her. Here, numb and shocked, with her shields thin and the aftermath of the Power she'd jacked and the magick she'd worked pounding in her pulse with insistent need, she drowned in what *he* was feeling.

Agonizing pain. Nausea. Sick aching in his chest, the heartburn that wouldn't go away—*she shouldn't have to see this, shouldn't have seen it.*

Jack sighed, his shoulders slumping. "It's bad, Selene. Something I ain't never seen before. And Nikolai says it's not human. Which means..." His brown eyes were almost black in the uncertain light. "Christ," he finished, when she just stared at him, her mouth slightly open. Her breath rasped in the chill rainwashed air. "Just go home. Come by the station tomorrow to sign your statement. I'm sorry."

Selene shrugged. "Great. Just go home, he says." She heard the funny breathless tone in her own voice. She was close to the edge, so close—did Jack think she was numb and grieving? Or did he guess that she wouldn't be able to grieve until the need pounding in her blood was blotted out?

*Grieve, hell.* There was something sharp as a broken bone in her chest. *I'm going to get whoever did this. I'm going to make them* pay.

Nikolai stepped forward. His eyes were depthless. "I will take her, Jack. Thank you."

Jack nodded. "Go with—"

"Like a good little girl, right?" Her tone sounded shrill even to herself, it bounced off the alley's walls and came back to her through a layer of cotton wool. "What I'm hearing is that you're not going to work too hard, because it's a P-fucking-C. Right?"

Jack's shoulders hunched as if she'd hit him. "Paranormal cases are technically not the jurisdiction of the Saint City police force, until the new laws go into effect. They're the jurisdiction of—"

"Of the reigning prime paranormal Power in the city." She stepped away from Jack. "Which means Nikolai. Which means I can kiss any hope of finding out who did this to my brother goodbye." *You bastards. All of you, bastards.*

"Not necessarily." Nikolai's eyes never left her. He moved closer, not precisely crowding her, but stepping past Jack without so much as glancing at the detective. "Cooperate with me, Selene, and I will see the killer brought to you, for your revenge. Will you take that bargain?"

Jack coughed, uncomfortably. "I've got to go. Sorry, Selene."

*You son of a bitch. Both of you. Fucking men.* "Are you really," she said, flatly, and turned on her heel. She put her head down, started to walk. At least she wasn't staggering. *Oh, God. Danny. Who did this to you?*

Nikolai murmured something behind her—no doubt talking to Jack, something along the lines of *women, irrational, what can you do, she'll see reason in the morning.*

It was too much. Rage and something like a sob made flesh drew tighter and tighter under her breastbone, and the tension snapped.

Selene ran.

# FOUR

BY THE TIME she reached Cliff Street, she was stumbling. She'd fallen once, scraping her palms on pavement, and scrambled to her feet, looking up to see a shadow flitting over a rooftop above her. He didn't even have the decency to try and conceal himself.

Her hands jittered. Her keys jangled, her scraped palms singing in pain. Her heart threatened to burst out of her chest. Sweat rolled down her spine, soaked into the waistband of her jeans.

She checked the street behind her, deserted under the orange streetlamps. It took her three tries to unlock the door to her apartment building, her breath coming high and harsh and fast, expecting to feel a hand closing on her shoulder at any moment.

The run up her own stairs took on a nightmarish quality, moving too slowly while something chased her from behind. Those had been the worst dreams when she was little, an orphan huddled in a cold camp tent with her brother, running through syrup while the monster snarled behind, gaining on her.

Her own door. She fumbled out her keys, tried to unlock it, made a short sound of agonized frustration when her fingers slipped.

Finally the key slid into the lock.

She twisted it, opened her door, yanked the key out, kicked the door shut with a resounding slam that shook the building. She threw the deadbolt, then turned around and hurled her keys down her dark hall.

Nikolai plucked the keyring out of the air, his signet ring glittering. One moment her pretty, spacious one-bedroom apartment was empty—the next moment, a slight breeze brushed Selene's cheek and she let out a strangled scream. The protections placed in the walls of her apartment and the whole building shuddered with a sound like a crystal wineglass ringing, stroked just right. *Don't worry, nobody will hear it, I'm the only Talent in the building. A merry little party, just Nikolai and me.*

*And whatever he's going to do to me.*

Selene whirled and started trying to unbolt the door. Her sweat-slick fingers slipped against cold metal. *Christ why can't he leave me ALONE?*

"Stop." He was suddenly *there*, laying the keys down on the small table by the front door. His fingers bit into her shoulder and he yanked her back, locked the second deadbolt with his other hand. The sound of the lock going home was the clang of a prison cell closing.

Selene heard her own harsh sobs, the low moaning sound of a strangled scream.

Nikolai slid the coat off her shoulders while he dragged her along. Tossed it over the back of the couch as he pulled her into the living room. Then he grabbed the canvas strap of her bag, wrapped it around his fist, and jerked it up over her head. Selene let out a short cry, cut off midway when he clamped his free hand over her mouth. He dropped the bag on the couch as well, and looked down at her.

Silence, except for the muffled sounds slipping past his fingers. Fire raced up her side, tearing through her ribs—the stitch in her side, getting worse. Her calves were burning too. Her lower back ached, and her palms were scraped raw.

Worse than that was the miserable, hot, prickling need slamming through her. The low, relentless burn between her legs, spreading through her entire body. Now that she wasn't running, it returned. When would she start to beg?

*I'm a whore, and my brother is dead.* The sobs turned into a slick stone in her throat.

He considered her, cocking his head to one side. A few soft strands of black hair fell over his forehead. "I told you not to look." There was no inflection to his voice, it was a passionless murmur. "But look you must. Are you happy? Are you *satisfied?*"

Selene's shoulders slumped. *I could bite him. What would he do if I bit him? Would he hold me down and...*

Nikolai let out a low pent breath. It was for effect—he didn't need to breathe, did he? He only did it when he *wanted* to.

He slid one hand around her waist, flattened it against the small of her back. His fingers scorched through her sweater. "I forgive you much." His hand exerted a little pressure, enough that she shifted back away from him, resisting. "I forgive you because you are young, because you are unique, because you amuse me, and for other reasons." A ghost of a smile touched his lips. "Sometimes you even surprise me, which is rare. But sometimes, my Selene, I wonder if I forgive *too* much."

She tried to twist free, but he had her, one hand on the small of her back, the other over her mouth. Tears trickled down her cheeks. He pulled her close to him, closer, until she could feel something very definitely alive pressing against her belly, through his jeans and her sweater. *I could give a lecture on this,* she thought hysterically. *Vampire Anatomy: Dead or Alive? I never even knew a Nichtvren could* get *a hard-on—they didn't cover that in the textbooks.*

It was her effect on him—her effect on any man. Maybe it was pheromones, maybe it was only her cursed Power making sure it could complete itself. Nikolai had known what she was the first time he smelled her.

Or so he said.

"Now," he said, leaning down just a little, whispering in her ear. "You disobeyed me. You tossed my last gift to you away like a piece of trash. You also acted as a complete fool, dropping your defenses and working the Art while you sat in the back of a police car. And I saw where you found the Power for that trick, my sweet." He was murmuring, and Selene shut her eyes. Her entire body shook now, straining against his, recognizing that here was something it *needed.* Something that could take the ache away. "I wonder how you're feeling."

He took a step, and let her move too, back toward the bedroom. Only the nightlight in the hall broke the darkness of her apartment, but that would present no difficulty to him. Not to a Nichtvren, who could see in complete dark.

"Well?" He moved, his legs bumping hers.

Selene's body betrayed her. Her hips jerked forward and her hands came up, sliding along his arms to find his shoulders and clenching, trying to pull him forward. Her lips parted, and she sobbed in a breath behind his hand. Two.

*I hate myself.* It was the only clear thought in the straining welter of sensation she'd become, her curse awake and alive under her skin. *I hate him and I hate myself.* She tasted salt, and kissed his palm, her lips softening, unable to help herself.

"I see," he continued, pitilessly. "The succubus needs her food."

*That's not what I am!* She wanted to scream, but his hand was still over her mouth.

"You are the only *tantraiiken* of adult age to walk the earth freely for five hundred years, and you do so because of my protection." He moved her back a step at a time, toward the bedroom. "If I were cruel, dear one, sweet Selene, I'd chain you in a stone cell and let you suffer. Let you burn for a little while, until you better appreciated me and the liberty I allow you." Then he gave a bitter little laugh, and Selene went liquid against him, relieved. She knew that sound.

He would give her what she needed. He would make it *stop*.

Then she could do what she had to do. Find out who had done...*that*...to Danny.

"Please," she mouthed against his palm, before she could stop herself. "Nikolai."

*I am such a whore.* Loathing filled her mouth like spilled wine, added another complex layer to the straining need pounding in her blood.

"Hush." He pushed her through the bedroom door, kicked it shut. She flinched, shaking so hard she couldn't walk, and he pushed her down on the bed. She landed hard, her head flung back, her back arching. The covers were still thrown back from when she'd leapt out of bed.

*Danny,* the part of her that wasn't crazed with need sobbed. *Danny. Oh, my God. My brother is dead, and what am I doing? God help me.*

He stood there, watching her shake against the cotton sheets. Selene bit her lower lip. That was a mistake—the pain now fed the loop of sensation, fear and hurt and lust driving in a circle that wrung shuddering little sounds from her.

Finally, he shed his coat, draping it over the chair set by the closet. Selene closed her eyes, twisting, her hips rising, falling back down. Her clothes were impossibly hot, confining, scraping against suddenly sensitive skin.

He knelt down, and worked her damp boots off, and her socks. Touched the inside of her ankle with a fingertip, under the damp cuff of her jeans. The touch sent a spark racing up her leg, through her entire body. "Selene." Why did he have to sound so *human*, so soft and reasonable? "I wanted to save you that sight."

"My *brother*," she whispered, and then moaned as the bed accepted Nikolai's weight next to her. He propped himself up on one elbow and used the other hand to pop the button on her waistband. *I'm going to kill whoever did that to him. Just get this over with so I can do what I have to.* She drew in a sobbing breath, her hips lifting helplessly.

"I would rather have you remember him alive." Nikolai slowly unzipped her jeans. The sound of the zipper was loud in the dark stillness of her bedroom. Tears leaked out between Selene's eyelids, and her sweater was drenched with sweat.

*Addicted to this, but I have no choice. I never have a choice.* The need would get worse and worse, a *tantraiiken*'s curse burning through her bones, until she was little more than an animal. She'd gone that far sometimes, when she was young and thought she could rule her own body, at least.

Before she'd learned how to use the curse for her own benefit. And before she'd met *him*. Since she'd come to Nikolai's notice, she hadn't needed to feed her curse in alleys or cheap hotel rooms. Even if she *could* forget it, he reminded her often enough. She owed him.

Owed, and was owned by. There wasn't much of a difference where Nichtvren were concerned.

"Nikolai..." It was a long despairing moan. It wouldn't take long before she started to beg. She'd drained her batteries and worked herself into a frenzy.

He slid his hand into her jeans, settling the heel of his palm against her mound. His fingers slipped down, and made a slight beckoning motion. Selene arched, her breath hissing in. But then, torture of tortures, he stopped.

"Why disobey me?" His breath was warm against her cheek. "Why, Selene? You leave me little choice."

"Nikolai—" It was all she had left, the pleading. He would give her what she needed, and then she could think again, ponder, consider, plan. But how much would he make her suffer, first, and how much of the suffering would she enjoy because of her traitorous body?

He took pity on her then, and made another little beckoning motion with his fingers, and another. He knew exactly what to do. It was all Selene needed, and she cried out, arching, her head tipped back and her entire body shuddering. It was like being dipped in fire, and the relief was instant.

Relief—and fresh need. She would need more. Much more. But now she could think, the first edge of her curse was blunted.

"Nikolai," she said, when she could speak again. "You were in there, what did you see?" *Give me something, you fucking suckhead. Get it, Selene? Fucking suckhead? You're such a whore.*

The image of Danny's apartment rose in front of her eyes again, and she struggled away from Nikolai's hand, curling into a ball, pulling her knees up while she hugged herself, making small sobbing sounds like an animal in a trap. Her wet clothes rasped uncomfortably against her skin.

Nikolai sighed again. He sounded frustrated. Good for him.

"Later, dear one. Right now you are in pain." He sliced her sweater up the back—his claws, extended delicately, not even brushing her skin beneath the wool. Chill air met her wet skin. Then his fingers, skating down the muscles on either side of her spine. His claws were retracted, but she could still feel the strength in his hands. He pushed her hair aside—the elastic band holding her ponytail snapped—and his mouth met her nape. She shivered, curling even more tightly into herself. He stroked her shoulder, touched the two dimples down low at the small of her back.

The first edge of pain was gone, and the burning settled back into a low dull agony. Her Talent wasn't like others, she *had* to fuel it with sex. It was the only thing that worked.

43

*Christ, do I have to let him touch me like this? He's not human. Can't he just fuck me and get it over with, leave me alone so I can do what I need to do?*

The rest of her ruined sweater was discarded over the side of the bed. He worked her jeans free and tossed them away too, then took her in his arms. His own clothes were gone—how he did that she couldn't guess, but it probably had something to do with his claws, and the fact the she was too busy trying to gulp down air and fight her body's need to really pay attention to him.

She was paying for the magick she'd done earlier. No preparation, no patterning—she'd simply dropped her defenses and gone for it, performed a major Work without any thought of the consequences. No wonder she was shaking with need.

*Everything has to be paid for.* She realized she'd said it out loud. "Everything has to be paid for, Nikolai, *everything.*"

"Do you think I do not know?" He pushed her onto her back, slid his hand between her legs. She was slick and feverish, damp with need. "Hush. Lie still."

It took a massive effort to do what he said. It would be quicker if she just let him—if she submitted, if she gave in.

Selene erupted into wild motion, trying to fight him off. He caught her wrists, stretching them above her head, and pinned her to the mattress. She would have been screaming, but his mouth was on hers, catching the scream, killing it. She tried to kick him, straining, but he slid a knee between hers. Then all of his weight, and Selene felt the edges of his hips against the soft insides of her thighs. He was much warmer now, his skin almost scorching hers.

The energetic discharge of sex would feed him, too. That was why a *tantraiiken* was such a valuable paranormal pet.

Pet? *Slave.* It was frowned upon, of course, but paranormals and Talents weren't that tightly policed, even though the laws were almost in effect to give them some protection and codify them. The higher echelons of the human world—the powerbrokers and politicians—knew about the slavery, of course, it was an open secret in some circles. No newspaper would ever report on it, and no television anchor would ever talk about the things that went on under the blanket of normality. How sometimes, people born with certain Talents were lost to the night side of life.

He found the entrance to her body, thrust in, and his hands tightened around her wrists, the small bones grinding together. Selene gulped back another useless scream, relief spilling through her. His fingers gentled, threaded through hers. He murmured something—maybe it was Russian, she didn't know, didn't care, the only thing she cared about was that the agony had stopped. He was in her to the hilt, stretching her, her hips slamming up, silently begging.

He moved, again, and Selene closed her eyes. Pleasure tore through her, a dark screaming pleasure wrapped in barbed wire and dragging hot velvet laceration through tender flesh. Soon enough she would be able to think about grieving.

"Get...it...over...with." She set her teeth together, even as her hips rocked and her ankles linked together at the small of his back. Her body betrayed her over and over again, that was the worst. Her body was an enemy, a traitor, it didn't care who he was as long as he had what she needed.

"Oh, no," he whispered into her ear, then caught her earlobe in his teeth, gently, delicately. A slight nip of razor teeth, and she sucked in a breath. He laughed, a low harsh breath against her cheek. "There are a few hours until morning."

"I hate you," she whispered back, even as her body shook and the blind fire took her again. And again.

# SELENE

# PART I

# PROLOGUE

*J'implore ta pitié, l'unique que j'aime...*  -Baudelaire

For all those who wrote to me, wondering about the
Nichtvren...

IN THE END, exhausted, she lay limp against the bed, hugging a
pillow rescued from the floor. Nikolai curled against her back,
sweat slicking his skin so it slid against hers. Her entire body
sparked pleasantly, and her shields were back up, thick enough
to protect her again.

If Danny had been able to shield himself, would he have
died? If he'd been able to run away from whatever had battered
his door down and torn him limb from limb, maybe he would
have survived. *Too late.* The thought she'd been avoiding the
whole time arrived, setting its claws just behind her ribs and
digging in. *I was too late.*

The image of her brother's door, torn to shreds, and
the...pieces...in his hall wouldn't go away. If Nikolai had
intended to distract her, it wasn't working.

Nikolai's hand polished the curve of her hip, something
cool and metallic sliding against her skin. He drew it up over her
ribs, under her breast, then the medallion lay where it used to,
half the chain spilling down to pool on the sheet. He fastened it
at the back of her neck, one-handed, and flattened his other
palm against the silver lying between her breasts. "This is

important, Selene. Without it, you're at risk. This gives you protection. You cannot throw it away. Understood?"

*I should have thrown it somewhere you couldn't get it back.* "Something killed my brother." Her throat rasped dryly, sobs caught and transformed into a stone. "What happened? What was it?"

He sighed, and she could predict his answer—the same one he gave every time he wasn't going to tell her a damn thing. "If I tell you what I know, it would be nothing. If I tell you what I suspect, it will be confusing, because I suspect many things." He yawned, burying his face in her hair, spread one hand against her belly. He was warm enough to pass for human now. The flush of sex had fed him. "If I tell you what I expect, we will be here for many hours, since I have learned to expect everything. It is far too soon to tell."

"My brother," she said, tonelessly. His knees were behind hers, one arm under her head, the other holding her to him. A yawn threatened to crack her jaw, changed into a sob she killed by locking it behind her teeth. It wasn't easy, but she was used to swallowing.

A *tantraïïken* had to swallow all sorts of things. "Something killed my brother, Nikolai."

*Something battered down his door and tore him into shreds. If you were watching over me, why weren't you watching over him? We're your pets, right? Or did you not care about him as long as you could get what you needed from me?* That was more likely. Nichtvren had once been human, sure—but most of them, if they made it alive to their Mastery, were used to taking what they wanted and damn the consequences for the mortals.

Especially when the mortals were useful.

Selene was very, very useful. It wasn't every day a Nichtvren found an unattached—*unowned,* her brain whispered, *call it what it is, you're old enough to call things what they are*—sexwitch wandering around. It was like a glutton finding a perpetual free hot meal under a tree.

"Cooperate with me, and I will find whatever killed your brother." Nikolai sighed again, relaxing against her back the way a cat might. A very big, very warm cat. Next would come The

Question, the one he asked every time. "Dawn is approaching. Will you come with me?"

"I have work tomorrow," she whispered, watching the edge of her pillowcase. *And a funeral to put together. And my brother's killer to find. Though you showing up puts a definite kink in things. As always. In every sense of the word.*

"Already done. You are not expected there for another two weeks."

*Damn you.* "I can't afford—"

"With pay."

"I don't want your money." They both knew she was lying. His money was the only thing standing between her and the gutter, and Selene had no intention of ever going back to being poor. Teaching barely paid the rent, for either her or Danny. He earned what he could as a Journeyman, of course, but there was only so much he could do when confined to the walls of his apartment— *Well, that's something you don't have to worry about now, is it?* The mocking little voice inside her head was familiar, loaded with self-loathing, and Selene flinched without moving.

Nikolai didn't take the bait. "It is not mine; it is from the college. You may call it a gift. For my Selene."

She closed her eyes. *If he was human, what would I do?* "I'm not yours." *You just own me because I'm weak. You like that, too, you like that I can't say no.*

As usual, he was too graceful to press the point. "You must belong somewhere," he said softly.

"I belonged with Danny." Poor, poor Danny. Locked in his apartment except for those times that he slipped the chain of his own body and went Journeying. How many times had Selene climbed the steps to his apartment to ask his help for the cold cases Jack Pepper brought her? How many times had she brought him meals, brought him little things he needed because he couldn't stand to leave the wards Selene had made for him?

*You undead jerk. Now he's gone, you wouldn't have even let me look at his body.*

If she was reading this situation right, Nikolai had neatly diverted the police from taking any real action. As the prime paranormal Power in the city, he could do that—and he could make Selene vanish from regular life too.

If he wanted to. If she made enough trouble.

"He was under my protection too." Nikolai's breath brushed her ear. She braced herself for him to do something, anything other than just lay there. "Come with me, Selene. You will be safer."

*Like hell I will.* "No."

"One day you will." He didn't push the issue, for once. Only asking twice? It was like some sort of record. "Jorge will come to offer you use of a car."

*Jorge? He'll make sure I don't get anything done tomorrow.* "And to keep an eye on me? No thanks, Nikolai." Selene bit her lower lip, bruising already. She tasted blood. She would ache tomorrow. It had been too long, she'd built up a heavy debt, and her body had exacted its toll with a vengeance. Not only had she cleared a poltergeist infestation and pulled the broken wards from Danny's apartment, but there had also been the work for that witch over on Seventeenth Street.

She'd needed the money. She always needed the money.

Nikolai paused, and his hand tensed against her belly. She held her breath, thinking of the prickle of claws against her skin; but he just tightened his arm around her.

For a bare moment it was like lying in bed with a human man, one she could pretend wanted her for her mind instead of for the sex, and tears prickled at her eyes. *Buck up, Selene. They all know you're weak, so let them keep thinking it. But don't you dare cry where Nikolai can see it. Don't you dare.*

"This is not a request. Jorge will come, and if you leave this place it will be with him. If you do anything foolish I will be vexed." His breath was soft against her hair, an intimate touch.

*Does he breathe because he knows it makes me a little more comfortable? I suppose he has to breathe to talk, doesn't he? I should ask.* Exhaustion crept in. If she fell asleep now she might be able to get a few hours of rest before...no. The fatigue blurred everything, made it difficult to think. "Vex all you want, Nik," she said, and his fingers tapped against her belly once, twice. Then he stopped. "I'm not your servant. I don't take your orders."

*Not without a lot of kicking and screaming. Or sometimes just screaming.*

He made a low sound against her hair, and Selene's traitorous body leapt. The medallion gave one scorching burst of heat. "Of course, if Jorge is incompetent enough to lose you, I suppose he will need punishment."

*You bastard. I should have known.* She'd made it a game at first, ditching Nikolai's trained dogs. Then he'd found the way to make her stop. "You wouldn't."

"I would, Selene. And I would make you watch." He sounded calm as if he was discussing a grocery list. "I dislike the thought of damage to you. I will take steps to avoid it."

*Everyone knows I'm your pet. Your prize little buffet, reserved for exclusive use.* "Nothing's going to happen to me."

But something had happened to Danny, hadn't it? Was it connected to Nikolai?

If it was, she might be dead in the water. She pushed the thought away. Now wasn't the time for planning. Now was the time for watching her step and letting Nikolai think she was resigned to him controlling everything.

"Especially not with Jorge watching over you." Neat, logical, precise. Just like always.

*Let him think you've given in.* Her throat ached, and her eyes were hot. "Fine. I'll wait for him. I'll be a good little girl. Now go away and leave me alone." *You've got what you wanted.*

Nikolai rolled away from her, his arm sliding from beneath her head. She heard him moving, getting into his clothes. She could imagine him getting dressed, pulling his jeans up, pulling his T-shirt back over his head, running his fingers back through his hair to push it back out of his face. Then his coat. She heard the heavy wool moving.

*Best of both worlds. He has to go home before dawn. Can't stay to make things sticky. And he's so fucking careful not to damage me. Though I can take it, can't I? It's hard to kill me. With sex, at least.*

The official word for people like her was *tantraiiken.* The working title was "sexwitch." The paranormal community, with its absolute genius for boiling everything down to essentials, called those like her *the beggars.*

Because they were always pleading and pleasing, born to be slaves. It was hard to mount a war for independence when your body kept betraying you.

He leaned over the bed to pull the sheet and the blankets back up, tucking her in gently and efficiently. When the covers were smoothed, he settled on the side of the bed and touched her hair. Ran his fingers through the heavy mass, lifting it slightly, and gathering it all up, pulling it back from her face. He stroked her cheek with his fingertips. His claws didn't prickle, but she knew they were there.

Selene kept her eyes shut. If she had to look at the face of a stone angel under a shelf of dark hair again, and see the lying concern in his dark inhuman eyes, she would start crying, and that would mean she'd broken. It was a familiar game, holding off any reaction until the client left. Making herself cold, putting a good face on her helplessness.

Her breathing evened out. She hugged the pillow. Her right hand was under the covers, and she made a fist, her nails biting into her palm. Squeezed. Tighter. Tighter.

Finally, Nikolai touched the corner of her mouth with a fingertip. Selene didn't open her eyes—but she did peek out through her lashes. Under the bedroom window shade, a faint grayness showed. Dawn was coming.

There was a slight sound—a breath of air. A cold breeze touched Selene's cheek.

Nikolai was gone.

She drove her fingernails into her palms and took in a shuddering breath.

Now, at last, she could cry. Except she couldn't. There was work to do.

Selene pushed back the covers, destroying Nikolai's tight, careful tucking-in job. She pushed herself up to a sitting position, swiped angrily at her wet cheeks, and slid out of bed.

# ONE

SHE TOOK A long shower, rinsing away sweat and stickiness. Her palms hurt, her legs hurt, her back throbbed; there were various other aches and pains. If she'd gone to work today, she'd be miserable and stiff.

That reminded her of Nikolai, quietly taking care of rearranging her life. Selene swiped condensation from the mirror and looked at herself.

Dark blue cat-tilted eyes—just like Danny's—in a pale face, two spots of color high on her cheeks. Her mouth, shaped just like Danny's too, with the same full lower lip. Blonde—well, maybe that was too ambitious a word. Maybe just brown with blonde pretensions. There was nothing special about her face.

Of course, that wasn't how they would see her. All of them, from Nikolai to Jack and down to anyone she passed on the street, would see a pretty woman, a desirable woman, a woman who smelled like something fragrant and wanting. Her cursed talent would take care of attracting willing partners so it could feed itself.

Men would whistle, women would gather and glance at her. The openly lesbian would approach sometimes, the straight women would simply stare with envy and longing.

Selene shut her eyes, holding the towel to her chest. Who was she, now that Danny was dead? He had been immune from her as a *tantraiiken*, thank God, and had done his best to protect her when she'd hit puberty and the boys in the refugee camps and orphanages had started to notice her. Selene hadn't understood what was happening; the Power had been so delicious, so warm, and she had been able to do things. Unfortunately, she hadn't known about the price.

Selene shivered. *Don't think about that.*

The silver medallion hung against her skin, warm from the heat of the shower. It was a flat disc of glittering silver, with a maybe-lion's head etched into its surface. The back of it held a few squiggles. Nichtvren writing.

*Vampire language. I wonder what it says. No Trespassers? Property of Nikolai? Best if opened by this date?*

She'd never asked. The medallion was supposed to protect her from other paranormals—the nonhumans that might be tempted to scoop her up as a pet. She'd never had it put severely to the test since he'd given it to her all those months ago; Nikolai ran a tight ship. Everyone who would be tempted to snatch her inside the city limits had been warned away. She'd heard little whispers, here and there, especially when plugging into the paranormal network to do her freelance work. *Don't touch that. It's owned.*

Throwing it away when Nikolai tried to stop her from seeing her brother's body had been just a useless defiance, like all of Selene's other useless little defiances.

*Great, Selene. While you're standing here, mooning over your own reflection, the marks are fading. Come on. Get busy. You've got a few hours before Jorge gets here, use them!*

She left the towel hanging up neatly in her cream-and-rose bathroom. Her hair dripped against the small of her back as she came out into her bedroom. The bed was neatly made, showing no signs of the hours she'd spent with Nikolai. And there was weak rainy sunlight against her window shade. Daytime. Not the best for a full Work, but it would do.

Selene shrugged into her black silk robe. It stuck against her damp skin. She swept her hair up and thrust two enameled chopsticks through a loose chignon. Then she went into the living room.

It took only a moment to move the coffee table aside and roll up the rug. The space revealed was hardwood floor, with a complicated chalk diagram drawn on it, a triangle within a circle and various runic symbols around the edge of the circle. The chalk was as clean and crisp as the first day she'd traced the diagram, kept there by the Power trapped in Selene's apartment. She'd christened the diagram by sleeping atop the rug with a Refugee Restoration lawyer she'd brought home from a bar on the East Side. Drained and happy, he'd gone home the next morning, and still sent her flowers occasionally. A good contact, a *useful* contact when handled correctly.

*I wonder if I could use him again? No, it would get sticky; I'm fairly sure Nikolai will show up in the middle of it. Again. He ruined the last date with that stockbroker, I could have gotten a good charge off that man. And some cash, too. Goddamn Nichtvren, as if he's the only one allowed to touch me.*

Although it was comforting, to know you weren't likely to catch anything. She was remarkably resistant to all types of diseases, but Nikolai was completely immune. It was one less thing to worry about, even if he was a possessive scumbucket.

Selene carried her canvas bag into the middle of the diagram, stepping carefully over the chalk line. Her pulse quickened just a little; her body knew this was where she did her Work. Her "batteries" were fully charged—Nikolai had seen to that—and what she was going to do would take them down by about half. She would need him again in a week or two.

"Need him," Selene murmured. "Yeah. Like I need a—"

Then she shut her lips firmly. Whatever she spoke here would come true, since this was her Place of Power. *An arrogant, overbearing vampire screwing up my life. I need to find a real boyfriend.*

The trouble was, most human men didn't have the required endurance. Plenty of them wouldn't like her keeping a stable of three or four. And one-night stands were dangerous on more than a potential-disease level. You never knew what you were getting. Danny had chased off more than one sicko with his trusty switchblade, back before they'd met Nikolai.

Back when she'd been reduced to taking clients off the streets to feed her curse.

*Stop it, Selene.* She settled down, her sore legs crossed and her robe pooling around her. She pushed a strand of wet hair back, and opened her bag, drawing out her athame and contemplating it. Some witches liked ornate fantasy knives, but Selene had always preferred something functional and simple. Of course, few of the others who called themselves witches had her handicaps or her specific gifts, though plenty of people were doing things they couldn't before.

The Awakening had changed everything.

None of them had grown up in the camps, either. Here on the West Coast the camps were Recent, though Unpleasant, History. And unpleasant history was always easy to forget. Especially with the Paranormal Species Act and the Parapsychic Act signed into law. The War and the Awakening was done and over with, and nobody wanted to think about nasty things like the sudden exponential jump in psychic ability. Or the War's hungry, dark aftermath.

*Except the kids who grew up in the craters. We can't stop thinking about it.* The handle was plain dark wood, the blade eight inches long and razor-sharp in its sheath.

And it held the remains of the wards from her brother's apartment, careful delicate work she'd pulled away and stored in the physical fabric of the knife so she could look at them later.

*It's later now.*

Danny had been dead for less than twelve hours now. The trail was only going to get colder, and this was the only clue she had.

Selene turned her athame over and over in her hands, and closed her eyes. Tears rose behind her eyelids, filled her throat. She'd always been good at promising herself "breakdowns later, work now."

*Just get this done and you can cry. You can't cry now, it will ruin your concentration.*

She swallowed against the lump in her throat. Then she lifted her head and spoke the Word that made the circle come to life.

The chalk lines shifted on the floor and began to writhe prettily. *I am a true artist.* Selene felt the ghost of a smile touch her lips. *Not bad for learning most of my magick from books and in trade.* Then she lifted the sheathed knife from her lap.

She clasped it in her left hand while she began to speak the language of her magick, the spell falling from her lips in a stream of syllables that was never the same twice. Her right hand passed over a section of the floor in front of her, and the hardwood rippled just a little, like heat haze on pavement. Then she lay the knife down and spread both her hands over it, took a deep breath in, and felt the first few glimmers of feeling down low in her belly. The Power started to drain from her, taking shape in the spell. Like Nikolai's hand between her legs, careful and just a little rough, touching her in exactly the right way.

Selene's head tipped back, and she gasped. She liked her privacy while she Worked, because it was so close to sex even she couldn't tell the two apart. The sensations blurred, and her hands, held over the knife with her fingers spread, began to shake.

*Show me,* she whispered, she cajoled, she seduced. *Show me. Show me.*

The wards rose, shimmering, little sparkles of crimson energy. It was her Work, with the blurring of Danny's personality overlying. It unfolded in a complex matrix, dimensions spreading up and out, threads of Power unweaving here and there once the wards weren't anchored in a physical object.

Selene struck, plunging through the matrix of energy, the pattern taking its place in her mind.

*Danny's apartment. Knock on the door—he doesn't answer, shaking, he's shaking. Flood of chemical fear, salt against her tongue, he's cold. Selene. He has to warn Selene. "Cold—Lena, don't—don't. Dangerous..." He says it into the phone. His fingers are numb. He's been out a-journeying, traveling on the astral, and yanked back into his body, that's why he's freezing. Panic threading through his bones, spilling through his veins, loose cool terror. He has miscalculated.*

*Darkness, spilling into the apartment, filling the hall, the door burst off its hinges. It roared in the hall, and Danny looked into the laughing face of evil before it was on him.*

*"Give my regards to Nikolai," a soft, deadly voice purred. Beads clacking against shoulders, a hook nose, clamping of razor-sharp fingers in Danny's throat. Screaming, muffled and choked.*

*"The book!" He tried to scream, a wet garbled sound. "Selene, the book, the book!"*

It threw her back. Blood flew. She made a muffled choked sound too, and her curse blazed into life, slamming into her nervous system like a freight train. She hit the bottom of her sturdy, scuffed leather couch and slid down to lie on the floor, her cheek against the floor, the robe falling open. The medallion lay against her chest, scorching hot, and it stayed hot while Selene grayed out for a little while, losing consciousness, drifting back and forth.

When she finally came back into herself, she blinked something warm and wet out of her eyes. Selene levered herself up, the dull ache pounding between her legs and—thankfully—subsiding when she pushed it down.

The curse was well fed, and it would obey her. For now.

Blood dripped into her eyes and trickled out of her nose. She'd bitten her lip too, blood smearing on the floor and her hand as she wiped blindly at her face. There was a thick smell in the air, and she sniffed deeply, filling her nose with the stench.

It was a distinctive scent. Now she had her quarry. Never mind that it was probably a quarry who would kill her too, if she managed to track it. That was the least of her problems right now.

The thing that had killed her brother smelled like death and pain and blood, something male, ancient—and hungry. Wet ratfur and a kind of musk. Selene made it up to sitting and rested her fevered forehead on her knees, blood soaking into the loose silk of her robe. Whatever it was, it was hungry. She shivered, her teeth chattering, even though she was sweating freely again.

*Give my regards to Nikolai.*

She waited until the shivers eased, and used the couch to pull herself up. She sat primly on the old leather, her fingers interlaced in her lap like a schoolgirl. Thank God she was fully recharged, or that might have drained her to the point of madness.

The medallion cooled, pulsing between her breasts. Nikolai might be able to tell that she'd worked magick, but he wouldn't be able to tell *exactly* what she'd done.

*I hope he won't, at least. What was Danny talking about, the book? So Nikolai's mixed up in this?*

It was simple once she thought about it. Danny's little black notebook, the one that held his secrets. As a Journeyman, he was an information broker for certain parts of the city, certain clients who needed particular talents. Selene had turned a blind eye to it, mostly because they both needed the money Danny brought in from selling what he knew.

It was the only book Selene could think of that might explain what had happened. If Danny had come across the wrong piece of information—or sold to the wrong people—it could have been very dangerous. And Nikolai was mixed up in it somehow.

No wonder he hadn't wanted a report filed, and hadn't wanted Selene near the body. How deeply was he involved?

Right now it didn't matter. She'd put it off as long as it could.

*Oh, Danny.* Her eyes brimmed with fresh hot salt water. Tears slid down her cheeks, mixing with the blood. *I'm so sorry. If we hadn't...if I hadn't...oh, Danny.*

She cried for a good half-hour, while the apartment building woke up around her. Smells of coffee brewing, sound of footsteps, water beginning to run through pipes, Pippa Shelton next door turning her hip-hop radio up. All of them going on about their normal lives. Selene was the only Talent in the building—and if they knew, they would probably kick her out. Oh, they would find something else to pin it on, for sure— a discrepancy in the rental agreement, something in the lease— but she would be out on the street again and maybe lose her job again too if they found out. It was illegal, of course, under the terms of the new Parapsychic Act, to deny someone lodging or employment because they had Talent...but nobody cared about that. It was like being accused of being a Gilead sympathizer, nobody gave a damn if it was true or not. They just reflexively cut you loose.

Now that Danny was dead, she had nobody else in the entire world to depend on. At least, nobody who wouldn't exact a price for anything she asked of them. Nobody who would take care of her, nobody she could relax with.

When she finished crying, she just sat there for a few minutes, struggling to breathe. If she didn't stop soon she would need Nikolai again. Either him or someone else, the curse didn't care. Fear and pain changed directly into desire, and that fed her power...but the desire itself had to be fed, too.

*I wish I'd killed myself when I had the chance. Before I knew what this would do to me. Before I became a fucking whore.*

When she finally had herself under some kind of control, she got up, wiped up the blood on the floor with a handful of her robe. She picked up her athame again, stepping carefully over the chalk marks. They were still and faded now, and would need recharging. She'd expended more Power than she'd thought. She rolled the carpet carefully back, put her athame away, and replaced the coffee table. Then she hobbled slowly into the bathroom. She needed another shower, and she had to get dressed.

Her face was a mess of tears and half-coated with blood from a shallow slice along her hairline. The snapping backlash of Power had been flung at her, needle-sharp and potentially deadly. She was lucky it had missed her eyes. Her nose was still trickling blood, and her lip would probably swell. She looked worked-over, to be sure. Maybe she would have a black eye.

*That will be great, a shiner to add to the fun.* The silver medallion was warm against her skin. It glittered once, angrily, and she touched it with a bloody finger.

The lion's head—was it a lion? Whatever it was, etched into the front of the silver disc, shifted slightly. Selene frowned and touched it again. The warmth coming from it intensified, and a sudden rush of sensation crawled down Selene's skin.

Power. Stored in the medallion? Maybe.

*Well, isn't that useful.* She clutched at her bathroom counter, looked up into the mirror. The medallion glinted, subsided as she took a deep breath. She was wet between her legs, slick and swollen.

Another deep breath, forcing it down. Making the curse obey her.

The curse retreated. She stared at the silver disc and wondered again exactly what it was.

*Get going. Jorge will be here soon. And if he sees you in this state, he'll report it to Nikolai. You don't want that.*

*Give my regards to Nikolai.* The soft voice was etched in her memory, tied to the sick twisting smell of whatever had killed Danny. Long hair, beads clacking. Selene shook the memory away.

Now she had a lead, it was time to work it.

For the second time that morning she stepped into the shower. She twisted the single knob over to "hot" and yanked it outwards. The water gurgled and sprayed into life, stinging needles of cold water hitting her shrinking flesh. It warmed up quickly, became scalding-hot, and she stood under the painful spray and kept crying.

SHE WAS DRESSED by the time a courteous knock sounded at her door. Charcoal wool skirt hemmed just below the knee, black heels, black nylons, a crisp white dress shirt and a charcoal wool blazer. It screamed *professional*, though she'd bought the suit at a thrift store. Prices were finally going down all over as the infrastructure recovered from the Republic's slash-and-burn, and the black market was withering to drugs and illegal weapons. A few years ago it had been impossible to even find bread or butter without knowing someone. And clothes? Forget it.

She opened the door to find Jorge Czestowitz looming in the hall outside.

He wore, as usual, a dark-gray Jarmani suit and a tasteful wine-red tie. He was built like a football player, wide shoulders and a bull neck, a bald head that gleamed in the yellow electric light from the hall fixtures, and a diamond earring that winked merrily at her from his left ear. "Hi, Jorge." She smiled, leaning against the wall. "Come on in. Want some coffee?"

"Hello, Miss Selene." Always with the formality. He was one of Nikolai's thralls, but Selene liked him anyway. He was quiet, and didn't try to force her into doing anything. Instead, he asked politely, and Selene usually could see the logic of his requests. "Tea, if you have it. Thank you."

"Come in," she repeated. "You okay?"

Jorge stepped his Trestoni loafers over her threshold and into her apartment. "You've been working magick in here." He sniffed deeply. "And you've changed your perfume. You used to wear Chatelier."

*Knockoff Chatelier, you mean, since I couldn't afford pre-War perfume if I tried. How very observant of you.* "Nikolai said he liked it, so I had to change." *Not to mention I could finally afford something real instead of tramp-juice.* Selene shut the door behind him. "And I had Work to do. The world doesn't stop just because my brother gets m-murdered." She cursed the quavering in her voice, flipped both locks, suddenly squeamishly glad for Jorge's presence. He was big, and a Nichtvren's thrall; between that and the locks on the door she was as safe as possible.

"I was told of your loss." Jorge followed her into the kitchen. It was another reminder of just how big he was, the way her apartment suddenly seemed too small around her. "I am sorry, Selene."

"Me too." She took her battered green enamel kettle from the stove, filled it with water and set it back, turning the gas on. Flame burst into life. For a moment, just like she did every time, she marveled at heat you could get just by twisting a dial, instead of scrounging for waste wood. "The worst part of it is the cops probably won't touch it. Nikolai's pulled a few strings and Jack's declared it a Paranormal Case. And Nikolai won't lift a finger."

"How do you know?" Jorge reached up for the chipped and scarred metal canister of teabags. He didn't look at her legs or her breasts, which Selene was grateful for. He treated her like a person instead of a cut of meat; that was rare and precious indeed.

"Because I won't 'cooperate' with his game plan, whatever it is." She set a coffee cup down on the counter. "Make yourself at home. I want to put my hair up."

"You look beautiful." Jorge said it quietly, as a compliment instead of a come-on. "Selene, your brother was under Nikolai's protection too. The Master has to answer this killing, or it will be seen as weakness. He won't let it go."

*Thanks for reminding me Nikolai wouldn't be interested unless it affects him somehow.* "Great." Selene's mouth twisted. "So he'll go out for revenge, but not until he uses this to get any leverage he can on me. How utterly typical. How did you get involved with such a bastard, Jorge?" She leaned against the kitchen counter, combing her fingers back through her wet hair and gritting her teeth as she found tangles. "I mean, you seem like a decent fellow." *For a thrall.*

Jorge looked down at the scarred Formica counter. "Nikolai took me from my native land after he saved my life. I asked to go with him. He is an honorable man."

"I'm not sure the term 'man' applies." The kettle began to make its usual pre-boil sounds. "I'm going to go put my hair up."

"Thank you, Miss Selene." As usual, he said her name almost stiffly, as if it was a foreign title. He had a thick, round face and heavy black eyebrows over hazel eyes, wide lips, and a nose that had been broken one or two times. "Nikolai wouldn't like it if you were hurt. That's why I'm here."

"I know why you're here," Selene tossed over her shoulder as she headed across the living room. *To make sure I behave like a good little slave and don't get any ideas about investigating on my own.* Pearly rainy-day light came in through her windows, the shades open wide. She didn't get much light since her windows only looked out onto an alley. "I'm not mad at you, Jorge. I'm mad at *him*."

"That's the usual state of affairs." Jorge muttered, and she pretended she didn't hear, pacing into her bathroom. Her hair was still damp, and if she had it down today it would cover the shallow slice on her forehead. It would also tangle, and invite people to touch it.

So she had to put it up.

The swelling over her eye had gone down. Thank God for little favors. She combed quickly, yanking at the tangled bits. Her lip stung. Then she French-braided the whole mess back, a thick rope reaching almost to her waist. *Why am I being nasty? It's not his fault he works for Nikolai. He's also one of the more decent of his thralls. There was the one that wouldn't even let me go outside, I could have died of embarrassment.*

When she came out, Jorge had a cup of tea in his hands, and was studying one of her cheap metal bookcases—the one with the reference texts. "I've never seen your books by day before. You have quite a collection."

Selene shrugged. "Goes with the territory. I had to find out what I was, and then I had to research in college. I can't stand to throw a book away." *Especially since I didn't see a real one until I was twelve. Just the chapsheets at the orphanage. It's a wonder I'm literate at all.*

He nodded, his bald head gleaming. She looked past him to the window. It was a gray, nasty, drizzly day. She would have to wear a coat.

Her conscience pricked her. He didn't deserve the sharp edge of her tongue, he was just as helpless as she was. One of the slaves, just like she was. "I'm sorry, Jorge. I shouldn't take it out on you."

He didn't look away from the shelves. "It's all right. You have a right to be upset."

She stopped by the entrance to the kitchen, staring at her black leather purse. It sat obediently on the counter. "I don't think *upset* quite covers the way I'm feeling. I..."

*What exactly do I feel?* There was a hollow place under her ribs, a whistling emptiness, just like a very cold stream. One that could numb your feet while sharp rocks slashed them to ribbons. *I don't know how I feel. Isn't that strange.*

"Ah." Jorge took a sip of tea, transferred his gaze from the shelves to the cup's interior. It was probably tact, giving her the only space he could. "Nikolai will answer this, Miss Selene. I know he will."

Selene nodded. The simple faith shining in the big man's eyes was uncomfortable to witness, like watching a kid who still believed in Santa Claus or Kochba bar Gilead. *He'll answer it if it serves a purpose for him to do so. That's how Nichtvren work.* "Not before he gets whatever he can out of me for the service."

Jorge shrugged. It was an evocative movement, expressing regret and resignation all at once. "Thank you for the tea."

She felt a small smile lift up the corner of her stinging lips. "You're so polite, Jorge. I suppose I have to go to the police station."

"To sign a statement. Nikolai also expressed that you would wish to visit a funeral parlor. To select a suitable...container."

Selene shivered. The morning's magick hung in the air, like the smell of spiced rum. And darkness, the lingering reek of the thing that had burst into Danny's apartment. "An urn, because they incinerate paranormal victims unless the family has a release on file. It'll have to be a memorial service, if he has a funeral at all. I can't imagine anyone else would attend." Her voice shook slightly. *Listen to me. I sound bitter.* Grief twisted inside her, down in the dark place where her curse dwelled. She couldn't afford it. It would drain her, and raise her to a pitch where she would need someone, anyone.

Even Nikolai.

"You might be surprised," Jorge replied, kindly enough. "I take it you're ready to go?"

"I just have to find my coat." The hall closet door squeaked slightly, familiar. Nikolai had hung her camel coat up, neatly, and it was still damp from last night's desperate running in the rain, trying to reach Danny's apartment in time.

She lifted it down, still on the hanger, hung it back up. "Fuck it. I don't need a coat. I suppose Nikolai sent a car, huh?"

"Of course, Miss Selene." He set the mug in the kitchen sink, carefully. "Since you don't have one, he sent one of his. He also sent Bradley to do the driving, and Netley is waiting."

*Wait just one skin-pickin' minute here. Just what the hell is this?* "Netley? Nikolai sent *three* of this thralls? One of them his chief attorney?" Selene folded her arms. "What aren't you telling me?"

Jorge shrugged again, spreading his hands. "I only know Nikolai ordered the three of us to accompany you today." The words were careful, but his grim expression spoke volumes.

"He expects trouble?" Selene's eyebrows drew together. A chill finger touched the base of her spine. Her skin tightened and her nipples hardened, and she was glad she didn't start blushing.

*Goddamn fear. Control yourself!*

"I don't know what he expects, really." He looked so worried Selene actually believed him. "Sending us with you will make it clear that he intends to find out who killed your brother, and to answer the attack. It will also make it clear that he takes the threat to you very seriously. Or so he said."

Hearing Nikolai's reasons for anything always made her feel like she was playing chess with a very hungry tiger. Chess had rules, and even a tiger could be trained to play, she supposed. But if a tiger gets hungry enough, all the rules in the world wouldn't stop it from eating you. "Well." Her throat was dry. "I have to go by the precinct. And I need to...to go by Danny's apartment. There are some things I want to have."

Jorge nodded. "I suppose Nikolai expected as much."

Selene waited. When it became apparent Jorge wasn't going to say anything further, she looked up at him, letting her eyes open all the way, softening her lips. She'd done this so many times, and most men had a very hard time concentrating when faced with it.

It wasn't fair, but neither was Nikolai forcing her to trail around behind two of his shaved gorillas and his head attorney today. "What else did he expect?" *And are you going to let me into Danny's apartment? Or has Nikolai banned me from seeing it?*

*And what aren't you telling me?*

He shrugged again. Selene blinked, but Jorge's hazel eyes were steady. He wasn't even sweating. She would have to do a little more than flutter her eyelashes to drag anything out of him, and that was dangerous. If she touched one of his thralls, Nikolai would know.

He *always* knew.

The sour taste of failure scoured her tongue, but she wasn't beaten yet.

Selene scooped her purse up. "Fine. I get the score. Let's go."

# Two

IT WAS AN uncomfortable, mostly silent ride. Jorge didn't speak in front of Price Netley, Nikolai's chief attorney, a short thin man in a dapper dark-blue suit. Netley was blond, bland, and smooth; he stared at Selene's legs, making no attempt to hide his interest. She began to wish she'd worn a coat—even a coat Nikolai had touched—when Netley transferred his gaze to her chest, and she was actively longing to punch him by the time he coughed and glanced up at her face, realizing she was watching.

"See something you like?" She wet her lips with her tongue, just to play. The sweet musky perfume of her skin would be filling the car, making it damn hard to think, and the fact that he was Nikolai's thrall only added to the nasty squirming sense of satisfaction under her breastbone. *Go ahead, Netley. Keep staring. It won't do you any good.*

He flushed, and Jorge glanced at him. He had been watching out the window as the limo pulled away from the curb, the heat of him comforting on her right side. "Selene?" Jorge's tone was careful, mild, and held just a hint of a grumble.

Selene shrugged, settling back into the seat and crossing her ankles. Netley looked away. She'd made her point. *Don't stare at me like that. I don't like it.*

The black limo was the one Nikolai had sent for her before, one of the new hybrid antigrav-petroleo models, quiet and rolling on a cushion of invisible antifriction instead of tires. The reactive paint along the underside would keep it sliding along two feet from the pavement. Nothing but the best and newest for the prime paranormal Power. A pale leather interior, a dry bar, and smoked glass between the seats and the driver's section.

The first time she'd ever been in a limo, it ended up wrecked into a flaming ball of twisted metal, and Selene herself had barely escaped.

It had been one hell of a prom night. A couple of pro-Gilead reactionaries had decided to show their disapproval of the refugee camps by disrupting the one party the kids got, since it was "sinful" to dance. Selene still wasn't sure if they'd picked her group because her Talent had just begun to show. But then, they'd hit the whole line of donated limos, old things that still ran solely on petroleo, and seventeen kids had died. The others...well, hospitals in the camps weren't the best. Not by a long shot.

She shivered, remembering screams and the smells of burning rubber and scorched metal. The medallion warmed against her skin. There was a trickle of Power coming from it, seeping into her skin. *That* was new. Had she triggered something in it with the Work this morning?

Selene snagged the chain and drew it out from under her shirt, cupping the medallion in her palm. The almost-lion's head was the same, and the Nichtvren squiggles on the back. She touched the engraved head, running her fingertip over the curve of the mane, testing the edge of the disc. Smooth and hard, impenetrable.

*Just like Nikolai.*

Netley made a small sound. Selene looked up. He had gone chalky-pale under his expensive razor-layered haircut.

"What?" Her heart lodged in her throat. *Don't have a heart attack, I'm just looking at it.* "What is it? Netley?"

He didn't answer, just looked hurriedly out the window. His Adam's apple bobbed as he swallowed.

She tried another tack. "Jorge?"

But he was looking out the window too. A faint sheen of sweat showed on his bald head.

A deep sigh worked its way out of her. "Someone will have to tell me what this is all about," she said to the thick silence. Then she dropped the medallion back down inside her shirt and pulled her purse up onto her lap, hugging it. Maybe she shouldn't have dressed professionally. Jeans and boots would have served her better, especially if she had to escape.

If she escaped them, Nikolai would punish Jorge. The thought made Selene's stomach flip. The nausea, true to form, made her flush.

*I've really got to find a way to get out of here. There's got to be somewhere I can live and not have to sell myself, someplace I can go where I won't have to be what I am.*

Yeah. If she moved out in the country she'd go mad once her charge ran out and her curse had no sex to feed on. That had almost happened before she and Danny had gotten clearance to leave the camp. They'd made it out just in time, right before mandatory Matheson testing became law. Selene might have been scooped up and sent to a parapsychic lab, or forced into one of many government programs meant to figure out just what the Awakening had done and how Power worked now.

As much as Selene hated the city, it kept her alive. At least being Nikolai's slave left her largely able to do as she pleased—and kept the government from swallowing her for experimentation.

Besides, she *liked* dressing this way. Nylons had been impossible to get in the camps, and heels? Forget it. Not to mention any decent lipstick.

She stared unseeing out the window, and it wasn't until Jorge discreetly handed her a crisp white handkerchief that she noticed she was leaking again. Tears rolled down her cheeks, slick and hot.

She just finished mopping at her face as the limo braked to a smooth stop in a No Parking zone directly in front of the South Side Precinct house, a concrete rectangle reinforced with chunks of the new plastic-steel stuff that was all over the city these days. Selene started to move, but Jorge's fingers closed around her wrist. He was between her and the door, anyway.

The medallion suddenly flared with heat, but Jorge didn't seem to notice anything. "Let me, Selene. Please."

She settled back into the seat. It was pointless to argue.

Jorge got out, then Netley, and she was finally able to slide across the seat and duck out of the limo's quiet cocoon, taking Jorge's broad warm hand to steady herself. Heels weren't the ideal footwear for struggling out of a car. Still, they were armor. Of a sort.

She set off for the stairs that led up to the front doors of the precinct house, her heels cracking against the pavement. There was a knot of people standing off to one side with a TV van. That was usual, since the cop show was full of excitement these days, with the postwar reconstruction going on and weapons all over. So Selene ignored it—until they caught sight of her.

There was a mad scramble that ended with flashbulbs popping and Jorge pushing through a sudden crowd. Selene, shocked, stumbled behind him, Netley's hand suddenly around her elbow. *They must mistake me for someone else*, she thought, and when they finally gained the safety of the doors, she tore her arm out of his grip. "What the *hell?*"

"I was afraid of that," Netley said grimly. "I'll tell Bradley to use the parking garage to pick us up. How long will you be, Miss Thompson?"

"I don't know. It depends on what Jack says." The precinct was linoleum tile floors and fluorescent lights, cops passing back and forth, people moving like tides. There was a brass statue of Justice tucked into a niche, her eyes covered by the obligatory brass handkerchief, and a carved motto in Latin. Something pretentious about the truth setting you free. "Netley? What's going on?"

His eyes were dark and troubled. "I'll come back up every fifteen minutes. Jorge?" Jorge nodded. The attorney plunged back out through the glass door and into the waiting knot of reporters.

Selene watched this, mystified. "For Christos's sake, I know where to go—" she began, but Jorge was already speaking to the desk sergeant.

The Sarge—a tall plump mustachioed man whose uniform badge said *Parker*—glanced over Selene, glanced again, licking his lips with a bloodless tongue, and proceeded to stare at her breasts while he told Jorge to go up to the third floor, turn right, and find office 312. Selene suffered this in silence and let Jorge lead her toward the brass-mirrored elevators. He punched the "up" button, and Selene glanced back, casually, to see the Sarge hook up the phone and talk into it while staring at her ass.

It was so depressingly par for the course that Selene didn't even bother sighing, following the bald thrall into the elevator. Her eyes felt hot and grainy from crying. "Jorge, what the *hell* is going on?"

"Maybe they just liked your looks." Completely deadpan.

*So he does have a sense of humor. Good for him.* Selene bit the inside of her cheek. "Would Nikolai tell me what's going on?" She reached down, gripping the round handrail at hip-height. Her knuckles were white.

"Probably. You'd have to ask him. I'm sorry, Selene."

Meaning, *I can't tell you a damn thing, and even if I could I probably wouldn't.* "Me too. I thought you were a decent guy."

He had no snappy comeback for that.

Selene could have told him where Detective Jack Pepper's office was, but she wasn't in a mood to play tour guide. Sarge had given Jorge good directions, and it was only a few minutes until she was standing in Jack's tiny cluttered domain, looking at the familiar eternally-dying plant—a wandering-Judic that Jack had been trying to kill for two years now—and the stacks of paperwork, teetering dangerously on every horizontal surface, even the floor.

She looked up at Jorge, whose large hands folded one over the other in a classic bodyguard pose. "I'm not going anywhere," she said, dully. "Can you go down to the corner and get me a latte, please? I think I'll need the caffeine." Coffee had been hard to get after the War, at least for the first few years. It was still worth its weight in flesh or gold out in the camps. Or it had been when Selene left.

Funny how some days it felt like she hadn't left at all.

He considered this. "Do you promise not to go anywhere else?"

Selene would have been furious if she hadn't been fighting back more tears. "I give my word."

The tall bald man nodded and disappeared, closing the door behind him. Selene stood at the window, looking down at the front steps of the precinct house. The limo pulled away from the curb on its cushion of air, and she was suddenly, powerfully, tempted to run. Her heart leapt, and she rested her forehead against the chilly glass. Condensation spread out from her breath touching the cold slick surface.

She breathed slowly, struggling to contain the frustration. *If Nikolai was here...but that's ridiculous. He wouldn't be here during the day. And anyway, if he was here he'd only make it worse, trying to order me around.*

The familiar song of the precinct—murmurs of voices, footsteps, phones ringing, doors slamming—blurred together as Selene glared out the window, not seeing anything except clouds and the street below, empty cardboard people walking through their empty cardboard lives. The lump in her throat crested, and she wished that she was home, curled in her warm bed, watching whatever rain could make it into the alley bead on the window. This was definitely a day for staying in bed and forgetting about the rest of the whole goddamn planet.

*Oh, Danny. I'm so sorry, I wasn't there in time. I should never have left you alone. I should have lived with you, I should have found a way.*

The door banged open and Jack Pepper stalked in, his mournful hound-dog face drawn up in a grimace under a grim, thinning quarter-inch of brown hair. He saw her and stopped dead, a steaming cup of ash-smelling coffee in his hand. "Ah. Thompson."

"Hi, Jack." Selene turned from the window and hopped up to sit on the ledge, crossing her legs. "Mind telling me what the fuck is up? I just got mugged by press vultures."

"Aw, Christos." Jack rolled his eyes. "Good morning to you too."

Selene, settled in the window, just looked at him. He kicked the door closed and got right down to business. "My hands are fucking tied, princess. The word is down from on high that this is a Paranormal Case, and no exceptions. I can't do a goddamn thing, even on my off-hours." He stalked over to the desk and shoved aside a stack of paper to make room for his coffee cup. His suit jacket—the same one he'd been wearing early that morning at Danny's apartment—hung on the wooden chair behind his desk. His shoulder holster snagged on the thinning material of his dress shirt, which was holding up remarkably well. Selene only counted one hole in it, a small cigarette burn on his right cuff.

"Why would this be declared untouchable even if it is a PC, Jack?" Selene asked, reasonably enough. She rubbed at her forehead with her fingertips, thin skin moving over the bone. The floral musk of her skin filled the office by now. She watched Jack's shoulders come up and his head drop a little, like a turtle, and her eyes dropped to his pants.

Nothing yet, not even a telltale twitch. Jack was remarkably resistant to her. It was one of the best things about him.

He shot her a withering look. His buzzcut was wilting, lying flat against his head, and that disturbed Selene more than anything else. "'Cause something's going on, that's why. And it's probably your bloodsucking boyfriend behind it. God knows he's behind everything else in this fuckin' town."

"He's not my boyfriend—" she began, pitching her voice deliberately low. *He's my owner. Get it straight.*

Jack shivered. "Oh, come *off* it, Lena! Every time you get in trouble, he shows up and bails your ass out."

*Goddamn you.* "Jack, I'm warning you." Her voice was rising. So was his. Jack's cheeks were flushed and his hands shook. Selene sat bolt-upright on the window sill, her own hands curled into fists. She didn't glance at his crotch. She was fairly sure he had a hard-on by now. The anger would make him easier to affect.

"Christos, Selene. *Don't* start."

"I need your help," she said, softly. *Come on, Jack. You like me. I'm like your little sister, remember? I babysat your kids. Maureen likes me. You want to help me.* "You knew I'd ask, Jack. I *need* you to help me on this. I want the fucker that killed my Danny. I *want* him, you *help* me." She folded her arms, her fingers digging into her biceps.

"I can't lose my job, Lena." Jack stalked over to the window, looking out over the rain-slick street below. His jaw was working, a muscle twitching high up in his cheek. "I got Maureen and the kids to think about. The word's out, both officially and off the record. *Leave the Thompson case alone.*"

Selene's lips compressed into a thin line. She looked down at the street too, turning her face away from him. Silence stretched between them, a thin crystalline quiet full of the things they never said. She could have moved closer to him, brushed against him, but she didn't.

"Alton Gresham," she said, finally. "James Darryl Gray."

"Selene—" Jack took a half step away from her, along the window.

"Tyreese Nottingham. Lee Merrick Jones. Jimmy Dobbs Creech." Selene's voice broke. "Jerril Hightower. Allan Bowen. Do I need to go on?" *Should I start listing the names of their victims, too?*

Jack's head dropped even further. He looked down at the window ledge. She didn't move. If she did, he would look at her legs under her skirt. *I'm sorry, Jack, I really am.*

"You've helped me," he said. "That's right. You got scumbags off the street. It was the right thing to do."

*The right thing to do? And you wouldn't leave me alone once you found out I could track the bastards, even after years and the War and the death of witnesses and Jesu alone knows what else. And it doesn't matter to you that I have to sell my fucking body to do it, does it? No. You got what you wanted and now it's too bad for me. Just like always. Just like a man.* "Yeah." *Come on, Jack. Prove me wrong.* "And catching the scumbag that did a fucking Gilead Inquisitor job on my *brother* is the right thing to do. Whoever it is *tore him apart*. Into little tiny pieces. Just like a Heretic's Tangle."

He actually went pale. Jack was old enough to have seen footage from the Republic's public mass ceremonies of purification. He was old enough to remember all sorts of things.

He turned around, picked up a slim manila folder from his desk. "For God's sake, don't let anyone but Nikolai see this. I *can't* help you, Selene. But I'll look the other way, okay? It's all I can do. Come on."

*Well, that's more than I hoped for, at least.* She shoved the folder into her purse, mashing to make it fit, and pulled the zipper closed. "All right. I guess." She couldn't help herself. "You bastard." Her voice broke, and she swallowed harshly.

"I can't afford to piss Nikolai off. I got a mortgage and two kids, Lena," He was still staring at the window ledge. "And Maureen."

"Yeah. You're lucky. All I had was my brother." *That and a sucktooth breathing down my neck, wanting to own me.* She hopped down off the window ledge. Jack's eyes shifted up to her breasts, and color began to stain his flat cheeks. "What *can* you tell me, Jack? Anything?"

There was a tap on the door, and Jorge opened it, a sixteen-ounce latte balanced delicately in one large hand. "Your coffee, Miss Selene. Detective." He nodded to Jack, his bald head gleaming. He must oil it to get that sheen.

*Dammit. Just when I was getting somewhere.*

"I take it you're Nikolai's representative." Jack's shoulders went back and he dropped into the only chair in the office that wasn't buried under a drift of paper—the one behind his desk. The ancient wooden thing creaked alarmingly as he leaned back. "I have your statement from last night, Lena. Want to eyeball it?"

Selene slid down from the window ledge. She slid her purse strap up her arm, taking the papers Jack held up over his shoulder. "I suppose if I want to make corrections, you'll tell me not to waste my time?"

"Take it up with Nikolai, not me," Jack snapped. "So, Mister...?" He looked up at Jorge, trailing off.

Lena scanned the statement. As the official version of last night's events, it left out about three-quarters of what actually happened and didn't mention Nikolai at all. She picked up a pen from Jack's cluttered desk and bent down to sign it. Jack's eyes skittered over the desk, touched her face, and Selene glanced up to see the detective look hurriedly away.

"Czestowitz," Jorge said. "Jorge Czestowitz."

"Jesu Christos." Jack sounded half impressed. "Gesundheit. Nicetameetcha."

Selene tossed the signed statement onto Jack's desk. "Ciao, Pepper. I'm going to pick up some mementos from my brother's apartment. Unless I'm not allowed to even grieve for him."

"Why don't you get out of my face, Thompson?" Jack snarled back. There were half-moons of sweat on his wilting shirt, under his arms. "Go and play with your bloodsucking boyfriend, why don't you?"

*Oh, I'd love to. I'd love to take a stake and about fifty gallons of petroleo to the bastard. And I'm not going to forget this, Jack.* "Fuck you," Selene tossed over her shoulder as she took her latte from

Jorge and opened Jack's office door. "You can hunt your own goddamn murderers from now on. Don't call me, Pepper. I'll call you." *So I can tell you to go to hell.*

"Yeah, likewise," Jack muttered, and Selene heard Jorge's heavy footsteps behind her as she clicked out into the hall, swallowing the lump in her throat. *That went well. Better than I thought it would, really.*

*So why do I feel like screaming?*

# THREE

YELLOW CRIME-SCENE tape stretched across the doorframe. Jorge contemplated the plywood boards some thoughtful soul had nailed up. "I don't know, Selene. It hasn't been cleaned, or anything."

"Come on, Jorge." Selene eased herself another half-step closer to him. "I have a right. He was my *brother.*"

Jorge's eyebrows beetled together. He looked a little confused, and miserably certain he was going to get in trouble one way or the other. "Nikolai will not like this."

"He expected it, and he didn't tell you to stop me. I'm not in any danger." She actually *wheedled,* stepping even closer and pushing stray tendrils of her hair back. Her shields were thinning, she could smell Jorge's acrid lemon worry and the faint flavor of delicious chocolate wickedness that meant he was Nikolai's. She inhaled, filling her lungs with the smell.

Nikolai.

*Stop it. Business, get down to business. Quit thinking about him. You'll deal with him soon enough, I'm sure.*

"Well..." Jorge looked at the door. A slight shudder passed through his broad shoulders.

"He didn't tell you to stop me, Jorge. I have a right to go into my brother's home." Selene grabbed at the crime-scene tape and tore it down, the plastic stretching and biting her hand. "Yowch." She curled her fingers over the edge of the plywood, wriggling them through a gap. She pulled, grimacing, but couldn't move it. She hissed out through her teeth, frustrated. It wouldn't budge.

She yanked again.

Jorge shouldered her aside and thrust his fingers through the small space. Nails squealed and the plywood ripped free. He spent another moment on the piece of plywood nailed below it, and Selene let out a pent breath. "Thanks." There was a coppery, awful smell boiling out through the smashed doorframe. "Do you do parties too?"

Jorge's hazel eyes met hers. He magnanimously refused to reply.

Selene had to bend down to slip through the hole he'd made. "Wait—" Jorge began, but she was already through. *Too late. Thanks, Jorge. I owe you one for being a decent person after all.*

The cheap carpet was soaked with blood, still tacky-wet. Selene's heels slipped. *I'm going to have to burn these shoes.* Her stomach flipped under her ribs, her hands were slick with sweat.

There were footsteps out in the hall, and she heard Jorge's voice saying something about an investigation. Another voice, querulous—an old woman, maybe a neighbor. *Where were you last night?* Selene wanted to shout. *Huh? Where were you when he needed help? This had to have made a fuck of a lot of noise, where were you when he needed someone, anyone?*

*Where were you when he needed* me?

Selene edged down the hall. Rainy daylight glared in here, showing her the pools of blood, drips and spatters on the walls. The air swirled uneasily. Murder, and Selene's own magick, and the highly-charged fear and nausea of the cops and forensics personnel who had photographed and measured the scene all mixed together, a heady stew.

*I could tap in and use that, stave off having to feed.* A trickle of heat spilled into her belly, overwhelmed by revulsion at the idea. *Dear God, Danny. What did you do?*

She didn't have much time. At any moment, Jorge could rip off another piece of plywood and come in, deciding that Nikolai wouldn't like her in here at all even if he hadn't specifically banned it.

*Just look at it like any other scene. You've done this a million times, maybe more.*

A panicked, breathless little thought rose up after that. *I can't look at it like any other scene, it was Danny, Danny was lying right there—or what was left of him, anyway.*

*Stop it. You have to be calm, Lena. Do what you have to do, then you can cry. Save the weeping and whining for later, okay?*

She found herself in the kitchen, crouching down. On one side of the stove, there was a cabinet. There was very little blood here—Danny had died in the hall and the single room of the studio, maroon splashed on walls, soaking into the carpet. In here there were only a few trailing drops.

*Give my regards to Nikolai.* Selene let out a soft shapeless sigh, pushed the memory away. It didn't want to go.

Her footprints marked the linoleum, the dots of her heels, the rest of the shoe making a softly rounded triangle against the hard surface. *I'm tracking around his blood. It isn't even dry yet. God.*

She opened the cabinet and pulled the mixing bowls out. Behind them was a shapeless cloth-wrapped bundle. There was something hard in there as well as the softer edges of the notebook—Danny's little black book.

*I can't hide this, my purse is already full.* She cast around for something else.

When she finally ducked back out into the hall, carrying a small blue canvas bag she'd often used to bring Danny his library books, Jorge was still looming with his arms crossed over his massive Jarmani-clad chest. The dingy orange-carpeted hallway was quiet around him, a midday sort of quiet. Someone's television was turned way up, and Selene heard a newscaster's voice rising and falling through the thin walls. It sounded rich, not tinny—maybe someone had one of the new three-dimensional holograph sets Danny was always talking about.

"Did you retrieve what you needed?" Jorge asked, kindly enough.

Selene nodded. Her throat constricted. The medallion warmed again between her breasts, the silver shifting slightly against her skin. "Thanks, Jorge. I mean it." *I shouldn't have even had to ask anyone to bring me out here, and I shouldn't have had to twist your arm and wheedle...but thank you.*

She'd taken two pictures of Danny and his threadbare teddy bear Carson—named after the camp where the rebellion happened, who said refugee kids didn't have a sense of humor?—as well as a red button-down flannel shirt that had been tossed over his foldout bed. It had a few speckles of his blood on it, good for tracking. She could use it for Working if she had to.

There were a few other things she wanted, but those were the most important and space was limited. She also took a little blue glass apple, found in a dumpster the week after they'd left the camp. It had perched proudly on Danny's desk for as long as he'd had the apartment. She'd played with it every time she'd come over, tossing it up in the air, catching it, running her fingers over the slick glass. A useless bit of pre-War glitz, but he'd loved it.

"Nikolai suggested we might visit a funeral parlor," Jorge said, turning to the plywood sheets he had set to the side. He put the first back in place and held it for a moment, metal nails squealing, and when he took his hands away, it stayed. A breath of Power brushed Selene's skin. Jorge repeated the process with the second sheet of plywood.

It was mighty handy, having a thrall around.

*Was that an order, or was Nikolai trying to be polite? What's the etiquette for this? I bet he'd know, wouldn't he.* "I don't..." Selene trailed off. That would make it too real. Picking out an urn, scheduling a memorial service, and dealing with Netley and Jorge looming over her at the same time... Christos, no. Her stomach rose in revolt, the latte churning against her back teeth, she managed to push it down with an effort. "I just want to go home, Jorge. Please?"

Jorge deftly knotted the torn crime-scene tape together. "Of course. Would you like Netley to stay with you?"

"I'd rather get eaten by an epileptic shark." Selene hitched the blue canvas bag and her black leather purse higher up on her shoulder. "I suppose Nikolai wants someone to stay with me, right? Just to make sure I don't head for the bus station or do something silly like try to find out who killed my only kin." *Settle down there, Selene. It's not Jorge's fault. It really isn't.*

Jorge shrugged, let her go first down the hall toward the stairs again. Selene's blood pounded in her ears, nervous sweat running down the shallow track of her spine to the small of her back, soaking into the waistband of her skirt. Her nylons rubbed against the inside of her thighs, damp and uncomfortable. *God,*

*I just want to go home. Why am I so nervous? What was Danny hiding in there?*

The foyer downstairs looked even more dingy and depressing with pearly rainy light coming in through the glass doors. The phone box crouched obediently in its corner. A chill finger touched Selene's nape.

The medallion warmed against her skin, vaguely comforting. She wondered if she'd tracked blood out onto the thin orange carpet. Her stomach roiled again, doing its best to declare an insurrection, quelled only by the fact that she would go to hell before she let Nikolai's thralls see her puking her guts out.

Jorge opened the door for her. The limo idled quietly at the curb, right next to the red painted strip. *The driver seems to have a thing for No Parking zones, doesn't he? Maybe it's working for a Nichtvren that does it.* Selene's ankles hurt, and her lower back. The sweat was starting to spring up underneath her breasts, soaking into her bra. Lace and the underwire began to chafe.

She looked down at the cracked pavement, her shoes gleaming black and dotted with rain. How much of Danny's blood was she tracking over the pavement now?

The thought made her stomach flip again, and something acidic boiled up into her mouth. She stopped on the sidewalk, looking down at her feet. *Am I really going to puke? Please don't let me throw up. Let me keep a little dignity, God, please? I know I'm not supposed to have any shame, but please let me have this one shred of dignity. Please.*

The limo's engine hummed obediently. The sound of another car shushing wetly through a puddle made the hair on the back of her neck stand up. Selene, frozen, stared down at her toes. Her intuition prickled, the same chill panic she'd felt last night when the phone rang and Danny—

Someone yelled. Jorge pushed her and she fell, heavily, her teeth clicking together. Training brought her head down, she tucked and rolled along the wet pavement. One shoe skittered off. Her elbow sang with pain. The back of her head hit concrete, she literally saw stars, bright pinpricks of light flashing through the gray mist the day had become.

Pocking sounds—*pop! pop! pop!* Chips of concrete flew. Selene heard a scream, realized it was hers. Copper and the flat iron of adrenaline filled her throat.

Jorge's hand closed around her left arm. He yanked her up from the ground so hard her shoulder gave a screaming flare of pain. Her right arm clamped around the blue canvas bag and her purse. Something hard and round that must have been the glass apple bounced against Selene's ribs as he spun her around, sheltering her behind the bulk of his Jarmani.

He shoved her into the limousine. There was an acrid smell—*gunfire,* Selene thought, recognizing it from childhood violence and the firing range where Jack had taught her to shoot. *Someone's firing a fucking gun. At me. Why?*

Glass shattered. The limousine pulled away from the curb. Selene looked over her shoulder, through the broken window. Jorge grabbed her arm and pushed her down against the leather seat, but not before she saw a low-slung black shape—someone on an old petroleo motorcycle, gloved and helmeted, hunching down, stuffing what might have been a semiautomatic into his jacket.

Netley calmly shoved another clip into a silver automatic— *9mm, maybe, probably legally registered too*, some part of Selene said with chilling, lunatic calm. Her body burned, little prickles of electricity crawled over her skin. The latte rose hot and insistent against her back teeth again, sour and tainted with the taste of false hazelnut.

She was lucky she didn't crave sweets like Danny did, after the perpetual scrounging for food that was living in the camps. God, how he loved sweet things—the first time she'd ever been paid for sex she'd bought him twenty candy bars. It had seemed like so much money, back then.

Selene's own hungers were darker. The flush of fear pouring through her was enough to make her curse half-wake. She struggled to breathe deeply, scrabbling for control.

Netley took aim and fired twice out the broken window, deafening thunder in the small space. Selene clapped her hands over her ears. Her nylons were destroyed, a thin trickle of blood slid down from her right knee. She couldn't get enough air in with her throat shrunk to the size of a straw.

"Check her," Netley snapped. "God, tell me she's not hit."

She was on fire, the fear biting into her belly and making her entire body liquid and hot, clothes rasping against her skin. Selene heard her own shallow, panting gasps and curled up around the blue canvas bag and her purse. Jorge spared her a single look. He was bleeding from his cheek and his shoulder, a crimson wetness spreading across his gray jacket.

"Selene?" His gaze was dark, and for a moment something moved in its depths, something ancient and dangerous. She wondered, not for the first time, if a Nichtvren as old and powerful as his master could look out through a thrall's eyes. "Are you hurt? *Are* you?"

She couldn't tell. Her entire body was numb and throbbing at the same time, her curse hard to control when she was this terrified. "I..." she began. Had to take another deep breath. "No. I don't think so...what *was* that?"

"That," Price Netley said, his hazel eyes wide and sparkling and his hair wildly mussed, "was why Nikolai told us to accompany you, Miss Thompson."

THE LIMOUSINE PULLED into a cavernous garage, rows of sleek cars lining either side of the central aisle, and Selene raised her head.

"I don't want this, I want to go home, I want to go *home—*" she began again, and had to take another deep shuddering breath as fresh fit of trembling seized her. Her teeth chattered.

"Orders, Miss Thompson," Netley said, his bland blond face unusually severe. Darkness swallowed the limo. The garage didn't have windows and the door was going down, shutting out daylight. "Nikolai's orders."

*And we all obey when Nikolai orders, don't we. All his little puppets, dancing on strings.* "I don't care," Selene gasped. "I want to go home. I *don't want to be here.*"

"If they've marked your brother's home, then they've probably marked yours too," Netley pointed out, sounding maddeningly calm. "Ah, here we are. The Master will want to see if—"

Selene put her forehead down on her knees again. Both knees were scraped raw, but the right one had bled all down her shin. "Shut up," she whispered, and Netley did.

Nikolai's nest was on the east side of town, across the bridge. Every mile that slipped away under the limo's humming bottom would make it harder for Selene to get home. She'd tried cajoling, wheedling, and even begging. No dice. Jorge simply closed his eyes—Selene didn't blame him, he was bleeding pretty bad, his left hand clamped over the wound—and Netley kept repeating, with the same quiet finality a teacher would use with a third-grader, that they were just *obeying orders*. Nikolai *wanted her safe*. This was *for the best*.

The limousine drifted to a stop, its engine powering down and the landing gear creaking as weight settled. Doors opened, closed, there were quiet male murmurs exchanged. Selene curled even more tightly into herself. Her knees were bleeding, her ankle and her elbow throbbed with pain. Worst of all, though, was the smell of Jorge's blood and the insistent perfume of fear and danger in the air. It teased at Selene's shields, tapped at them, begged for entrance. If she used it as fuel, it might make her even more frantic.

And she knew where that would lead.

"Selene." Quiet. A dark voice like old whiskey.

The medallion sent a tingling shock through her entire body. Selene's head jerked up. Half her hair fell in her face. *Well, if that isn't par for the course.*

Nikolai stood by the open door, bending down a little, looking in at her. His hair was a soft mussed sheaf of glossy black over the same hurtfully beautiful features, and the black silk button-down shirt he wore had the top two buttons torn free, exposing his throat and the vulnerable space between his collarbones. The shirt was loosely untucked over a pair of jeans.

He put his hand into the gloomy interior of the car. The carnelian ring ran with a dim wet gleam. "Come," he said, softly, soothingly. "Are you hurt?"

Selene stared at him. "It's day," she whispered. "You— you're..." *You're up and awake during the day.* Her entire body went cold. Nichtvren just didn't come out by day; the sun was deadly and they needed their deep, hibernating, rejuvenating sleep. To see him during the day was...

Terrifying. It was the only word that fit.

He shrugged, still holding his hand out. "Come, Selene. Let me see you." Still that soft tone, as if she was a frightened animal he was trying to calm.

She reached out blindly, his fingers closed over hers, and he steadied her as she scrambled out of the car. Netley supported Jorge as both limped across the garage. The driver—Bradley—followed them, his dreadlocks bouncing in time with his slow steps. Selene only had one shoe, and she stumbled, twisting her ankle again before she stepped out of it. Cold concrete made her feet ache. Her ankle rolled to one side, she swayed drunkenly. The blue canvas bag and her purse bumped against her side. *He's up during the day, someone just shot at me and he's up during the* day, *my God, what's happening?*

Nikolai reeled her in, closed his arms around her, and rested his chin on top of her head. "Selene," he whispered, and she slumped against him, her knees shaking. He cupped the back of her head in one hand and held her. It was like standing next to an electrical transformer; there was a fine humming tremor going through him. He was *shaking.*

She had never felt that in him before. *It's daylight. He shouldn't be awake. He should be sleeping. He should be sleeping like the dead.*

*Or the undead. Whatever.* "What the hell is going *on?*" she whispered into his chest. And as much as she despised it, she had to admit it felt safe to be here.

Much safer, at least. She knew it was dangerous in a different way, but right now she didn't care much.

He simply held her. Concrete chill worked its way into her feet. "I thought you lost," he muttered, his lips pressed against her hair. "And I had to *wait* here, useless."

Her ribs hurt, he was holding her so tightly. A hard lump, maybe the glass apple, dug into her aching side.

Selene's teeth chattered. His arms finally loosened, and he tipped her chin up and examined her face, one thumb smoothing her bruised cheekbone. His eyes were flat and lightless, dark circles scored under them. His lips were drawn tight into a thin line, and his cheeks hollow. He looked at her shoulders, examined her neck, touched her bleeding knee. Then he straightened and took her shoulders again, more gently. "This happened outside the apartment building? Danny's building?"

*Why is he asking me? His thralls were there, he knows. He probably knows everything, if he can be up during the day it's no big deal for him to look out through a thrall's eyes. Christos. I knew he was old, but...* She nodded. Strands of her hair fell forward into her face. "Just as we were c-coming out. J-Jorge pushed me down, and into the c-c-car. They were *shooting* at us."

Nikolai closed his eyes and tipped his head back. A muscle flicked in his cheek. Then he took a deep breath, and looked back down at her. His eyes were *black*, so dark that the bruised circles underneath eyes seemed almost greenish in comparison. "Why do you do this? Do you think this is a *game*, Selene? Why did you disobey me?"

*You don't own me. At least, not completely. Not yet.* "I d-d-didn't." Her teeth were still chattering and her knees threatened to give way completely. "You n-never s-s-said not to g-go there, J-jorge said y-you e-expected... I j-just wanted some of D-D-Danny's things—"

"I would have brought you anything you wanted." It sounded like he was actually grinding his teeth, and his fingers bit into Selene's shoulders. "All you must do is ask."

*Ask you? I never asked you for anything. Never. Except for you just to go to hell and leave me the fuck alone, but we both know that won't happen. Since I'm so fucking valuable. Such a nice source of food for you.* She grabbed at the anger, nursed it, but it still wasn't enough to cover up how badly she was shaking too. "I shouldn't have to ask *your* permission. He's my brother. I have a *right*."

Nikolai's lips peeled back from his teeth. His ribs flared as if he was taking a deep breath. A low rumbling sound, like a freight train crossed with a lion's purr, made the air hot and thick. There were two old petroleo cars nearby—a low-slung cherry-red Viper and a boxy green Morris—and the cars leaned back on their springs, glass in windshields and car windows rattling. Metal popped and rang, as if cooling down after a hard race.

Selene choked on the rest of the sentence. She would have backed up, but her ankle rolled again, sending an amazing red flare of pain up her leg. Her knee buckled, and Nikolai caught her as she leaned back, frantic to get away. As quickly as it had appeared, the fury was gone, submerged with frightening swiftness.

He examined her face, then set his jaw and nodded. "Come," he said, as if he hadn't just been snarling. "You're cold, and wounded."

"Nikolai..." *Why won't he tell me what's going on? I just got shot at, for Christos's sake! And my b-brother...* Even her thoughts stuttered. *I think I'm in shock.* "I just got shot at. Will you *please* tell me what's going on?"

"When you are bandaged and have been fed I will discuss this with you, not before." The medallion sent another tingling rush down Selene's skin. Oddly enough, it made her feel a little steadier. "You didn't have breakfast. You must take greater care with yourself."

"How are you up during the day?" The chattering of her teeth eased a little bit, now that she was moving. She limped, but Nikolai managed to take most of her weight, his arm turning to oddly-flexible stone. He stopped, once, and kissed her temple, pressing warm lips against her skin. Selene flinched away, but he seemed not to notice. "Nikolai, goddammit, stop it."

"What?" He threaded his fingers through a strand of her blonde hair, lifted it to his face, and inhaled deeply. A thin wire of warmth slid into Selene's belly. *Why does he keep doing that?*

Anger and the will to resist drained away. Abruptly, none seemed particularly important. "My shoe. Can you burn it? Please? I don't want to see it again." *It's got Danny's blood smeared all over it. Oh, God, I stepped in his blood.* Bile rose in her throat again. His arm tightened around her. He started for the back corner of the garage, opposite to where Jorge and the other men had vanished.

"If you like, Selene."

It took forever to reach the door to the house, and Nikolai lifted her up over the steps as if she weighed nothing. Selene pushed her hair back with one heavy hand. Her nylons stuck to the inside of her thighs, were gummed to her shins by drying blood. Her skirt was torn up the side, and her jacket might be beyond repair. It was tempting—she could just sink down, curl into a ball, and let the world do whatever it wanted without her.

She couldn't even scrape up the will to care about Nikolai's hands on her.

He kicked the door shut behind them. A hardwood floor was only slightly more forgiving to Selene's battered feet, and she saw a low cedar bench and a utility closet. There was a rack of car keys to the side, and another, larger closet. The house smelled of lemon furniture polish, beeswax, and dust.

She closed her eyes, leaning on Nikolai's shoulder, and heard him say something very low, muttering as he bent down to slide his arm under her knees. Then she was cuddled in his arms like a sleepy child.

"What?" she asked. The bag bumped against his hip, cut into her shoulder.

He said nothing. Selene laid her head against his shoulder and closed her eyes. "Nikolai?"

"Quiet." He pressed his lips to her forehead. Her heart leapt behind her ribs. "I think I am beginning to believe you are alive and unhurt."

*What does that mean?* The trembling in her arms and legs was beginning to ease up. "I think I'm going to pass out."

"If you must." Now Nikolai sounded amused. His even footsteps didn't alter, even though she could tell they were descending stairs. She was curious; she'd never seen Nikolai's nest. Her eyes just wouldn't open. When he finally laid her down on something wonderfully soft, easing the strap of the canvas bag up over her head and freeing her purse from her arm, she sighed. Then he unzipped her skirt, easing it down over her hips. His fingers hooked into the top of her nylons, and he slowly peeled them free of her legs. The feeling was exquisite, and she sighed, making a little throaty sound of relief.

"What did you find, in your brother's home?" He touched her scraped knee delicately. His fingers brushed raw skin, and the spike of pain made her catch her breath. "What were you searching for?"

"A teddy bear. His glass apple. His shirt. Just things to remember him." Her throat closed. *I'm lying. Only a little, though. Can he tell? Maybe he can. I don't care. It's none of his business.*

"I did not forbid you to go there. You are correct. I was simply...upset. Forgive me."

His fingers slid up her thigh, and Selene's eyes opened. The room was dark, with dusty red velvet draping the four-poster bed. The walls were bare, paneled in heavy dark wood, and she saw an empty fireplace. There was a vase atop the mantel, a restrained curve of black porcelain, and a single dead rose lifted from the vase.

*I gave him a rose once.* She made herself look at him. He sat on the bed, his black eyes now sheened with green and gold, the cat-shine that was the mark of a night-hunting predator. His warm fingers paused on her left thigh, high up. He had combed his hair back and it fell obediently away from his forehead. "Not now, Nikolai," she whispered. *God, don't you have any decency? I just got shot at and stepped in my brother's blood. His blood's not even* dry *yet. Can't you control yourself, for once?*

His fingers tensed, sank into her flesh. It wasn't painful; it trembled on the edge, sparking through her nerves, waking up her curse so it rolled uneasily under her flesh. She was wet already, aching, but she swallowed against the feeling. *No. Not now. I can't. Please, not now.*

"Very well." His hand didn't move. He watched her, his eyes faintly glowing in the darkness. There was no sunlight coming into the room, of course, but there was a dimly glowing lamp with a red-lace shade sitting on the nightstand, probably out of deference to her human eyes. "You need bandaging. And food."

"I just want to sleep." She pushed herself slowly, painfully up to a sitting position. Her entire body twinged, an orchestra of bruises and scrapes. Her palms sang with pain. She unbuttoned her dress shirt, and Nikolai's hand slid away from her leg.

Selene struggled out of her shirt and jacket, hissing out between her teeth as her shoulder seized up. The medallion flared with heat before settling against her skin, quiescent. She was bruised, red-purple mottling spreading down her chest in the front and her shoulder blade in back. Her wrists were bruised too. She pushed her hair back and Nikolai's eyes snagged on her face. The shallow slice along her hairline had re-opened, raw and painful but thankfully not bleeding.

Her bra-strap slid down her unbruised shoulder. Nikolai still said nothing. His face was blank, or maybe she just didn't know how to decipher his expression.

"Can I sleep here?" she said, finally. "Please? I just want to lie down and sleep. I don't want anything else. I can't eat."

He took this in. "This is my sanctum. It might be...disconcerting for you to remain here while I rest."

Selene dropped her shirt and ruined jacket over the side of the bed. *Well, since I'm here on the bed, I don't think it's very likely you'll let me find somewhere else to lie down. Besides, with someone trying to kill me, this is probably the safest place on earth. I just hope you're not thirsty when you wake up tonight.* "It's okay. I know you look like you're dead when you're...sleeping. Besides, what did you bring me down here for, if you didn't want me to stay?"

His mouth curled slightly on one side. His eyes dropped to the silver disc between her breasts and the white lace of her bra. "At least you are safe here. As safe as possible." He stood up, and she scooted away slowly and awkwardly as he pulled the covers down. The sheets were white silk, and Selene couldn't help herself. She laughed. The weary little chuckle didn't echo, just fell into the still air. Of course—the sanctum would be underground.

"White silk. You're *so* weird, it's like a huge cliché. I bet you had silk even during the War, too." *Who's trying to kill me, Nikolai? Do you know? Would you tell me if I asked you? You've finally got me where you want me, right?*

Amazingly enough, he laughed too. Selene slid her legs under the covers and lowered herself back into the bed's embrace. He sank down into the bed himself, pulling the sheet and velvet coverlet up as Selene tried to reach her bra clasp with one hand. "Here," he said, softly, and slid his hand under her, setting the clasp free. The relief was instant, and Selene sighed. She tossed the bra carelessly down to the end of the bed, her shoulder giving one last flare of pain. *I know he's not human, but sleeping with him so many times makes it hard not to relax around him.*

"Why am I being shot at?" she asked through a yawn. Nikolai settled himself on his back, looking up at the dusty velvet canopy. His eyes half-lidded.

"Later, Selene. For now, rest."

"I don't suppose I could wait for you to go to sleep and leave the house." She wriggled, turning toward him to lie on her side, gasping as her shoulder protested.

"The door to my sanctum is barred. Inside, and out." He stared up at the canopy.

"I thought so." She studied his profile. Nice nose, the dark hollows of his eyes, his mouth eased a little but still thin and tense. "Are you going to...um, be hungry when you wake up?"

*In other words, are you going to want to fuck me when you wake up? Is it going to be dangerous to be around you? Are you going to want to bite something?*

His face didn't change. "You are safe enough, Selene. You are not prey meant for draining."

*It'd be silly of you to kill me, since I'm such a nice little buffet table for you. Well, isn't that comforting.* "Great. Go to sleep, Nikolai." *Maybe I can find out if the door is barred once you drop off.*

"Soon enough."

Selene closed her eyes. Exquisite relief. She hadn't realized how tired she was. *I'm lying in Nikolai's bed for the first time.* She yawned, sinking into the softness. *I shouldn't be here. Why is he awake? It's daylight, he should be asleep... I wonder if Jorge is all right. Why am I so sleepy? Being shot at, and two major Works this morning...of course I'm tired.*

The last thing she felt, before she fell asleep, was Nikolai stroking her hair. It was a comforting touch, warm fingers occasionally touching her forehead, threading through, smoothing down stray strands.

*Why did he bring me all the way in here?* But blackness took her before she could finish the thought.

# FOUR

HE WAS PALE, cold and still, unbreathing, his hair falling back from his forehead in a soft charcoal wave. His cheeks were almost white as the sheets; the circles under his eyes had faded. So had the gauntness in his cheeks.

Selene lay curled on her side, facing him, her shoulder stiff and throbbing. Her face hurt, and her knees felt sticky.

Nikolai just lay there.

It wasn't precisely sleep. There was no pulse, he didn't breathe, and a chill stillness spread out from him, thickening the air in the room. She was glad for the heavy red velvet comforter.

His inky eyelashes lay against his cheeks in perfect arcs. His pale lips were loose and relaxed, and Selene examined the white marble curve of his right ear. There was a small, hurtful mark in his earlobe—he'd had it pierced, at one time. *I wonder what he'd wear. A diamond? Maybe an onyx stud. Or a gold hoop. He'd look nice with a gold hoop. Kind of piratical. A movie pirate, not a real one.* Strange to think of a time when he *could* be pierced, could be hurt.

Also strange to see him like this. If she had a cigarette lighter or a wooden stake she could hurt him, maybe even kill him if she was extraordinarily lucky and the stake managed to stick in the thoracic cavity, causing enough hemorrhage. Selene chewed on her lower lip, ignoring the pain. Her lips were cracked and probably bruised, too. *Just like the rest of me. I feel like I've been through a week's worth of ditch labor.*

She slid her hand out from under the covers. Paused before touching him, her fingers hanging in midair three inches from his cheek. The cold radiating from his skin made gooseflesh stand out on her arm.

*It's a toss-up. I hate him almost as much as I need him.* She touched his cheek, resting her fingertips against skin.

Strangely enough, his cheek wasn't cold. The chill was more psychic than physical, a simmering curtain of Power.

Her heart hammered. She licked her dry, stinging lips. *When will it be dark?* A tired, drained Nikolai during the day she could handle. Maybe. If she had the advantage of a few wooden stakes, maybe a crossbow or a rifle, and a whole lot of luck and Power.

*But when he wakes up, it'll be full dark and he'll be hungry, maybe. And here I am trapped in his nest. How am I going to get out of this one? I need a quiet place so I can go over Danny's book.*

Her fingers were still against his cheek. Selene drew in a short, aching breath. She'd stiffened up, muscles protesting the unaccustomed running, tearing up stairs, and getting shot at.

*If he wakes up and I'm here, he might drain me. Nobody knows how thirsty a Nichtvren is when he wakes up, especially an old one. No matter how many Paranormal Anatomy classes it becomes necessary to take to keep your funding.*

That would be silly. He'd never bitten her before, and she'd been banking on the fact that biting her would reduce her usefulness as a buffet table. Still...

Selene slid across the silk, her skin running with prickles as the power blurring through the air pushed against her. She slid closer, and closer, and ended up next to him, her scraped knees against his jeans, her breasts pressing against his arm.

His arm was taut with muscle, even when he was asleep. The silk sleeve rubbed against her nipple. She shivered slightly, the sensation spilling through her familiar as an old coat. He had lain next to her through so many nights, it was hard not to feel comforted.

Even if he did think he owned her. Or, if she was to be absolutely honest, he *did* own her. If it wasn't him it would be some other Power. She'd been lucky to stay under the radar, moving from city to city to collect her college credits. Nobody powerful enough to grab her and use her like a battery had ever noticed her and Danny.

Until Nikolai.

Memory swallowed her whole.

*Nikolai, waiting until the man gave her the roll of cash and went away with a spring in his step. Danny melted out of the shadows, his switchblade out to protect his sister—and Nikolai twisted his wrist, shunting aside Selene's attack of razor-toothed Power and grabbing her by the back of her neck just like a mother cat would grab a kitten. He bent down, inhaling, smelling her hair, his own candy-spiced, wicked scent filling her head. The silken weight of his attention closed around her, a psychic and physical predator scenting prey but not feeding.*

*Yet.*

*Simply watching, making the point that they couldn't harm him, that he could do what he wanted with them both.*

*"Peace," he finally said, the Power in his voice stroking and teasing her skin. She went limp, trembling, the curse making her own body a traitor, liquid heat pooling between her legs. "Peace, Selene. And you too, Daniel. You are under my protection. I am Nikolai, and you have heard of me, verscht za? Now we will discuss a few things, and you will go to your new home."*

*He had handed Selene a thick roll of bills, enough to cover first, last, deposit, and several more months of life in a decent apartment. Tossed her brother the keys to a temporary room in the apartment house on Flight Street, along with a receipt for two weeks' rent. And to finish everything, he flushed her with enough Power to last her for weeks.*

*And afterwards, she never had to feed in alleyways again. There was always Nikolai, even when she tried to find another source of sex for the Power she needed. Nikolai, who had, she suspected, smoothed the way for her teaching job and some of the other...less normal jobs she took to bring in some cash, like helping Jack track cold case criminals and cleaning out poltergeist infestations or hauntings. Always showing up, always bailing Selene out, always Nikolai pushing her, seducing her, cajoling her—*

She brushed her knuckles against his cheek. His skin wasn't like hers. A different texture, slightly rougher, but with a finer grain than human skin. It was why he looked so pale, and so perfect. If he had been awake, he might have leaned into her touch, rubbed his cheek against her. Then he might have turned on his side and touched her too.

If he was hungry. If he needed the charge feeding off sex would give him. And maybe he even liked it. Most people liked sex, they just felt guilty about it afterward.

Still, he wasn't strictly a *person*, either. He had been once—every Nichtvren was before they got Turned—but he wasn't now. He was old, possibly ancient. The older a Nichtvren got, the more their psyches changed.

Immortality was hard on humanity. Or anything that might be called humanity surviving in a pale, perfect, bloodsucking shell.

She brushed his lips, shivering again as her finger sank past the skin and met the smooth enamel of his teeth, careful not to touch the sharp edges. She was wet again between her legs, her heart pounding and her breath coming in light, quick bursts.

Selene trailed her fingers down his chin, touched his jaw, slid her fingers down his throat. No pulse. His collarbones were still, not moving with human breath. Daylight sleep. She could see where the stories of corpses rising came from, centuries of Nichtvren living in the shadows, merely rumors and bad stories before the Awakening, when everything in stories turned out to be all too real.

And very, very dangerous.

She skated her fingers over his chest, felt muscle under the silk. The Turn gave them denser bone and muscle, greater endurance, greater speed and agility. And, of course, enough paranormal magick and Power to run a block generator. The juice only accumulated, the older they got.

She touched the waistband of his jeans and bit her lip again, ignoring the pain. *Human enough for some things.* Her fingers traced the brass button on his waistband. *Alive enough for some things.*

The medallion rested chill against her skin. She still didn't know what the damn thing said. Although it did seem to frighten off most of the small-fry paranormals. Even some of the bigger ones. If it held Power, there might be a way to charge it, and use the trickle of energy to stave off the worst effects of her Talent. Somehow.

The cold in the air stilled, lying heavily over the bed. Selene traced the edges of the brass button, thinking.

*It's very tempting. After all, he's been hanging around for how long? Acting like he owns me, but Jorge and Netley saved my life. I suppose I should be grateful.*

Then again, how was he involved with this? *"Give my regards to Nikolai."*

She looked at his face again. With his eyes closed, and without the flush of life, he was carved out of some white rock, polished to an unforgiving matte finish. His lips were pale, barely darker than his skin, and the shadows of his eyelashes and eyebrows were ink lines, drawn carefully by some Renascence artist. A stone angel.

*I don't even know when he was Turned, or where he's from, or who he was when he was human.* She worked the brass button between her fingers. *Or why he follows me around. I'm a* tantraiiken, *and valuable, and he's the... I don't know. Am I just easy food? A good lay?*

*"Give my regards to Nikolai." Another Nichtvren, most likely. Dammit, I have enough trouble with this one.*

The cold prickling power in the air pulsed. Selene gasped and scrambled back, her entire body singing a three-part chorus medley of pain. To top it all off, she was hungry, and needed the bathroom.

She propped herself gingerly on her raw hands and looked around. A bed, two leather wingback chairs in front of the empty fireplace and mantel with its single vase and dead dried rose perched atop it, a table between the chairs, a closed set of doors that looked like a closet, an iron-bound door made of some dark wood with a bar of iron as thick as both her legs together across it, and another door, this one slightly open, showing a yellow slice of electric light and the edge of a mirror.

*Bathroom.* The situation immediately looked brighter.

She slid out of bed slowly, wincing as her feet hit chill hardwood. Limped over to the double doors and found that they were indeed a closet, complete with a light switch that turned on some very dim overhead fixtures, with suits and silk T-shirts hung in neat rows, jeans and chinos and—she raised her eyebrows—ten pairs of leather pants all neatly hung up, as well as racks of shoes, from loafers to engineer boots, and several pairs of Nikos sneakers.

*What a clotheshorse.* Selene bit back a laugh. The sound was thin and weak in the absolute quiet.

She took a gray cashmere sweater down from a hanger, and contemplated the pants. *Doesn't this man have any sweats?* Another tired giggle escaped her. *Christos. I wish I'd worn jeans yesterday.*

There, on a set of shelves, were a few pairs of sweats and some tank tops, neatly folded. They looked like workout gear. A pair of padded gloves lay on top of the pile.

She took a pair of gray sweatpants, trying not to feel like a thief. *I can't run around naked, and I didn't bring anything with me,* she told herself sternly. *I wasn't allowed to bring anything with me. I need a shower, and then I'll look at Danny's book. I can't have slept that long, Nikolai should still be out for a good while.*

With her course of action decided, she hobbled out of the closet and left the doors open. He'd be able to tell she'd been poking around in there anyway.

She glanced over and saw him lying on his back, still and cold. The bed was rumpled right next to him, with a dent in the white pillows where her head had rested, and a warm feeling crept up from her belly. Her cheeks flamed.

*Stop it. He's not human, and he wouldn't even let you go and see Danny. Finding whoever hurt my brother is the goal here. And keeping one step ahead of whatever leverage Nikolai's going to use on me next.*

The image of Danny's broken apartment rose up in front of her again, and Selene closed her eyes, swaying. Her ankle ached. She'd have to be careful unless she used some Power to help her body heal. But that would only speed up the inevitable.

She'd need Nikolai again. Or someone else.

She limped into the bathroom. It was functional, even if it was done in black lacquer and dark-blue tile. *I don't think much of his color scheme.* Her forlorn little giggle bounced off the tiles and echoed in the huge shower stall. The sunken bathtub was big enough to keep koi in, and the bank of mirrors and vanity space along one wall would have been kind of amusing if it wasn't so chill and clean. There was nothing personal about this room, and Selene shivered. *He probably doesn't use it. Nichtvren don't need a lot of cleaning up.*

She closed the door, tossed the new clothes over an acre of counter space. Stepped out of her panties, wincing as they slipped past her raw knees. Hobbled to the toilet, and for a minute or two, all other considerations were lost in sheer relief.

*I will never*, she told herself for the ten thousandth time, *go camping. Or go anywhere without basic toilet facilities. So help me God and Jesu Christos.* Basic plumbing in the camps was a luxury, now one of those things she was determined to use to the fullest wherever she found it.

A shower would be best. She might drown in the huge glossy black bathtub, and they wouldn't find her for days.

It took her a second to figure out which set of knobs went with which side, and hot water was soon cascading down, filling the air with steam. There were black towels hung up on a rack, and she took down two of them and tossed them on top of the clothes.

Hot water stung her cuts and scrapes but felt wonderful against her bruises. It was hard to wash her hair, with her shoulder aching every time she moved her arm, but she managed. Some European kind of shampoo, with the bottle done in French. It smelled strange, like musky roses, but it got the job done, and she stood for a long time under the heat, water beating on her nape, running down her back, sliding over the curves of her body.

Hot water, another luxury. It cost two candy bars or fifteen cigarettes for five minutes in a shower, double for a warm one. Why bother when you could bathe in a bucket? When she got a little older, she could shower for free if she didn't mind an audience. Selene shivered and let her mind go blank, enjoying the sheer, gratuitous extravagance.

Her eyes closed. She lost herself there for a long time, swaying on her throbbing ankle, the medallion glinting under the hot water. Pure heaven.

It was a shock when fingers brushed up her back. Selene whirled, her ankle giving out, and almost fell against the slick tiles.

Nikolai caught her, his arms sliding under hers. He set her carefully on her feet again. She hadn't even heard the shower door, assuming he'd opened it and not just materialized in the damn stall using that shimmer-thing he was so fond of.

"Goddammit, Nikolai!" she yelled, the sound bouncing off the tiles. Her own voice made her flinch. "Don't *do* that!"

He cocked his head to the side, water beating against his shoulder. His hair was already starting to stick to his skull, weighed down with water, and he smiled. It was the good-natured grin again, white teeth gleaming, and Selene's knees give out as her heart give a shattering leap. *Oh, Christos, don't tell me he's naked, of course he's naked, we're in the shower.* She glanced down, then just as quickly glanced back up.

There seemed to be no air left in the entire room.

He still watched her, black eyes fixed on her face. "I see you've made yourself at home." His voice cut through the sound of rushing water and made Selene's already-burning cheeks flame even hotter.

*Why the bloody hell doesn't he leave me ALONE?* A traitorous bubble of excitement burst at the base of her spine. He was definitely interested—completely erect, a hard length pressing into the softness of her lower belly. Her throat was absolutely dry, and she couldn't back up. The only place to go was against the tiled wall, and that would make the situation even more interesting.

*Time to beg a little. Christos, can't he leave me alone?* "Not now. Please. Not now, Nikolai."

"Then when?" he asked, softly, crowding her even more. She only reached his collarbone, and even if she tipped her head back and looked up at him it was uncomfortably like admitting defeat. She did it anyway, shoving her wet hair back over her shoulders, her elbow bumping into his chest. It was like hitting a rock, and she flinched.

"It's bad manners to even ask at a time like this." She set her jaw and glared at him. *For Christos's sake, my brother was just murdered and all you can think of is sex? Just like a goddamn man.*

He actually laughed, and slid away to the side. Selene's entire body swayed, leaning after him. But he turned his back on her, stepping under the jet of hot water, and she crossed her arms over her breasts. Her nipples were as hard as chips of rock.

*Well, he's got a cute ass, at least.* She watched muscle move under his skin as he reached up for the shampoo. The signet ring gleamed on his hand, but that wasn't what caught Selene's attention. There were four silvery scars down his back, running from his shoulders almost to his hips. Jagged, and they must have been deep. *Never seen those before. And Nichtvren don't scar; those are from before he was Turned.*

Before she knew what she was doing, she had stepped forward, flinching as her ankle sent up another burst of pain, and laid her hand flat across two of the scars. They were smooth and hard, different from the rest of his skin. She moved her palm up gently a few millimeters, wondering where they had come from.

Nikolai was completely motionless, his hand raised halfway to the chrome rack holding the soap. He might as well have been a statue. Liquid heat pooled in Selene's belly. She licked her lips, tasted water. And oddly enough, him. It was as if he'd kissed her, night and dark and something not quite human on her tongue.

"Where did these come from?" Her voice bounced eerily off the tiles.

He said nothing, but his head dropped forward a little, dark hair running with water.

*Oh, I get it. I'm good enough to fuck, but he won't tell me a goddamn thing. Because I'm only human, even if I'm a paranormal.* She swallowed the lump in her throat again. *I'm just off-balance because of Danny, that's all. I should never have asked. He's just playing games. Fucking sucktooth games.* "Fine. Forget it."

She fumbled for the shower door and wrenched it open. *Thank God this thing is big enough for a hippo to bathe in.* There wasn't a bath mat and she didn't want to slip and crack her head open, so a fresh towel got flung on the floor. One of the towels she'd thrown on the counter went around her hair. The third towel she used to start patting herself dry, avoiding some of the scrapes and dabbing gingerly at others until she was reasonably sure she wouldn't freeze to death.

Selene couldn't stop calculating the cost of the laundry, or the sheer volume of hot water still running in the shower behind her. She struggled into the gray sweater, her shoulder grinding, stepped into the sweatpants. The water just kept on pounding, and the air was thick with steam. Nikolai said nothing. Through the glass of the shower door she could see the pale shape of him against the wet blackness of the tiles, his arm still upraised. He hadn't moved.

Her ankle threatened to give at any moment, but she managed, leaving the wet towels tossed on the floor. *Why bother being neat? He's rich enough.* She yanked the bathroom door open and limped out into the sanctum. *Bedroom. Sanctum. Whatever.*

She scrubbed at her hair as she hobbled across the room. The bed was neatly made, and there was—*surprise, surprise, how does he do it, folks, he's a miracle worker*—a fire in the fireplace now. She settled gingerly in one of the chairs and let the heat leach into her. Scrubbed at her hair fiercely, and was surprised to find hot tears welling up again.

*I don't care. He's only a sucktooth, anyway.*

NIKOLAI'S THRALLS WERE human, so there was food in the house. Best of all, Jorge brought a covered tray into the bedroom. He was pale, but seemed all right, even though he moved very slowly. Selene leapt up as soon as the sanctum's door creaked open. Or she tried to, anyway, she had to stop halfway and hold onto the chair. "Jorge!" She hobbled as quickly as she could across the floor and tried to take the tray from him.

He shook his head and stepped past her, crossing the room with long mechanical strides to set the tray on the table between the two chairs with finicky precision. The thoughtful, glazed look on his face didn't change.

If her ankle hadn't been so swollen she might have hopped from foot to foot. "Hi, Jorge. How are you? I mean, you just got shot, but...God, I'm glad you're still alive."

"I am too." Jorge settled the tray to his satisfaction. The red polo shirt strained at his massive shoulders, and he was barefoot in immaculate khakis with creases sharp enough to slice bread. It was the first time she'd seen him without a suit on, and he still looked dapper.

Selene held the back of the chair, staring at him. *He looks drugged. Of course, he's probably in pain, but if he's carrying trays around it can't be that bad, right? Right? Nikolai wouldn't make him walk around if it was serious, would he?*

"Nikolai usually has coffee when he rises, and I brought something for you." His hazel eyes were flat and dull, his mouth bloodless. The burn on his cheek looked old and half-healed instead of fresh, and a chill touched her neck. Thralls healed quickly, if their Master let them. It was a fine time to wish she'd studied more about thralls than Nichtvren themselves.

*Why does Nikolai have coffee? Nichtvren like acidic drinks, but it probably gives him stomach cramps.* "What's wrong with you? Why didn't you go to a clinic?" *They have good ones in the city, not like the death-holes in the camps.* "I would have gone with you."

Her eagerness sounded pathetic, she realized. *I would have loved to go with you, I could have caught a cab home. I could have been in my own bed.*

Unless someone or something did indeed know where she lived, and was waiting there for her. Now there was an awful thought.

"I'm expendable," he said, steadily. "You're not. Don't worry, I'm fine. It was only a flesh wound, and I'm not feeling it now." His bald head gleamed. The lamp by the side of the bed was glowing brighter now, and there were recessed track lights on the high ceiling, spotlighting the chairs and the bed.

Selene's fingers curled into fists, resting on the leather. "You got shot, Jorge. We should have gone to a hospital. And what the hell is wrong with you? You're..." Her mouth worked for a moment, not finding any applicable words. Her hair lay chill and wet against the back of her neck.

"He's a thrall, and his Master is fully awake." Nikolai said from the bathroom door. "He's also in some pain, which I am keeping from him. As a Master should. He performed well, it is not right to allow him to suffer." He wore a white button-down dress shirt and a pair of jeans, and his hair was slick with water. That made his face look even sharper, aquiline nose and high cheekbones standing out, black eyes glittering with the green-gold predator's shine.

The ever-present urge to smooth her hair and check for loose threads almost made Selene glance down at her own clothes. Or his clothes, whatever way you wanted to look at it.

*He performed well? Now there's a thought.* How much "performing" could you do to get a little freedom? Selene leaned on her good ankle, watching Nikolai carefully. He barely glanced at her, crossing the room and settling into the other leather chair.

Jorge took the lid off the tray. He moved like a mechanical waxwork, each gesture stopped with a tiny jerk.

She backed up, limping a little, until she was a fair distance from the fireplace. Then she turned on her heel. Her purse and the blue canvas bag were lying against the wall on the far side of the bed, untouched. Or at least, apparently untouched.

"I thought you would want to see Jorge," Nikolai continued. Her back prickled at the thought of him behind her, even sitting down. "To reassure yourself. He seems to be the thrall you find least threatening. Thank you, Jorge. Go and rest."

Jorge nodded, and marched out of the room with the same weird, stop-stepping gait. Selene bent down slowly, curled her hand around the straps, and hauled both the bag and her purse up. *Well, isn't that mighty kind of you.* "Thanks for the chance to catch some sleep. Can you have one of your little mechanical-toy boys drop me off at home? I've got some things I need to do."

"Selene." Nikolai's voice changed, dropped into a lower, more caressing tone. "You *are* home. Come and have something to eat."

Selene's stomach dropped toward her ankles, somersaulted, and completed its acrobatics by flipping a few more times and sending out a definitely mixed signal. *I can't tell whether to throw up or cry.* She took a deep breath. Her palms sang with pain, her ankle buckled, and her entire body twinged as she faced the door.

"Thanks very much, Nikolai," she said, formally. "But I've got a home, and I want to *go* home. I don't want to stay here. It's dusty and too dark and you're scary. Not to mention the fact that I have a job that I'm due back at in two weeks and my brother's killer to hunt down. I've got kind of a full ration-card, you know. So just tell one of your nice little slaves to drive me home, or I'll call a cab, or I'll walk. I don't care."

Nikolai picked up the silver coffeepot balanced on the tray and poured a cup of coffee. There were two black-lacquer coffee cups, and a peanut butter and jelly sandwich. A tall glass of milk. An apple, a bunch of grapes, and a bowl of something that looked like granola. Just what she'd want for breakfast after a long couple of days and a sidewalk shooting. *This is ridiculous.*

*Whoever heard of a Nichtvren stocking granola? Christos. Has someone been following me to the grocery store, too?*

"I regret to inform you that you will not be leaving my nest until I determine your safety is assured." He settled back into his chair and took a sip of the gently steaming liquid, his eyes half-lidded. "Your apartment can be cleared, and your belongings, including whatever small amount of Power you have managed to sink into the walls and floor, can be brought here. Your employment will be discussed later." *Much later*, his tone said.

*And that*, Selene thought, *is that*. "I don't think so." She struggled for the same quiet tone. "I've got a life, Nikolai. It doesn't include you. You can't hold me here against my will." *Man, I say that as if I believe it. It might even be better to stay, if someone's waiting to shoot me at my apartment. But still.*

"I doubt you will have much will left if I set myself to break you, dear one. Do not push me."

Selene's jaw ached. It was a little difficult to speak with her teeth grinding together. "Don't you dare. If you want me to hate you, Nikolai, you're doing everything exactly right."

"If you are still alive to hate me, I am satisfied." He still stared into the fire, like he was barely paying attention to the conversation. "Come, have something to eat."

Selene counted to ten. Her shoulders felt taut as bridge cables. She counted to ten again.

It wasn't working.

She set her jaw, settled the canvas bag and her purse over her unwounded shoulder, and pivoted back toward the door, left invitingly, tactfully open.

"If you try to leave the nest, Selene, I will stop you. If you attempt to leave more than once, I will Turn you, and your obedience will be easier to enforce." He didn't raise his voice, but the room shivered, the wood paneling groaned. Selene's body recognized the Power and wanted to melt, changing into something soft and pliant. Something that could be shaped. Her heart hammered. It would be so easy to drop down on the bed and let him do whatever he wanted.

Everything inside her rose in rebellion. "If you Turn me you'll lose what you want. I won't be a nice little battery anymore. No more pleasant little feedings. And no more status from controlling the only *tantraiiken* around. It's not nice to play with your food, Nikolai."

He apparently didn't take offense, his tone as silken as the sheets. "You don't know what happens when a *tantraiiken* is Turned."

*You can't do that to me. I'm human, goddammit. You just can't.* "And you do?" Her shoulders hitched up, one of them flaring with pain.

He said nothing.

*Now or never, Selene. Get yourself out of here.* "Thanks for a lovely evening, Nikolai. Don't expect to see me for a week or two. I've got some business to take care of."

"This is the last warning, Selene. I have been patient, and I have been gentle, and I have been as kind as my need will let me be. If you would simply trust me to avenge your brother's death, none of this would be necessary."

"Tell me what's going on, or I walk." She took another limping step toward the door. *How far is he going to let me go this time? Any of his thralls would be chained up by now.* Her breath evened out. If she had to run, would she make it out of his bedroom?

*Not on a busted ankle and carrying whatever this is, whatever killed Danny. What was he holding, and who was he holding it for?*

*And what did Nikolai have to do with it?*

He didn't sigh, but her skin prickled as if he'd exhaled. "Sit. Have something to eat. And I will tell you what I know."

Once again, a show of rebellion had gotten her something. *That's more like it. Of course, he could be lying.* She stood, irresolute, and finally swung back around to face him, her ankle rolling and sending another bright copper spear of pain up her leg. "You promise? You swear to tell me everything, fully and completely, holding nothing back and answering all my questions to my satisfaction?"

You had to be a lawyer when dealing with Nichtvren. She'd learned that much, at least.

Nikolai paused. When he spoke, it was very quietly. "I swear on my Bloodline. Will you swear to remain under my protection, wearing my sigil?"

*His sigil? Does he mean the medallion?* She racked her brains, decided it was worth it. "I'll swear. I promise."

"Good." His eyes stayed half-lidded while he sipped at his coffee. But his hand shook just a little. The cup jittered, and coffee sloshed against the sides. It was so unlike him she decided not to mention it. Nichtvren were funny about any perceived weakness, with all a predator's touchy pride and a formerly human ego.

For all Selene's study and a hard-won degree as a Paranormal Species teacher, she was woefully underinformed when it came to him.

She limped back to the empty leather chair and laid the bag down beside it, in front of the fire. Lowered herself down, slowly, reached over to pick up an apple. "I'll eat. You start talking."

"Danny was tracking objects for me. I paid him well enough, happy in the knowledge that what I paid him also helped you."

*So you are involved with this, and admitting it too. The two of you, keeping cozy little secrets.* She bit into the apple. Crisp skin and white flesh crunched between her teeth. "Danny said he had a good client, the work was complex but not dangerous." She took another bite, chewed and swallowed, and looked at him, wiping her mouth with the back of her hand. "He was going to buy me a car. One of the new ones, with hover tech instead of petroleo."
*It was a nice pipe dream, wasn't it?*

Nikolai's mouth firmed slightly. He took another sip. "Danny did so well with the initial objectives that I set him to finding something slightly more difficult."

Selene waited, taking another bite of apple. Wiped the juice from her chin. Instead of watching the fire, he now watched her from under his lashes. She ate the apple down to the core, bit the core in half, and chewed.

*Don't talk with your mouth full, Selene.* But she was so hungry. "What was he supposed to find?" She was beginning to think she might have survived getting shot at and sleeping in a Nichtvren's bed.

"A certain Talisman."

"A Talisman?" She shivered. Danny knew better than to fuck around with Talismans; ever since the War and the Awakening those sorts of things had been far more powerful—

not to mention far more dangerous. Just like the rest of the world. "Which one?"

"The Seal of Sitirris."

The remainder of the apple core dropped into her lap. "The Seal of..." *That's been lost for ages.* She frowned, trying to remember. The Sitirrismi were called Timewalkers, and rumor had it they were the only force the Nichtvren had ever collectively feared.

Of course, what would immortals fear but time?

Not to mention the Sitirrismi's nasty habit of popping out of a temporal whirlpool to strike where they were least expected. They were paying the bills with assassination these days, or so she heard. It was one of those little pieces of information picked up on a job that she could have done without.

"It was a relatively simple operation," Nikolai said. "He was only to locate the Seal. Instead, he made arrangements to steal it."

*Yeah, Danny always was an overachiever.* Her fingers pressed against her mouth, she had to peel them away one by one. Her bruised lip throbbed. Gooseflesh slid down her skin, for once not spurred by Nikolai's nearness. Hell, next to the Sitirrismi, Nikolai was damn near warm and cuddly. "He *stole* it?"

"He made arrangements to steal it," the Nichtvren corrected, a trifle pedantically. "Where the Seal is now, I have not been told." Nikolai's cheeks were white. His eyes flicked down Selene's body, back up to meet her gaze. "I am uncertain if that is the reason he was terminated."

*You know, euphemisms don't really work for you, Nik.* "You mean murdered."

"I mean terminated. This was professional, dear one. As was the attack on you. Premeditated and flexible, with hardware and paranormal ability to slip past even my vigilance. You have been under heavy guard for quite some time now."

*Now you tell me. And since when does that little Nichtvren jackass you set outside my apartment building qualify as "heavy guard"?* But she knew the more serious of Nikolai's help wouldn't be visible to a human, even one as Talented and sensitive as Selene. She swallowed, picked the apple core back up. *Don't waste food,* old habit prodded her, and she bit the rest of the core away from

111

the stem, chewed it to bits. Set the stem on the tray, and clasped her hands primly in her lap. "Maybe your vigilance isn't all it's cracked up to be."

It didn't come out the way it had sounded in her head. *Great, Selene. Accuse him of being a weakling. You know Nichtvren are really touchy about this sort of thing.*

Nikolai shrugged. It was a fluid movement, catlike. As if amused. "All the more reason to take additional measures for your safety." He took another sip.

*If it wasn't for you meddling with my life, I wouldn't need protection. Though I admit only having you to worry about brightened my days considerably, I still wouldn't call it perfect.* "What do you need the Seal for?"

He looked down into his coffee cup. "I have a...habit, of acquiring such items. The original owners of the Seal contracted me to find it, since they suspect a Nichtvren of the original theft."

*Oh, Jesu. This just keeps getting better and better.* "You collect cursed Talismans? You're a lot braver than I thought." Selene's fingers knotted together, as if she was still in the camp orphanage listening to a lecture. *The Sitirrismi hiring a Nichtvren to bring back the Seal, which they suspect was stolen by another Nichtvren—although what sucktooth would be suicidal enough to do that, I don't know—and hiring my brother to locate it. Perfect.*

That made Nikolai's lips curl up. It was a different smile than his usual good-natured shark grin. Instead, he looked wry and amused, acknowledging the humor. "I am already cursed, what do more curses matter? And if I possess these items, they are far less likely to cause havoc in the world."

"Nikolai Nichtvren, the altruist." *I don't even know his last name. If he has one. Just one name for him, like a movie villain.* "You've been watching too much 3D primetime. When did this happen?"

"Five years ago. It's a relatively new obsession for me."

The medallion quivered against Selene's skin. "A relatively new obsession," she repeated, picking up the black ceramic plate. The peanut butter and jelly sandwich, neatly sliced on the diagonal, bleeding strawberry jam. Just what she'd wanted, really. That was unsettling.

Still, peanut butter was another one of those luxuries she couldn't get enough of nowadays. Right next to hot water, lipstick, coffee, decent wine...really, there was a whole list of things she never wanted to be without.

*Including Danny.* Her heart did a funny wrenching sidestep. But she couldn't put the sandwich down.

"Absolutely." Something in the tone of Nikolai's voice sounded like a smile.

Strawberry jelly leaked over her fingers, she had to balance the plate in one hand while she wolfed the sandwich. *Danny used to make a great grilled cheese.* Tears rose hot in her eyes. *And he never would have taken this job from you, Nikolai. What did you tell him to make him take it? What lie did you give him?*

Only she could imagine all too well that Nikolai hadn't lied. Danny always wanted to protect his older sister; it had damn near killed him to have to retreat to his apartment and let her walk the streets alone.

*And the only reason Danny didn't worry more was because Nikolai was "looking out for me." But I kept complaining, and Danny thought he'd score a job, a big one. He probably had another buyer lined up. Enough money for us to get a start somewhere new, or maybe even a house.*

Her heart contracted to a black hole inside her ribs. *It's my fault.* "You seem to have picked up a lot of obsessions these past few years." She sounded steady enough. *All things considered, I'm doing really well with this. So why are my hands shaking?*

"It must be my age. Selene, there is another reason why I believe this attack was a premeditated termination."

"I'm all ears," she mumbled, and took another huge bite. He was smiling, that same ironic, amused half-grin.

"The media has been alerted. They know you and your brother were...*are* paranormal. Your name has been plastered over the evening and morning news. The press were lying in wait for you at the police station. They may have found your apartment building." He paused, just to let that sink in. "There is a reward for news of your whereabouts. Quite a large one, too."

Her stomach filled with cold lead. "Oh, Christos." Selene swallowed dryly, picked up the glass of milk. It curdled her uneasy stomach immediately, but she knew better than to ignore a meal in front of her. "There goes my job."

*And any hope I had of quietly finding out who killed him. But why alert the press if you think you've killed me outside Danny's apartment?* But no, they'd been waiting for her outside the police station.

There was only one answer. *It's a message.* "Give my regards to Nikolai."

"The university will keep you, Selene," he said quietly. "I will see to it."

Yeah. As usual, he thought that would make her feel better about the mess her life was becoming. "I don't want you to pressure them into keeping me on. That's like the playground bully picking me for a friend. It just makes things harder." *Besides, I think I've got bigger problems than that right now. But thanks for the thought.*

He persisted, and for once, he actually sounded a little anxious. "When you go to work, I'll send Rigel with you as your assistant. That should ease your—"

"No, Nikolai." She finished the sandwich, licking her fingers. The jelly clung, sweet and sticky, and her eyes half-lidded. "The job's done. Forget it. I'll get something else." *As soon as I finish sussing out who killed my brother, I'll blow town. I'll find a way to live under the radar, even if it kills me.* She sucked on her two first fingers, making sure every little bit of jam was gone. *So this is a vendetta someone's got with you. Figures.*

Nikolai's watched her face. Selene's cheeks prickled with heat. She slipped her fingers out of her mouth. That was even worse, because his gaze fastened on her lips. "Don't look at me like that, okay?" Instead of sounding like an order, it came out half-breathless, plaintive.

His eyes had the predator's shine again. "Like what?" He leaned back in the chair, steepling his fingers in front of his chest. He didn't look away. Selene's battered body felt the chill in the air and responded, her nipples peaking and her flesh suddenly sensitive. She glanced away, at the fire.

She could still feel his eyes on her. He had so much goddamn Power, and she responded to it, especially if he wasn't careful.

"Like you're hungry," she heard herself say. And of course, that was it exactly. He stared at her like he was starving, and she was dinner.

"Perhaps I am."

"You fed last night." It was the same breathless little voice she seemed to only have when he was around, not her usual confident tone. *Isn't it enough that you helped kill my brother? When did you decide to take over my life and treat me like your personal entertainment center? Poke the poor stupid sexwitch, listen to her beg.*

"I do not think it was enough. And you need Power, Selene. To heal your wounds."

*You know, I think I'd like to heal normally. Since you put it that way.* She took another drink of milk. Her entire body ached. "I have to start finding out who killed Danny. If I... If you feed, if I let you feed, then you'll leave me alone to go hunting whoever—"

"No. But if you...allow me to feed, I will allow you to come with me while I acquire information that will lead me to whoever killed your brother and sought to rob me of you."

*As if I'm a color television lifted from the back of a truck. "Rob" you of me. Charming.* She licked her lips, wished she hadn't when his gaze rested on her mouth again. "Fine." She set the half-full glass of milk back down. Her stomach closed tighter than a fist. *Well, I got the information, I have to pay for it. Oldest law in the universe: nothing's free. And the second oldest law is that everyone wants to screw you. Literally, in my case.* "What is it you want, Nikolai?"

"I think the bed will do," he said, meditatively. Power roiled and weighted the air; the sudden heaviness blurred her vision, set her heart to pounding, teased at her skin. He *had* been careful, keeping the full weight of Power from escaping him, knowing how it affected her. Go figure.

The door, which had obediently sat half-open all this time, creaked closed, swinging on its hinges and latching shut with a hollow boom. Selene started, her shoulder twinging.

Nikolai's smile widened slightly.

"Fine." She struggled to her feet. Her ankle rolled again, sending a flare of pain up her leg. "Christos, just fuck me and get it over with, don't make a huge production out of it!"

He rose in one fluid motion and caught her as she swayed. His hands somehow found their way under her sweater, slid against her belly. They molded the shape of her ribs; Selene's head tipped back. One hand moved against her back, pulling her against his body, the other slid slowly up to cup the weight of her breast, gently, his thumb rubbing over her nipple and drawing a startled gasp from her.

Nikolai bent down, his lips touching her throat, right where the pulse beat. "Now, now," he whispered. "Do I not treat you well, *dorogaya moya*?"

Fire raced up her body, and the curse woke up, pounding in her veins. It wasn't as overpowering as it had been last night since she wasn't crazed with need...but still, he knew just what to do. Just how to make her helpless.

"Yeah, you're a real prince," she managed. His thumb kept stroking evenly. Her hips strained forward, seeking.

Her body had betrayed her again.

*God, Jesu, whoever you are, whoever made me like this, I hate you. And to top it all off, I hate him too. Why won't he leave me alone?*

"I feared the worst," he murmured, his lips flirting delicately with sensitive skin. She was wet by now, dripping down the insides of her thighs. Her hips pushed against him. The radiant warmth of the fire stroked along her hip, her back, only slightly less delicious than the heat of his mouth against her throat. His tongue flicked delicately against her skin, rough and catlike, taking in her scent.

*The tongue of the Nichtvren species is full of barbs that closely resemble a cat's. These barbs have a dual function, both to prepare the skin for the teeth and also in—* Her own voice, as she stood at a lectern with eager faces in front of her. A degree in Paranormal Studies was still almost like admitting that you believed in the Tooth Fairy or worshiped some huge hairy beast. Some of the smaller universities, especially the ones which had been "religious" before the War, wouldn't offer the course, no matter if you needed it to qualify for federal funding.

"What?" she gasped. *God, the least you could do is leave me alone, my brother's dead because of you and your sucktooth games, do you have to rape me too? Only it isn't rape if I enjoy it, is it? That's why it's okay for you to use me, right?*

*But it's not. It's not.* It was useless. She couldn't think with him so close, her curse rising and tearing at rational thought, drowning her in sensation.

He tore the sweater up the back, his claws extended, in one swift movement. *He's getting hard on clothes, thank God the sweater's his.* "I feared you injured, or dead," he murmured, kissing up her throat. She swayed, he caught her again, moving with her, a hard length pressing through his jeans. It wasn't his fault, really, she was *tantraiiken*. The same old story, she'd been born addicted to sex, hooked on a drug she'd never chosen to taste. He kept murmuring, a steady low sound. "—centuries."

"Hmm?" It was a low inquiring sound, she pressed against him again and he swore, something low and vile in whatever harshly-accented tongue his sentences were occasionally salted with. "What were you afraid of?" A gasp tore at the end of the question.

*Even that's a whore's question, I don't care what he's afraid of, I just can't stop talking.* Self-loathing crawled through her belly, tainted the harsh air as her breathing quickened.

The sweater came free. He stopped caressing her breast long enough to slide his hands beneath her bottom and pick her up, his fingers biting in, her legs wrapping around his waist. She clung to him, he bent his face to her breasts and licked, making her squirm. She found that she had threaded her fingers into his hair and was pulling him into her, making little throaty sounds of need.

They fell on the bed, Nikolai disentangling himself long enough to tear his shirt off over his head. Selene found she was laughing. It was the only time he was less than absolutely graceful. She slid her hands into his jeans and found the smooth curve of his buttocks, muscle flickering under her fingers. He hissed something. Her laughter was beginning to take on a hitching, gasping, sobbing sound.

"Shhh," he soothed, as Selene wrapped her legs around him. His skin was volcano-hot, they lay tangled together, his fingers in her hair, Selene's ankles locked at the small of his back. Her injured ankle flared with pain and her shoulder was a sharp throbbing agony. He went completely still, looking down at her, propped on his elbows, his eyes gone dark and deep. "Selene?"

At least the space inside her head was her own. "Go ahead and feed," she whispered, and closed her eyes, shutting him out. Hot tears trickled down her temples, sank into her damp hair. "Don't mind me." *It doesn't matter to you, it never matters to any of them. Christos, just hurry up and take what you want, the sooner you do the sooner you'll leave me alone.*

"You're weeping." As if surprised.

Selene went limp under him, resigned. *Just get it over with, will you? Fuck my body if you have to, but leave the rest of me alone.* "Of course I'm crying," she said, her body gone hot and prickling with a sudden flush of Power. "My b-b-brother—" *Shut up, Selene. That's not his business.* The bed was soft underneath her, she sank down helplessly.

"I did not want you to see..." He sounded, of all things, uncertain.

Nikolai, uncertain? *No. I didn't hear him right.* "I had to. He's all I had."

*And it's my fault, sucktooth. Someone else tore him into bits, but it's my fault. And for once I'm not fucking blaming you, either. Even though I am, you got him involved in whatever killed him, but if I wasn't what I am you never would have been interested in me and—*

He freed his fingers from her hair long enough to stroke her cheek, a gentle and completely unexpected touch. "A bargain is a bargain, dear one." But still he didn't move, though she could feel him pressing against her inner thigh, hot skin against slick dampness. She was wet and the low constant ache had started again. She wasn't drained, but her body wanted completion now.

*Again. My curse.* Selene's throat was blocked with unshed tears. "Just get it over with." It took work to force the whisper out.

"Do you still hate me?" He kissed along her throat. His teeth scraped above the pulse and Selene's heart slammed against her ribs.

"Don't," she began. "Nikolai, *don't!*"

"Too late," he whispered, and his hips came down. She was so slick and wet with need that he had no difficulty—and at the same moment, he drove his teeth into her throat.

A bolt of fire slammed through her nervous system, she tried to scream, couldn't find the breath. Instead, a low reedy sound escaped. Her hips jerked up, helping him, he drove into her body as if he wanted to hurt her, long rough thrusts that pushed her down into the velvet softness of the bed. Selene, caught between the sheets and his teeth, arched and tried again to scream.

The first climax shook her, white fire exploding behind her eyes, lack of oxygen making it even longer. It seemed to take forever, her fingernails driving into his shoulders hard enough to bruise if he'd been human, Power rising through her entire body and spilling through every nerve channel, static crackling in the air. Sparks rang against the edges of the bed, electrical energy spilling out and mixing uneasily with the close, still air.

Warm velvet blackness folded around her. It was the blood-dark, she'd read prurient accounts of it in research texts. Loss of blood and the overcharge of electromagnetic energy driving the brain into a sort of storm; sometimes humans got addicted to it, craving the pulsing.

*It's nothing like they told me.* The second climax slammed into her, even harder than the first. Her entire body arched, and a long breathless howl burst from her throat.

Nikolai's fangs retracted, slid free of her flesh. His tongue rasped against the small wounds he'd made, the barbs and coagulant combining to shut off the flow. He kissed her mouth, a kiss flavored with Nichtvren and the copper taste of her own blood. It sang through her, wine and spice and darkness and blood, she shook her head, trying to tear her mouth away from his. *You bastard, I wish I could kill you. You weren't supposed to bite me, you were just supposed to rape me!*

His fingers slid against her cheek, forced her mouth back up to his. Nikolai settled into her body, pulsing inside her, he moved slightly and she gasped again. She stretched around him, her internal tissues rubbed raw and exquisitely sensitive, the slightest friction sending waves of sensation sliding through her. Her throat burned.

*He bit me, oh God, oh no, he BIT me!*

Even now she couldn't stop. She strained against him, his mouth against hers, his tongue sliding against hers, she was kissing him, tasting her own blood on his lips. He broke away from her mouth, kissing the corner of her lips, her cheek, along the corner of her jaw. Each kiss was a brand pressed against her skin, white-hot. The sparks were still crackling in the air when the third climax took her, long and low like a freight train at midnight, her body shuddering and jerking. Nikolai barely moved, Selene's own frantic response doing all the work for him. He did kiss her, over and over, printing blood-flavored kisses on her cheek, her throat, her jaw, her mouth, as if he couldn't stop.

It finally ended. Selene shuddered into stillness. Her eyes closed. Power spilled into bruised and torn flesh, knitting together, repairing bruises and torn muscles. It was Nikolai—she didn't have any of the control required to perform even the smallest act of magick right now.

*I've been infected, oh God, please help me.* "Stop," she gasped. "Stop it. Please—"

It was all she could say, all she could even think. *Please, no please, please no, please.* Begging, pleading, entreating, imploring, helpless.

Too late.

"You agreed to bear my sigil," he murmured in her ear. Her fingernails tore at his shoulders. He didn't even have the grace to pretend he noticed.

Her eyes flew open, met his. He was smiling again, that amused, slightly ironic smile, his dark hair falling forward, brushing her face. His lips were stained dark.

"But the...the necklace—" *Jesu fucking Christos, I sound like Mizzie the goddamn Mouse. I wasn't ready, I thought he wasn't going to do that, I thought he was just going to use me again.*

Panic beat underneath everything else. Infected. She was *infected.* Good luck getting a job, good luck getting away from him, good luck doing anything now. He'd *bitten* her.

"No," he said, and he kissed the sore spot on her neck. "This. My sigil."

"Then what—" Her body went liquid around him. It burned on her throat, the wound, a new fire spreading through her bloodstream.

"The medallion is something else." He nuzzled her cheek. Selene's skin roughened with gooseflesh. It only excited her more. She moved, her legs clasping him, even while she raked at his skin with her broken fingernails and tried to push him away. "Shh, be still."

"Get off me." She tried to fight him, it was no use. He simply caught her wrists, held them down, used his weight to keep her pinned to the bed until the breath was pressed out of her again. Then he took pity on her, maybe, and let up a little. But he did not slide free of her. Instead, he moved again, a shallow thrust that made her entire body jerk against his.

A thread of exquisite, helpless, glassy hatred boiled through her, deepened. *I might not be able to fight you, but I can dream about killing you.*

"You gave your word," he whispered in her ear, kissing a strand of her hair. "I gave mine."

"I hate you," she sobbed, even as he gave her what she needed. "I fucking hate you."

He didn't even pretend it mattered. "Hate me if you like. As long as you *live*, I don't care."

# FIVE

THEY BROUGHT HER a dress. If she wanted to go with Nikolai, she had to wear it.

*Of course,* Selene thought numbly, pushing her hair back. She had needed yet another shower, this one scalding-hot, and she sobbed while scrubbing until her skin was pink and raw. Nikolai was nowhere in evidence when she emerged from the bathroom. But the dress lay on the bed, mute and accusing.

The same glass ball of calm that had descended over her at the sight of Danny's body was around her now, but it was cracking. A scream beat inside her chest, she swallowed it. *Don't you dare break now, Selene. Don't you* dare.

Silver and black, silken and lovely, a long skirt and low neckline, skimming over her hips to fall to the floor, bell sleeves that would fall over her hands. She pulled it over her head, slowly, and smoothed the soft material over her shoulders and hips.

The tender place on her neck throbbed. The feeling sent a wire of cloying, nauseating warmth down into her stomach. She made it back into the bathroom like a sleepwalker, the glass ball cracking even more.

Selene tilted her chin up to one side, examined her throat in the mirror. The mark was distinctive, two pinpricks in the middle of an oval of purple-red bruising with a serrated edge. One hell of a hickey, the chemicals of Nichtvren saliva mixing with the Power Nikolai had used to make a mark nobody could possibly miss. Just like a brand.

*Infected.*

Selene combed her hair back, roughly, yanking at tangles. Her entire body glowed, not caring that she had just...had just been...

*Infected. That's the word you're looking for. Bitten by a monster. And you still fucked him.*

Everything inside her revolved, fruitlessly. There went all her dreams of escaping, of getting out somewhere, of finding a place where she wasn't a slave. There went everything she'd ever hoped for since she realized what she was. It was all gone, finished, burned up, because she was *infected.*

What if she Turned?

How long would it be before she couldn't even pass for human anymore, if Nikolai kept playing with her?

*Trapped.* Again.

She pivoted, letting out a short cry that bounced off the tiles, and flung the comb across the bathroom. It hit the floor and skittered out the door into Nikolai's bedroom, followed by a towel. She looked around wildly for anything else to throw. Found a bar of creamy soap perched in a pretty brass dish, hurled those too. There was a glass bottle holding lotion, she pitched it at the mirror and listened to the sound of falling glass. The heavy smell of roses filled the room, runnels of lotion leaking down the cracked mirror.

*Seven years bad luck, I'm infected, infected. Why did I have to be born like this?*

She stalked into the bedroom, the dress fluttering around her bare ankles, and overturned both of the chairs, hurled the tray across the room to splatter against the far wall, then leapt onto the bed and kicked the covers off, jumping up to try and tear the curtains from their rails.

That didn't work, so she hopped down, almost tripping on the sheets pooled on the floor, stalked to the mantel and swept the vase with its dead rose away. The sound of it shattering as it hit the floor was not nearly satisfying enough.

The door to the rest of the goddamn place was open. She couldn't escape the confines of the house.

But *inside* the house was fair game. Fury boiled up inside her, the beating of wings against the inside of a cage. If she was lucky she'd batter herself senseless.

Outside the bedroom, a long hall with stairs at the end, dimly lit by tasteful wall sconces. She couldn't find anything to throw at them, so she raced down the hall and up the stairs. Her breath came quick and hard by the time she reached another hall, this one with dusty red carpet.

There were pieces scattered along both sides—a porcelain vase on a stand, paintings on the wall, and best of all, a slim brass sculpture of a half-naked woman holding up a bowl of flowers. This was about the size of a baseball bat, and its top fit snugly in Selene's hands.

*He bit me!* The scream shrilled inside her head. *The bastard, the absolute bastard, it's not enough that he fucks me, he has to BITE me too!*

She swung the brass statue. The porcelain vase shattered, probably a priceless artifact now dust and splinters. Just like a riot in the camps, a fruitless raging. Selene skipped back, avoiding the shower of pieces. Her lips pulled back from her teeth, an aching-cheek rictus imitating a smile.

Two paintings ripped free of the wall, and she came to a choice. She could go down a hall with bedroom doors on either side, or she could go down another short flight of stairs into something that looked like a gallery, with different glass cases and other things scattered around. *Stairs it is.*

The first glass case shattered, and Selene skipped back again. Her heart hammered madly, her ears full of a sound oddly like ocean waves roaring up and retreating. Footsteps echoed through the halls. An awful keening yell rang in the dark, cavernous room. It was her own voice, screaming.

Trapped. Trapped again, like she'd been trapped all her miserable fucking life.

*Get it, Selene? Fucking life? So funny. You're such a funny little slave girl.*

Another glass case shattered. She caught a glimpse of what was inside it—a bucket? Rusted and old, but there was a heady breath of Power in the air. Dust swirled, twisted into hieroglyphs, settled, rose again to writhe in complicated patterns. Something magickal was in this room. Or several somethings.

Selene couldn't care less.

There was a low hulking shape covered in a dustcloth, and Selene ripped the cloth free to find a small red car. The little plinth in front of it had a brass plate that read *J. Dean. Acquired #053.*

She swung the brass sculpture (the base a little scratched now) and the windshield gave in a shower of pebbly safety glass. Running footsteps echoed through the halls.

She lifted the sculpture again. It thudded into the hood, once, twice, leaving huge dents in the pristine red paint. Then she bolted, pausing only to smash a case that had something that looked like an Egyptian collar in it. She didn't read the card for that one. *He's been collecting for five years,* she thought, coldly, *and now he's branching out into keeping pets. Paranormal pets.*

Well, if she was a pet, there was no reason not to chew on the furniture and piddle on the rug.

"Leave her alone!" someone shouted. It was Price Netley. There was a gallery running upstairs along one side of the huge room, and Netley leaned over the heavy carved banister to shout at whoever was behind her. His bland blond face was twisted into a feral mask, his eyes dark holes and his mouth moving far too much. "The Master says she's not to be touched!" His voice boomed and echoed.

*Yes, leave me alone. I'll break everything in this goddamn mausoleum.* Selene let out another sharp scream, a falcon's cry, and broke one more glass case. Her arms were burning now. She swung again, the heavy brass base smacking into an ornate wooden Ouija board that splintered under the impact, the sheet of glass laid over it shivering into an odd spiral pattern.

And again, another scream, the shattering of yet another case. This one held six or seven withered clawlike things that some rational part of Selene recognized as Hands of Glory. All of them had scorch-blackened fingers, and she shuddered, leaping over broken glass. *My feet are going to be hamburger if I keep this up.* She swung the brass statue again. This time it rebounded from a heavy stone sarcophagus set upright on a black curlicued wrought-iron stand. The shock grated all the way into her shoulders. Her throat felt as if a red-hot collar had been clipped around it, and the medallion swung as she lifted her arms again.

Another cry burst out of her, and she brought the statue down.

Nikolai caught it in one hand, his fingers closing around the square base. The statue stopped, but Selene's arms didn't reverberate with the sudden shock. It simply *stopped*.

Her ribs flared with deep, gasping breaths. *I wish I had a gun. Only I can't tell who I'd use it on. Him, or me, or just the whole goddamn world.*

Nikolai's eyes flicked over her once, from head to foot. "Bring her shoes, and a coat, and her purse," he said, apparently to thin air, but Selene heard motion in the shadows. There were only a few lights burning in this cavern of a room. Someone scurried to do what he said.

*Scurry, scurry, the Master's said so. Polly put the kettle on, master's come to tea.* A lunatic singsong revolved in her head, and she let out another sharp cry. This one wasn't a scream; it died halfway out of her mouth, broke on a sob.

Selene tried to wrench the statue away. It stayed immobile, though he held it in one hand with no apparent effort. "Let go," she said, acutely aware of the heat against her throat. Broken glass crunched under someone's booted feet, but she didn't look back, staring at Nikolai's face. *You bastard. You undead piece of shit.*

A muscle twitched along his jaw. But he didn't look angry. Instead, one corner of his mouth tilted up, and his eyes crinkled just a little at the corners. His hair fell over his forehead in a soft wave, melding with the darkness, and he wore the same jeans and white button-down that he'd changed into after his shower. He'd added steel-toed boots with heavy tarnished silver buckles against the black leather. Very fashionable, no doubt. "Only if you will. I understand your anger, Selene. Be still, now."

An electric shiver spilled through her body. The bite burned on her throat, a spreading fire. Nikolai's tone had turned dark, and full of cold steel—the voice of a Master Nichtvren, old and powerful, expecting complete obedience.

"You don't understand *jackshit*." *He didn't give me his blood, I'm not a thrall.* Selene jerked on the statue, accomplishing exactly nothing. "I will smash everything in your house, you son of a bitch." Her lips were strangely numb. "You *bit* me. I'm *infected*. One day I'll drive a stake through your heart. I mean it."

"No doubt." His fingers tightened on the statue. "You are to come with me, to continue the hunt for your brother's killer. Unless you would prefer to stay here."

*What?* She swallowed dryly. "Aren't you going to punish me? Isn't that your undead thing? *Punishment?*"

He looked away then, back at the trail of broken glass and smashed wood she'd left behind. "I value the trinkets less than I value you, Selene." He twisted the statue free of her fingers and tossed it, carelessly, to his left. Glass smashed and tinkled. Selene glanced, automatically tracking the arc of destruction, and when she snapped her gaze back he was next to her, catching her around the waist and lifting her free of the litter of glass and splinters. His boots crunched into broken glass. "Besides, there are far more enjoyable things to do than *punish* you."

The medallion grew abruptly chill, then scorching hot. *Why? What is this goddamn thing?* "Leave me alone, put me *down!*"

"You may hurt yourself." He paused, lifting her smoothly over another diamond glitter of smashed glass. "You look lovely."

It was the first time he had ever said anything even remotely complimentary about her appearance. On any other day she might have been pleased.

"You *bit* me!" She balled up her left fist and punched him.

It was a good hit, right on his cheek. Something crunched in her hand. His head snapped to the side, but he didn't drop her. Instead, he simply stopped and brought his chin down, the cat-shine folding over his black eyes again.

Her hand started to throb. A thin trickle of blood, black in the dim lighting, slid down his chin. One of his fangs must have cut his bottom lip. *I just made him bleed. He'll kill me for sure.* She felt nothing but a type of dazed wonder. "You *bit* me!" she screamed. He didn't even blink.

"I did," he agreed calmly. "Now, will you come with me to find whatever killed your brother, or would you prefer to waste time with this display?"

"Put me down, you fucking sucktooth," she snarled.

"When your feet are safe, I will set you down. Will you come with me?" Not giving an inch, of course.

Something inside her head, a little voice that oddly, painfully, sounded like Danny, was trying to tell her to calm down. Rationality reasserted itself.

What could she do? Other than wait for him to let go of her and destroy something else?

*You could go with him. Find out all you can. Smash his things later. The more you know, the better you can fight him. And you'll have to fight him with everything you've got, now. He's infected you, that means he's serious about keeping you. For the rest of your goddamn life you'll be trapped here.*

*You'd better start thinking, Lena. You'd better start planning.*

Her throat was dry. Every muscle in her body quivered with the need to strike out again. "I loathe you. I *despise* you," Selene said. She ached to spit in his face. "Where are we going?"

Nikolai moved, glass crunching like small dry bones under his boots. He carried her between silent glass cases, past a tall bookcase in a glass rectangle. *I could have broken that.* She shivered. Old leather spines showed and a venomously-glowing yellow glass orb perched on one of the shelves. Another, smaller case held a squat black statue, probably obsidian, that looked like a mad cross between a Tiki god and a Cubist spider. It gleamed wetly in the dim light, like Nikolai's signet ring.

When he reached the far end of the room, he stopped and set her carefully on her feet.

Her throat burned afresh. "Why the hell are you fucking with me? Can't you find someone else to torment?"

"You are a mystery, Selene." He held her left hand, folding both of his around it, and Power stirred. Selene's body leapt. She stared at his pale, perfect mouth. It felt like a small animal was stirring under her skin, and the Power he used tingled at the edges of Selene's shielding. He was *healing* the wound—she had never seen that before, either. "You will not start to rot and become a grave-head, nor will you be a thrall. I did not drink that deeply. Your heart still beats, you are still human. Were you wounded near to death, there is only a small chance you would Turn. And were you to become a grave-head instead of a full Nichtvren, I would dispatch you personally." He let go of her hand and she let it drop nervelessly to her side. Whatever had broken in her hand was now fixed, even if it ached a little.

"That's comforting." And oddly enough, it was. *If I can get to the hospital and get an enzyme treatment in time I might even be okay.* "Why, Nikolai? You *planned* this, didn't you." *You were going to bite me when this whole thing started, you've just been drawing it out. Playing with me.*

"I have always intended to Turn you, Selene, and make of you a full Nichtvren. But not yet." He smiled slightly, his good-natured grin, the one that made her want to frantically retreat and find a wall to put her back to. Then he offered his hand, palm-up. "Come with me. I am hunting your brother's killer."

Selene flinched. She turned the movement into a mincing step away. *Give my regards to Nikolai.* "I'll walk on my own."

He nodded, his dark hair falling forward over his forehead. His eyes had the predator's sheen again, and his sharp handsome face was set into that jolly smile. His hand dropped back down to his side.

*Someday, you bastard, I* will *get free. And I will make you pay for this.* She stared at him, her heart thudding. "Where are we going?"

His smile widened, and Selene took another step back, hardwood cold against her feet. The dress made a low soft sound, sliding against her legs.

"We are going," Nikolai said, "to the House of Pain."

# SIX

THE SHOES TURNED out to be black spike-heeled sandals and the 'coat' was a velvet wrap Nikolai slid over her shoulders. Her purse was handed to her by another one of his thralls—Rigel, with a lean dark expressionless face.

Rigel was an enigma, quiet even for a thrall, tall and thin and usually dressed in a black T-shirt and jeans, moving far too silently to be strictly human though Selene could never smell Power on him. Tonight he wore black leather pants and a long black coat, boots that matched Nikolai's. His dark hair was short in the back and sweeping longer in the front, very punk and almost cute. A diamond earring winked from his left ear.

Selene's purse was still closed. She unzipped it and checked, ignoring the fact that Nikolai, Rigel, and two other thralls were waiting for her to get into the long, gleaming limo waiting quietly in the huge garage. Ranks of cars stood on either side, most of them hybrid, a few antique petroleo model scrouched on gleaming black tires.

*I hadn't pegged Nikolai for such conspicuous consumption.* She tapped one heel against the concrete. *I wish he'd brought me some boots instead of these things.*

The manila folder was still there. Her wallet was still there. The tarot cards, wrapped in their hank of red silk, were still there. Her purse didn't *smell* like a thrall had gone through it.

"What are you looking for?" Nikolai asked. It was as if he had closed a warm hand over her nape, his thumb stroking the most sensitive part. Her stomach flipped, settled.

"I'm checking to make sure you're not a thief as well as a total bastard." She zipped the bag closed. The medallion hung between her breasts, warm and reassuring. Nikolai tilted his head back and regarded her, and to save him the trouble of replying, she got moving.

Selene ducked into the limo, clutching the purse to her chest. At least it was black leather, and not too scruffy. *Why do I care?* She swallowed hard against the lump in her throat. *Scruffy or not. Nikolai's scruffy little pet. His property.*

Selene scooted all the way over to the window on the other side, her ankle twinging a little bit. The Power unleashed by Nikolai's feeding—*and my own, let's be honest, I fed too, like a good little sexwitch*—had repaired muscles and torn tendons and taken the swelling down, but she would still be a little sore. The slice on her hairline was closed and healed over, and her lip was no longer sore and puffy. She was in better shape, but nowhere near full health.

And the baffled, helpless rage was a steady blowtorch high in her chest, like indigestion. *I wish I had a gun. A big one.*

There was a murmur outside, and Rigel ducked into the limo. He sat opposite, stretching out his long legs. Nikolai took his place next to Selene and settled in, almost close enough to touch her. The medallion was hot against her skin, pulsing underneath the dress.

The door closed. The two other thralls would be up front, one driving, the other on watch. And Rigel. Selene looked for telltale bulge under Rigel's arm. Yes, they were armed. Probably all of them, except for her.

*Great. Of course, if I had a gun, I'd shoot Nikolai. He probably wouldn't find that so amusing.* Or he might, and that prospect sent another shiver down her spine.

Nikolai touched her shoulder as the limo crept smoothly across the garage floor. She jerked away from the contact, but there was nowhere else to go except through the window, and she couldn't do that. Not yet, at least.

*It must be full night.* But when the car slid out through a reinforced garage door it was only dusk, the sun drowning its daily death in the bay. Nikolai's nest was set on a hill overlooking the river and the city, a metaphorical and physical height at once.

*I could open a window and let the sun in.*

Except they would anticipate that, wouldn't they. Her brain shook like a rabbit in a cage. Gone mad. Gone to lunch. Gone buzzo.

He smoothed the velvet over her shoulder, a gentle touch. "You're angry." A soft dark tone caressing even the upholstery. The mark on Selene's throat and the medallion both burned.

Selene stared out the window. *God, I wish I had a gun. A Glock-Stryker, that would do it. If the calibre was big enough.* "Shouldn't I be? You *bit* me."

"I gave you my sigil, which marks you as mine. You agreed to it." He sounded calm and reasonable, and his fingers never ceased their stroking.

"I don't belong to you." The words choked her. *Who are you at war with, Nikolai? Who wants to kill you so bad they'll settle for killing Danny? Or me?*

"If it does you good to think so, Selene, by all means, continue." Now he sounded amused. "I am being patient. Any other Master would have you trammeled in the nest, chained if necessary." His gaze met Rigel's. The thrall didn't even have the grace to look uncomfortable.

Selene turned away from the window. "I could break the glass and let the sun in." Her voice broke, she cursed herself for being weak. "I wish I had a gun. One day I'm going to pound a stake right through your black little heart."

"Nothing worth having comes easily," he replied obliquely, still watching Rigel. "Eternity has taught me that, at least."

*Now what the hell does that mean?* "How old are you?" She hugged the purse to her belly. The dress shifted against her skin, rich pretty silk that she might have liked if *he* hadn't given it to her. "Who were you when you were human? What are those scars on your back? And why are you *doing* this?"

"Doing what?" The limo slid down the paved drive, winding down the hill, shimmers of Power riding the air now that the sun was going down. There were layers of invisible defenses on the nest, standard for any Prime Power. And besides, Nichtvren took their nests seriously.

"Why did you give Danny work you knew would kill him? And why are you so obsessed with screwing around with me?"

She glanced at Rigel, who looked away quickly, maybe not daring to meet her eyes. So maybe he *was* uncomfortable.

Good.

"I did not know the work would kill him. I did everything possible to keep him safe." Nikolai's eyes half-lidded as his fingers continued their even, soothing motions.

Selene took a deep ragged breath. Her heartbeat, rabbiting under her ribs, slowed a little. Her lungs stopped burning. It seemed almost possible that she might be able to just sit for a minute and collect herself.

*Give my regards to Nikolai.* An evil voice, as evil and self-centered as the creature sitting right next to her. Goddamn Nichtvren. They played their games with other people's lives, and never paid the price themselves.

Rigel moved, leaning forward as if he would say something.

Nikolai glanced at him and Rigel immediately sat back, his mouth thinning. "I am sorry, Selene. You have trusted me this far." His fingers continued touching her shoulder, making little patterns on the velvet. "You may as well continue." Then he did something strange. He leaned over and pressed his lips against her cheek, crowding her against the side of the limo again.

Heat spilled through Selene's entire body. She drew in a short, sharp breath, closing her eyes. *It's just a kiss,* she told herself, but her entire body flamed, a trickle slipping down between her legs. *Stop it, it's just a kiss.*

Her body didn't know that, though. The *tantraiiken* part of her knew only that he was powerful, and that he had fed her. Her body responded, changing into liquid. He might as well have branded her and put her on a leash.

Selene's head tipped back, and she melted. "Nikolai..." It was wrung out of her, a despairing moan. *Not in front of Rigel.* Panic swimming through her. *Please, not in front of Rigel, this is private. Don't do this to me in front of someone else.*

As if it mattered.

"Who else would not use this against you?" His lips moved against her cheek. "I *know* you, Selene. I know more about your need than you do. Be a little kinder to me, if you please."

She shut her eyes, a delicate shudder running down her arms and legs. Her pulse pounded in her ears and wrists and throat, hammering against the mark he'd left on her. She pushed the curse away, her muscles locking one by one as she fought with her rebellious body. "Get off me," she whispered. "Goddamn you, get *off* me."

He did, moving slightly away, but his hand came up and stroked her shoulder again. Now a steady, comforting heat came through velvet and silk, sinking into her skin. "We will have to discuss this, Selene, when I have finished and ensured your safety. I am no longer willing to be quite so patient with you."

"You can't break me." *I may be a* tantraiiken, *but I have my pride. Or at least my dignity.*

*Yeah. Sure.*

Rigel moved again, restless. He was looking out the window, but a faint flush had risen in his sallow cheeks. The diamond earring glittered at Selene, who blinked and filled her lungs again. There wasn't enough air, she was suffocating. Suffocating and trying not to sob out loud.

Nikolai didn't say anything. He didn't need to.

Everyone in the car knew she was wrong.

THE ALLEY CAME off Heller Street, and there was a crowd. Since the Awakening, the press and a certain slice of jaded pleasure-seekers had started clustering around every place the Nichtvren were known to gather, hoping for all sorts of things. Most of the world had worshiped celebrities before the rise of the Republic of Gilead, and after the War things had gone back to business as usual—only with different famous faces to make the little people feel better about their drab, rationed lives. Now that the rationing was being lifted and the world was starting to recover, the hunger for celebrities was growing exponentially.

The limo sliced through, shadows pressing away, and Nikolai's hand slid down Selene's arm, his fingers loose around her wrist. "Listen to me, dear one," he said, his voice soft instead of chill and hurtful. "This is a Nichtvren haunt. Do you know what that is?"

*Of course I know.* Selene's throat was dry and smooth as glass. "A communal feeding-ground," she said, slowly. "Serves a dual function, social and..." Her voice broke again. This wasn't a lecture-hall. This was *real*.

He nodded. His skin was warm. He could almost pass for human, except for the perfection of his skin and the sheen of his eyes, and the Power that cloaked him. The vamparazzi probably loved him. "You will see many things here. Know that I will not allow you to be harmed. But you *must* stay close to me, and you must obey. Otherwise we will never find Danny's killer."

*Carrot and the stick, right? Okay, I'll play.* Selene set her jaw. She nodded.

Nikolai let go of her wrist to slide his fingers through her hair, pulling some of it forward. Then he stroked her cheek. Selene submitted, her skin crawling. The Power prickling in the air around him scraped against her, moved over her skin under the silk, slid between her legs. "This will be disturbing for you, Selene."

*How could I get any more disturbed?* "I've got a degree," Selene said numbly. "It took a hell of a lot of work to get. I might as well get some field experience to go with it."

The limo came to a smooth stop. The front passenger door opened, and Nikolai shifted slightly. He was smiling, the amused and ironic half-tender smile she had just recently begun to see on him. His fingertips touched her face again, tracing the arc of her cheekbone. Then he took his hand away and glanced at Rigel, who nodded.

The limo's door opened. People milled around—*vampire groupies. If I start to laugh now I'll never stop, I'll keep laughing until I suffocate myself.*

She looked up at Nikolai. *Do I really have to do this?*

*Yes, I do. For Danny.*

"Courage, dear one," he said softly. Rigel had already unfolded himself gracefully out of the limo. Nikolai followed him, with one last lingering look at her, his eyes free of the catshine and suspiciously dark.

*I could just stay in here.* She stripped her hair back from her face with stiff, aching fingers. Then she slid across the seat, made sure her purse was secure and her long skirt was in place. *Only it isn't my skirt. It's Nikolai's.*

The mental image of Nikolai wearing the dress made a thin laugh well up inside her. She slid her foot out of the car, made sure she had good footing on the damp pavement, took Nikolai's hand. He steadied her as she slipped out of the leather-covered interior.

*Maybe I should have a drink or two.* Only she wasn't sure what they would serve in this place. The Nichtvren had always come here, even when they had to pay bribes to the Gilead enforcers. Even before the War. Nichtvren always had the money to grease the wheels, and the Republic hadn't been as pure as it wanted everyone to think.

Flashbulbs popped. Nikolai's hand was warm. Rigel closed the door behind them. The other thrall—a slim blond man tense and ready in his long black coat—stood to Selene's left, not-quite-posing.

Nikolai bent down and printed a kiss on her forehead. More flashes, a tide of them, pictures taken. Exclamations. "There," he said softly. "Let them feast their eyes on that."

He turned neatly, and somehow had her hand tucked into his arm. Then he paced forward, elegant as a panther, his step soundless. Selene's heels clicked on the pavement. He did not walk quickly, so she could keep up even in the heels.

There was a door made of black iron, with a blinking red neon sign whispering *Pain* over it. The door was slightly open, glitters of light pulsing out. She could hear a faint heartbeat, music booming. Two bouncers only slightly less massive than gorillas hulked near the door, glowering at all and sundry. They each had guns strapped under their armpits, and one of them had an axe that he held in a meaty, hairy hand. The double-curved blade was bright silver.

Selene smelled Power, and paranormal, and a loud zoolike stink. *Are they...they can't be. Not right out here in front of everyone.* She blinked. Nikolai shepherded her down a long aisle of people taking pictures and pointing excitedly. There were brass stands and red velvet ropes holding the crowd back. She heard her own name, called several times. Ignored it, holding her head high. Rigel and the other thrall flanked them. Nikolai managed to make it look as if he was accompanying Selene instead of the other way around.

*He must've had practice.* Hot bile-coated pressure rose in her throat again. She blinked, swallowed it.

There was a row of gleaming motorcycles along the wall, and a sinuous low gray hybrid car she longed for a closer look at. *That's a Reformed Lotus; Danny would like that.*

A spike of pain in her chest almost made her stumble. Nikolai's opposite hand came up, clamped over hers. It looked like he was enjoying himself, instead of steadying her as her feet faltered. He was smiling, the tips of his teeth hidden, nodding graciously as if he knew several of the reporters. Maybe he even did.

She'd seen pictures in the papers and magazines of Nichtvren haunts and the media circuses they caused, but she had never envisioned being in the middle of one. People screamed Nikolai's name, and one enterprising reporter vaulted the red velvet rope and ran for them, snapping pictures all the while. He was balding, overweight, in a long tan trench coat.

Selene inhaled sharply, bracing herself.

Rigel met the man halfway, made one swift movement, summarily dragged him back to the rope and dumped him over it, saying something in a low tone. The crowd hushed. Nikolai's steps never faltered.

They reached the door, and the huge paranormal with the axe looked down at them. *I'm seeing a werecain up close.* Dizzy wonder filled her head. She'd never seen one except in teaching films—they didn't care for the smell of *tantraiiken*, and didn't feed on sex anyway. Humans were too fragile to play with werecain. Even a *tantraiiken's* ability to heal after rough play wouldn't help.

The loud stink that followed 'cain around, shutting off only when the nasal receptors were overloaded, was also a distinct damper on any cross-species playing.

The werecain with the axe coughed slightly. "Prince," he rumbled, and nodded. "Apologies. No normals. Orders."

Nikolai paused and merely looked at him.

Selene glanced up at Nikolai's profile. His eyes had gone dark. Almost completely black, lid to lid. The crowd drew in a collective breath. Selene shivered as the cold wave of Power that was Nikolai's strength spread out in a single pulse.

The werecain lowered his axe. "Apologies. My mistake." But his yellow eyes slid down Selene's body, and he smirked. "Ya, Charlie," he said to the other werecain, who was watching with a great deal of interest, "we gotsa beggar here. Look at that."

"Charles and Algernon," Nikolai said calmly. "They are no doubt overwhelmed by the honor of meeting you." His eyebrow lifted a bare centimeter, and Selene's breath caught. The Power spilling out from Nikolai was enough to make her dizzy, her shields flaring in response.

Rigel rejoined them, and Selene almost flinched as the second werecain pushed the door open. A tide of light and music poured out. The vamparazzi strained forward, shouting, flashbulbs popping.

*No fear. I'm going straight into a Nichtvren haunt with Nikolai and his thralls. Great. Danny, if you weren't dead I'd kill you myself.* The black humor helped her hold her head up, helped her step into the House of Pain as if her legs weren't shaking and her entire body feverishly hot with fear...and excitement. *I'm about to see a Nichtvren haunt. I'm really going to see this. There are people that would give their eyes and hands to see this.*

*There are people that probably have.*

They stepped into the pulsing lights, Selene looked around. There were four more werecain here, one sitting on a tall three-legged stool at the end of a small enclosure hung with red velvet. The music was loud, a monstrous heartbeat thudding through the air, some kind of techno beat. Selene smelled heat, and the heady smell of Power hit the back of her throat in a rush. She'd done coke once, just out of the camps and in her first college program for refugee kids, and the brain-tingling chemical skyrocket had felt a little bit like this.

*I could feed off this,* she realized, and licked her lips. The outer edges of her shielding shivered and thinned, taking in the flood of energy. Electricity raced along the back of her neck, dipped down her spine, and Nikolai's warm hand was still clamped over hers.

Three of the werecain were sidling up on them. Rigel stepped forward. He cocked his head slightly to one side, said nothing, his dark hair falling down on either side of his face, framing him like a Byzantine ikon.

"No humans except preyfalls," one of the wereccain grumbled, a huge no-necked thug in a wool sweater dark with sweat under the armpits. "Not even prettybits."

Selene stared, fascinated. The werecain had hair on his cheeks and even growing on his knuckles, a short brown bristly ruff covering his head and vanishing under his collar. His eyes glowed yellow in the dim light. He wasn't even trying to pass for human. Instead, he was half-changed, somewhere between camouflage and huntform. His nostrils flared, scenting her under the layer of Nikolai's distinctive smell.

"Nikolai has brought his Acolyte." Rigel pitched his voice loud enough to be heard over the music. "She's marked, you can smell that. Cut the crap."

Selene glanced up at Nikolai, who now stepped forward, bringing her with him. Sweat, wine, hash, coffee, sex, copper. The reek of paranormals, of Nichtvren in particular, with different fascinating tangs. The zoo odor of the werecain vanished after a few deep breaths. Something about their scent filtered itself out quickly, like violets did for ordinary humans, something that had to do with certain sensory receptors. Selene had read about the effect, but never dreamed of experiencing it herself.

There was a whole lot happening lately she hadn't thought she'd ever personally experience. *Lucky me.*

Nikolai reached up, took her chin, and tilted it to the side, exposing her throat and the vivid bruised mark. Selene bit down hard, the urge to tear her arm out of his and back away trembling under her skin. He let go, and she shook her hair back, glaring at the werecain.

The massive fur-covered 'cain threw its head back and laughed, a snorting howling sound that managed to cut through the noise. Still laughing, he backed away and waved a hand. Nikolai pulled her forward, the red velvet billowing as he guided her down two steps and into a chaos of noise and light. Rigel and the other thrall flanked them, and Selene's jaw threatened to drop.

Four paces into the House of Pain, Nikolai stopped and half-turned. Selene, confused, didn't realize what he was doing until he had cupped her face in his hands and bent down, his lips brushing hers. There was only a bare moment's worth of warning before his fingers tensed and his tongue slid into her mouth.

Her traitorous body leaned into his, her mouth accepting his invitation, soft human flesh sliding against the rough catlike surface of a Nichtvren tongue. Her eyes closed, and she swayed into him, wishing she'd had a pair of panties to wear, because the insides of her thighs were wet already, and the Power hazing in the air around them made her entire body shake.

Nikolai broke free, and Selene blinked at him, remembering where she was. *What the hell was that for? Can't you keep your hands to yourself for—oh.*

Nichtvren. Bright eyes and pale flesh, groups of them at small tables, reclining on frayed purple velvet couches, laughing in the shadows. A group of werecain at the bar, calling for beers. The dance floor, a cavernous space hung with drifts of what looked like white chiffon that waved gently in the churning air, was crowded with writhing bodies. Four kobolding, their leathery grey-green skin covered with rough stonelike warts, hammered their tankards on the table and yelled for another round. There was even a contingent of swanhilds, their feathered ruffs standing erect; if Selene looked closely she would probably see other species too.

A tall, stick-thin Nichtvren female stalked past them, her sharp angles poured into a leather catsuit, her slim hand holding a leash that glittered in the revolving lights. Attached to the leash was her pet.

Bile rose in Selene's throat. The man was covered in sores and small cuts; he loped after the Nichtvren, an expression of dreamy happiness plastered on his chubby face. He wore only a pair of socks and a tasteful red silk tie, and his genitals swung as he followed the Nichtvren who twitched the chain absently, just as a human would play with a dog's leash.

Two Nichtvren males stood, deep in conversation, one of them in a Chinese-collared silk shirt and loose silk pants, his nose pierced with a gold ring. The other wore bottle-green velvet

Louis XIV might have approved of. Between them lay a naked woman, her eyes glazing as she convulsed, a thin trickle of blood slipping down from the mark on her throat, a mark very much like the one Selene could still feel pulsing uneasily on her own flesh. The woman's lips were blue, and she was deadly white, even her nipples oddly chalky-looking. Her long black hair tangled over the Chinese-collared Nichtvren's shoes.

Nikolai's hand folded over Selene's, and he pulled on her, gently. "Come," he said, not seeming to shout, but his tone cut through the din. "Walk with me, Selene. Trust me."

"Nikolai." Her voice was merely a whisper, a shadow. The Nichtvren male wearing Louis XIV glanced over at her. He had black eyes too, but without the electric charge Nikolai's gaze held. *He's a Master, but not like Nikolai. Nobody here is even remotely like him.*

A hot spike of anger went through her. But he was moving, and she had to keep up with him or fall over. He pulled her away from the door and they plunged into the crowd.

Something wet touched Selene's cheek. She glanced up, then just as quickly looked down, bile scorching the back of her throat. The smell of Power remained, making her stomach rise again. *There are cages hanging from the ceiling,* she thought, and felt the blood drain from her cheeks. The mark on her throat pulsed insistently. *My God, there are cages on the ceiling. Cages.*

The crowd parted, bright Nichtvren eyes eating Selene alive. A murmur ran under the music, and she saw a Nichtvren woman with a crimson-lipsticked mouth holding her hand up as she whispered to her neighbor. Between them was a graceful wrought-iron table that held a basket, with white silk falling over the side. There was a long dark stain on the white silk. *It could be blood, not lipstick. Oh, Jesu, what have I gotten myself into? Danny, oh, Danny, why did you have to take that job?*

Nikolai passed through the murmuring crowd, Selene matching him step for step. Her heels slipped against the floor; it had changed from concrete to slabs of marble. Must have cost a fortune. They were heading for booths hung with red velvet. The music receded a little, Selene's ears adjusting to the din, and she leaned into Nikolai as the Nichtvren pressed close, their faces lifting. She could smell her own fear, a sharp tang over the deeper smell of her body, the *tantraiiken* part of her responding to the presence of other paranormals, drenching the air. Her shields were thin as paper, Power flooding in from every direction.

Sudden sharp commotion. The slim blond thrall made a quick movement, and a young Nichtvren male went flying. He landed, rolling into a fetal position. The crowd stilled. Even some of the dancers were beginning to stop and look.

Nikolai stopped at a large booth. "Would you care to sit?" His eyes lost their gold-green sheen for just a moment, he sounded as calm as if they were at a restaurant.

He held her elbow while she lowered herself, silk whispering as she slid along the bench seat. There was a low ebony table carved to within an inch of its life, the bench seats were rosewood with watered-silk cushions. They would have been beautiful in any other setting. Here they were just creepy. The heat in the air was clammy, moving over her skin in prickling waves.

Nikolai dropped down next to her. As casually as if he was at home, he propped his boots up on the table and settled back, his arm sliding over her shoulders. He pulled her into his side, and Selene, yanked off balance, half-fell against him. It was like falling against a marble statue, he was tense, muscle standing out like tile. The cold prickling cloak of power folded around both of them. It seemed to distort the music, which was no huge loss as far as Selene was concerned. But still, she didn't like the feeling.

She ended up with her cheek against Nikolai's shoulder, his arm around her, just as if they were cuddling. *Awww, how cute, the Nichtvren and his pet,* she thought, and buried her face in his shoulder. She was shaking, and he was warm and at least familiar. Dangerous—but still familiar. White linen over hard muscle, and the musk-male smell of him. She took a deep breath. Her heartbeat slowed a little.

A fresh wave of shudders tightened the skin on her scalp and rolled all the way down her body. *Oh, my God. I never thought I would ever see this. Cages, Nichtvren, werecain...God.*

"Courage," he whispered into her hair. Funny how she could hear him, as if his was the only voice capable of cutting through the noise. "It shouldn't be long."

*No humans except preyfalls,* she heard the werecain say again. Preyfalls. Like the woman lying across the Nichtvren's feet as he calmly chatted to another. Like the man trotting after the tall black-leather Nichtvren, sores cracking on his body.

Like the things hanging over their heads.

The music fell away. It was still there, pounding away on the other side of a wall of quiet. It was a relief. Was it Nikolai blocking out the noise? She hoped so.

"Well. So the rumors are true." Someone settled on the bench on Selene's other side. Male, strangely accented, and a new wave of Power roiled under the words. "There *is* a pretty little piece taking your time now."

"Watch your mouth, Sevigny." Nikolai's fingers tightened on Selene's shoulder, comfortingly. "My Acolyte is none of your concern."

"I know that smell, Prince," the other Nichtvren said. His words blurred softly. Maybe French. "A tantric witch. Very nice. It is said you have gone soft for a human, my lord. Pity, if 'tis true."

Nikolai said nothing, but the tension in his body shifted infinitesimally. Selene swallowed dryly.

*I'm being ridiculous. I've got to find out who killed Danny. If Nikolai says we can find out here, then I might as well pay attention.* She managed to look up out of the comforting dark of Nikolai's shoulder.

It was Louis XIV, reclining next to her in his dark green velvet and icy white lace cuffs, short breeches and hose, shoes with fantastic gilt buckles propped on the table in an imitation of Nikolai's pose. All the same, this Nichtvren observed a careful distance from her.

He examined her face, then showed his teeth, delicately. He had a nice face under a mop of brown hair, even and regular, with none of the exceptional beauty Nichtvren usually looked for. He must have been vicious and imaginative to be Turned. "*Sacr'dieu*, Nikolai," he breathed, his eyes glowing blue in the dim pulsing light. "Exquisite. No wonder."

143

Nikolai's shoulder lifted in a shrug. "I'm sure your opinion will matter somewhere in the world. Talk, Sevigny. I am impatient tonight."

The Nichtvren yawned, theatrically. "Well, there is so little to report." He waved one limp white hand. Lace fluttered. "The Sitirrismi are in town, and they are so very angry. It seems someone stole their little toy. And the oddest thing, really, is that they blame you. Something about a retrieval gone wrong?"

"Very odd indeed," Nikolai agreed. He sounded amused.

*Sitirrismi? The Seal. It has to be. Did they*—Selene opened her mouth, but Nikolai's fingers tightened, this time warningly, on her shoulder. She shut up. *Let him deal with it. Let him do some work for once.*

Sevigny stared at Selene's face. "Oh, let her talk, Nikolai," he wheedled, leaning sideways a little. "I'm sure she has something *marvelously* interesting to say."

Nikolai said nothing. Selene bit her lip, wished she hadn't, because now the other Nichtvren was staring at her mouth, his eyes alight with predatory glee.

"Oh, what a waste," he finally said. "I hate to have to tell you this, Prince, but the particular incident you are inquiring about...well, the target was not hit."

"Someone died," Nikolai said, carelessly. Selene had to crane her neck to see his face—it was set into its usual straight lines. She could see Rigel and the other thrall standing guard at the entrance to the booth.

"Oh, someone died. But 'twas not the target. The *target* was that lovely little toy you have under your arm, Prince. She was expected to be there, nice and neat for disposal."

*What? I was supposed to be at Danny's? Of course, I'm on the lease so I can have a key, Danny insisted.* Bile rose in her throat. *It's even worse than I thought; they were coming for me, whoever it was, and got Danny instead.*

"Who ordered it?" Nikolai's eyes flared gold-green. *He's really angry. I've never seen him like this before.* She stared, fascinated, as a muscle jumped in his jaw and his fangs appeared, sliding out from under his sculpted top lip. She froze, fighting the urge to bring her knees up and curl into a ball, make herself as small as possible.

"Oh, one cannot be sure. But you hear things, you know. I've been told...well, 'tis still only rumor." Sevigny shifted a little, darting a glance at the dance floor. The Nichtvren had gone back to their business, but there were still bright glances pouring over the booth. They were on display, Selene realized. Nikolai was making a point. About her.

About who she *belonged* to.

*And you know, right now I don't really care as much about that as I should. I suppose it's a question of "better the devil you know," right?*

"Spit it out." The edge to Nikolai's tone made Selene shiver.

"'Tis being whispered that Kelaios Grigori is responsible," Sevigny said, all in one breath. "That he is coming to take his place as Master of this city, since you are his Acolyte."

*Grigori?* Her ears perked. *Who the hell is that? Nikolai's never talked about his Master before. He has to have had one. I never thought about that.*

Nikolai paused for the barest moment before replying. "Grigori is *dead*."

"Oh, certainly, because you say so," the other Nichtvren replied hurriedly. "*Rumor volat.* Anything else, my liege?"

"It would be useful to know where the Sitirrismi are making their nest," Nikolai said quietly.

Sevigny nodded. "Tomorrow, maybe. They are...cagey. Difficult, *n'est-ce pas?*"

"Set everyone to it, then. If they move against me, I will answer; not even Time will save them. Make that known." Nikolai pronounced this in a bored tone, looking out over the dance floor, his gaze moving in smooth arcs.

"You would declare war on the Sitirrismi?" For the first time, the other Nichtvren looked a little less than bored. As a matter of fact, his jaw dropped and he looked stunned; the lace of his cuffs trembled.

Selene fought the urge to smile. It looked like someone else finally felt the way she did about the Prime.

"This is my city. Mine *alone*. As is everything it contains." Nikolai's arm tightened on Selene's shoulders. "That will be all, Sevigny. My thanks."

145

Sevigny nodded. *All he needs is a powdered wig and a cane.* Selene had to bite the inside of her cheek to keep from screaming. *I don't think I'm going to be able to stay quiet much longer.* He stood up, backing away slightly, and said something. It sounded like French, and Selene wished frantically that she had studied something other than Latin. Latin was better for deciphering old texts about paranormals, but she would give a hell of a lot to be able to decipher what they were saying *right fucking now.*

Nikolai replied in the same tongue. Sevigny's eyes, blue and shining like oil on the surface of a dark puddle, widened. He looked like a frightened child. He asked one shorter question, and Nikolai nodded.

"You're mad," Sevigny said. "You have gone *mad.*"

"Perhaps. Sell that information where you please. I have taken her, and will Turn her. Any attempt made on her life is an attack made on me, and I will respond accordingly."

SELENE WAITED UNTIL the velvet-clad Nichtvren had walked away, shaking his head, his brown hair falling to his shoulders. She tried to sit upright, pushing away from Nikolai, but his arm was suddenly iron, pulling her even further into his side. "Wait," he said into her hair. "Stay close to me, Selene."

"What the hell were you talking about?" she whispered fiercely. Nikolai looked down at her, his eyes black from lid to lid. *Give my regards to Nikolai,* a chill evil voice whispered in her memory, and she shuddered again. This made no sense.

"It is the only thing they understand, Selene. Be calm. Just for a little longer."

*I have taken her, and will Turn her.* It was the second time he'd mentioned making her a sucktooth. It wasn't the sort of thing a Nichtvren said casually.

And who was this Grigori? Nichtvren society was intensely feudal, and few were the Masters who didn't owe someone obedience. If a Nichtvren's Master died or released them, they had a chance to become a Master themselves, but still, there was a net of obligation and alliance that kept them mostly-behaving, most of the time.

Nikolai moved slightly and pressed his lips to her forehead. Her heart leapt and her fingernails drove into her palms, sharp bright points of pain. Then he used his free hand to brush her hair back, looking down at her.

*What a performance,* the clinical part of Selene's mind purred. *You might almost think he cares.*

The music changed to a marginally-less-pounding beat. Something brushed across Selene's shields, a whisper of unease. She froze, closing her eyes, her nostrils flaring in unconscious reaction as her mental senses sharpened.

"What is it?" Nikolai's voice sliced through the dusty filtered sound of the music. "Selene?"

The unease crested, metal scraping against her skin, prickles spilling up Selene's back. She reacted, grabbing Nikolai, her fists bunching in his shirt. Rolling off the couch, dragging him, her hip hitting the stone floor and her head narrowly missing the table. Nikolai didn't resist her, but he didn't precisely fall. He somehow got his feet underneath him. Crouching, he shoved the table away so she wouldn't hit her head. Splinters flew. Selene rolled onto her back, the stone floor burning-cold through the silk of her dress, and saw the bullets tear into him. Blood flew black in the pulsating light.

"*Nikolai!*" she screamed, and he shoved the table onto its side, calmly, as if he wasn't being shot. More splinters flew.

Heavy pounding music broke into the thin protective shell laid over the booth. Selene flinched, curling onto her side, her purse digging into her ribs. She tried to push herself up on her hands and knees but Nikolai shoved her back down, his bleeding hand on her shoulder. "Stay *down*," he hissed. His white shirt was marred with dark holes—his right shoulder, two lower down on his belly, one on his left side along his ribs. A smear of welling blood marked his pale cheek, dripping down his chin.

Rigel appeared behind the table, shoving aside torn red velvet. He looked at Nikolai, glanced down at her. He had two guns, roughly the size of cannons, and he went down on one knee and started firing over the ebony table. His long black coat pooled on the floor behind him.

Gunfire boomed, ricocheted, Selene heard someone screaming. It was a high squealing sound, a Nichtvren death-wail.

*He pushed me down to protect me, give me some cover.* Her mouth was dry, she stared up at him with her mouth ajar. *He just let himself be shot and flipped the table around to make sure I wouldn't be hit.*

Nikolai stood up, blood streaking his shirt, and calmly brushed his hands together. The slim blond thrall was on his other side, reloading what looked like a military-issue infantry stopper. The noise was incredible, music played at high-decibel levels and punctuated by random explosions of gunfire.

Nikolai's right shoulder jerked again, blood flew, and Selene screamed, a thin high sound. *They're still shooting at him, Christos, and he acts like he doesn't even* feel *it!*

Rigel clamped his hand around Selene's arm and dragged her aside. Power crackled and flamed. The table chattered against the stone floor, moving on its own under the pressure of the Power Nikolai was pulling in. Splinters flew. Bullets whizzed through the air. A chip of stone flicked past Selene's cheek, whistling as it clove the air.

*I wish I had a gun. A knife. Anything.*

Rigel yanked her to her feet and pulled her along. Her heels chattered against the stone, and something flicked past her head. *Oh my God, I'm being shot at. Again. Why can't I have a nice boring life?*

The noise behind them intensified. It sounded like a mother of a fight. Rigel pushed her through another booth, the red velvet twitching as bullets stitched at it, and she lost patience with her heels, kicking them off. Barefoot was better than wrenching an ankle and staggering around uselessly for the rest of the night, unless she stepped in broken glass.

Always assuming, of course, that she survived.

Something leapt through the velvet after them and Rigel whirled, firing twice.

The werecain thudded to the floor, his long furry claws outstretched. Half his head was gone. The half that remained was a mess of hamburger. "Bloody hell," Rigel said conversationally, and Selene realized that the music had stopped, was replaced with gunfire and more screaming. "Come on, Selene. Let's move along."

Her heartbeat thundered in her ears. *I'm going to throw up. I know it, I'm going to throw up.* "Nikolai." Her voice was a thin shocked whisper. *Why am I worrying about him?*

"He can take care of himself," Rigel snapped, his fingers sunk into her upper arm. "He's about to cover our retreat, and we need to get you out of here."

"But—"

There was a sound like every key on a pipe organ being hit at once. Selene screamed, her legs failing her, her hands clamping over her ears in a futile attempt to keep it *out*. It was a psychic wall of resonance, a tide of Power, and the medallion hanging against her chest burst into red heat. The mark on her throat gave one agonizing burst of pain and she fell, her knees barking the stone floor. Rigel fell too, thrown off-balance by her sudden crumpling, but he rolled onto his back and was firing into a confused jumble of bodies. Someone chasing them.

*The werecain at the bar. Why? I haven't done anything to a werecain, ever.*

Something other than werecain stink tainted the air. Something that might have maddened them into lashing out. *Yeah, sure, something just* happened *to make them mad while I'm here. Great.*

Selene scrambled to her feet, her hands tingling and her knees giving out sharp bursts of pain. The dress tangled between her legs. Rigel rolled up to his feet with a quick, inhumanly-graceful movement. He gathered himself and leapt, kicking a werecain in the face. The force of the blow threw the gorilla-sized thing back—it was covered in hair, and its wool sweater was starting to tear across the chest. Its face was hairy, caught midway between human and *something else.*

*The door-guard,* she thought, dimly, casting around for anything she could use as a weapon. *If I'm going to die, I'm going to die fighting.*

One of the dead werecain had a holster strapped under his upflung arm. Selene dived for it, but something hard and hot closed around her bare ankle and she fell, her hip thudding into stone with bone-cracking force. Her skull bounced against her arm—she'd curled her arms protectively over her head, a reaction that probably saved her life.

She was being dragged backward.

*Ohgod NO—*

Selene kicked back with her free foot, screaming. Exquisite glassy terror slammed into her belly, and the desire rose too, a tide of red, her thighs wet, her breath coming in short little gasps that changed the scream into a hilarious series of hiccups.

The kick—mercifully, luckily—connected with something hard and cool and wet. *Just like a dog's nose.* A fresh burst of amazed hilarity; there was a shocked snarling howl of pain. Her ankle was released and she scrambled away, bolted, trying to make it to her feet and almost overbalancing, her eyes fixed on the shoulder-holster attached to the dead werecain and the ridged dark butt of a gun closed inside the dark leather.

Her fingers scrabbled at the release catch, and she freed the gun from the leather—*Glock-Stryker, military model,* Jack's voice said, chill and calm inside her head. *Fully loaded, there's no safety on that mother, be careful, Lena.* Rigel appeared, a gun in either hand. He glanced down at her. "Time to go, Selene." The words, clear and crisp, cut through the noise. There was a streak of blood on Rigel's chin, and his hair was wildly mussed, clotted with guck and dried blood. His long black coat was torn as if razor-edged claws had ripped it.

Selene got to her feet, stone cold underneath her. Rigel followed, walking sideways, his guns ready. "Are you hit?" he asked, as if they weren't surrounded by howling werecain and fighting Nichtvren. Chaos spilled through the House of Pain, Nichtvren setting upon Nichtvren, werecain changed into huntforms and blood filling the air. The swanhilds were gone, and the kobolding had barricaded themselves into a corner. She inhaled, the kick and tang of Power hitting the back of her palate like whiskey, going down to explode in her belly. Gooseflesh rippled her skin.

Her curse awakened. The image of Nikolai's face above hers, eyes closed, as he sighed and her body shuddered, spilled more desire through her veins, made her gasp.

*Don't get distracted.* The Power filled her; she wouldn't need Nikolai for a week or two now. The curse grumbled, subsided as she fought it. "No." She swallowed dryly. Her throat was a desert. "I think I'm ok—"

A huge painless impact slammed into her back. Selene was thrown forward, falling, the gun almost skittering from her hand. Luckily, her fingers went numb and clutched at it, she ended face-down on the floor, her back on fire, a long hissing breath slipping out of her. *What?*

"*NO!*" someone bellowed, and the ground shook. Crashing, rending noises. Screaming. All hell was breaking loose. *What hit me? What happened?*

Rigel went to his knees beside her. Selene tried to roll onto her back, but nothing below her shoulders seemed to work. Darkness started creeping in from the corners of her peripheral vision.

*What the hell just happened?*

"Lie still," Rigel said, from very far away. Then the pain came, a great rolling breaker of it, and Selene cried out weakly. This pain didn't mutate into a riptide of lust, it was *true* pain, deep and hot and like she never felt unless something serious had happened. She tried to arch away from its teeth even as some part of her was glad she didn't drown in it. "Lie still, Selene. God in Heaven."

"Wha...?" she started to ask, but a bubble of something warm burst on her lips and ran down her chin. *Ugh, did I throw up? I don't want to throw up, please, what hit me, oh it hurts it HURTS...*

The lights stopped swirling, and darkness slid over the cavernous interior. *Someone's cut the lights,* she thought hazily, before red emergency lamps came up, lurid, painting the stone underneath her. Hot blood splattered from her lips, pattering on stone, and she tried to roll onto her back again.

Then she smelled it. *Blood, and death. Male, ancient, a smell like dried ratfur and musk.* It was her quarry, Danny's killer. It was *here*. Selene tried desperately to move, she had a gun, and Danny's killer was *here*.

Cold. Cold seeping into her skin. *Why can't I move, it hurts me, my back hurts, owww Danny help me, help me.*

Rigel was saying something, but his voice was even further away now. All she heard was a mumble, and her name.

*What happened?* she wanted to ask, but her lips were cold and numb. *Where's Nikolai?* He would help her, he had always helped her before.

151

And one last thought in the swimming darkness made her try to stay awake. *Danny? Danny, is that you?* She failed, and fell into darkness, the pain retreating as night closed around her.

# SEVEN

"—CAREFULLY," A WOMAN'S voice said, soft and restful. She sounded tired. Scrape of metal. Smell of salt. "She'll heal, but she must have absolute rest."

Darkness again, a slow cold creeping darkness. Selene struggled up through it, a swimmer in deep water. The roaring noise retreated a little, and she could think again, if only a little.

*But I was dead. I know I was. I was dead. Am I in hell now?*

"—blood?" A dark voice, full of cold hurtful Power, a voice she would have struggled to get away from if she could. "How much more?"

"As much as you can give her." The woman's tone was very definite, but also respectful. Scorching-hot fingers resting against her forehead. "I've never seen healing this quick, even with my help. I see the mark, she is Acolyte?"

"*Tantraiiken.*" He sounded familiar, even if she did want to hide until the owner of that hurtful freezing went away. "And I... I..."

"Yes, I see. So the rumors *are* true." The woman sounded amused. Her tone was calm, smooth as satin. Selene smelled violets and musk, an odd combination. The voice wrapped Selene in comfort, sent heat through her cold, leaden body. "She's out of immediate danger. I'll leave you to it for a while, she can't take any more Power tonight. You must call me if she grows fevered. Now I'll go see if Jorge has left me anything to eat."

"As you like." Now a coolness pressed against her cheek, stroking and tender. Was it the woman?

*What woman?*

There was a sound of silk moving. Then a silence. Selene opened her eyes. Everything swam in front of her, a blur of color and shadow. "Prince," the woman said. "About Rigel."

*Rigel?* Selene thought, dimly. *I hope he's okay, what happened to me?*

"He is lucky." The Power in the cold hurtful voice was enough to strip flesh from bone, Selene heard a shapeless whimper. It was her own. "Were it not for your intercession, *sedayeenen*, he would be dead."

"It wasn't his fault." The woman sounded firm, but Selene detected something else. Was it fear? Maybe. But maybe not, it could have been anger.

The blurring in front of Selene's eyes slowly started to coalesce into shapes. Velvet, hanging across something. Dark blue.

There was a cold exhalation, and Selene's skin prickled. It was a shock to discover she was still breathing. "Jesu," she croaked, and blinked, her eyelids falling down. Then she opened her eyes again, and the shapes slowly started to settle into sharply-defined objects. "Am I dead?" It was a stupid thing to ask, but it was all she could think to say.

"You may have Rigel if you wish, healer." A snarl rose in the words. Selene's skin prickled again, but thankfully no wash of desire or Power rose in her. Her arms and legs felt cold and heavy. "I give him to you. May he offer you better service than he offered me. Now *get out.*" Deadly, deathly Power rattled the air of the room. Was it Nikolai's nest? It had to be.

"Rigel..." Selene coughed weakly. "Is he...is he okay?" She looked up at the blue velvet hanging. *At least it's not red.* She shuddered. Or she would have shuddered, if she hadn't been so weak. Her entire body was full of cold lead. *What happened? Oh yeah, someone shot me.*

"Better than he has any right to be," the chill voice said. Was it Nikolai? He sounded so...*dangerous.*

"He saved...my life," Selene said, softly. There was a rush and crackle, and the smell of smoke. A fire? In a Nichtvren's nest? They feared open flame, it was one of the few things even a very old Master might not survive.

"You almost died, Selene." There was something so familiar about that voice.

*Is that Nikolai? He sounds so scary.*

A door shut, and someone sat down on the bed next to her. Selene blinked again. Her vision blurred, everything losing its focus.

Nikolai leaned over her, his face marked with dried blood across forehead and cheeks. It looked like a strange kind of warpaint, and Selene examined him for a long moment. His hair was dirty, straggling over the black holes of his eyes. He looked gaunt, his cheeks hollow, pale skin stretched over aristocratic bones. He was still wearing a white shirt, only now it was in bloody tattered rags, and Selene had to look twice to make sure it was the same one he'd been wearing before. Pale unmarked flesh showed through the tatters. *Of course, he wouldn't scar after he Turned.* A dozy sort of logic filled her brain, and she felt the corners of her mouth tilt up.

"You look awful," she whispered. Hoarse, her throat full of sand and gravel.

He smoothed his fingertips across her forehead. His skin was chill, and hers was clammy. "Thank you, dear one." Something gentler passed over his face. The shadows over his eyes dispelled a little, though they were still black from lid to lid. "How do you feel?"

"Rigel saved my life." Selene took in a gasping breath. "Tell me you didn't hurt him."

Nikolai's mouth thinned. "He will live." He kept touching her forehead, his fingers slowly warming. "Twelve centuries I have roamed this earth," he said finally, quietly, "I have never feared immortality. I have never feared *anything* that walks in shadow or in sunlight. But you..." He trailed off, touched her cheek, with just his fingertips. His fangs slid out, pressing into his lower lip, and Selene began to feel a faint drowsy alarm. It wasn't like him to show his fangs without provocation. "I fear losing you, Selene." He stroked her cheek with the back of his hand. His skin was cold again, cold and perfect.

*You can't just pick up another* tantraiiken *off the street, after all.* Selene shivered, tried to stop the helpless little motion. "I smelled it. What killed Danny. It was *there.*"

Nikolai stilled, looking at her. "And how do you know this?" His fingertips brushed a stray strand of her hair.

"The wards," she answered, her eyelids drooping and heavy again. "The wards... I did them, they're mine. I took them. Looked at them the day after...yesterday? When was it?" She tried to remember, but it was so *hard* with the languid exhaustion weighing down every muscle, every inch of her skin. She had never felt so exquisitely, completely exhausted. There wasn't even a breath from the curse, and that was welcome relief.

A muscle jumped in Nikolai's pale, blood-marked cheek. "I am beginning to think I should chain you in my sanctum." He sounded serious. "What did the wards tell you, Selene?"

"Showed me...what killed Danny..." She was falling asleep again. Why wouldn't her arms move, and her legs?

"And what did you see?" Nikolai stroked her cheek. His fingers traced her jaw, dipped down to touch her throat. There was a faint, pulsing warmth at her throat. Why wasn't the mark burning?

"Tired." Selene's eyes drifted closed. "I smelled it. Something old, so old...and teeth...and..."

His breath against her cheek now. "Sleep, Selene. I will watch over you."

"Beads," Selene whispered. "In his hair... *Give my regards...to Nikolai*...he said...to Danny. Before...it killed...him."

Nikolai hissed a phrase that made the air quake. Wood groaned and glass shattered. She knew she should be frightened, but she couldn't work up the energy through the choking drowsiness.

Selene fell into darkness again, but before she lost consciousness entirely, she felt Nikolai's lips against her cheek, her chin, and finally her slack mouth. He was murmuring something between kisses, phrases she couldn't quite hear.

It didn't matter. Darkness, again.

"—WERECAIN." ANOTHER FAMILIAR voice. It was Jorge, he sounded like himself again. "What do you think?"

"I'm not paid to think about it." The woman's voice again, satiny and restful. A warm touch brushed Selene's forehead. "It's bad enough dealing with him as it is. If there's any intimation she might not survive he'll tear the house apart. He almost killed Rigel."

"Rigel's a thrall. It's a risk," Jorge sighed. "I can't believe he let you *have* him."

"Rigel is a person, Jorge. Not an object, though it matters little enough where your master's concerned. But for the record, I'm thankful." The woman sounded thoughtful. Her voice was so beautiful, clear and soft. "She's waking up. Hello, Selene."

Selene opened her eyes to find a woman sitting on the bed where Nikolai had been. For a moment she felt oddly...bereft, as if she'd expected to see him instead.

As if she'd *anticipated* seeing him.

The stranger had long dark hair, slightly curling, and she carried a breath of musk and violets. Her face was triangular, catlike, with large dark-blue eyes. The smell of her was strong and fragrant the way an ordinary person's never was—*paranormal*, Selene thought, staring. *Only not like me. Something else.*

"I'm Marina." That smile was like music, like dawn breaking over soft green hills. "I'm *sedayeenen*. A healer."

That explained it. A pacifist healer, capable of mending shattered bones and broken bodies, but incapable of using violence against anyone, even to defend herself. No wonder she was in the nest. She probably didn't go outside much. "Oh," Selene managed.

Jorge's face swam into view over the woman's slim shoulder. The healer wore dark-blue velvet, an empire-waisted dress that suited her pale skin and pretty eyes. She held her hand to Selene's forehead, and a warm tide of Power flushed down Selene's injured body.

The Power folded around her like a warm cloak. Thankfully, it didn't trigger the *tantraiiken* curse. It only filled her veins with new strength. The medallion lay cool and quiescent against her skin. "It's daylight." The healer's pretty mouth shaped the words quietly. "Nikolai is sleeping, but he will wake if you call. He's given you quite a bit of his blood."

Selene's head dropped back against the pillows. "He...gave me..." She was wrapped in cotton wool. None of it mattered.

"You shouldn't have told her," Jorge said mildly. His bald head gleamed.

"She has a right to know," Marina replied, unaffected. It didn't look like much affected her calm amusement at all. "Why don't you run along and fetch breakfast, cutie-pie, and tell Rigel to step on in."

"Nikolai won't like that either. He's irritated with Rigel." But he stepped back from the bed; it seemed impossible to argue with the healer's cool, beautiful voice. Jorge dropped his gaze from Selene's. He wore the same gray suit he always did, his dark eyes sharp and alert.

"Nikolai has abdicated all right to like or dislike what Rigel does. I'm responsible. Now do as I say, or I'll tell His Highness you disobeyed the healer. And since I've dragged his paramour back from the dead, my stock is particularly high with Nikolai right now." Marina's face didn't change, but her voice held just the faintest hint of contempt.

*I wish I could sound that sarcastic without dialing up my volume.*

Marina gazed back down at her. Jorge backed away, then stalked for the door.

The room was pretty, blue velvet and cream-colored silk. A black-and-white Japanese print of cranes flying over the moon hung on one wall. Four graceful torchieres gave an even light. There were three chairs and a loveseat, a huge pre-War rolltop desk made of pale blond wood, and bookcases ranged on the walls between long falls of blue velvet drapery. A restrained blue-and-white vase on an endtable—*must be a Ming.* Selene gazed on all this with a brand of weary wonder. *This is the most tasteful I've ever seen a Nichtvren get. I'll bet Nikolai didn't do the decorating in here.*

"You were shot in the back," Marina said. "You lost quite a bit of blood and might have been paralyzed, I can't tell. Nikolai had to give you his blood, even your ability to heal would have been...well, severely strained." The warmth flowing into Selene's body didn't stop. Marina's eyes were infinitely kind. "Besides, he'd already made up his mind to Turn you. You could do worse, you know."

The door closed, and Marina glanced away from Selene. "Here comes Rigel." The smile in her voice was just as calm as the rest of her.

"Did Nikolai hurt him?" *I'm super-infected now.* A shocked calm descended on her. *Gave me his blood. Am I his thrall? Oh, Jesu.* Her hands and feet seemed very far away, floating at the end of long strings.

"Not very much," Marina said. "I was able to stop him, but it was difficult. He values you, Selene. Nikolai has never had an Acolyte before. He's never even made a grave-head. He thought Rigel had let you be harmed, and he was furious."

"Jesu." It cost her precious energy to talk. The Power the healer was pushing into her crept through every nerve. *Sedayeenen* were almost as rare as *tantraiiken*, and had their own curse, their inability to fight back. Selene hadn't even known that there was a healer in Saint City. Most of them ended up attached to stronger paranormals, not quite slaves but definitely not free. There were superstitions about harming a healer, but Selene sometimes wondered just how useful a protection those superstitions were.

*There's a whole hell of a lot I don't know. Curse of an academic, getting some actual fieldwork makes you realize you're an idiot.* The fire creeping through her fingers and toes spread, tingling, up her arms.

Rigel's lean dark face appeared over Marina's shoulder. He had a black eye and a split lip, and moved very slowly. "Hallo, Selene." His accent made the words crisp. "My apologies. I should have acted more quickly."

"Oh, Christos," Selene whispered. "Did Nikolai beat you up?" It was getting difficult to talk, something seemed to be stuck in her mouth. Her tongue was thick and clumsy, too.

Rigel shrugged. His hand rested on Marina's shoulder and she glanced up at him, smiling. He didn't look down at her, but he straightened a little, self-consciously. Selene had seen that response too many times not to understand it. So Rigel...well, it was none of Selene's business.

Her chest ached, her ribs squeezed mercilessly. "I'm sorry," she whispered. *Dammit, Nikolai, if you've made me an enemy out of one of your own thralls it'll be the last straw. Why do you do things like this?*

"It wasn't your fault," Marina said briskly. "Now you just rest. Jorge will bring breakfast, and I'll take care of you. Don't worry. When Nikolai rises tonight..." She trailed off, looking across the room as if struck by a new thought.

Selene realized the velvet hung on the walls was probably covering glass. "The windows," she managed through her clumsy lips. "Sunlight. Open the windows. Please."

Marina leaned over. Her hand left Selene's forehead, she lifted up Selene's top lip and checked her teeth.

Selene thrashed up, teeth snapping together. Rigel tore Marina back, both of them falling on the floor as Selene flopped down on the bed, the covers flung back. Her body wouldn't obey her. The medallion was icy against her chest. She heard a long low hiss, like a kettle whistling with steam. *Is that me? Am I making that noise? What is* happening *to me?*

"*Ow!*" the healer yelled at the same time, and the sound of her landing cut off the cry midway. Selene lay against the pillows, dimly aware she was *snarling*, a low thrumming sound coming from her chest. Silk strained against her chill clammy skin—the sheets and a black silk nightgown. *Nichtvren have a thing for silk.*

Selene coughed again, rackingly. Her ribs twisted, and she heard crackling. Bones, re-forming.

Panic slammed through her, all her muscles contracting at once. *No. Please, no, tell me it's not happening. Please, no. I don't want to be a sucktooth.*

Rigel appeared. He bent down and helped the healer to her feet, hugged her, his dark eyes never leaving Selene. "All right then, love?" he asked her, his accent wearing through the words. "Rina?"

"Fine." Marina pushed her hair back, glancing up at him. "Just a bit shaken, that's all. Help me." She started forward, but Rigel almost lifted her off her feet and stepped back, quickly. Her dress swung with her. He set her down on her bare feet gently, reluctantly.

"You're not going near her. Look at her. She's Turning. Go get Nikolai."

"Open the drapes," Selene whispered. *I was trying to take her finger off. I wanted to bite her—oh, God. God, please...*"Please. God...help me. Please!" *Begging again, God help me.*

The healer tried to shake free of Rigel again, he pulled her back.

Selene coughed again, a dry deep hacking sound. *Thirsty.* Something was creeping through the horrible weakness that lay on her body—a merciless, slow-twisting fire. And with the flames rose the thirst. Deep as a mineshaft, her throat aching, her entire body a desert.

"Let go, Rigel." The healer's soft voice demanded obedience. "She won't hurt me. I *order* you to let go of me."

Silence ticked through the room. Selene's body jerked and twisted. "Open...the...fucking...curtains..."

Rigel slowly released the healer. His lean dark face was blank. "Be careful, love." His voice was husky. "Please."

Marina shook free of him, smoothing her robe down. "I can't open the curtains." Her voice seemed to make the slow creeping fire a little less. "You're too far gone. Sunlight will hurt you, might even kill you. You're very weak."

*I don't fucking care, if I'm weak it will be mostly painless, just open the goddamn motherfucking curtains!* "Open...them..."

"Get my bag, Rigel," Marina snapped, and stepped close to the bed. She leaned down, caught one of Selene's wrists, and Selene froze. The healer's skin felt scorching-hot against hers.

*Thud-thud. Thud-thud. Thud-thud. Thud-thud.*

The sound drove into Selene's head.

*Her heartbeat, it's her pulse, oh my God, I'm Turning.* "The windows," Selene gasped. "Sun. *Let the sun in.*"

"You'll die." The healer's fingers were skilled and gentle. Rigel dropped a small black bag onto the bed and tore it open— it was the kind of bag physicians used to carry a long time ago. "So don't be ridiculous. I haven't lost a patient yet, and I'm not about to start with you."

*Thud-thud. Thud-thud. Thud-thud.*

Selene's body lifted on its own, arching between her heels and the crown of her head without any direction from her, then dropped. "Hold her," Marina snapped at Rigel, who pushed Selene's shoulders down. He was stronger than he looked, even wounded. His hands bit her shoulders, bruising-hard. Fire twisted through her bones, racing toward her heart, reshaping crackling bone and sliding muscle in its wake. Her heels scrabbled weakly at the sheets as she bucked, trying to slip out of his grasp.

Marina's hands were quick and deft, tying something around Selene's arm and subtracting a hypodermic from her bag. "Hold her, she's going to thrash."

"Nikolai won't like this," Rigel said darkly.

"If she Turns now she'll be crippled, even with steady infusions of his blood. She's *too weak*. I know what I'm doing." Marina's long dark hair fell down, tickling Selene's arm, and she slapped the hypo on. "*Hold* her!" Marina snapped the tourniquet off, and a bolt of cold agony shot up Selene's arm.

Selene screamed. The medallion gave a livid flare, and blue sparks flew.

The door flew open, hitting the wall and splintering. Jorge strode into the room, and Rigel's hands left Selene's shoulders. The healer looked up, Selene's body twisted helplessly. Thundering, thundering, the healer's pulse had barely altered, as if she wasn't holding down a struggling almost-Turned Nichtvren.

"*Stop it!*" Marina yelled, her eyes flaring with blue-violet light. The entire room shook, velvet and silk billowing and snapping in the sudden breeze. "Jorge, don't be an idiot, haul your Polish ass over here and *help me*! Rigel, dammit, let *go* of him!"

Selene rolled onto her side. Marina had both her hands, fingers laced together and straining as bones cracked. Marina grimaced, her long hair falling forward as she climbed up on the bed, her knees on either side of Selene's hips. She leaned down, pushing Selene back, holding her hands, and was soon nose-to-nose with her. The healer's skin was fine and clear, her eyes glowing bright blue. Those eyes seemed to bore into Selene's skull. Heat slid from the healer's palms into hers, a soothing human heat.

"It's all right, Selene," she said, softly, as if she hadn't been screaming at the two thralls a moment ago. "I'm here. Squeeze my hands. It will hurt, but I'm here with you."

Selene stared at her. *Kill me. Let me die. Let me go so he can't hurt me anymore.* "Open...the...curtains," she whispered. "Please."

"In a minute." The healer kissed Selene's sweat-slick forehead, a gentle clean touch. "The enzyme will start to work, and you'll be drained afterwards. It's all right. Shhh, hush, it's all right." Her lips were warm. She kept talking, soothing little nonsense phrases, her voice full of a deep smooth Power that caught and held, mesmerized Selene. It was a thin thread, that Power, holding her to sanity while the Turn fought with the enzyme treatment for control of her body.

Selene's body arched. It was *cold*, it raced up her arm and hit the rest of her bloodstream in a mass of ice spikes, tearing through muscle and nerves. In the wake of the crushing freeze, the familiar bite of desire came, an old enemy she could never shake.

*I'd rather be dead than go on living like this.* But the pain rose again and Selene sobbed out a broken breath. She had a revenge to accomplish, Danny's killer to track down. There was time for death later, wasn't there?

*Oh, God, either kill me or let me get this done and over with, I don't care which.*

The shudders passed, convulsions lessening. The healer stayed with her the entire time, her gaze never leaving Selene's, her voice holding the *tantraiiken* to sanity while her body threw off the changes Nikolai's blood had produced.

Marina finally looked up. Her hair fell forward, brushing Selene's face, enfolding her with the smell of violets and white mallow. "Right. That's better." She cleared her throat. "Will you two please wait outside?"

Selene saw Jorge's face, chalky-pale. "What have you done?" He sounded like a little boy caught in a terrible nightmare.

Rigel stood in front of Jorge, his arm extended. The gun was absolutely steady, pointed at Jorge's face. "The lady said to wait outside. Let's go, old chap. Nice and easy. We'll have some coffee."

Jorge nodded. His hands trembled slightly. "I'm sorry, Selene," he said, pointlessly. His dark eyes never left Rigel's face. "Nikolai will—"

"If I would have let her Turn she would have been crippled, I've seen it before. *I'm* the professional here, you hunk of brainless muscle. Just *go*." The healer's hair brushed Selene's face.

Selene bit back a moan.

The two men left, Rigel holstering his gun. Jorge said something in a low tone, and Rigel replied in an equally soft tone. "Nothing personal, old son."

Marina waited until the door was closed. They had to rattle it to get it closed all the way, and the healer sighed. "Men." She looked back down at Selene, who was writhing against the sheets. "Driven by their crotches or their testosterone. They never *think*."

"I'm...*tantraiiken*," Selene gasped. Her body writhed, betraying her again. "I'm...sorry."

"It's all right." The healer leaned down, kissed her cheek. Ice slid through Selene's fingers, spread down her legs, and her muscles unlocked. The sound of the healer's pulse receded, faded altogether.

Selene realized she was squeezing the healer's hands as hard as she could. She tried to make her fingers unlock, couldn't. "My hands."

"Just relax," the healer replied. "It's the enzyme treatment. Partial paralysis in the extremities is normal. It will pass in a few moments. Breathe, Selene. Look at me. Breathe."

She did. The healer's hands were no longer scorching-hot. Instead, they were only warm. Marina's breath brushed her cheek. She smiled, looking down. It was a human smile, and Selene felt relief spill out into her chest with the ice.

A *human* smile. Not like Nikolai's good-natured grin or chilling little grimaces. Human. Whatever else she was, the healer was also blessedly human, and she was kind. She'd stopped Selene from Turning, and that put her number one on the list of Selene's favorite people just at the moment.

Her body strained again, arching up, and the healer rocked back a little, pressing her back down. "Good girl," she murmured. "That's it. Just try to relax. I should have given you the enzyme sooner, but I didn't think you were so far gone. He must have been coaxing you along for a while now, bringing you into the Twilight. Ah, well, hindsight's twenty-twenty, isn't it?" She looked thoughtful, chewing at her full bottom lip with small white teeth.

*The Twilight?* "I've never seen you before," Selene said. "What..."

"I direct the Free Clinic downtown," the healer replied. "But only for the past six months. I tried to negotiate entry into Nikolai's territory and had to wait for a while. I was living down the coast, in Altamira."

*So that's who she is, I've heard of her. How did she get here?* "You're the one that—"

Marina nodded. "I was the Prime of Altamira's prize pet for a long time. I understand, Selene. Truly, I do. Now just relax. I'll answer all your questions later." She cocked her head, watching Selene's face. "You'll need to feed when this is done," she said, softly. "I know you're *tantraiiken*. It doesn't bother me. Do you want me to call one of the thralls, or...?"

"No!" It burst out of Selene. If she had to lay under one of Nikolai's thralls... "Please."

Marina nodded. "I'll stay," she said, and smiled. "It should be quite an experience." Her hair brushed Selene's face, drenched her in that soothing violet-musk smell. Selene shut her eyes, trying to breathe deeply, failing.

Gradually the ice retreated, and inhaling became easier. Wherever the cold receded, a different kind of fire began. She stayed still for as long as she could, but her body betrayed her yet again, her hips rocking upwards slightly, pleading. She was wet, and now her skin turned to honey, dipped in warm oil.

The healer slowly slid her hands free. Selene's fingers curled into fists.

"Now," Marina breathed. "You need to feed. Have you ever had a *sedayeenen* before?"

# EIGHT

TEARS STARTED BEHIND Selene's eyelids. Her entire body was limp, drained: her heart was now thundering behind her ribs. She ached savagely, overstrained, but the ache just made the slick dampness between her legs worse. "N-n-no," she whispered. "Never." *I never have.*

The healer slid to the side and balanced on her knees on the bed, then moved slightly. Selene didn't dare look. Velvet brushed Selene's bare arm, then the healer lowered herself down and pulled the covers up, and took Selene in her arms. She was smooth and warm, soft, breasts and hips like Selene's own pressing against the slick silk of the nightgown.

*She's naked. I don't even know her. I never get to know them, the ones I have to feed the curse with.*

"This might be difficult for you," the healer said, quietly. "I don't have to fight my gift. But a *tantraiiken*...it must be so hard."

Selene's face pressed into the soft hollow under the healer's chin. Marina's fingers stroked her sweating back, the silk sticking to Selene's skin. Violets, spice, musk, and the smell of *female;* Selene had rarely used a woman for this. Most women didn't understand.

Nobody really understood. "Nikolai," she heard herself say. "He'll—"

The healer laughed. "He'll what? Probably want to watch. Or join in." Her fingers continued their slow, even massage, and Selene felt her body unstringing, muscles relaxing, the heat rising between her legs. The nightgown stuck and slid—she wanted it *off.*

"I need to take this thing off," she found herself saying. "Please."

"There's a lacing on the back." Incredibly, the healer giggled. Her body moved against Selene's, Selene caught her breath. Warm flesh and the curves that were so like her own, a comfort in the middle of the minefield of need and desire.

The healer's breathing was a little faster now, as she worked on the nightgown's laces. "I feel like a teenager again," she murmured, and Selene tentatively touched her hip, smoothing her fingers over satiny skin.

"Did you...while you were a teenager?" *Christos knows I did.* Selene's throat was blocked. She felt weak, her hands limp and her legs heavy, but the fire *demanded* that she move, that she touch the woman, find out what would make her respond, what would feed the curse.

"I did my fair share of experimenting. I was raised by Nichtvren, the Prime of Altamira took me when I was five. It does give one a different view of sex." There was laughter in her husky voice, covering a deep sadness in the well of her calm. Then the nightgown loosened. "There. I think that should do it. Help me, if you can, Selene. Lift your hips up...good. There. Now your arm."

It was as if she was a child again, being dressed by someone else. Or *undressed.* Her head was clearing rapidly. *Raised by Nichtvren? My God.* "Nikolai tried to Turn me?"

Marina ran her hand down Selene's ribs, her fingers leaving a trail of warmth in their wake. The gasping, electric sense of Power that Nikolai carried was very different from this gentleness. "It was a consideration. Mostly, he just wanted to give you enough strength to survive. The healing properties of Nichtvren blood..." The healer kissed her cheek, her lips sliding against the sweat slicking Selene's entire body. Then her hand slid between Selene's legs. "Listen to me lecture. Don't think about that now, just feed. You need it." Two of her slender, tapered fingers slid into the aching, throbbing need. Marina's thumb started a slow, even circling, and Selene's entire body jerked.

Marina laughed. It was a beautiful, husky sound. "Sometimes it takes another woman," she said, softly, breathlessly, and her eyes met Selene's, half-closed with pleasure. It was as if she *anticipated* what Selene needed, her fingers moving a split-second before Selene even thought to ask.

The healer's mouth met hers, a cool lipsticked kiss; Selene moaned, pleading. Marina's thumb moved fractionally faster, paused, and scraped down hard over the sharp swollen throbbing point.

Selene's body exploded. The first climax hit her, she half-screamed into Marina's mouth and the healer's delicious, wicked stroking went on. Power sparked and crackled between them, a soft violet glow instead of Nikolai's hard gasflame blue.

"There. Isn't that better?" A low, wicked laugh. Not Nichtvren-wicked, just a delicious little human noise.

Selene found she had wound her fingers in Marina's long hair and was kissing the taller woman's chin and cheek and throat, frantically, pleading, making soft little noises in the back of her throat. Marina's dark-blue eyes were half-closed, heavy-lidded. *Does she look at Rigel that way?* Selene did her best to push the thought away. She could feel another riptide of Power, but it was going in the opposite direction. The healer was feeding too, in a different way. *A perfect match. Altamira. What was that like, for her?*

The Power sparked, building, and her hips rocked forward. Marina kissed her again, a little harder, using her teeth to pull in Selene's bottom lip and scrape across sensitive flesh.

*It's like kissing myself.* The second climax slammed into her, nerves twisting and screaming. The *need* retreated more quickly than it ever had.

Marina slipped her fingers free with one last twist, making Selene shudder. "Now rest." She slid her arms around Selene and held her close, breasts pressing together, the other woman's nipples hard as her own, her flesh soft and blessedly human. Their legs tangled together. After a little bit of rearranging, Selene found her head on Marina's shoulder, Marina's arm around her, the healer's dark hair mixed with her own blonde. The comfort made Selene drowsy, luxuriating in the absence of pain and the aftermath of a full feeding.

*And she won't use it against me. I feel safe.* "When can I get up?"

"You'll break my heart." The healer yawned delicately. "After lunch, maybe. Your body's well healed, between Nikolai's blood and my talent, but you'll still be weak and tired. I'd counsel you not to get shot in the back again anytime soon."

"I'll try to avoid it." *Raised by Nichtvren. No wonder she's so easy with Nikolai.* "What did Nikolai do to Rigel?"

"Hit him a few times." The healer closed her eyes. "I refused to treat you until he stopped."

"Why?" *It's none of my business. So why do I ask?*

"Rigel bought me free from the Prime of Altamira. He bled to do it; he almost died. And he indentured himself to Nikolai for his aid in negotiating my freedom." The healer stroked Selene's forehead with her free hand. A quiet warmth wrapped around Selene's entire body, her arms and legs weighted with lead. "Now rest, Selene. You'll be all right."

Selene was about to ask why Rigel had done that, but deep velvet blackness slid over her. *She's putting me to sleep.* How had the healer staved off the Turn? *Even an enzyme treatment only has a seventy percent chance of working once it's reached a certain point. But she's* sedayeenen.

There, in the healer's arms, Selene finally had her first true restful sleep since Danny's death.

"NIKOLAI WON'T LIKE this." A slight, crisp accent. Rigel's voice.

"It's all right." Marina's husky, soothing tones. Velvet moved, rustling.

*Why do paranormals all dress so weird? Am I the only one who just wants a nice pair of heels?* Selene opened her eyes. She still felt human.

Selene lay on her side, and was greeted with the sight of Rigel tying the front laces of Marina's dress. He did this with an expression of pained concentration that made his dark severe face a little less harsh. The healer looked up at him, smiling, her dark hair mussed and her cheeks flushed. The blue of the room echoed the blue of her dress, and both shades suited her.

*I should ask her so much, I bet she knows all sorts of little tidbits about sucktooths. Why is she not Turned? Oh, right, she's a* sedayeenen, *and valuable.*

"He *really* won't like this." Rigel bit his lower lip, finishing the laces. Marina reached up and took his hands in hers. Her hands were smaller than his, and paler, but Rigel froze and stared down at her face, still biting at his lip. Color flushed his dark cheeks. She held him gently, smiling, and Selene could almost taste the Power rising through the *sedayeenen*, sinking into the tall dark man. Rigel was a thrall, fast and deadly, but he seemed curiously vulnerable next to the healer's self-possessed serenity.

"I find it very difficult to care," Marina said, softly.

Selene pushed herself upright, pulled the sheet up to her chest. "What won't Nikolai like?"

Rigel actually flinched. Marina let go of his hands, lightly, and faced Selene. There was a fire in the fireplace, more open flame in a Nichtvren's house.

Selene blinked. One of the velvet drapes was pulled aside, and afternoon sun slanted down into the room, making the wood glow and bringing out chestnut highlights in Marina's tangled hair. The *sedayeenen* belonged here, in the middle of antiques and rich textures, graceful and slim.

"He won't like that I didn't allow you to Turn." Marina moved away from Rigel, picked up a silver tray that lay on a table near the fireplace. "But he'll understand. Rigel, can you find her clothes? I think Nik put them in the closet with the blue canvas bag."

Selene's heart gave a painful, twisting leap. The medallion was dull and cool against her skin. "The bag. And my purse. I need them both."

Rigel didn't even look at her. Instead, he looked at Marina's long, beautiful hair as she brought the tray to the bed. He seemed lost in thought, staring at the *sedayeenen* as she set it down on a pale baroque ashwood nightstand. "All right." Marina took the cover off the tray. "The blue bag, and your purse. Meanwhile, you eat. Here, it's broth, and good for you. The more you can eat human food, the better."

Selene accepted a steaming blue pottery mug from the healer's hands. A hunger-cramp seized her, and she crouched

over, smelling the steam. *Chicken broth. Of course. Cure for everything.*
A bitter, unwilling grin pulled up one corner of her mouth.

Marina smiled. "That's a good girl." She pushed a few stray
curls of Selene's hair back, with warm soft fingers. "Drink it all."
Her blue eyes were dark and thoughtful. She half-turned, velvet
sweeping the floor. Rigel still stood as if nailed in place,
watching. "The bag, Rigel. If you don't mind." Patiently, as if
she was used to his staring.

The tall dark man blinked, as if he was having trouble
remembering where he was. "Right. The bag. Clothes. Right."
He'd found another long black coat, and was fully armed. Selene
saw knives strapped to his waist and the butt of a gun under his
armpit as he pushed his dark hair back. His lip was whole and
his eyes weren't bruised anymore. *She must have healed him. Wish I
could do something that useful. Instead, I'm the paranormal equivalent of a
scarlet woman.*

"I'm curious. Why *didn't* you let me Turn?" She sipped at
the broth. Her fingers felt cold and shaky, and the big muscles
in her thighs felt limp as wet noodles. And the medallion—it lay
under the silk of the sheet she'd wrapped around herself. It had
never felt so still and cold. "He'll be furious."

"Amen to that," Rigel muttered. The healer ignored him.

"Well, if you'd Turned, you would have been crippled.
That's my professional opinion, and I've seen enough Turns go
wrong to know. It would have been too hard on you." There
was a restrained green porcelain teapot and two Japanese tea-
bowls, Marina poured delicately. "Nik's sensible. As long as
you're still alive and whole, he won't be *that* difficult to deal with.
The Prime of Altamira would be a different story." Amazingly,
the healer shuddered, a little of the color leaching out of her
pretty cheeks. "Besides, you didn't seem too enchanted with the
notion of immortality. I hate to see a woman forced. I always
have." She settled onto the bed, blue velvet pooling around her.
With her long tangled hair and her cat-tilted eyes, she looked like
a Pre-Raphaelite painting. Sunlight glowed through the room.
"Rigel, what on earth are you doing?"

The tall man had stopped and was simply staring at her
again. Selene sipped at the mug, watching. It hurt to see, right
behind her breastbone. *I'll bet he watches her sleep, too.*

Rigel blinked, for all the world as if just waking up. "Um...nothing much. The bag, and her clothes. Right."

"And her purse," the *sedayeenen* supplied helpfully. "Please?"

He nodded. "Right-o, love." He stalked over to a door painted with cherubs Selene hadn't noticed before and pulled it open, revealing a closet. Marina sipped at her tea. Her gaze stayed on Rigel, a faint line between her dark eyebrows. Her cheeks were pale. Probably remembering Altamira.

What would make a *sedayeenen* go pale and shiver? It must have been horrible. The Prime of Altamira had a reputation for psychological cruelty even among other Nichtvren. The rumors were bad enough; did Selene even want to ask? It wasn't polite, but...

That was the trouble with sex. You never knew what you could ask afterward.

Marina sighed. "Not a very good memory, that man. Mind like a sieve." A faint smile touched her lips, a little color coming back into her cheeks. "So what are you planning, Selene?"

"What makes you think I'm planning anything?" She tried for a tone of blithe innocence and probably failed miserably, hunching her bare shoulders and stared into the blue pottery cup. *For being shot last night, I think I'm doing really well.* Her skin roughened in instinctive response. *I could have died. Nikolai tried to Turn me. He probably knows who had Danny killed and is just playing around. Bastard.*

"Drink that, Selene. That blue bag of yours stinks of darkness and Power. Something's in there Nik either doesn't sense or is waiting for you to tell him about." The healer took another sip of tea and stared into her cup. "Either way, it's trouble. I know your brother was killed, and that you're hungry for revenge, and Nik stopped you." Marina shrugged. "It doesn't take a genius to figure out that you might have something in mind."

Rigel brought the blue canvas bag, and Selene's black leather purse. He also brought Marina's little black physician's bag and a stack of clothing.

"I brought a pair of jeans and a T-shirt. They're mine, so they'll be a little big for you." Marina's eyes met hers. "There's one of Rigel's coats in the closet. I brought boots too, in the bag, I hope they fit. *Don't* tell Nikolai, or both Rigel and I will be in hot water." She set her cup down and stood up, gathering her velvet skirts. "As far as I know, I've tended you as best I can and left you to his thralls once you were out of danger." The healer took a deep breath. "There's a business card in the pocket of the jeans that marks you as a friend of mine. You might find it useful if you run across anyone who knows me, or owes me a favor. There are a few in the city—not as many as I'd like, but a few."

"He'll find out." Rigel stood with his hands stuffed in his pockets. "They always do."

Marina looked up at him and shrugged, combing her hair back with her fingers. "I won't see a woman forced and do nothing about it, Rigel."

He nodded, his punk haircut falling forward into his face again. "He'll know."

She held her hands up, and he took them, pulling her to her feet. He didn't step back, so she was close enough to hug him, but he simply looked down at the top of her head until she tilted her chin up, her face inches from his. Selene stared at them. Her heart twisted, a sharp pain in the center of her chest.

"Whatever he guesses," the *sedayeenen* said very quietly, "I'll not tell him anything. And neither will she." Her chin came up a little more, and Selene saw her blue eyes flash.

"I won't say anything," she told them around the old familiar lump in her throat. Rigel still looked down into Marina's face, ignoring Selene. "I promise. My word's good."

The healer nodded, but she still looked up into Rigel's eyes. "I believe you, Selene. Thank you. And now I'll take us out of your way, and you can do what you like." She pushed at the tall man, who backed up slightly. It was disconcerting to see him staring at her, backing up without looking until she broke eye contact and glanced at Selene. Then he watched Marina's profile. The look on his lean dark face was startling—hungry and intent all at once.

Still a familiar expression, though. Blessedly, completely human.

"Be careful, sister." The *sedayeenen* looked grave and serious now. "There are things hunting now in Nikolai's city that wouldn't think twice about eating either of us."

Selene nodded. "I'm good at going around unnoticed." She began gathering the sheet, willing away the obstruction in her throat. Rigel kept quiet, but his eyebrows rose slightly, and she glared at him. "I *am*."

"You have three hours of daylight left." Marina pushed at Rigel's arm. "Come on, Limey, let's go. You can talk us past Jorge and Tierney, I want to go get a cup of coffee at Lonbard's."

"A pleasure." Rigel moved obediently in front of her, his black coat swinging with his long-legged strides.

At the door—it had been fixed, no longer splintered and jagged—Marina looked over her shoulder. The velvet of her dress glowed on the other side of the shaft of sunlight, just like a painting. Rigel was already out of sight. "Do you know what Nikolai wants?" Marina asked. "Really wants out of you?"

"Other than feeding rights on a rare piece of ass?" Selene downed the rest of the broth and grimaced. It burned all the way down. *Do you?* "I haven't a clue. He said he's twelve centuries old."

"It's more like thirteen, I guess." Marina didn't smile. "But he's never, *ever* shown the kind of interest in anyone that he has for you. Strange, isn't it?"

With that, she slipped out the door and shut it quietly.

Left alone, Selene looked down at the tray. There was a grilled-cheese sandwich—*Danny,* she thought, and her eyes filled with tears. She looked at it for a few minutes, left it where it was, and pushed the sheet away. The air was cool against her naked skin, and she could still smell Marina, violets and musk, in her own hair. Strangely enough, it was comforting.

*Why couldn't I have met someone like her ages ago?*

It took only a few minutes to get dressed, and when she fetched Rigel's black coat from the almost-empty closet she found one pocket was strangely heavy. She reached in tentatively, and her fingers touched cold metal.

They'd left her a gun. Or Rigel had, Marina wouldn't like guns, being *sedayeenen*. How had the healer talked him into that?

Of course, it looked like she could talk him into just about anything. Lucky girl.

She shrugged into the coat. It was ludicrously long on her, the cuffs falling forward over her hands like the silk dress had.

Selene shivered. The medallion was still icy-cold. It hadn't warmed since she'd awakened. She yanked the socks on, and the boots, they were a little too tight. *Her feet must be smaller than mine,* she thought, and tasted the other woman's mouth for a moment. If she'd met Marina before she'd met Nikolai...

*Forget it.* She looked toward the window. *Nikolai's the problem I have. He tried to Turn me, the bastard, and he probably got my brother killed too.* Sunlight streamed through in a thick golden bar. She stepped into the warm light, settling Danny's bag so the strap lay across her body and stuffing her purse inside the blue canvas. *Let's just concentrate on getting out of here. All I've got to do is escape his nest during daylight and figure out what to do next.*

Outside the window, a slope of manicured lawn fell away toward a hedge. *Does Nikolai have dogs? Will they bite me?* She unlatched the window and swung it open, wishing she had time to take a shower or visit the bathroom. But her skin crawled with the sudden need to be *away* from this place. The memory of the slow, awful, creeping fire of the Turn—and the spiky ice of the enzyme treatment, fighting for control of her body, Marina's Power a tenuous bridge to reality—made the blood drain from her cheeks and her knees go weak. She swung her legs out through the window and jumped down. It wasn't like Nikolai to put her in a room she could escape from. *Unless he'd planned on me Turning, which would mean that I couldn't escape during the day. Fucking bastard.*

The first step was getting more money. You couldn't run without cash.

She was full-up on Power, so the cold tide of terror didn't make her wet and needy. But her breath caught and her hands shook as she closed the window from the outside. Her boots were crushing a thick spiny bush, and as soon as she moved, it sprang back up.

It was a nice sunny day, but clouds were scudding in from the west. From the sea. *It'll probably rain tonight.*

*Crap. I'm going to have to climb a wall. And catch a cab.*

# NINE

IT WAS A beautiful day, mostly sunny, seventy-one degrees according to the bank thermometer. She waited for a good half-hour across Cliff Street from her apartment building, safe in the shadow of a doorway. People walked the streets. She watched them carefully but none of them seemed to notice anything out of the ordinary. There was no sign of the press, a police presence, or of any paranormals watching her building.

Thank God for small favors. She closed her eyes, sending her senses through the familiar halls and corridors of her building. Nothing except the glow of her own wards on the fourth floor.

She crossed the street, watching for cars, and ducked into the alley on the left side of the building. The dumpsters hulked here, a strong simmering smell rising from their open maws. Her boots slipped greasily against crud on the cracked pavement. No sunlight, the buildings blocked it. Cold kissed Selene's face, a slight breeze. There was rain on the way, the tang of it rolling in from the bay.

She wasn't tall enough to reach the fire-escape ladder, so she had to spend a little Power to unlock it. Physics took over, it slid down and banged on the concrete. The noise was incredible, but at the end of the day with everybody at work, her chances of being noticed were slim to none. A few schoolkids might see her, but precious few people would ask them.

Her building was mostly refugees or kids of refugees, living in rent-controlled havens. Selene's kind of people didn't talk to the cops much. The word for someone who did wasn't a nice one, and it meant you weren't trustworthy enough for anything.

You could run with a bad crowd, sign up with a gang in self-defense, murder and loot, even rape. That would make you dangerous, but not outside the pale.

Talking to the authorities would put you in a scarlet robe all its own, dressed up like a Gilead heretic ready for the burning or the Tangle.

She climbed the ladder, the chill of rusting metal making her palms ache. Her arms shook a little, and her legs hurt slightly. Marina was right, she would be weak for a while. Power couldn't heal everything, couldn't replace physical reserves.

*If I use too much Power, I wonder if the bullet hole will open back up?* Selene shivered. She knew it was theoretically impossible...but still. *Getting shot in the back kind of makes you wonder about all sorts of things.* Her lips pulled back from her teeth. Fourth floor—and her own window.

She touched the glass, crouching on the metal platform. Her monthly drills—an escape route was always a good idea, but useless if you didn't practice using it—had only included going out through the window, not getting back in.

She ran her fingers along splintery wood. The window came up just enough for her to fit her fingers under, Power tingling and sparking along her hand. She heaved up, and in a trice was shimmying through, the blue canvas bag knocking against her hip.

Her feet crunched as they landed on the floor. Selene straightened, looked around.

*Oh, no. No.*

Someone had been in her apartment, and they'd trashed it. Her collection of cheap post-War porcelain geisha figurines lay scattered and broken on the floor; that was the crunching under her borrowed boots. Her bed was torn apart, her dresser drawers yanked out and emptied, her desk disemboweled. Her computer monitor was smashed, the hard drive tossed over on its side. *Goddammit, all those grades gone.* Her closet was open, everything yanked off the hangers.

Her nostrils flared. A powerful zoolike smell assaulted her queasy stomach. *Werecain. Well, that's how they got through my wards. Good too, not to leave any marks.* Her eyes smarted, filling with hot salt water.

*No. I'm not going to cry*, she told herself, sternly. *No more. I'm done with that.* She wiped at her eyes, the denied tears greasing her fingers. *Goddammit. This was my place, my safe place. Everything's gone.*

*Well*, the voice of practicality replied, *you were only here to pack a suitcase and pick up your cash-stash. You were going to be leaving this all behind anyway. Don't bitch so much.*

Selene's heart leapt against her ribs. She heard a low, grinding growl.

From her living room.

She reached down blindly, digging for Rigel's gun. Her fingers curled around it and she tugged it out of her pocket. It got caught in the material; she yanked, tearing the dark fabric.

There was a crash. *Sounds like it's in the kitchen. Lucky me having hardwood floors, easier to break shit, what is a werecain doing in my house?* She swallowed dryly. *How much noise did I make coming in here? Why isn't it on top of me by now? It hasn't heard me?*

*I can't be that lucky.*

Maybe she was due for a little luck. Jesu knew it had been a fucking disaster for a long time now. She was owed a break.

She edged toward the bedroom door. Broken porcelain ground under her borrowed boots. *It hears me, it has to hear me, its senses are much better than a human's.*

There was a roar, a growl, another crash—*living room.* She raised the gun, slowly, through a dreamlike syrupy haze. *Must have been the coffee table. Goddammit, I carried that up the stairs myself.* Selene heard her own breathing, harsh and light and quick, something blurred through the door, a slice of darkness.

Selene squeezed the trigger. There was an incredible coughing roar and the smell of cordite, a jet of blue smoke. *Rigel likes automatics. Is it the gun of choice for werecain hunting?*

The first shot went wide, splinters scattering through the air from the jamb, the door hit the wall and started to bounce back. She kept squeezing, tracking in front of the target's head, like Jack had taught her. With paranormals it was always safer to shatter the skull if you could.

The second shot took it in the shoulder, and the third in the head. A hairy shape with a long snout and awful claws, a tattered pair of jeans hugging its hips. *Must have Changed in helluva hurry*, Selene's brain howled with a sort of lunatic glee.

It thudded to the floor. Half its head was vaporized. Hollowpoints, most likely; you had to use a special kind of ammo to cause enough damage to kill 'cain or really anything paranormal, they healed so quickly. The smell was awful, Power and blood and animal and the copper-tainted stink of death. Selene heard a faint breathy sound and realized she was trying to scream, couldn't find the air. She gulped it back, her heart hammering. Her entire body was tingling. The curse was awake with a vengeance, making her hand shake slightly and her throat dry out.

*Nikolai.* She shoved the thought away. It would only make the burning between her legs, the swimming weakness, worse.

She skipped nervously over the werecain's body, hoping it was dead. Its fur was dark and matted, blood sprayed against the framed print of Vermeer's *The Letter* hanging next to the door. Danny had bought it over the Intranet and had it delivered last Christmas, a splurge to celebrate a particularly successful job. She peeked out past the shattered door into her apartment.

*Are there more? Please, God, throw me a bone, let this one be the only one.* Her shields thinned. The wards on her apartment resounded, vibrating with her nearness. *Throw me a bone for no more werecains? Ha.*

Nothing else in her apartment. Nothing living. How had she missed a werecain, for Christos's sake? The smell alone should have hit her before she came into the apartment.

*I'm not dealing with this very well.* The thought was faraway and dim. *I think I'm in shock.*

Whoever the werecain was, he'd been in her home for a while. Everything was smashed. It was an orgy of destruction, all right. Even the couch had been chopped up. Everything bigger than a breadbox had been destroyed.

*They were looking for something. It*—he *was looking for something, no wonder it didn't hear me. It was too busy tearing my entire apartment to shreds, making enough noise to cover me breaking into my own house. Dear God. What was it looking for?*

Selene crunched over broken glass. All her dishes were smashed. That wasn't looking for something, it was pure terrorization. If she'd come in her front door...

*Don't think about that.*

Nobody in the kitchen, nobody in the bathroom, though her medicine cabinet was cleaned out, bottles lying on the floor, the mirror spiderwebbed. Even the shower curtain had been torn down.

*First things first.* She closed the door and flicked the light on, set the gun on the counter next to a shattered bottle of Vickle's VaporRub, then unbuttoned her jeans and plopped down on the toilet. *I live my life by the dictates of my bladder.* A strained giggle bounced off the tiled walls. The pretty little pink ceramic dish for her talcum powder was shattered on the floor, powder scattered everywhere, the marks of her borrowed boots and the werecain's tough furry pads scraping aside the delicate white drifts. The smell of powder, Vickle's, baby shampoo, and werecain mixed together uneasily, overlaid with the perfume of Selene's skin. She was emitting.

The medallion was still chilly against her skin.

*I've got to get out of here. Where can I go? I could call Nikolai's nest and...*

"Goddammmit!" she yelled, flinching as the sound bounced off the tiled walls. Here she was calmly sitting and pissing when she'd just killed a werecain in her bedroom, and she was thinking about Nikolai, of all things.

*Is it really dead?* She chided herself as she stood up and flushed, buttoned her jeans. It was ridiculous, half the werecain's head was gone, of course it was dead. Rigel had filled up the gun with good ammo. Had he guessed? Or was it just business as usual for a thrall to load up with paranormal-killing bullets?

*There were werecain at the Nichtvren haunt. So the werecain have it in for Nikolai. Not that I blame them, but why? And what the hell did it have to do with this Grigori?* Her brain skipped between questions, trying to find the right one to frame the situation. *Of course the werecain's dead. Even a Nichtvren would have a hard time surviving a shot like that to the head.*

But what if it's not dead? What if it's waiting for me outside the door?

*Stop.* Nikolai's voice infiltrated her head, quiet and cool and logical. *Do not freeze. You are safe enough, this is your Place of Power. Open the bathroom door and check the werecain's body again. You would have heard him by now if he had awakened.*

She swallowed against the lump in her throat. Why was it that the voice of cold logic inside her head sounded like his? Irritation boiled under her ribs.

Her left fingers curled around the doorknob. She ripped the door open, the gun held level.

Nothing. Her shattered apartment was empty, except for a corpse.

She paced through the wreckage again, a lump in her throat. Her figurines, all gone, her books dumped over the floor, the cedar chest that served as her altar hacked apart and magickal implements scattered.

*Looking for something.* Her left hand reached up to touch the strap of the bag. *What do you want to bet the Seal of Sitirris is what he was looking for? And what do you want to bet Danny put it with his little black book? There had been something with the book, something heavy and hard, but she hadn't had a moment to herself since...*

*You idiot, Selene. You've probably been carrying a Talisman all this time.*

The thought made her entire body go cold again. She shivered, her teeth chattering, and lunatic laughter pressed against her throat. *I've got a dead fucking werecain in my bedroom and a whole host of problems and once dusk hits Nikolai will rise and I'll be in even more trouble. Jesu Christos.*

She lifted her left hand to her mouth, set her teeth against the soft flesh below her thumb, and bit down hard.

Red pain jolted her nervous system, swilled through a sharp flare of desire, and subsided. *First things first,* she heard Danny's voice, from the very center of her skull. The All-Dead Hit Parade was playing inside Selene Thompson's head, come on and get your tickets now.

She let out a shrill, barking sob. Then she lifted the gun again and sidled over broken wood and porcelain and glass. *I need a pair of my own shoes.* The boots pinched her toes unmercifully. *Some clothes, see if they found my stash. Then I'll drain the wards and the altar and leave everything here like I planned to anyway. That's safest.*

Safest. Yeah.

The werecain's body still lay slumped against her bedroom floor, mostly headless. *Just as well I have to leave, I never want to sleep here again.* A lake of blood spread out from the body, vivid red. *It looks fake. Like paint. Christos, I wish it was.*

She found some of her own clothes—a pair of jeans, a sweater, a white dress shirt—and changed hurriedly, stealing glances at the dead werecain every few moments. She found her boots tossed, one under the bed, another on her chair by the closet. The chair was miraculously still upright and not reduced to a pile of matchsticks.

She thought about it, left Rigel's coat there too. Her camel coat was in the front closet, she'd pick it up on the way out. Its pockets were deep enough to hold a gun.

The cash she'd stashed—no refugee child trusted banks—behind the headboard was luckily still there when she slid aside the flimsy panel. She kept glancing at the werecain's body, imagining she saw it twitch every time she made a noise.

Then she left her bedroom, carrying the blue canvas bag, with only one last nervous glance down at the werecain.

It took her only a few moments to transfer everything in her purse into her black canvas bag, which was dumped unceremoniously out across the shattered couch. She repacked it quickly. Her athame, a small glass container of salt, the vial of consecrated water, her tarot cards.

Then she stuffed everything from Danny's blue bag in as well, making sure her wallet was on top. The file folder fit in there too, just barely. *I need a quiet place to sit and go over this.* She closed the bag's flap, tested it gingerly. Not too heavy.

It was just like packing to leave the filtration camp, the last stop before they were "re-entered." As if they could ever be normal after living there. As if anything could be normal after the War. They could only take what they could carry, and rumor had it everything else would be burned.

*How many years of my life am I leaving behind again?* She breathed in the violated smell of her shattered sanctuary. *What did I do to deserve this?*

There was no answer. There never was.

She took one last long look, then she stood up and closed her eyes. Spread her arms a little. *Come to mama.* Dropped below the surface of conscious thought. These were her own wards and defenses and she was standing in the middle of them, so they didn't cost her to pull back and disassemble, Power flooding her, replacing what she'd used. The chalk marks on the floor would be writhing madly, and they would fade as soon as she was done. She scanned them quickly—*he had a key, and he jacked in through my wards there. I didn't even know there was a loophole. Going to have to fix that next time...if there is a next time. Hours. He was here for hours, tearing everything apart and probably waiting for me. Stupid and sloppy, just like a dog.*

She came back to herself, coughing, her eyes watering. The tang of werecain was overwhelming. Now, naked, without the defenses on the apartment, the echoes of what she'd done and the magick she'd worked sent up flares all over the spectrum. It would be a miracle if nobody noticed.

With that happy and comfortable thought keeping her company, she stamped through her apartment, grinding porcelain shards underfoot. She kept her right hand curled around the gun in her pocket, unlocking and opening her front door with her left. The hallway was deserted.

Selene took one last look over her shoulder at her ruined life, stepped out into the hall, and slammed the door shut.

# TEN

THE BUS STATION crouched under a blue sky, the sun tending westward and the shadows getting long. Lumbering silver hybrid buses, gliding on pockets of frictionless space, nosed steadily past. Selene stopped at the pay phone, picked it up, and fed two credit-coins into the slot. Her finger trembled as she dialed, and she leaned against the side of the pay phone's box. The shakes were beginning to hit in waves now.

She stared blankly at the phone's numbers as she took a deep breath, trying to steady herself. How had she gotten here? She couldn't quite remember. Walking aimlessly, one foot in front of the other, working her way toward the bus depot.

But before she left town, one small thing. Was there still someone she could trust? Her hands were shaking too badly, and her throat was on fire. She probably looked like a junkie.

*Something is very wrong with me.*

Four rings. Five. *Not the voicemail. Don't let it go to voicemail.*

"South Side Precinct, Pepper speaking," he barked into the phone. Selene squeezed her eyes shut, tears leaking between her lids. *Thank you, God.*

"Jack?" she whispered into the phone. Her fingers and toes were so cold. "Jack, it's Selene."

"Can't you stay out of trouble for one fucking day?" he hissed, his voice dropping. Did he have someone else in his office? "Where are you? Nikolai's thralls are jumping all over us. He's going to be pissed, and guess who he's going to come down on?"

She winced. So they'd found out she was gone. Of course—Jorge would have come and checked on her, brought her more food or something. Or even just to make sure she was behaving, Nikolai would have given orders. "Don't tell them. I need a safehouse, Jack. Someone tossed my apartment. There's a dead werecain in my bedroom, I shot him in the head."

"Jesu fucking Christos!" Jack whisper-yelled. "Ain't you got no fucking sense? Goddammit, Selene!" Papers in the background, the sound of someone moving, a clicking sound. "Where are you?"

"Safehouse, Jack. I need a safehouse. Something's wrong with me." Her teeth were chattering too hard and her skin burned. "I think...oh, goddammit, please, Jack, for the love of God, help me."

There was another click, then nothing. Silence. Total silence. The dial tone sounded in her ear. The sound of her money clicking into the innards of the phone was lost under the roar of traffic. Sirens screamed in the distance.

*Can't really blame him. He's got a wife and kids to support, he can't afford to do anything that might piss Nikolai off. Thanks a lot, Jack. Wonderful.*

She looked up Farris Avenue to Eighth. Then down to Tenth, opposite. There were flophouses around her, but she might end up robbed or beaten if she went to any of those. And the shakes were beginning to intensify. She'd attract attention if this kept up. Getting on a bus and having a seizure didn't sound like a good time. What was wrong with her? She was thinking through mud.

*Jack...Danny...* The sum total of her support network, gone.
*Wait a minute. Danny.*

It was idiotic. There was blood all over Danny's apartment, and it was just as naked as her own now that she'd torn the wards down. She couldn't go there.

*But nobody would expect it, would they.*

No, she couldn't go there. Couldn't look at the blood, drying into the carpeting. Her own footprints in her brother's blood.

Where else could she go? She had no real friends, simply showed up to teach her classes, graded her papers, went home carrying her work with her. Even the fellow teachers wouldn't talk to her, because she taught the class nobody wanted to take:

the mandatory Paranormal Studies you needed to keep federal funding since the paranormals with their big lobbyists—funded by Nichtvren treasure, the rumor was—got the vote. Even if they didn't think she was paranormal she was still contaminated, and imposed on them.

*Where can I go?*

There was nowhere to go except out of town. She just had to keep it together long enough to buy a ticket to somewhere, anywhere.

*I'll sleep under a bridge if I have to.* She leaned against the pay phone. The chaos of a city street resounded around her, the transit hopelessness of the bus station. *What is wrong with me? Shock, or...* The thought wouldn't finish itself, and the shakes started to jitter under her skin as if her bones were dancing.

She glanced up at the sky, shivering, and the searing sunlight struck through her eyes, all the way to the center of her brain. It *hurt*, gouging at her eyes, and her skin prickled.

*Oh, no.*

The enzyme treatment hadn't worked after all. It had only staved off the inevitable.

She blinked, her eyes watering furiously. Then she trotted down the cracked pavement, leaving the phone receiver dangling from its cord. It swayed gently in the breeze.

Blind animal instinct plunged her into the bus station. *Should I buy a ticket or find a closet?* She hitched in a breath, swallowing it as she broke free of the sunlight coming in through the glass doors and into the fluorescent lighting. The relief was instant, but it made the burning and crawling over her skin even more intense.

*Closet. If I have to wait for a bus I'll start to convulse. Christos.*

The bus station was familiar from other hunting trips— she'd fed down here, in the alley behind, hooking and desperate to get enough cash to feed Danny, who could barely stay in his body while he was away from her. And not so incidentally, feed herself, both her stomach and that other, deeper hunger between her legs. It was a wonder she hadn't been knifed or robbed during that nightmare time. Then she'd landed the teaching job, and Danny had sold a few bits of gossip, and they had moved into the rooming house on Sarvedo Street...and a few weeks after that, she'd met Nikolai in that alley, and her life had changed overnight again.

*Just look how much good that did me.*

She walked purposefully down the bright-lit hallway toward the bathroom, inserting herself into the midday crowd. There were a few homeless people, and the travelers of course, mostly younger women with children. There were also a fair number of men in uniform—Army, mostly; the Navy boys were further south and the paramilitary organizations were quietly being absorbed wherever the infrastructure needed rebuilding. *Good prey*, her curse whispered faintly, and her skin prickled again. A rush of Power slammed across her nerves, and she spotted a door that most probably gave onto a utility corridor. *Got to find a dark place*, she thought incoherently, and her fingers tingled.

*Hide me*, she prayed. *Oh, God, hide me.*

The Power answered, cloaking her in a faint blur. It would be draining to keep it up for any length of time, but she only needed to make it into the corridor. The janitorial staff wouldn't be out in force until well past dark.

Cold, creeping fire started in her palms. Her toes were numb, she was dragging her right foot behind her like a cripple. *Oh, Christos.*

She made it to the metal door and blindly put her hand on the knob. Nobody was looking; the blur should hide her unless they were paranormal, and she seriously doubted she could hold off a werecain—or anything else—while she was jittering and jiving from the Turn.

*I'm going to be a Nichtvren.* A weird image of birthday candles and a pink-frosted cake sprang to her mind. *Gonna be a Nichtvren, gonna be a Nichtvren, heigh-ho the dairy-o, gonna be a Nichtvren.* The knob gave under her fingers, the Power she was pouring into it trembled at the outside of her control. If she didn't Turn she was going to be so drained as to be useless.

*And won't that be fun. Christos. Someone, anyone, help me.*

There was nobody. As usual, she had to help herself.

Selene ducked through the door, taking care to close it quietly behind her. A sharp noise would dispel the blur and cause questions.

She was in a long, concrete-floored tunnel that went down into the bowels of the bus station. The prickling cold spilled up her arms and legs. She'd have to crawl soon.

*Why didn't the enzyme work? It only delayed the Turn, goddammit. Seventy percent is bad odds after all? Oh, God. Jesu, help me, I'm going to be a bloodsucking fiend, I'm going to be like Nikolai, I'm going to be awful, a damned soul, damned, damned...*

Amazing how childhood religious training came back to haunt her. They were big on Jesu in the camps. Big on suffering in silence instead of taking up the Gilead sword of righteousness.

Sometimes Selene wondered if the Republic had the right idea, fighting so hard. She wasn't the only one—but she was probably the only paranormal who ever wondered. The others probably counted their blessings to be out from under the Gilead thumb. It was a sentence of death to be paranormal during Gilead's time; nowadays you were only shunned and shunted into menial jobs or taken for government experiments. What a choice.

*There.* A broom closet or something like it. She fumbled with the door, the lock throwing itself open in response to a blue-white spark of Power, and she saw metal shelves with assorted things on them. Light fixtures, light bulbs, there were fluorescent tubes stacked in racks bolted to the wall in back. Selene stepped in and drew the door closed, locked it, plunging the room into complete darkness except for one small strip of light coming in under the door. She had to try several times before she could focus enough, forced her attention to one still small point.

One of the Greater Words was in her repertoire, the Word of Closing, syllables that would bar an entrance. She sketched the symbol that went with it on the door with a numb finger, feeling the Power bleed down her arm and into it, her lips stuttering over the Word. It had to be pronounced right or it would fail, and she'd be out the Power as well as with a ruined Word and backlash on her hands.

Light slid out from her fingertip, a violet glow reminding her of Marina, and Selene let out a choked laugh. Draining herself this rapidly meant the Turn would speed up. It was already up to her biceps, and her legs below the knee were cold and unresponsive.

The glyph wavered, guttered...

And held.

Sighing in relief, Selene collapsed against the door. Cold fire swept up her legs, racked her pelvis, and the crackling of bones re-forming echoed in the closet. Selene drove her teeth into her tongue. *Don't scream. It will break the binding. Don't scream. Don't scream. Jesu, just don't scream, don't scream, don't scream.*

The chill fire spread up her neck, and Selene's jaw locked.

Now she couldn't scream even if she wanted to.

Her scalp crawled. Bones continued their cracking, her muscles sliding and writhing under her skin, the cold prickling working its way into her very core.

She tasted blood, and some other chemical tang. Then, dimly, she felt the medallion warm against her chest. The heat didn't stop the prickling, fiery, nerve-wrenching cold of the Turn, but it was...comforting.

*I'm going to make you pay for this, Nikolai. I'm never going to be able to get a regular job now.* It was her last coherent thought before the cold raced through her belly and down her chest, toward her frantic-beating heart.

# PART II

# ELEVEN

*KA-THUD. KA-THUD. KA-THUD. KA-THUD.*

Teeth. Sliding free. Nerve impulses, slow and sluggish at first. Prickling in her flesh. Light...against closed eyelids.

*What...is...*

Groggy, Selene tried to open her eyes. It took another two tries before she could actually do it.

The closet seemed glare-lit by floodlights. Every detail stood out in sharp relief: the sheen of the fluorescent tubes stacked in racks against the back wall, boxes of light bulbs and fixtures, the writing on their sides crisp and clear; the concrete below her veined with little sparkles, walls lit from within by a soft sick green glow.

*I didn't switch the light on.*

The thought brought her up to a crouch, immediately. She shook her head to clear it, her hair sliding and swinging in her face.

*ka-THUD. ka-THUD. ka-THUD. ka-THUD. ka-THUD.*

It took her a moment to realize her knees were sticking out grotesquely to either side, her elbows bent and palms flat against the concrete floor. Either her hip joints had decided to go floppy on her in a way that would make a hop dancer die from envy, or...

*Oh, Christos.* The regular, mechanical thudding sound intensified. And along with that sound came something else.

Thirst. Terrible, burning, racking thirst that made her throat a desert, her head an aching bomb cradled on her neck. Her nostrils flared. She could smell it, copper liquid thudding through living veins, hot and salty.

*I'm thirsty.* She held up one hand. Her fingers wriggled, long and slender in the greenish light. Then the claws burst free, and she almost fell over backwards, choking back a cry. Her coat brushed a box of light bulbs sitting on a low shelf, and the box fell.

Selene's hand arrived before it could hit the ground, scooped up the box, and set it neatly back on its shelf without any conscious direction from her brain.

*Reflex. I've got Nichtvren reflexes.*

She stared at her hands in disbelief. The thudding sound was getting louder. She could also smell the source of it—*male, older, dark hair*, she thought, without knowing quite how she knew. Getting closer. Probably a janitor.

Selene's first meal.

She stuffed her hand in her mouth, forgetting her teeth would be sharper than a human's, and tried to muffle the choked mewling sound of need springing from her throat. Her body demanded blood. Older Nichtvren could live on sex or violence, but the fledglings needed blood. Hot, pulsing, coppery, straight from the vein. Her teeth scraped her skin, but didn't break through.

Yet.

She stared at the closet door. The knob jiggled.

*Go away! For the love of God, go! Run away!*

The glyph on the door flared, holding it closed. A small metallic snap sounded.

"Fuck," someone said, clearly audible through the door. "Key broke. Goddamn it."

Selene's eyes rolled. *It's prey. It's blood.*

So close.

Her breathing slowed, stopped. She couldn't stop breathing fully until she fed for the first time and the Turn was completed, so red pinwheels revolved behind her closed eyelids. Oxygen deprivation. Her body would start to cannibalize itself unless she fed, and after twenty-four hours she'd be a rotting brain-damaged hulk without even the sense to stay out of sunlight.

*Oh, God...*

The medallion, hanging between her breasts, sent out a silent pulse like the warm push of air in front of an explosion. It scorched at her skin and settled comfortably, pounding out the rhythm of her own frantic heart.

A new smell filled the closet, sweet and cloying, fermented. Her body, dying, the human cells committing mass suicide, the Nichtvren cells splitting, filling up, altering, taking their place. She could feel it, consciousness invading every atom of her body, as if her mind was stretching. Mental silicon-putty gooping and glorping all the way through her liver, her kidneys shrinking and self-destructing now, because Nichtvren didn't need them.

*No wonder they have such great reflexes, they think with their whole bodies.* She stifled a moan. The thirst set her throat on fire, like greasy petroleo smoke.

The knob jiggled again. *Go away!* She couldn't concentrate enough to raise any Power to push the man away from the door, or—

She blinked.

That was all it took, one blink. Her body slipped the leash of her will, bolting, and the door crumpled like tinfoil, the hinges and lock tearing free with one crunching noise. She burst out into the hall, knocking the portly man with his bucket and mop onto his ass. Then she was on him, her bag bumping her hip, something crunching as she grabbed his hand, instinctively jerking the man back into the dark hole she'd just vacated. The fluorescents overhead tore at her eyes until her pupils contracted.

SELENE CAME TO with her teeth driven into the man's throat, hot blood filling her mouth. Her jaw distended, cartilage popping so she could get a better hold on him. Her slim hands held him down, overriding his struggles, batting away his ineffectual punches.

It poured down her throat, hot life, it tasted like fresh bread and chocolate and red wine, everything good and wholesome she'd ever had. A tide of strength exploded from her throat, filled her stomach, tingled in every finger and toe as the Nichtvren cells finished the task of converting her body into something else.

Something inhuman.

It didn't stop until the dried husk dropped from her hands. Selene backed up, crouching, along the wall. Boxes of light bulbs fell onto the thing. It lay slumped on the concrete, a round blob in a blue jumpsuit, the name Carl stitched with white thread on its left front pocket. A lifeless husk.

*No, not husk. Body. It's a body. I've committed a murder.*

He had a metal brace on one leg. It looked like a War wound; the Army prosthetics all had that weird shine to them. She stared at him for a long moment, her lower lip trembling. She wiped at her mouth, a futile movement, as if she could clean away the stain. *Oh, God...*

There was no God to hear. There never was. Nikolai had Turned her after all. Made her a Nichtvren.

*I just killed a man.* She looked down at her fingers, stained with a few drops of crimson. The urge to lick them rose up inside her, and she had her finger halfway to her mouth before she realized what she was doing.

She let out another strangled little cry and wiped her hand on her sweater under her coat, uselessly. Her fingers tingled. When she lifted them again, they were white and smooth, her nails looking like a human's. Camouflage. The blood had vanished, drawn into the surface of her skin.

"I'm sorry," she whispered.

The body on the floor didn't reply.

CASSIDY'S WAS OPEN late, and Selene got a back booth.

The restaurant was on Klondel and Eighth, in a part of town the university students frequented since it was close to the U District and had cheap beer. She ran the risk of being recognized, but the warmth of a cup of coffee and some good dim lighting, not to mention some humans—

*Prey.*

—humans drew her. It seemed like a safe enough place to sit and collect herself.

*Where else does a murderer go after her crime, anyway? To the nearest cafe, where she coldly orders a cuppa joe. Good thing we're not still on ration cards. I wonder if they'd have one for blood banks?*

The hostess showed her to a red-vinyl booth and gave her a glass of water Selene suspected she'd be unable to drink. Selene ordered coffee and, as soon as she'd gotten rid of the waitress, dug in the bag she'd been hauling around all this time, and pulled out the battered manila folder.

*I killed a man. I'm a murderer now. Takes one to catch one, maybe? You think?*

There weren't many students in here on a weeknight, especially this early. The lighting was low, but still glaringly harsh to Selene's new senses. It even hurt her *skin*. No wonder Nichtvren preferred silk, dim light and rich colors. Their vision was so acute it was painful for them to sit under fluorescent lighting or look at bright color.

Pictures of old silent-screen stars on the walls stared down at a few scattered customers. Red vinyl booths and glass-topped tables reflected the light bulbs. The entire front of the restaurant was glass, looking out on the top of Klondel Avenue—the nice part, the part where you wouldn't get mugged or raped past dark. South of Twentieth Street, the Ave became a cesspool, choked with poverty and cheap liquor. Not to mention other, darker things.

She opened the folder. The rasp of paper against her newly-sensitive fingertips was like sandpaper.

*I killed a man, and I'm sitting here like it doesn't matter. My God.*

Responding officer's report, a copy of the report Jack had typed up from her, a transcript of the emergency-dispatch call she'd made...autopsy report.

*Well, there wasn't that much left to autopsy.* Selene flipped the report over with one convulsive movement. Her eyes prickled, but she set her jaw. *Don't do it, Selene. Don't dissolve now.*

*I won't even get to go to a memorial service, they hold them during the day, don't they? And I'm a fugitive. A criminal, even though nobody knows it yet.*

She glanced over the rest of file, her skin going cold in instinctive reaction.

*Demoskenos Kirai Nikolai, Turned by Kelaios Grigorivitch Grigori.* A picture of Nikolai exiting a limo, his collar up against wind. A few paragraphs, detailing everything Jack had been able to dig up.

No wonder he couldn't tell her. Nikolai had been Turned by this mysterious Grigori. A little bit about Nikolai's financial holdings, and the extent of his territory. He wasn't as powerful as she thought.

No, he was far more than he let on. Selene shivered, glancing through the information. She'd been lucky to escape him. He was a very busy boy, and a very rich one.

Selene turned the page.

It said Nikolai had killed his maker. As far as Selene understood, that was a mortal sin among Nichtvren. *Patricide among immortals, how very mythic.* Black humor bubbling up in her throat.

Except for one little thing. Grigori didn't appear to be dead.

Selene flipped another page. This was a photograph, poorly done in black and white, pixilated as if an old-fashioned printer had run it off. Underneath it were a few more lines—the date taken, a month ago. The location, down on the docks on the west side of town, a tanker from the Venezuela Republic, docked at the same time. The name?

Grigori Kelayos.

*They're not very creative, are they.* Next was the memo from the top, detailing that the Thompson case had to be lost. *The sister might be a problem*, she read, her skin roughening into large goosebumps. *She will be dealt with by the Prime Power. She is to be left strictly alone.*

Well, wasn't that nice of them. Would they leave her alone now that she was a sucktooth, and a murderer to boot?

"Anything you need?" the waitress said. She had high cheekbones and a straight fall of crow's-wing hair that brushed her back. Like Nikolai's hair, with a blue sheen to it.

And her pulse echoed in Selene's head, a lighter flutter than the janitor's heavy drumbeat. Healthier, younger, richer. *ka-THUD. ka-THUD. ka-THUD.*

"No, thank you," Selene said, politely enough, and tried to smile. But her fangs were aching to slip out, and she didn't know how to stop them. She settled for a sort of smiling grimace.

The waitress stared at her for a long moment, as if wanting to say something, but shrugged instead. "Okay. I'll be back with more coffee in a minute."

"Thanks." Selene's eyes dropped to the file again. The waitress, mercifully, went away.

She flipped back to the picture.

Grigori had a nice face, at least. Broad cheekbones, strong chin, straight eyebrows. He looked vaguely Asian, his eyes slightly elongated. Beardless, his hair braided into long strings. Braided or beaded, she couldn't tell, the picture quality was poor.

The face seemed familiar. Her skin roughened, instinctive reaction, and she flattened her palm over the picture. Intuition ran a river of ice cubes right under her new, pale, perfect skin.

*Give my regards to Nikolai.*

Selene shuddered. Was this her brother's killer? He looked familiar. Had she seen him before? But that was ridiculous. Or was it? She knew better than to discount her instincts, but they had to be severely fucked-up by shock now.

*No wonder Jack didn't want this getting out.* She picked up her cooling coffee cup, raising it to her lips as if she was taking a sip. *Sensitive information on the Prime of Saint City, it's pure blackmail material in the right hands.* Her back crawled with shivering gooseflesh. "Grigori," she whispered into the cup.

*He's probably got a huge grudge against Nikolai. So do I, come to think of it.*

That still didn't solve the question of who killed Danny, though. Unless this Grigori did it, because Danny was working for Nikolai and popped above the radar.

It was the only possible explanation. Which meant she had a picture of her brother's killer, even if he hadn't personally ripped Danny's body to shreds.

The other Nichtvren—Sevigny—had said something about Grigori. Just before all hell had broken loose at the House of Pain. And then all the werecain had turned on the Nichtvren. And the dead werecain in her bedroom...

*I'm woefully behind on my werecain research. Not to mention a few little things about Nichtvren I wish I'd known before now. Nothing like field experience to make a good teacher into a great one.*

Yeah. Good luck getting hired now.

She glanced out over the restaurant. Nothing out of the ordinary. Still, she was uneasy, the back of her neck prickling. That always meant bad news.

Selene dug in her wallet, pulled out a fiver credit to pay for the coffee, and swept the file together, jamming it back into her bag. What was it about werecain and Nichtvren? They weren't quite enemies, and some Nichtvren could control werecain, couldn't they? Or so it seemed. None of Nikolai's thralls were werecain—not that she'd seen, anyway. But there was something else, too, something she was forgetting.

She couldn't dredge it up. Her memory wasn't what it used to be, what with all the murder and screaming and changing into the walking dead. No, not dead. Undead. And bloodsucking.

*I'm really dealing with this quite well,* she thought, and laid five carefully on the table. Her wrists ached savagely—the spurs and bone formations there were the last thing to Turn and solidify on a Nichtvren. The fine mechanisms of the claws were there, and nobody knew why they were the last thing to finish changing.

*Can the lecture, sister, and get the hell out of here.* Danny's voice, urgently whispering in the center of her head. The medallion warmed against her chest. *Something's wrong. Something's tracking you.*

She eased out of the booth, sliding the strap of the bag over her head. Her nostrils flared. It was only a breath of scent, but she recognized it instantly, and the recognition froze her in place for a few precious seconds. Her pupils shrank, and the entire restaurant seemed to darken, a cloud passing over the booths and the few customers, who continued on with their meals, oblivious. One of them—a man in the window, his dark brown hair sleek as a seal's head—lifted a cigarette to his lips. The smell of the cigarette mixed with that other reek, the one Selene recognized.

Death and pain and blood, something male, ancient...and hungry.

Danny's killer. Whatever it was.

Selene straightened. She stuffed her hand in her pocket and closed her fingers around cold metal. *The gun. Is it out on the street? And why is it tracking me?*

Another realization hit her at the same moment.

The curse. She hadn't felt the swimming weakness or the slow burning since she'd murdered that poor man at the bus station.

*Am I not a* tantraiiken *anymore?*

She was still standing there, her fingers around the butt of the gun, looking down at the fiver on the table and the full cup of cold coffee, when every window along the front of the restaurant crashed inward on a shockwave that threw Selene back against the wall.

HER BODY MOVED on instinct, the fierce joy of action slamming into her stomach. If she'd been human the thing would have killed her.

*Well, it still might*, Danny's voice said peevishly in her head.

Her fingers dug into the plastered ceiling. She hung on it like one of those cartoon images of cats. *If I had a tail it would be puffed up by now.* Her bag hung down, the strap digging into her neck. It was a good thing the ceiling was pre-War plaster rather than shoddy acoustic tile, the tiles would never have held her.

The thing was fluid and low, a shape of hairy darkness. It didn't smell precisely like a werecain—that other smell, the reek of Danny's killer, cloaked its furry stench. *A hired hand.* The helpless urge to giggle almost swallowed her whole. *Or hired paw, har de har har.*

The ceiling was too high. The werecain thudded back down onto the floor, too heavy to leap straight up at her.

*Here I am clinging to the ceiling in a restaurant after I've murdered a bus-station janitor, and I don't even know what this thing wants, except to kill me. Why? What did I do to deserve this?*

It leapt again, blindly, claws outstretched, twisting to thud down on the floor once more. The entire building shuddered when it did that. *It's dense, denser than even a Nichtvren.* The lunatic desire to laugh rose up again, she shoved it down. This wasn't funny, but her brain just wouldn't quit. *And boy golly, they're pretty dense.*

She didn't have the faintest idea of what to do now. Her feet hung down, she could fold in half and get them up out of the way, but how long could she hang by just her fingers? The medallion burned against her chest, growing steadily hotter and hotter.

The werecain leapt again and she flinched. The bag swung, and the creature's claws whooshed through empty air, a low deadly sound.

*Is it after my bag? It doesn't like my accessories? If it eats my feet can I grow them back?*

Her fingers slipped and the werecain growled. The sound made the tables rattle. Selene dimly heard screaming. Of course, some of the waitstaff would be left alive. Had it killed the customers? She craned her neck to look, could see nothing but shattered glass and tables, smashed wooden chairs. *God, what am I going to do? There's no way I can fight that thing, and sooner or later—*

The little bell over the door jingled. Selene twisted, trying to look. Couldn't, she had to twist her legs up out of the way as the werecain leapt again and thudded back into the floor. Another wounded howl. Her fingers slipped again, and she jackknifed, trying to get her legs up around a light fixture, something, anything.

Her fingers slipped free of the ceiling. White dust pattered down. She twisted in midair. *If I land on top of that thing I'm as good as dead.*

She hit the ground, her feet thudding into a litter of broken glass and a tide of spilled coffee. It was amazing, her body moving without thought to let her land lightly as a cat. The black-furred werecain-thing scrabbled, doubling on itself. Claws and teeth, and a stink of something both physical and magickal.

Realization struck her. *It's being used. That's why it doesn't smell like a regular—*

"*Move!*" He slammed into her from the side, knocking her down, the breath leaving her in a *whoof!* that would have been funny if she hadn't been flying through the air and skidding across a glass-topped table to hit the wall.

The beast snarled and leapt at her, but Nikolai moved first, something blurring silver in his hands. There was a solid meaty sound, and the werecain thudded to the floor, this time limply. It made a horrible little mewling sound and Selene gasped, sliding off the table, scrambling to her feet. Nikolai knelt in a swordsman's crouch, the bright length of metal making a humming sound. Then he rose like a dark wave.

Nikolai grabbed her arm with his left hand. In his other hand he had...*well, why should that surprise me?* A sword. She wasn't up on her metals, but it looked slightly curved, a slashing blade far too large for a human. A type of longsword, maybe. His eyes burned black and her knees went weak.

He held her by one arm, his hand clamped painfully around her bicep, and examined her from head to foot, his eyes flaring with deadly catshine. Then he nodded, shortly, and turned on his heel. Selene caught her breath again. *The human habit of breathing*, she thought, and tried to pull her arm out of his grasp. Even her newfound strength couldn't help her. He simply shook her as if she was a kitten in a mama cat's mouth, her teeth clicking together painfully, and dragged her away from the creature. A spreading pool of black tarry stuff was sliding out from the furred hulk. The smell was awesome, biblical, a roiling stench that would have made Selene gag and puke if she'd still been capable of it. Power boiled in the air.

Nikolai's hand around her arm sent a prickling wave of heat through her. The medallion was burning, white-hot, the mark on her throat suddenly flaring to life. *I thought this was over with.* The familiar weakness spilled through her. Nikolai's face was set and white, his eyes an incandescent black, if such a thing were possible. He carried the sword as if it was natural and normal to walk around dragging a woman with one hand and carrying a bright unsheathed blade with the other.

Nikolai kicked the restaurant's door open and dragged her out into the street. Sirens whooped in the distance. He smelled like gunpowder and musk, the scent hitting the back of her throat like strong liquor. The familiar dampness between her legs began to throb.

He chose right, south on Klondel, and set off down the sidewalk. Selene pulled fruitlessly against his grasp. He barely even slowed down, even when she tried to go limp and resist him that way. Though when she did that, he did put the sword away, and stopped for long enough to shake her again, her head wobbling back and forth, and he slapped her, once, a light sting across her face.

*He could have broken my neck.* Another wave of terror-soaked desire washed over her. "What are you going to do?" she gasped.

He said nothing, but showed his teeth, fangs sliding out from behind his upper lip, his aquiline nose wrinkled. It was a silent snarl. The medallion was still white-hot. She was afraid it would start to cook her skin soon.

"Nikolai?" It was her pleading voice, the one that she only seemed to have for him, the breathless begging. *What if I'm still a* tantraiiken? *Oh God, Nichtvren live forever and if I have to do this forever I'll...I'll... He killed it. Did he kill it?* "Did you kill it?"

Nikolai shrugged, dragging her along. "It was werecain once," he said, shortly, and his steps quickened. "I don't know if it's dead."

"What the hell? It was *controlled*! By whoever killed Danny!" She sounded shrill and terrified even to herself.

"It appears so." His jaw set. He didn't even break stride. He had Selene's right arm, so she couldn't dig in her pocket for the gun without him noticing. "I doubt that even cursed steel can kill it completely, but the Power I used perhaps worked. Come along, Selene." He jerked on her arm, hurrying her down the street. People stared, but the sirens behind them seemed to fade. Or maybe she just couldn't hear them through the rushing in her ears.

"You Turned me!" Still trying to twist her arm free from his iron grip, and still accomplishing nothing. "You bastard, you *Turned* me!"

"I did." He stopped and pivoted. "I should have done so long ago." He dragged her into a convenient alley, stepping over piles of refuse and puddles of oily liquid. The smell rose around Selene and she choked, but the medallion cooled against her skin and the stench became more bearable. "You were shot twice in the back, Selene. You would have died had I not shared my blood with you."

"I suppose it never occurred to you to let me die rather than Turning me into a sucktooth," she blurted, horrified at herself but unable to stop. *You made me into a murderer, I killed that man, my God, you* made *me do it!*

But she could have stayed out in the sun, couldn't she. Her own weakness disgusted her. Again. She wanted to survive, was that so bad?

He took her shoulders, his fingers biting into her coat, and shoved her against the wall. "No. It never occurred to me to let you die, Selene. You should thank your gods it didn't."

"Fuck you," she spat at him. "I hate you!"

"Master." He shook her, lightly. Her head bounced off the brick behind her, a brief flare of pain. "That's the proper way to address your Maker. *I hate you, Master.* Say it." His face, lit with the same light that blurred over everything now that Selene's eyes were a night-hunter's eyes, was drawn tight, his eyes burning holes, his fangs extended and pressing into his bottom lip. It should have looked ridiculous, corny, the image seen through the lens of every bad B-movie and pulp paperback cover that had survived the fire of Gilead and the greater fire of the War.

Instead, she slumped against the brick, her fingers plucking at the pockets of her coat. She shook, great trembling waves of shudders passing through her from head to foot, her entire body becoming liquid again. *I thought I was done with this.* "Go fuck yourself," she whispered, and closed her eyes. Maybe if she shut out his face she could stop shaking like a windblown leaf.

The sirens whooped closer.

The blow came out of nowhere, not a light slap this time but a hard smack against her cheek, it rocked her head back, bouncing off the brick, and she literally saw stars, bright little silvery points of light. "That was a warning," Nikolai said quietly, propping her up against the wall again. She'd almost toppled over. Her breathing came in short little gasps. Heat pooled in her belly, raced through her veins. "You can take much more damage now, Selene. Do not force me to prove it to you. I have Turned you, you are angry. Very well. Better you survive to hate me than I mourn your passing. Why do you not understand this?" He sounded fractionally calmer. At least he didn't hit her again. "You are not *tantraiiken* anymore." His right hand left her shoulder, brushed back straggling strands of her blonde hair. His fingertips felt good, cool against feverish skin.

"I still..." She trailed off, licked her lips.

"Yes. But only for me now, since I Turned you. My blood in your veins, your curse in mine." He stroked her cheek, touched her lips. "That is what happens when a Nichtvren Turns a *tantraiiken*. That is why you are such valuable pets, when you're human. A bargaining chip, a counter, or a companion to while away eternity with." His fingertip traced the sensitive outline of her lower lip.

Selene's breath jagged in, out. *I don't have to breathe.* Her right hand fumbled for her pocket. *So why do I feel breathless?*

Nikolai paused, retraced the line of her lip. "I am lonely, Selene, and I recognize much of myself in you."

Familiar heat flooded her. He was fucking with her head, again. She would be free of the curse if it wasn't for him. After so little time without the need pulsing in her body she couldn't stand the thought of going back to it.

*You bastard.* Selene's hand found the cold weight of the gun. She slid it out of her pocket, moaning a little, her head tipping back. Nikolai's touch almost drove all rational considerations out of her head.

She pressed the barrel to his chest and pulled the trigger in one motion. There was a coughing roar, and Nikolai stumbled back.

*How many shots do I have left? Enough to kill him? Probably not.* She squeezed the trigger again, and again. How many were in the clip Rigel had left her? How many could she afford to spend on Nikolai? And the werecain, was it even now hauling itself up off the floor of the restaurant and sniffing for her?

Blood. She smelled it, the paranormal tang to it, and it smelled like food, as familiar as her own smell. Nikolai's blood.

*You made me a murderer and got my brother killed, you wouldn't leave me alone, you USED me!* Why were tears standing out in her eyes, and why was she making the hurt little sound as if she'd been the one shot?

Selene fired twice more. He staggered back, dropped to his knees, his arms spread. His head flung back, she saw the line of his chin and a flash of pale throat. His body jerked as she squeezed the trigger one more time.

*You bastard. Now I'm free, if I've killed you. I hope I did.*

She bolted, scrambling for the end of the alley, her boots slipping in crud and muck but her new body leaping and running with preternatural grace and speed. The curse pounded in her belly, every nerve in her body screamed that she go back to Nikolai, let him do what he wanted, stand still while he caressed her, slid his fingers under her shirt and...

Selene burst out of the alley and fled south, leaping along Klondel Avenue with all the speed she could possibly force out of her new body. Wind sang in her ears, and a crazy exhilaration burst inside her chest. She'd shot him and escaped.

She'd finally escaped him. Whatever else happened now, she was free. For the first time in her miserable, awful, poor, hungry, dirt-trodden, whoring life.

Free.

Laughing like a madwoman, her hair streaming behind her, Selene streaked down the street faster than a human could, the sound of pounding feet and screeching laughter making the humans crowded in doorways or strolling on the cracked pavement flinch and scatter.

*I'm free at last.* The tears spilling down her cheeks didn't matter.

Nothing mattered. Not now.

Liberated, sob-laughing, Selene fled into the night.

# TWELVE

THE ABANDONED CHURCH on Trivisidero Street sat under gathering clouds, its windows blind and boarded. It was surrounded by a long stretch of pitted wreckage, the remains of carpet-bombing still echoing in the ground twenty years after peace was declared. There weren't enough people to fill this part of the city yet, but it was only a matter of time. Another baby boom was right on course, though casualties had been mostly civilian in this part of the world and the sexes were now roughly equal because of that simple fact. In other places there weren't any men left. And in some—like in parts of what used to be Russye—there weren't any women, mostly because of the huge community burnings after the Awakening.

*Thank God I wasn't born over there. I wouldn't have made it past puberty.* Selene hefted herself over the ruin of the fence, some of it even old wrought-iron that hadn't been salvaged, and landed balanced on two feet. Only an hour left till dawn.

She'd read that Nichtvren had an internal clock that told them of the sun's approach. It was another thing entirely to have that clock beating inside her pulse, an irrational compulsion to get under cover hunching her shoulders and quickening her steps.

She found loose boards nailed over an opening, spent a little time carefully pulling two aside enough so she could slip through. When she was inside, standing on a set of wooden stairs, she pulled the boards back and hoped they would stay.

Then she eased down the steps. The stairs were cloaked in blackness, but the greenish light everything emitted was enough for her to find her way down to a cellar full of boxes and other things stacked in close ranks. There was an old rust-pocked boiler furnace standing against one wall.

Selene made a circuit of the whole place, chose a spot behind a pile of rotting wooden boxes labeled *Lent* and *Easter* in antiquated, faded handwriting. It was in the farthest corner of the cellar, no windows to spill sunlight in at her, and hidden from the door by which she'd entered.

She slumped down, her legs trembling, and propped herself against the wall, sitting down with her legs splayed in front of her. The exhaustion was beginning to set in.

Selene pushed her hair back and opened up the bag, pulled out the lump of material Danny had hidden his book and something else in.

Her fingers shook as she unwrapped it.

*No wonder it's heavy.* Fabric fell aside and revealed a mellow shine.

He'd stolen it after all.

The Seal of Sitirris was pure heavy gold, studded with emeralds, Greater Words carved all around its circumference. In the middle, an unfamiliar glyph twisted, the gold shifting soundlessly as the carved contours changed like a Mobius strip. The gold was set in a shallow black steel dish, with a small iron loop set on the bottom. Selene let out a low breath of wonder, setting the Seal down in her lap. She pulled Danny's notebook out.

Paging through it, she was vaguely surprised she could read down here. The black spidery strokes of Danny's cryptic handwriting—a code only he and Selene knew, since they had invented it in the camp orphanage, scribbling in the dirt—showed up in clear contrast to the greenish-white of the pages.

The last page was full of thin spidery marks, done messily and hastily. Selene traced them with her index finger.

*N. only wants me to find it but I'm going to steal it myself. Greater Word of Awakening. Wakes up all sorts of shit. Useful, powerful. Sell to highest bidder... Got it! It was easy... Guy named G. wants it too, will outbid N. Finally gonna buy Lena that car. Move somewhere warm.*

Tears spilled down Selene's cheeks. "You jackass," she whispered. "Why couldn't you just have done what he told you to? Why'd you have to steal this and get yourself killed?"

LILITH SAINTCROW

*Delivered by KM but something wrong, cold in the apartment. Danger. Not going to call Sel. Got to get it out of my house. Stole the wrong thing. G. wants N. to suffer. Something's wrong.*

There was one last scrawl.

*Danger. G. coming to collect. Took fifteen had to get it out of here.*

There was a long string of numbers, and one last hurried sentence. *Gonna buy Sel that car.*

Selene thought she knew who KM was. Kristian Mueller, one of Danny's contacts. He lived over on the other end of the bridge on Sommersby Street; the rich side of town.

Nikolai's side of town.

The numbers puzzled her. She traced them, her sensitive fingertips feeling the little divots in the paper, almost tasting the chemical composition of the ink.

Comprehension hit. She felt slow and stupid. *Bank account. It's a routing string and a bank account. Who did he sell it to?*

*G. Grigori?*

The mysterious Grigori, popping up all over. If Danny was known to be one of Nikolai's people, someone with a grudge against Nikolai might want to interfere. But Danny was a small fish at best. Why go after him?

Nikolai said the Seal had been stolen in the first place, and Danny only hired to locate it. Did she believe that? And what about this Grigori? His face nagged at her memory, something she couldn't quite remember.

If Danny had stolen the Seal, why did he have the bank account number? Had Nikolai paid him up-front, and Danny thought to double-dip? It wasn't out of the question. Dear Danny the overachiever, always with an angle. God knew they'd both needed every angle they could get.

Bitterness touched her tongue. Now she was free, and strong enough—probably—to defend Danny, and he was dead. There was no justice in the world, and if there was a God or a Jesu like the Gileads had said, he was a monster. She might as well be a hell-fiend.

*Tomorrow night I'll visit Kristian.* Getting out of town was a good bet, but finding Danny's killer was an even better one. What did she have to lose now?

A whole lot of nothing. Especially since she'd shot Nikolai. She didn't think he'd forgive that.

She closed the notebook, wrapped it with the Seal in the hank of material, and slipped the resulting package back into her bag. Then she pulled her knees up and rested her forehead against them, taking a deep breath.

*Oh, God, I shot him, it won't kill him but he'll be so angry. I hope I didn't kill him. That would make two men I've killed tonight.*

But some part of her hoped she *had* killed him. Most of all, she wanted to be completely free. She wanted to get so far away Nikolai could never make her weak again.

She shook the thought away, her forehead knocking against her knees. The medallion warmed against her chest. Her breathing slowed, slowed, and stopped. Nothing happened. She didn't have to breathe as much, but after a long time she inhaled again. The habit was just too strong. Her pulse was slowing too, strong evenly-spaced thuds of her heart marking off time.

Sleep fell over her, a kind of death she welcomed even as it drove her down into darkness.

༄ ༄

"GET UP." A hand around her throat. Clamped down. The zoo stink of werecain. Lots of werecain. "Look at this. In a *church*."

Selene lunged into wakefulness, her fist instinctively blurring up in a strike that would break the nasal promontory and drive it into the brain—

His hand closed over her wrist, warm iron fingers squeezing hard enough to break bone if she had still been human. "Lovely. Let's just chain her, and bring her along."

Her eyes fluttered open. The exhaustion was still on her, a sheet of lead weighing her down while her body shook off the effects of the daytime. Lethargy receded, but not fast enough. Steel clamped around her wrists, and something that burned. "*Ow!* What the—"

Her pupils dilated. The greenish light returned. She looked up, blinking furiously. Broad cheekbones, strong chin, straight eyebrows. He looked vaguely Asian, his eyes slightly elongated. Beardless, his hair braided into long strings threaded with black lacquer beads gleaming wetly in the faint green glow. A cuff of yellowed lace came up through his collar, framing his throat. He had a long black coat on, just like Nikolai. Pale expressive hands held whatever was clasped around her wrists, whatever was burning almost down to her bones.

The air was full of the smell of werecain, and the heatless power pouring off him. He smelled old, like dust and dry tombs, spice and open steppes. And he also smelled like dry ratfur and blood, ancient Power clotted and dammed-up, a lake of force. She recognized the smell, even without its overlay of stinking black werecain.

*Oh. My. God.* Her throat went dry.

Everything clicked into place.

"You're *him*," she whispered. "Grigori."

He caught the chain, looped it over her wrists again. The cuffs and the length of chain sent a flare of agony down her arms, jolting in her shoulders. "Very good, sugar puff." His accent was thick, heavy on the Eastern Europe, light on the cuteness. This was a soft, evil voice to make you slit your own wrists and smile as the blade parted flesh. "And you are Nikolai's little love-bird." The words almost staggered under a weight of sarcasm as dark as a silted-up river.

She knew that voice. *Give my regards to Nikolai.*

"I hate Nikolai!" she screamed desperately. *He's going to kill me, he's going to kill me, the werecain was in my apartment to kill me think fast Selene think fast!* "I just shot him! He Turned me and I *hate* him!"

He yanked on the chains. Selene jerked to her feet. His dark eyes met hers.

Selene screamed again, an inarticulate sound of agony.

Those eyes were lakes of black fire, burrowing into Selene's head. *He is of my Bloodline,* Nikolai's voice said inside her head. *Do not resist him, Selene. Tell whatever lies you must, but do not resist.*

She had a brief flash, so vivid it was like being in two places at once. Nikolai, driving his fingers into a brick wall, the world rippling slightly around him. The psychic cord between them stretched taut, a refuge in the very back of her mind, a well of strength she had never imagined existed. Was it his, or her own? Did her mind just use him as an image, a mental walking-stick?

*You hate me, Selene,* Nikolai's voice reminded her. There was pain, he was biting his own lip with razor-sharp teeth, and she wondered hazily why she was thinking about him when she had other things to think about, like surviving this. *Remind him that you hate me. You hate me.*

"I hate him!" she screamed again. The scraping inside her head intensified unbearably, tore at her skull, pounded at her temples from the inside. But didn't crack the safe little corner of her where something crouched, some essential core of darkness that made her think of Nikolai's eyes. "I *killed* him! *Goddammit stop it, I killed him!*"

The chains fell away, sizzling. The older Nichtvren cupped her chin in his hot hand.

There was a low growl. "Quiet," Grigori said. "Don't mouth off to me, dog."

*Grigori is* abseyatein, Nikolai's voice whispered urgently, blood in his mouth and his fingers aching from driving into the wall, a low sound like a strangled scream locked in his chest. The psychic cord stretched again, thinning, but held. *Beast-master. Be careful, Selene, I beg of you.*

*Leave me alone!* she screamed inwardly, to both of them, yanking her between them in a horrible game of tug-of-war. Grigori didn't know she had reserved a corner of herself from him. He thought she was completely open to him.

Completely submissive.

And Selene knew all about submission, didn't she? Knew all about reserving a corner of her mind, some small part of her soul, while her body wept and went pliable with hot need. Wherever the strength to keep that corner of her safe and inviolate came from, she used it gratefully, unquestioningly— and let Grigori rummage through the rest of her mind.

It was no different than letting them use her body, was it? No different, and no less of a rape, made more horrible by the fact that she acquiesced, that she needed it. God was a monster, and she was trapped here again. But this time she had a chance, and she used it, withdrawing into the small safe little corner of herself she could lock everything else out of.

The only part of her that didn't beg.

"What else can you tell me, little girl?" Those eyes blazed, but the intensity behind them was a little less. They weren't digging into her head like a raccoon going through a garbage can. Instead, they were thoughtful, scorching away dust. "Don't lie. I can smell falsehood. It is like candy."

*Give my regards to Nikolai.*

"I've got the Seal." Her voice trembled. "My brother sold it to you. I'd like my fifteen, I give you the Seal, and we go our separate ways."

Grigori nodded. His beaded hair fell forward, clacking like bones, rustling against the shoulders of his coat. Beads. Beads in his hair. The texture of the wool glowed. "That is one option. But I have a score to settle with my wayward son, little girl."

Selene settled her back against the cellar wall. Her wrists ached furiously. *If I can just keep him from killing me I'll be happy.* "How did you find me?"

"I've tracked falcons and werecain," he said, and there was a low growl in the cellar. Selene's eyes darted past him. Six fur-heavy shapes squatted on the dusty floor, near the stairs she'd crept down last night. Cool night wind poured down the stairs, past the boxes, flavored with rain. They must have broken in. No need for subtlety, not for a creature this old. "You are no trouble. As long as Nikolai kept you human and under his hand, I could not See you. He must value you, to have made an unbroken fledgling in defiance of the Law."

She wanted to rub at her wrists, didn't let herself. *I'll be damned if I let you see that.* The thought was like a slap, waking her up. It felt as if the metal bracelets were still on her, burning sensitive skin. "What was on those handcuffs?"

"A little mixture of my own. Induces a simple allergic reaction, painful but nothing more. Unless it's swallowed." He shrugged. "And now I'll have to request that you come with me."

*You killed my brother, you son of a bitch. I'm going to kill you.* Selene shook her head. You never, *ever* gave in the first time a client named a price. "I give you the Seal, you give me the money, and we go our separate ways." Her heart hammered. *And I thought Nikolai was a tiger. This thing could eat me alive and suck my bones dry...if he thinks I don't know about him killing Danny will he let me live?*

Or if he doesn't care that I know?

"I have you, and the Seal, already," he pointed out.

Selene's throat was as dry and smooth as glass.

*Why don't I want him?* Sudden confusion made her blink. *If this was Nikolai, I'd be a little puddle on the floor.*

"Nikolai trapped me. He's been using me for years. I want him out of my life," she told the old Nichtvren, her pulse hammering in her ears. "All the way out of my life. Forever."

*Give me something I can use.* She huddled in the tiny corner behind the smooth invisible wall keeping her safe. *Please, please. You wanted to kill me, but see how useful I am? Don't kill me, please God, don't let him kill me.*

*Let me stay alive so I can fucking rip his heart out. Somehow.*

"Of course." Grigori's thumb stroked her cheek. "And I want him. Six hundred years he served me faithfully, as a friend and lover, and I want him *back*. I want him fettered at my feet as I break that regrettable pride." He cocked his head thoughtfully, examining her. "Now, if you'll help me acquire him, I'll set you free. You can wander the world as a Nichtvren without a Master."

Selene's entire body shook. "What do you want me to do?" she asked. Her throat was parched, desert dust. *The thirst. I want...oh, God, I have to feed. God help me.*

"Oh, nothing much. One phone call. He'll come, I'll have him, and you'll go free." He smiled, a purely beautiful, terrifying smile that looked just like Nikolai's—if Nikolai had been nailed onto a cross and hung snarling down on the populace. Just waiting to tear free of the nails and run raving—and *feeding*—through them. "I wanted to kill you to prove to him there is nothing of his I cannot destroy, but having you betray him is ever so much better. I think that will go a long way towards breaking him."

*Christos, this guy's a real winner, ain't he?* Danny's voice whispered in the little corner of sanity left in her head. Why couldn't she think in her own voice for once? *Agree with him, Selene. You can juke him out. I'd bet my panties on it.* It was just the sort of thing Danny would have said, too.

"He won't come," she told him. "I shot him. And he's too smart."

"He would not have Turned you if he would not come for you. I know him well enough to know *that*." Grigori's hand tensed on her chin, his thumb sinking into her cheek. His claws pinpricked her skin. "What say you, sugar puff?"

*I say you killed my brother and I'm going to make you pay. I'm going to make you both pay for fucking with our lives.* Selene buried the thought in the very bottom of her mind. *Can he read me? God, help me?*

God couldn't help her, but the small corner of her mind Grigori hadn't invaded pulsed reassuringly. Selene drew a deep breath, another sudden crazy mental image of Nikolai standing, his claws sinking into a stone wall and his eyes closed, rose in that deep small hidden place. If he could do that, reach across distance like that and crawl into her head, would there be anywhere in the world she was safe? Or was her psyche breaking under the strain, feeding her sudden hallucinations to make sense of what was happening to her?

Great. She was either crazy or totally fucked, again.

"You've been working on your slang," she managed, without the faintest idea of what she was going to say next. Her own smell faded under the onslaught of the smell of werecain and the basal fiery aroma of an ancient Nichtvren. It was like vanishing. Panic rose under her breastbone. She pushed it down with a hysterical effort. *Why don't I want him? Why am I not a pile of pudding? He fucking terrifies me, why am I not begging him to fuck me?*

She didn't know.

*I'm not a* tantraiiken *anymore. Not a...my God. Oh my God. I reacted to Nikolai. Is it only him now? Jesu. He said so, didn't he?*

*I'm not thinking very fast right now.*

"Of course. We must change with the times, no? There is no point in staying still while the river flows on." He smiled, not showing his fangs, his eyes dancing with red streaks like crimson oil on a puddle of black mineral water. The beads clicked and clacked against his shoulders as he moved. Danny had heard that sound before he died. "One phone call. Do we have a bargain?"

Selene swallowed, her throat clicking. "I'm thirsty."

"If we have a bargain, you can feed, little girl." He kept stroking her cheek, his thumb digging in. The touch should have made her melt. Instead, loathing crawled under her skin. A spiked mass of disgust made her shudder. Maybe he thought it was desire. What did he know about her? What did he guess? Had he ever Turned a *tantraiiken*?

"Deal," she whispered. The thirst twisted in her bloodstream, clawed at her belly, locked its greedy hands around her throat.

His hand left her chin. He lifted his wrist to his own mouth, bit in, and offered it to her.

Selene moaned. Blood dripped, black in the greenish glow. The thirst woke up fully, and her mouth fastened on the cut. Grigori's hand slid through her hair, cupped the back of her neck, just like a man stroking a puppy while it ate. "Drink deep, granddaughter," he whispered. There was another low growl that had a weird modulation, as if a wolf was trying to speak. It ended on an inquisitive yip.

It scorched down her throat like pure fire, Nichtvren blood, intensely powerful. Exploded in her stomach, under her breastbone, a bombshell that spread and tingled through her nerves. *He must have fed tonight.* Her sensitive mouth tasted the sweet lingering effects of human blood.

"He'll come, Thorvald," Grigori said. His pulse thudded in her ears, forcing her own heartbeat to follow it. She gulped, and gulped, her jaw distending so she could take as much as possible, greedily. *If I feed enough I'll be able to run.* "I know Nikolai. He'll come to see her one last time. He will think he is freeing her." A low chuckle. "I may even keep you, exquisite one. And use you to torture my son."

*Use me? I've been used all my life. It's nothing new.* She kept that thought carefully buried, her mouth drawing frantically against the fountain.

Fresh life surged through her veins. "That's enough," Grigori said, and the flow stopped. Selene snarled, wanting to bury her fangs into his wrist, but he made a quick movement and she was pinned against the wall, hanging, his hand clamped around her throat. "I said, that's enough. You have no manners. I'd half like to teach you some."

He dropped her, but her new reflexes kicked in and she landed on her feet. Wiped at her mouth with the back of her hand. *You killed my brother. But to make you pay, I've got to get away from you. You and Nikolai can kill each other for all I care.* "Where do I call him from?"

"Come with me. What possessed you to take your daylight rest in a church?"

"It seemed as good a place as any." *And deserted, after the War. They pretty much all are. Once people forget the Republic they won't be.* A numbness settled on her, one she recognized. It was the feeling of waiting while a client decided how to start the game.

*He's a beast-master. He rules werecain.* Her entire body went cold. The medallion pulsed, strangely subdued. That was what she'd been unable to remember. Werecain were peculiarly vulnerable to psychic pressure anyway, but some of the Nichtvren could control werecain without it, become a dominant member of a pack. And Grigori, immensely ancient and powerful, was one of them.

*Don't do it, Selene,* Danny's voice whispered. *It's suicide. Don't do it—yet.*

The six werecain lumbered up the stairs, hair swaying off their frames. Dust pattered down. Selene followed, moving automatically, her heart thudding in her ears.

They reached the top of the stairs and ducked out, one at a time. They had torn the boards away, the gaping hole was open to let in the night.

*I'll never see the sun again.* It was all pointless. Then again, half the world was always in night-time. Could she run fast enough to outpace the sun? Just keep moving?

"Give my regards to Nikolai," Grigori said softly, chuckling. The air changed, grew still and cold and dark.

Selene bolted. Four lines of fire whipped across her back, but she exploded up the stairs and out the door into the chill wet darkness. *Made it!* She leapt, whirling as one of the werecain grabbed for her, he piled into the door behind her. *He just ran into Grigori. The bastard tried to hit me from behind!*

*Do not worry about that,* Nikolai's voice whispered, exhausted. Why did he sound so tired if he was only a voice inside her head? *Run. Run for your life. My dear one, beloved, my only hope,* run.

Snarls behind her, pounding footsteps, Grigori's roar. It sounded like an enraged freight train. Something whizzed past her head—*shooting at me again goddammit*—she leapt again, grabbing the top of the leaning, trash-stacked fence. One of the sharp edges sliced across her palm, she soared over.

*How fast am I?* The baying began behind her. It was a footrace over the shattered terrain around Trivisidero now. Her back was on fire, blood soaking her jeans. If he had snagged a claw in her ribs he could have caught her. *I can probably outrun the werecain, but him...he's old. How fast can Master Nichtvren move? Christos. Run, Selene, run.*

The terror was dark wine at the back of her throat. New power slammed through her, fueled by Grigori's blood. *Shouldn't have let me drink even if you did expect to get it right back.* A giddy exhilaration began in her middle, her entire body tingling. *Beastmaster. He controls werecain. He looked familiar because I saw him through Danny's wards.*

She reached the edge of the bombed-out section and plunged onto an actual street, flashing through pools of streetlamp light, as thunder began in the distance. The air was damp, heavy, storm electricity tingling under the heavy low sky. *Nikolai.* The resulting flare of desire between her legs almost made her stumble. *Let you two kill each other, and then I'll be really, truly free.*

First, she had to escape.

Selene put her head down and kept running.

# THIRTEEN

THE IRON GATE was slightly ajar. Selene squeezed through, her canvas bag knocking against it and producing a hollow muffled clang. Lightning lit the sky overhead, forked diamonds thrown across the dark-orange glow of a cloudy city sky. The air was pregnant with storm.

She limped, her left calf spiking with pain. *Good thing I found that car.* She winced when she thought of the way she'd wrecked it. *I hope they had insurance, I haven't driven in years and those hybrids are stupid. They wallow like politicians.*

She shuddered. *I'm a thief as well as a murderer now, just to top off a life spent being a paranormal tramp. Christos. Really racking up the score here, Selene.*

The nest loomed up at the top of the hill, defenses shimmering in the rain-laden air. Selene's nostrils flared. She smelled like petroleo, and her camel coat was scorched almost beyond recognition. She ran her hands back through her hair, trying to smooth it down, flinching when she felt crispy, charred bits. *I always did want a short haircut.* Her breath jagged in. *Maybe I'll cut it all off.* When would she learn not to breathe?

*Give it a little while. I've only been Nichtvren for two nights.* She limped up the graveled drive. *Two wonderful nights. My entire life's gone into the Sarajevo DMZ. Well, more than usual.*

The nest was huge, a sort of neo-Victorian spread out in two wings and a main complex, with the windowless garage off to the side. There were no lights, no signs of life, just dark empty windows and the exhalation of some cold Power living here. The manicured grounds lay uneasily under that chilly cloak, Power flicking in Selene's peripheral vision.

*I'll be lucky if his defenses don't fry me.*

By the time she reached the front door, dime-sized drops of rain were beginning to plop down onto the paved drive. Rosebushes bowed under the sudden wash of cold wind. Obedient ranks of them folding away on either side, as well as low laurel hedges, an ornamental fountain standing dry and cold off to her left. The fountain sent up one metal spike like a warning finger. Selene shivered. Her coat steamed.

She climbed the seven granite steps between the two stone lions, walked across the flagstones leading up to the door. Carved gargoyles watched her from heavy iron-bound wood, their mouths open in silent screams. *The man just has no taste.* She shivered, raised her hands and was about to pound on the door when she noticed the button for the bell tucked to one side on a copper plate.

The shivers had her again. *I can't believe I got away. Maybe I'm luckier than I thought.* The hair on her nape rose up. Her knees buckled, and she almost fell against the door, catching herself just in time. Her palms sang with pain, she pulled back as if the door had burned her.

"Nikolai," she whispered, and rang the bell.

Nothing happened.

She waited, her heart pounding in her ears. Pushed the button again.

Still, nothing.

The rain began to come down in quarter-sized instead of dime-sized drops. Her face throbbed with pain. Had she been burned? She couldn't remember. Shock was closing in, cotton wool wrapping her ears and nose.

She rang the bell a third time, a short sob escaping her. "God," she whispered, "don't tell me you're not home. If I have to break *into* your house after all this... Jesu, Nikolai, open up."

Nothing again. The house rose up over her, a wave of stone and glass about to break.

Selene stepped up to the door, found the handle, and pressed it down. It swung open easily, on eerily quiet hinges. Revealed an expanse of white and black marble, checkerboard squares, a narrow strip of red carpeting running up two flights of stairs, one on either side of the foyer. Fred Astaire could have danced down those steps.

She stepped inside. The cessation of the rain's pounding made her head ring. The door swung closed behind her, latched shut.

Relief made her knees weak and her hands cold. Now she was here, in Nikolai's house. At least here, she could sleep for a little bit. Wait for him to come home...maybe.

Then he and Grigori could kill each other all they wanted, and she'd be able to go on her way. Only where would she *go*, now?

And would Nikolai let her vanish? That was the million-credit question, wasn't it.

Selene's legs gave out for the last time. She slid down the inside of the door and sat on the floor. The marble was cold, and her ass went numb almost immediately. There was a grandfather clock set off to one side, an awful, heavily carved thing ticking and tocking like a demented rocking chair.

"Nikolai," she whispered. "Please be home." *I didn't shoot you enough to kill you. Go figure, I'm suddenly okay with the idea.*

Light seared through her eyes and she blinked, resting her head against the door. There was a chandelier overhead, tinkling crystal drops that were now glowing from several incandescent bulbs. It hurt to look at, but she was too tired to glance away.

"Jesu Christos," Price Netley said. "Selene? My *God*. Call the Master. Tell him she's here. Selene, we've been looking *everywhere* for you." Running footsteps.

Her eyes fell closed, shutting out the glare. "I ran into some trouble," she husked, her throat far too dry. "Netley—I've seen Grigori. He killed Danny. You've got to tell...got to tell Nikolai." *So they can fucking do each other to death and leave me alone.*

And yet she came running back to Nikolai's house, hoping he was home so he could take care of this, bail her out like he'd done so many times before, all the time she'd known him. Or maybe because it was the only halfway-safe place left to her. Between what Grigori wanted and what Nikolai wanted, she'd probably pick Nikolai every time. Since Nikolai seemed to want her alive so he could fuck with her.

*Selene, you are a piece of work, aren't you.* She was too tired to feel the bite of self-loathing under the thought. She had a whole lifetime's worth of things to loathe about herself. One or two more wasn't going to make a damn bit of difference at this point.

"You need blood. Come on, Selene, stay awake." Netley patted her cheek. The feel of warm damp human flesh against her skin made her fangs slide free, and Selene made a small pleading sound. "Here." He pressed his wrist against her mouth. Her eyes slid open. She saw the lawyer's blond face, his hair mussed, his cheeks paper-white. "Come on, feed. Nikolai will come back as soon as he gets word. Whatever you did knocked him for a loop, he's searching high and low for you."

Selene clamped her lips together. Netley's legs stuck out of the bottom of his flannel shirt and blue boxers, hairy and knob-kneed. He wore a pair of fuzzy blue slippers too, and smelled like pipe tobacco. The smell took her back to the war profiteers in the camps, they'd smelled the same way.

Selene's throat closed up.

*Bite him,* Nikolai's voice whispered in her ear. *You need blood, and he is my thrall. Take what you must, what is mine is yours.*

Selene shook her head again, but Netley jammed his wrist against her mouth again. "Don't make me cut myself, Selene, please. Drink. You *must,* or Nikolai will be very angry with me." Running footsteps behind him. Someone was talking; it sounded like one half of a phone conversation.

"—right here," Jorge said. "She's talking about Grigori. Master—" The sound of a cell-phone flipped shut was sharp in the quiet. Fabric moving, people running. "Damn. He's on his way. Bring a bloodpack. Selene, you need to feed, you're going into shock."

Tears trickled out between Selene's eyelids. *Of course I need to feed, but Netley...I know him, goddammit, I know him, I can't bite him.*

*DRINK!* Nikolai's voice, a gong ringing in the very center of her head, rattling her skull. Selene found herself opening her mouth, her fangs driving into Netley's wrist. Blood filled her throat, hot and tasting of human, and she choked. Then her body took over, drinking, swallowing, it tasted *good.* She made a small mewling sound while she drank, like a kitten.

The entire world faded out, replaced by the sound of Netley's pulse. *That's enough, Selene.* Nikolai's voice, again, filling the world, impossible to disobey. Selene retracted her fangs. Her tongue lapped across the marks; the coagulant her tongue secreted would help take care of the wounds.

She let go of his wrist. Choked on the last mouthful of blood, gagged, swallowed it. The world returned, a fresh rush of color and sensation. New heat blurred through her veins, tingled in her fingertips. The blood she'd taken from Grigori had done something funny to her, sealed some part of her away. He hadn't expected her to keep it, so much power.

What would it do to her, so much precious fluid from an ancient Master? It had given her the strength and speed to run without her heart bursting, but maybe there were deeper effects.

*If it made me fast enough to outrun him I'm all for it. I'll figure out the rest of it later. If Nikolai doesn't kill me for shooting him.*

*Great. What a lovely thought.*

Jorge was dragging her over to the stairs. She was denser now, he grunted as she gained her feet and tried to help. "Lock down the defenses," he said. "Bradley, help Netley. We've got a transfusion pack in the medroom. Clark, get me some alcohol swabs. Jesu, Selene, what did you do to yourself this time?"

The doors boomed as something hit them from the outside. They shuddered theatrically and swung open. Nikolai strode in from the rain, water running off his black hair and long coat. He didn't bother to close the doors, they simply slammed shut without any help.

The air ran with hot prickles of tension. Nikolai's footsteps echoed against the marble.

Selene dropped down on the steps. She could sit up now, and she pushed her hair back, tucking charred strands behind her ears. The bag miraculously rested against her side, slumping against her, a faithful little dog.

Jorge stepped back. She didn't blame him.

"Leave us," Nikolai said. Footsteps resounded, running away, someone dragging Netley. Jorge stayed long enough to look at Selene as if he wanted to say something, but then he shook his head and retreated up the stairs.

Nikolai halted six feet from the steps. Water streamed off him. He slicked his hair back with one hand, looking down at her, his eyes black from lid to lid, sparks of blue-green glittering on the surface of the blackness.

Selene swallowed dryly. "I saw Grigori." Her voice sounded very small. "He wanted...he said one phone call, to lure you into a trap. He's a beast-master, isn't he? I forgot about those, we didn't cover them much in school." She dug in the bag at her side, came up with the lump of fabric and its terrible secret weight. "Then he tried to kill me. I have this." She unwrapped the fabric with shaking hands.

The Seal glowed under the warm electric light from the chandelier. Its emeralds sparked. She tossed it at him, and his white hand flashed out and caught it. "Danny had it hidden in his apartment. It's why he died, maybe. I don't know. But Grigori...he killed Danny, Nikolai. He tried to kill *me*, I..." *I heard your voice inside my head. Did you help me?*

*And if you did, do I owe you for that? What the fuck do I have to pay you now, Nikolai? You're a monster, I'm a monster, even God is a monster. We're all in this together.*

"Why did you not betray me?" His voice slid through the air, made Selene's entire body go cold. He sounded bored. Goosebumps rose on Selene's skin. She shivered, unable to look away from him until he blinked, deliberately, his lids closing over his eyes and releasing her.

She looked down at her hands. Her palms were black with soot and there were little beads of scorching marching across her fingers. *Would I have tried to, if he hadn't tried to kill me? Who knows?* Her face ached. "He said he wanted you back. T-t-to *serve*." How could she explain it, to him of all people? "I know what it's like to be trapped. I don't want to do that. To anyone. Ever. Not even someone I...hate." Her palm was slashed too, from the fence at the church. That wound was rapidly closing, flesh knitting itself back together now that she had a few seconds to rest. Then she tipped her head back up, looked directly at him. "If anyone kills you," she whispered, "it's going to be me."

*Unless you and Grigori take care of each other. I can't be that lucky.*

His gaze met hers. Heat slammed into her belly and she bit her lower lip, forgetting her teeth were sharper now. Something warm trickled down her chin.

He approached cautiously, his boots making wet squeaking sounds against the marble tiles. Then he crouched down right in front of the bottom step. He reached up, touching her chin with his free hand, smoothing the blood away. His fingers were warm and hard. "Why do you fight me so hard, Selene? All I wish for..." Here, maddeningly, he stopped. "You saw Grigori? How do you know it was him?"

"I know, I saw him through Danny's wards. He wanted me to feed from him."

"Did you?"

"I..." She stole a glance at him under her lashes. How could she tell him she had heard his voice during the whole thing?

He was watching her face. "I see." He nodded.

Then he took her scraped and slashed hand and held it up, placed the Seal in her palm. "There. Hold it until we can give it back."

"I don't want to. You had Danny steal it."

"I wanted Danny to *locate* it for the Sitirrismi," he corrected. "You are so willing to believe the worst of me."

Did he sound *hurt*? Wonders never ceased. "You're a bastard." The rain was a distant drumming against the roof, muffled by the bulk of the house. "You deliberately Turned me. I'll never be human again."

"I sought to save your life, since a Nichtvren's blood can cure many ills. Now you are immortal, and what you call your curse does not rule you. I should think you would thank me, but you are ungrateful as well as spiteful—"

"Thank you," Selene said immediately, interrupting him.

He smiled, the black shrinking until his eyes were normal again. Or as normal as Nikolai's eyes ever got, the catshine across his pupil and iris contrasting with the perfect whites. The smile was gentle, tender, and ironic, the most human expression she'd ever seen on him.

It was terrifying in a whole new way.

Her heart thudded in her throat, a red tide of fear slamming up her spinal cord. "I hate that you Turned me."

He nodded. "Hate me if you like. As long as you are *alive* to do so, I can bear it."

"You keep saying that." Her head dropped forward. A few strands of singed hair fell in her face. Her heart pounded harshly. Why? She wasn't running anymore. Or was it thunder from outside echoing in her bones?

"You need more blood. How did you escape Grigori?"

"I ran. He caught my coat—I outdistanced the werecain, then I stole a car. They almost caught me on the bridge, but the car wrecked and blew up. I barely got out. I have this thing for cars blowing up, I guess. Did I ever tell you about my prom?"

He was still brushing her hair back. He murmured very softly, Selene didn't hear quite what. Then he cleared his throat. "Come. You need to feed, and to rest."

"There was a werecain in my apartment. It tore everything up. I had to hide in the closet at the bus station."

"If I were mortal, you might kill me with worry," Nikolai said dryly, brushing her shoulders. "Your coat is ruined. Come with me, Selene."

She nodded. Held her hand up to him. "I don't think I can stand up," she admitted. "He's scary, Nikolai. He's really scary. I wish you two would kill each other and leave me *alone*."

There. It was out. It was said. Her hand quivered in midair.

Nikolai nodded, his black hair slicked back from his face. The warm electric light glowed down, highlighted his hair, his charcoal eyebrows, glimmered in his black eyes. His fingers threaded through hers. "Indeed he is frightening. More terrifying than me, I would suspect, since you have run from him straight to my door."

"He said he couldn't see me under your hand." Shivers racked her. Her palms were sweating. His voice did something strange to her head, her entire body changing into warm oil.

Nikolai let go, took her shoulders and stood up, which dragged her upright. The Seal weighted down her fingers, bumped against her hip. "I hate this thing," she continued. "You can have it, I don't want it."

He nodded. "You'll have to feed, Selene. You used more Power than you should have, running from him. I shall teach you better."

*I just fed, from Netley. You mean that isn't enough?* "I can't do this." Selene leaned into him. "I don't want to be a bloodsucking monster."

"We are all God's monsters. You only doubt yourself." He folded her in his arms. Selene's body unstrung, her arms and legs weighed down with exhaustion. "It will pass."

"Did Grigori make that thing kill Danny?" She tipped her head back to look up at his face.

"It is certainly possible. The spent shell casings inside Danny's apartment would lead me to the conclusion that altered beast was simply to *find* Danny. Danny was shot twice before Grigori worked his will. I did *not* want you to see his body, Selene. You had enough to bear. You are more fragile than you think."

Selene blinked. *Fragile? I don't think so, but if you...* "Shot? But I didn't see that in the wards."

"Did it ever occur to you that the wards would not have cared about bullets? Or that the presence of a werecain *and* a Nichtvren might have confused the issue? And that you were already shocked by grief and drained of Power, perhaps the wards did not tell you the complete tale?" His voice rumbled in his chest, stroked her skin, slid down her back and ruffled her hair. "Had you simply let me do what I intended, we could have discovered all, with little trouble and effort, and Grigori would have been forced to show his hand."

"Did you intend on me getting shot, then?" Her cheek was pressed against his chest, so there wasn't much of a challenge except for her tone. *I don't think anyone else could talk to him like this.* She was going to bite at her lower lip again before she remembered her teeth were much sharper now.

Her legs completely failed her, and she dropped against him, her head lolling. The Seal bumped her hip again. Her fingers wouldn't quite let go of it.

"I am a fool. Come, dear one."

He half-carried her through the halls, carpet barely muffling the sound of crisp measured steps. Her boot-toes dragged against the floor, but Selene was past caring. For the moment she was warm, and Nikolai was carrying her, and she felt reasonably safe.

*Funny how my idea of safe changes from minute to minute lately*, she thought dimly. *He's definitely not safe. He's as dangerous as Grigori.*

"Stay awake, Selene." He set her down on something soft. A door creaked closed, and there was the sound of an iron bar clanging. "Here, take this off." His fingers, stripping her bag away, the Seal slipping away from her hand and hitting the floor with a clang. The rags of her coat were torn off, and the sweater and dress shirt were charred and useless. Her back ran with pain.

He hissed in a breath. "You're burned. And he marked you." He sounded shocked.

"Always trying to get my clothes off," she heard herself say. Her voice had a funny breathless tone she didn't like, dreamy and disconnected. She smelled something very sweet, fermenting. *That's my blood decaying. Weird. How do I know that?*

"Drink, Selene," he whispered, his fingers closing around the back of her neck. "Take what you need."

The pulse beat against her lips. It wasn't his wrist, it was too strong, and his skin was too soft.

Her fangs slid out, her jaw distending, and he pushed gently on the back of her head. *Drink, Selene.* His voice whispered in the center of her head again. *For the love of God, drink.*

It was like breaking a crust, his skin cool and resistant until her newfound fangs cracked through and the taste of him flooded her mouth. Heat poured down her throat. Selene's eyelids fluttered, shutterclicks of light burning through her eyes. His hair brushed her face. Her entire body pitched forward, melding against his, the sliding perfect texture of his skin now rubbing over hers. His pulse pounded, forcing hers to follow, a tandem beat that strained at her ears and wrists and throat.

His pulse continued for an eternity, blood murmuring in her ears, and Selene's entire body flushed with heat.

And then she fell.

*ROUGH WOOD AGAINST cheek, screaming of the crowd, chanting deep voices. "Recant! Recant! Recant!" Smell, human stink and sweat and garlic and the cold.*

*The first lash. For a moment the impact didn't hurt, it was so deep and huge, but then the skin tore and the agony ripped flesh from bone.*

229

*Screams of a wounded animal, a familiar voice. Knees against stone, slipping greasily in ice and the offal the crowd hurled at the heretic.*

*The sun had fled behind a bank of cloud, premature winter darkness falling. Uneasiness slid through the chanting voices. It was dangerous to be out after dark. Screams bounced off the ice-frosted flags, knees aching, back on fire, hoarse sobbing, throat cut with screaming.*

*"Recant! Recant!" The chanting of the crowd frayed, dissolved into an animal roar. The whip cracked again. And again.*

"Enough!" The voice roared through the crowd.

*But the animals bayed. They wanted blood, and death, and more blood. There was not enough red in the world to fill their thirst.*

*The whip descended one last time. Blood, dripping onto the flags. A red haze descending.*

Selene slammed back into her body. Her fangs slid free of Nikolai's throat. He hadn't told her to stop, she was simply gorged with blood, a queer bloated feeling under her ribs as her body tried to cope with the sudden influx.

Nikolai fell back onto the bed, landed against the pillows. Her back and face crackled, shedding burned tissue, fresh healthy skin suddenly shrinking from the chill.

Selene stood at the edge of the bed, a sharp edge digging into her shins. Nikolai was paper-white, wheezing. He was old, and powerful, but even a Master could die of blood loss. She'd taken too much.

Nikolai's eyes were shut, sharp black lashes in an arc against his too-white cheek. He drew in a shallow gasp. The horrible choked sound rattled inside Selene's head, bounced off the walls.

*Call for one of his thralls.* She looked at the heavy wooden door. It was barred inside and out, probably. She could see the heavy iron bar, set in brackets driven deep into the dark wood paneling. *Oh, no.*

"Nikolai!" Before she knew it she was on the bed, her knees on either side of his hips. His back arched, his fangs distended, his skin was almost translucent. The pulse beat under the thin skin at his temples, swelling and retreating strongly.

She had her wrist halfway to her mouth before she realized what she was doing, her teeth set just against the skin. *I bet I could break the door down or figure it out,* she thought blankly, looking down at his face. He was choking on the still air. *He would probably survive. Then he and Grigori could fight it out and I can get away.*

*Maybe.*

"If anyone kills you," she repeated softly, "it's going to be me." Her throat closed against the words, her pulse suddenly racing, rapid and thready, something uncomfortably like bile pressing against the back of her throat. *Nichtvren don't throw up,* she heard herself saying in a lecture hall years ago, heard the shocked titters of the students. *There is no gag reflex, since they have no need to void; there is no such thing as poisoning a Nichtvren. They can rupture their stomachs, though, with gorging.* She shook the memory away. She'd probably never teach again.

*What are you doing?* her own voice shrilled inside her head. *You can't, you won't!*

*He'll be crippled if he goes for too long without feeding on something. He gave me too much.*

Why would he do something like that? Probably to trap her again. He never did anything without a reason, did he. It was the only thing he understood, the planning and the reasons.

So maybe she should do something just for the hell of it. Like saving his life.

Her teeth scraped over the throbbing in her own wrist. Nikolai's blood wasn't silty and thick like Grigori's. Instead, it was like brandy, a smooth fire that exploded in her stomach and tingled against her skin. And it fed her even deeper, flushing her body with even more Power. Most fledgelings didn't get to drink more than once from their Master, she'd fed from two Masters now. And Jesu alone knew how much of Nikolai's blood she'd taken down when she'd been shot in the back.

*You'd better start thinking about why he would do these things, Selene. And why you're doing what you're doing.*

The dim lighting of Nikolai's sanctum was now perfect for her night-hunting vision. The greenish glow that was almost-total darkness retreated under the faint light from the lamp with the red lace shade, and the red velvet was soothing. The blank dark walls held none of the painful brightness of the human world.

Inside this cocoon, then, she looked down at the pale dish of Nikolai's face. He drew in a long shallow rattling breath, his body tensing under hers.

Selene drove her own teeth into her wrist. A bright spike of pain made her eyes roll up.

*What are you doing? You hate him!* Her own voice scraped against the inside of her mind. *He Turned you into a sucktooth! Made you a murderer! And he...he...*

*He protected me. From my own Talent, and from Grigori.* So she owed him. And she needed him to settle things with Grigori so she could escape. For good this time. Her fangs retracted. Blood dripped down her arm, and she shoved her wrist against Nikolai's mouth. "Come on," she whispered. "Come on."

He fastened on the wound. The feel of his mouth on her skin, drawing from her, made her gasp, fire pulling against her veins.

*I didn't know.* Her head dipped forward. Her body settled against his, she felt the definite start of something hard pressing against the juncture of her legs. Warmth flooded up, and she felt wetness trickle down, threading along and soaking into denim. Sweat sprang up along her forehead, under her arms. Selene moaned.

He drew in another long mouthful and she arched her back. This was familiar, the swimming weakness, fear and a slight edge of pain making her legs faraway and dim, her wet jeans and her singed bra too confining, rasping against her skin.

He took another endless pull against her wrist, swallowing four times. His eyes closed, his face losing some of its translucence. Selene cried out, the sensation exploding through her body, her head now flung back. *If he does that again I'll die.* But it was an eager disconnected thought. She didn't care. Dying of this kind of sensory overload would almost make it worthwhile.

Nikolai pushed her aside, one hand clamped around her wrist, Selene's entire body unstrung and languid, falling through space. Her nerve endings sparked like Roman candles, and she wondered vaguely if her hand would glow in the dim light if she held it up enough to see. He knelt on the bed, holding the wound on her wrist closed, his other hand pushing her shoulder. She fell against the velvet, cloth rasping at her skin.

"Enough," Nikolai said, harshly. "Stay here. I'll return."

"No." It was out of her mouth before she could stop herself, Selene caught at fingers on her wrist with her free hand, her own fingers clamping home with more force than she thought possible. "Nikolai."

He went still, looking down at her. His face was gaunt. *He gave me too much.* An incoherent haze, her mouth falling open as she looked up at him. *I could have let him die here.*

She pulled at his hand. *More.* She wanted *more.*

He still didn't move. He might have been a statue, unblinking, unbreathing. His cheeks were hollow, and there were dark bruised circles under his eyes. *How much did I drink?* Selene stared at him. His eyes scorched the darkness around his face, a pulsing haze of cold Power. His hand fell away from her shoulder.

Selene swallowed. The tang of his blood still stained the inside of her mouth. It took an effort of will to let go of his wrist, one finger at a time. "Where are you going?" she asked, barely believing that she would even care. A shudder raced through her entire body. Aftershocks.

*That was one hell of a feeding. We know exactly what that is, too. It's the curse again.*

He moved then, brushing strands of sweat-damp hair back from her forehead. *Well what do you know?* The cheerful, lunatic side of Selene said in a bright jolly voice. *Nichtvren do sweat. All it takes is a little sex, and they sweat buckets. As in buckets of blood? Ha ha?*

"I have thralls, and bloodpacks. Time to use them, *verscht za?* I will return to let you feed again. Until then, I will leave the door to my sanctum closed, for your safety. You have escaped Grigori, dear one, and he will not take that kindly." Nikolai's black eyes with their layer of predatory shine met hers. "He will, in fact, be furious. If the nest is attacked and broken, you will find a safe passage out. It is hidden behind the bed, and will respond only to the medallion." He looked as if he would say more, shook his head, smoothing back another charred strand of her hair. "I would ask that you stay, Selene. Please."

*Miracles do happen. Now that it's too late to do any good, he starts asking instead of telling me.* A hazy amazement settled over her. She nodded, curling into the velvet coverlet. Her cheek slid against the velvet. She nodded again, to feel that slight touch against her quivering skin. "I'm sorry," she managed. "I took too much."

"I allowed it, did I not?" He slid away from her to come to his feet, soundless and lithe as a giant cat, on the other side of the bed. "Rest, Selene. You are still new to this. No other fledgling has escaped Grigori's pursuit in over six centuries."

"Great. Bully for me," Selene muttered, suddenly acutely aware that she was wearing a torn, stained bra and a pair of ragged jeans that were slick and damp, wadded between her legs. "How do you know?"

"Because I was the only one who ever did, before."

Selene swallowed, curling into a ball. Her body slumped gratefully into the softness of the bed. "Maybe he let me escape." But Grigori's roar, and the marks of his claws on her back, told her otherwise.

"That," Nikolai replied, "is why I will bar the door. We cannot trust each other too much yet, *dorogaya moya*."

With that, he left. Selene lay in the half-dark, thinking it over. "No," she finally said to the silence of his absence. "I guess we can't."

# FOURTEEN

SHE RAIDED HIS closet again, finding a black button-down linen shirt and another pair of sweatpants. Ducking into the bathroom, she eyed the toilet for a moment before turning the shower on. *Three days ago the porcelain god would have been the first thing on my mind.* She shivered, gooseflesh spilling down her back and up her arms. *He Turned me, and I'm a sucktooth now. And I just...what the fuck did I just do?*

Testing the water gingerly with one hand, she finally stepped into the shower, sighing with relief. The medallion bounced against her chest, skin-warm. The remainder of Nikolai's blood tingled in her fingers and toes, her heart still pounding too hard. Her stomach bulged out fractionally just under where her ribs met her breastbone.

*Jesu, I'm bloated with blood.* She rested her forehead against the slick cold tiles. *Oh, God. Nichtvren can't throw up.* Was she sweating? The warm water beat against her shoulder, ran down her hip. Chills slid down her skin.

The feeling—was it a memory?—of a rough wooden post and the crack of a whip rose again. Selene shut her eyes. Was that where the scars had come from? Was she going to drown in Nikolai's memories now?

A thin squealing sound rasped against her ears under the roar of the water.

*Shut up,* Danny's voice barked in the middle of her skull again. He sounded, of all things, alarmed. *Get out of the fucking shower. Stop moaning. Keep it together, Lena. Come on.*

She nodded, her forehead squeaking against the tiles. A swelling, hitching laugh bounced out of her, echoed against the tiles, was followed by the collapse of a slow moan.

*Keep it together, Lena. Come on. Get out of the shower.* Now Danny's voice was cajoling, wheedling. Just like when they were kids and he was trying to cheer her up, or talk her into taking part in some game or another—

"Shut up," Selene heard herself say, over the rush of water. She reached out blindly and turned the shower off. Slowing water plinked down onto the glossy dark-blue tiles. "If I'm going to live forever, do I want you whining at me all the time?"

*You're the one who's talking to a ghost,* he came back smartly. It was just the sort of thing Danny would say. The loneliness rose to choke her. *Get dressed, Selene. Come on.*

"Okay," she whispered. Her lips slid over her teeth. "Goddamn you getting yourself killed."

*They were after you, Lena. I was only an afterthought. Bait. Stupid bait, at that.*

"Stop that. Jesu, I'm even insulting my dead brother now." She dried off with angry swipes, her skin shrinking from the rasp of terrycloth. Finally, she stalked out into the sanctum, the towel balled up in her fist.

Her charred clothes lay on the floor by the wrinkled bed, sending up a powerful stink of Nichtvren and fear. The faint but thunderously lingering odor of werecain filled her nose briefly.

She balled the pitiful remainders up with the towel, wrinkling her nose, and shoved them through the door into the bathroom. Her black bag was scorched at the edges. It had been under her in the wreck of the car. The Seal glittered on the floor, its emeralds sending up thin needles of light.

Selene shivered, copper filling her mouth. *I could have died.*

It was too much. Too many shocks, too close together. The All-Dead Hit Parade inside her head didn't help either.

She took a deep breath, plopped down on the bed with the bag cradled in her arms.

After a few seconds of sitting, staring fixedly at nothing, Selene fell back onto the bed, curling on her side and hugging the bag to her chest. A few sharp edges—file folder, her athame, her wallet—poked into her chest, but she wriggled a bit until the softnesses were in the right place. Carson the teddy and the flannel shirt...had Danny worn the shirt the day he died? It had been tossed on the bed.

Selene squeezed her eyes shut and hugged the bag. The pressure behind her eyes was familiar, natural, normal, *human*. She wanted to cry.

*I wonder, will they be blood tears?*

Oddly enough, that was the last straw.

The low keening sound of grief began somewhere in her belly and rose up through her spine, dragging broken glass with it. Selene's throat swelled. She buried her face in the rough canvas of the bag, curling her knees up and coughing out an endless scream.

*How strange. So I do have to breathe after all.*

"Selene?" Nikolai's voice.

*I didn't hear the door open*, she thought dimly.

The bed creaked as he lowered himself down behind her. "Selene?" He cleared his throat and touched her shoulder. His fingers burned through the linen. Then he touched her hair, running his fingers through the charred bits.

The keening sound coming from her stomach wouldn't stop. Selene squeezed her eyelids even tighter, bringing her knees up, something wet and warm trickling from her eyes. Her nose was full.

"No." Nikolai's voice made the entire room go cold. "Selene? *Selene!*"

*Leave me alone. You've ruined everything. Go away.*

"You can grieve all you like later." His hand clamped around her shoulder. "Not now. Not like this. It's dangerous, shock can kill a fledgling. Selene, for the love of God, *don't* cry."

*I'm not crying. I'm screaming, can't you hear it?* A kind of wonder filled her at the thought. *I should have let you die. I wish I'd let you die.*

*Why didn't I? Oh, right. I need you to kill Grigori, and I need Grigori to kill you, and then...*

The future was a blank empty wasteland stretching in front of her. It always had been, but now there was so much more of the emptiness to contemplate. An ocean of it, a desert she would have to keep plodding through, day after gray endless weary day.

"Do not waste your tears on a pillow when I am here. Would it make you feel better if I let you try to harm me again?" He squeezed her shoulder even more tightly. Muscle ground against bone, pain slicing down her chest. But the pain melted, changed into liquid heat, pooled in her lower belly.

The scream broke, jagged into a hoarse sob. "Fuck you," she managed around the dry heaving sounds. "Leave me *alone*."

"No." His fingers ground in even further. Her breath caught halfway, she sobbed again. Would she bruise? *Did* Nichtvren bruise? "There is no comfort in *alone*, Selene, no matter how much you may wish for it. Cease this. You will damage yourself, and that I will not allow."

Selene pulled away, trying to wrench her shoulder from Nikolai's grasp. He didn't let go, but his fingers eased up a little. Then he leaned down, his breath brushing her ear. "If you do not fight now," he whispered, intimately, "I *will* break you, dear one. It takes very little effort. A few days without feeding, some pain. How would you like to be a mindless thrall to my will? A submissive Consort?"

She tore away from him, pushing up on her hands, and scooted across the bed. The bag came with her, clinking. She faced his back across the expanse of wrinkled red velvet. He didn't move, his spine perfectly straight, sitting on the edge of the bed, one pale hand dropping to his side. His hair was still damp, slicked down with rain. Selene flipped her bag open with trembling hands, and her fingers curled around the wooden hilt of her athame.

"Try it," she whispered. Cool air touched her wet cheeks. Her heart hammered, pulse pounding in her ears, the medallion burned against her chest. Her bones crawled with Power, shifting inside her skin. "You're such a fucking bastard."

He was utterly still, unbreathing.

"I wish I'd killed you when I shot you," she said. She took a deep shaking breath. "How can you be such a...such a..."

"Think of some more creative epithets, Selene." He did not turn. The air shimmered around him like the haze on pavement on a summer day. "You are beginning to bore me."

*Bore you? What the fuck?* Her hand shook inside the bag.

*If I stabbed him, it wouldn't matter. He'd shake it off. The knife won't cause enough damage. I* shot *him, and it didn't even make a dent.* Determination caught fire inside her chest. Her breathing evened out. *I'll give it the old college try, though. Let's see if that* bores *him.*

New life flooded her arms and legs. "Like I ever wanted you to be interested in me." She slipped off the bed and rocketed to her feet. "I don't know why I even *came* here."

"Because you have nowhere else to go." Pitilessly, no quarter given. "Grigori will hunt you down and use you before he makes you beg for death. I simply require your presence. I am by far the lesser of two evils."

"Evil's a good word for you," she flung at him. "Add manipulative, ugly, arrogant, delusional, chauvinistic, sex-crazed fucking little *freak*—"

"There," he interrupted. "That, at least, is something new even from you." He rose from the bed slowly, still not bothering to look at her. "Now you should feed, and rest. Dawn approaches."

"Hour and a half," she said, automatically. Pointlessly. "I wish you'd just leave me the fuck alone."

He shrugged. "You keep saying that. What would you be without me? Still combing the streets to find the men to feed your precious curse? I have given you shelter, and yet you curse me. If I were crueler to you, would you be kinder to me?" He took two steps away from the bed, tipped his head back. She could see a pale slice of his forehead, the coal-black wave of his hair falling back.

"How could you be any *worse*?" she yelled. The sound bounced off the paneled walls, made the entire room shake. *Will you look at that? I'm doing his trick, the I-can-shake-the-walls trick. Holy shit. But no, there's nothing holy about it.*

He rounded on her, his eyes full of black fire, his face a twisted mask. "*I could be Grigori!*" he yelled back. Selene's shoulders hit the wall. The echoes boomed. Glass shattered in the bathroom, tinkling.

In one graceful, inhuman movement he was over the bed, his entire body pressing hers against the wall. *Well, isn't this familiar,* a snide little voice caroled inside her head and was quickly strangled.

"I could be Grigori," he repeated, venomously, his cheek laid against hers and his breath hot in her ear. "I could take you, break you, and *keep* you; I could become what I fear most. I could lose you to my own hunger and smash your spirit, trying to chain what I cannot live without. What I cannot buy or steal or win, what you will not *give* me even though I do not *take*, I only ask." His voice rose harshly, spilling out as if he could not help himself. "I am trying to be better than Grigori was to me, and you make me wonder if perhaps I should follow in his footsteps and simply take what I must have, what you *deny* me—"

"You *are* like him! You've tried to break me all this time!" Selene lunged away and actually succeeded in throwing him off-balance. It was a small victory, but she immediately froze, terror and fresh arousal flooding her.

*What did I just do?*

"I could be much worse." His lips moved against her cheek, teeth gently scraping her skin. The ragged tone was gone, he had mastered himself. "I could have taken you and Turned you the first night I found you. I could have stretched out my hand and taken you at any time after that, but I refrained. I played your games and took instead what crumbs you gave me, and in return I gave you *time*. I was far more patient with you than you deserve, you ungrateful little beggar."

The fact that he was kind of right, that he *could* have forced her and hadn't—much—didn't help. "You *manipulated* me. You never took no for an answer."

"I kept you safe. I allow you far more than a Master has ever allowed a *tantraiiken*. There is no freedom to be had in this world, Selene." He kissed her cheek, a strangely gentle movement.

Selene shoved him again. The possibility of being stronger—almost as strong as him, strong enough to stop him from overrunning her—dangled in front of her.

This time he didn't even move. "Next time," he said quietly, his dark head dipping down, lips trailing over her jaw, "hit me with Power as well as physical force, Selene. Anything else is useless."

"Get away from me," she gasped.

"There is an hour and a half until dawn." His lips moved against her jawline. Selene's cheeks flamed. Her knees threatened to buckle. "I suggest we spend the time doing something pleasant. I have waited, and I have made you immortal, Selene. I risked losing you far too many times. I will not lose you now to a fledgling's bloodsick despair."

"Doesn't anything ever stop you?" She sagged against the wall. *And could I have, if I didn't stop? Why did I stop?* "Why won't you just leave me *alone?*"

"There is no comfort in alone," he repeated, and peeled her away from the wall. She let him, then erupted into wild motion, kicking, screaming, her teeth clicking together as she tried to bite him. He backhanded her, his hand blurring, her head snapping to the side. Blood flew—her lip was cut. "*Stop*, Selene. Now."

She found herself crumpled on the floor, shaking her head to clear it. A gigantic shivering sound like the inside of a huge brass bell filled her head and receded, leaving a disorienting weakness in its wake.

Nikolai crouched before her, his hands hanging loosely. "That is a Master's *command* over a fledgling. Disobey me again, I will use it again. Stand up."

The bell rang again, her entire body shaking with the inaudible, world-cracking sound. Selene found herself swaying on her bare feet. Nikolai caught her, his arms closing like a steel trap. "Shhh," he crooned, "it isn't so hard, is it, to cry on me instead of a pillow? Trust me a little, a very little. Please, Selene. *Help* me."

*Me? Help him? Is he crazy?* Selene crumpled, folding into him. He moved back a little, as if surprised, and his arms tightened. The stone egg of grief in her chest cracked completely open. "*Danny...*" It was a long, drawn-out moan.

Nikolai held her, stroking her hair. He moved slightly, rocking from side to side, making a low thrumming noise that shook her bones into jelly. She sobbed into his shirt, messily and completely, while he crooned to her, occasionally stopping to kiss the top of her head and whisper soothing nonsense in whatever harshly musical native tongue he used just for her.

# FIFTEEN

"KRISTIAN MULLER." SELENE stared up into the red velvet. Nikolai traced the curve of her ribs, spread his hand against her side. His skin slid against hers, two perfect textures. Selene caught her breath. "I wanted to visit him, see what he knew. Danny wrote that G. was coming to collect the Seal, and..." She gasped again when Nikolai's hand trailed fire across her belly. Her eyes were dry and full of sand, her cheeks raw and inflamed. Even a Nichtvren couldn't cry prettily.

Dawn was coming. Lead weighed her arms and legs, started creeping up her limbs.

"G as in Grigori." Nikolai set the manila folder on the nightstand. The picture of Grigori stared up until he turned it over and tightened his arms around her.

Selene shuddered. Her head moved slightly against his shoulder. She shut her eyes. "I guess so. Grigori killed Danny. Played with him and killed him."

"It would appear so. Grigori stole from the Sitirrismi, they contracted me to bring the Seal back without telling me who had stolen it. I contracted Danny to find it, he stole from Grigori, and Grigori... *You* were expected to be at his apartment, Selene."

*Cold... Lena, don't...don't... Danger...* Danny's voice on the phone echoed in memory. The smell of the rain, the heat of her panic as she raced to his apartment—the front hall, bloodsoaked and scattered with little bits. *Nikolai said Danny was shot before...that.* A shiver spilled through her. Nikolai was silent. *I hope so. Jesu, I hope it was quick for him.* "What if Grigori *was* in the apartment? If I hadn't run across Bruce I might have been there earlier, and he alerted you, didn't he? Or if I'd caught a cab, I'd have been there."

Nikolai's hand tensed. "I owe both Stirling and the cab service distinct gratitude, then." He didn't sound as amused as he usually did. He sounded, in fact, like he had something in his throat.

*I don't have to breathe. Why am I yawning?* "Nikolai?"

"Hmm?" He moved, his hair sliding against the pillowcase and making a low sweet sound. His lips met her temple.

"When I...fed from you, I saw—no. I *felt* like...or maybe I saw something, like it was a dream."

He was utterly still. "A dream?"

"I was tied to a post and being whipped while they screamed for me to recant." She swallowed dryly. "Is that where the scars come from?"

Nikolai didn't move. The silence returned, and she knew it had been the wrong question to ask. If there were any right questions, she hadn't learned what they were, and he probably wouldn't answer them anyway.

*Just like a Nichtvren.*

Selene finally sighed. *I don't know why I even try.* It took every scrap of energy she had left to hitch her hip up, as if she was about to move away. "Fine. Keep your secrets."

"No." His arm tightened under her head. He pushed her hip back down with his free hand. "I do not like to speak of it. Before I was Turned...yes. I was tied to a stake and lashed as a heretic." His voice was low and even, emotionless. "It was dusk." The rhythm of another language wore through the English, accenting strangely. "There were dark clouds in the sky. Dark comes early in winter, that far north. Then Kelaios Grigorivitch Grigori came."

"He saved you?" The blackness of approaching dawn swamped her. She couldn't feel her hands anymore, or her legs.

He kissed her temple again, the touch burning through the lassitude creeping up her body. "Yes." Very softly. "But you see, it was Grigori who arranged for the punishment when I would not submit to him. He wished me broken so he could Turn me. But the torture, starvation and whipping was too much for mortal flesh, he had no choice but to Turn me unbroken. He thought he could finish the process at his leisure."

Selene would have spoken, but the blackness was closing over her head like deep water.

The last thing she heard was Nikolai's sigh. "I will not lose you to him, Selene. I swear it."

Irritation flooded her. *Goddammit, Nikolai. As if I'm a bicycle chained to a rack, and you don't want him making off with me.* But the words refused to come.

Darkness, then. Dawn.

# SIXTEEN

SELENE FOUGHT UPWARDS through sleep, layer after layer of black water, sand swirling in darkness, the sound of Nikolai's voice. He was saying something very important, but she couldn't quite hear. A ragged tone she'd never heard from him.

Fire, a lash laid along her nerves. She cried out weakly, her body convulsing. The feeling was familiar. Movement, the taste of him in her mouth, his fangs brushing hers and sending a jolt of pleasure down her spine.

Selene moaned into his mouth, her hips arching up. He slid into her, exquisite friction, and her eyes half-opened, drifted closed again, drowning. His breath ran into hers, shallow and labored. She arched her back and he murmured, soothingly, said something harsh and accented like poetry. Then his mouth broke away, kissed down her throat.

*Don't.* Selene knew what was coming, tears slipping out of her eyes. "Nikolai," she whispered. *Please...*

His hips slid down, driving into her, and his fangs drove into her throat at the same moment.

Selene's breath tore out of her in a long howling scream, her entire body shaking, shivering to bits. Power exploded along her nerves, sparking, swirling, filling all the empty hollows and bleeding out in a spreading haze of gasflame light. Sparks popped, showering from her skin.

He didn't take much, just a single mouthful, but the pulling against her veins sent another jolting tide of flame through her. His fangs slid free while she was still bucking under him, her entire body flushed with sweet sugared volcanic heat.

"Feed," he whispered in her ear. "*Feed*, Selene."

Her own fangs slid free, and he bent lower, thrusting into her so that she arched her back and gasped again. "Feed," he repeated, and Selene dug her fingers into his back, pulling him down. Her fangs broke his skin and blood sprang free, burst into her mouth.

Nikolai stiffened, a hoarse scream wrenching out of him. Blood and Power mixed, drove through Selene's nerves, she drank until Nikolai collapsed onto her, spent. Her fangs retracted, easing free of his flesh. She lapped at the small wound, once, twice, her tongue rasping. Nikolai shuddered, and she blinked.

*What a way to wake up.* She hugged him, his weight sinking into her. *Good thing I don't have to breathe. Wow.*

"Stay with me," she whispered. "Don't fall asleep. I hate that." As if he ever had. A small prickle of chill ran down her skin.

Nikolai laughed, surprising her, kissed her temple. He shook slightly, his entire body trembling. "Time," he said into her sweat-damp hair. "How many nights I have waited, and now I have no *time*."

"What's going on?" Her body sparkled, purring with Power. *God, that was something else. I had no idea.*

"Grigori will come tonight. Or I will find him." Nikolai kissed her temple again, slowly slid to the side. The bed accepted his weight, silk moving slick and cold against her skin. "Jorge and Netley are taking the Seal to the Sitirrismi."

Selene nodded, her hair stuck to her forehead in sweat-soaked little curls. "Good riddance to the goddamn thing." Her heart was beginning to slow down. "You're not keeping it?"

"Of course not. I never wanted it in the first place. I simply wanted it *located*, since it had been stolen from them. Then Danny stole it from the thief, and so you see."

*Here we are. Why am I not trying to get away from you?* Selene rolled onto her side, propped herself up on her elbow. The silk and velvet slid away, she yanked at it, clutched the sheet to her chest. "Grigori stole it in the first place."

Nikolai lay on his back, his chest rising and falling with deep breaths. His eyes were half-lidded. His black hair raveled wetly over his forehead. A low rumbling sound emanated from him.

*Purring.* Selene realized, and wondered why she wasn't shivering. *Nichtvren purr sometimes. What just happened? I'm not thirsty at all.* Her entire body glowed.

Literally glowed. When Selene held her hand up, her skin shimmered alabaster in the dim light from the red-lace lamp. *I'm a goddamn night-light. And you...you protected me. It was you in my head, when Grigori started rummaging through my brain. You kept me from having to feed in alleys and bars, you scared off everyone who might have thought of hurting me...and I still want Grigori and you to fucking deal with each other.*

*You know, Nikolai, this is a seriously messed-up relationship. If it even qualifies as one. The sex is great, but the rest of this sucks.*

He appeared deep in thought. "I have given the matter careful consideration. The Sitirrismi were once the only force on earth the Nichtvren feared. It would be like Grigori to challenge them to prove his survival."

"*Were* the only force on earth? And what the hell *is* the Seal anyway?"

"It holds one of the Greater Words of Awakening." Nikolai laced his fingers behind his head. Selene rested her cheek on her hand and watched him. *I should be getting up and getting dressed and getting the hell out of here.*

Instead, she made sure the sheet and comforter were pulled up over them both, smoothing the velvet over his chest. The texture was soothing; he didn't move but seemed to arch slightly into her touch anyway. *Where would I go? Both of them would come after me, and isn't that a prospect to make a girl tremble.* "So it what, raises the dead? I thought the Sitirrismi messed around with time."

"Among other things. The Seal holds its own curse, though. It consumes the one who uses it." Nikolai watched her hand moving on the coverlet. "Usually...grotesquely. From the inside out."

*Oh, ugh.* "You knew this and you let me haul it around all over hell and creation?" Selene pushed her hair back from her face, stroked the velvet over his chest again, her fingers trailing.

"Your scent covered the marks of the Seal's presence. And you could not unlock it, there was no danger to you." His eyebrows dropped another fraction. "Selene?"

She snatched her hand back, pushed herself upright, yanking the sheet up. "Okay. Well, I'd guess we'd better get started, then. If this guy killed my brother, I want him dead." *And you too. But I'd give you a pass if you would just quit messing with my head and my hormones. Not to mention controlling every little thing I do.*

"You will stay here in the nest. I will dispose of Grigori." He lay very still, Selene glanced back over her shoulder to find him still watching her.

"What if he 'disposes of' *you?*" She slid her legs out from under the covers. Pale, perfect skin over her knees, still with that foxfire glow. *I don't suppose Nichtvren shave.* "What about that?"

"I killed him once, or close enough to send him underground to recover for a long time. And I am no longer a fledgling. In any case, you will be safe here."

"No. He killed *my* brother." Her voice bounced off the walls, made the velvet on the bed rustle. *You are not going to control me any longer, Nikolai. I've got some power now, I might as well use it.*

"My grudge with him is older." Nikolai still lay on his back, his eyes heavy-lidded. The pale expanse of his chest showed, muscle flickering under the skin. "You will stay here, *dorogaya moya.*"

"You can't make me," she pointed out. "Go ahead and use your magic-command thing on me. I'll just wait and escape you later. You'll have to tie me up permanently to keep me here. Grigori won't have to kill you if you keep this up. *I'll* do it." *Come on, Nikolai. Be reasonable, for once.*

Nikolai sat up, a single fluid motion. The coverlet fell away, pooling between them. "You seem determined to harm yourself despite all my care." He touched her shoulder, ran his fingers down her bare back. Selene closed her eyes, exhaling. His fingers burned all the way down to her bones, pleasantly, as if she was an instrument and his the hand of a master musician. "If I *asked* you to stay, Selene, would you?"

Surprised, she leaned back into his touch. *Well, that's a distinct improvement.* "I can't. Any more than *you* would if I announced I was going to go and get medieval on this Grigori guy all by my lonesome." The thought made her flinch. *There's no way. He's too scary.* Remembered pain bit at her wrists, her head throbbed once, remembering his pale mental fingers slipping through the inside of her skull. "I told him I wanted you dead, and all the way out of my life."

His fingers stopped their steady caressing. "And?"

Her throat was dry, she swallowed against the lump lodged right above the notch where her collarbones met. "I guess the first place I ran to get away from him was here." Her eyes squeezed shut, hearing Grigori's silt-dark, painful voice. *Six hundred years he served me... I want him back. I want him fettered at my feet as I break that regrettable pride of his.* She scrubbed her hands together, trying to rub away the burning settling into her wrists. "All I could think of was...what if you weren't home? Jesu, Nikolai. Don't try to make me stay here. Danny..." Her voice broke, she had to swallow hard. Took a deep breath, rubbed her hands together. "Besides, I'm not entirely useless. I know how to use a gun."

"Grigori—" he began, but she shook her head, her hair brushing her cheeks. The crisped bits were gone, her hair was a little shaggier but so silky it seemed not to matter.

"Yeah, I know. Won't do any good against him. But what about all the werecain? Huh? And I know how to cast Power." She laced her fingers together and squeezed to stop them shaking.

"Too dangerous." Nikolai shifted his weight. It was a small, restless movement. "No, Selene. Please."

She shrugged. *Are we actually having a discussion instead of him giving orders and me whining? My God. It's a miracle. And far too fucking late to make any difference.* "I'll either go with you or follow you. If I go with you, you'll know where I am and be able to keep an eye on me, right?"

Nikolai resumed stroking her back, his fingers scorching-hot. The entire room rattled with silence. "This presents an interesting choice. Do I risk your enmity by ensuring your safety, or do I risk losing you to your foolish pride?"

*What does it matter if I hate you? You never cared how I felt before.* "Look at it this way." Selene shook away from his hand and stood up, letting the covers fall back on the bed. "If you be a good boy and take me along, I'll let you help me get dressed." *How about that? Isn't that the way to get around you?*

Nikolai sighed. "Grigori warned me never to make a fledgling." The bed creaked as he levered himself out of its embrace. Selene ran her fingers back through her hair, grimacing as it tangled. "He told me, *they break your heart.*"

"Considering that you want to kill him, it was probably good advice," Selene heard herself say, and flinched slightly. *I'm talking to him as if I know him.*

Amazingly enough, Nikolai laughed. He paced around the bed and took her shoulders, turned her to face him. His hands were gentle, so she didn't fight him. He ran his palms up her shoulders, up her neck, and cupped her face in his hands. Selene drew in a sharp startled breath.

He looked thoughtful, his eyebrows drawn together, no gold-green catshine over his pupils. Her entire body was liquid, and she leaned into him. *He used to be cold. Why is he so warm now? Because he Turned me?*

*Why don't I want to back away?*

"I do not want your enmity, dear one," he said, very quietly. "Grigori earned mine and to spare, I do not wish for yours. Why such stubbornness?"

A fine tremor ran down Selene's entire body. His face seemed suddenly familiar. *How the hell did I get here? I just spent the day sleeping next to a Nichtvren, again. And now I'm actually insisting on going with him.* "I'm not stubborn." Her voice sounded very small. "You're just a manipulative, spoiled sucktooth."

His lips thinned, turned up at the corners. The corners of his eyes crinkled slightly. Oddly enough, the smile didn't make Selene want to back up and find something to hide behind. "Be kind to me," he murmured. Leaned forward, and kissed her forehead. "I am at your mercy, *milaya.*"

Power settled over Selene, a thick warm cloak of it. "Don't think we're going out or anything. You—"

Nikolai stiffened. His spine straightened, and he cocked his head as if listening. The air stilled, dust settling and scorching, Selene gasped. She tried to pull away, but he held her still, as casually as he might hold an inanimate object. "Someone's here," he said. "Get dressed, Selene, and come with me."

He let her go. Selene stumbled back, regained her balance, crossed her arms defensively over her breasts.

"Do you have anything that will fit me?"

≈≈

"*NIKOLAI!*" A CRASH, something breaking. "Goddamn you! *Nikolai!*"

Selene followed Nikolai's back through the dim halls. Hardwood floors thudded beneath her boots. Nikolai moved soundlessly, blurring through space, the chill breeze of his passing ruffling velvet curtains and brushing against antiques set in niches.

"*Nikolai!*"

*It's Rigel. What the hell?*

The hallway opened up, and Nikolai moved silently down one of the staircases that led into the foyer. Selene followed, looking down over the balustrade.

Rigel stood in the middle of the checkerboard squares of marble flooring the foyer. A huge porcelain vase—it had been standing on a cherrywood table by the door—lay in dust-ground pieces on the floor. There was a tide of spilled water, the heavy scent of the lilies crushed under Rigel's boots vying with the heatless static of Power in the air.

He whirled as soon as Nikolai became visible, the gun coming up. "Nikolai," he said, hoarsely.

*He's a mess.* Selene gasped. Rigel's face was bruised and torn, blood threading down from his nose and the corner of one eye, and he held his free hand clamped to his ribs, where blood leaked out and down his shredded jeans. The entire left side of his lean face was covered in blood from a deep gash along his scalp. The smell of the blood rose, mixed with the smell of the flowers, and made Selene's fangs ache slightly. His long black coat was torn and scorched, and the powerful additional stink of violence, smoke, and fury that clung to him was enough to make Selene's eyes prickle. For a moment, she saw something like a skitter of Power around him, then it was gone. She wondered, once again, just what he was.

Nikolai barely paused at the bottom of the stairs. Selene saw the tensing in his shoulders and arrived behind him, her hand shooting out and catching his arm. He stopped, so quickly she almost ran into him.

*Wow.* Her eyes fastened on her pale hand on his arm, too slender and frail to stop a Master Nichtvren in his tracks.

"They took her." Rigel sounded like his throat had been scraped out. "Goddamn you, they *took* her. I'll pay you. I'll pay you anything you want, they *took* her!"

Selene's heart dropped into her stomach. "Oh, Jesu," she said. "Marina? Rigel, who took her?" She tried to slide around Nikolai, but he was suddenly right in front of her, crowding her back up another step or two. She hadn't even seen him move.

"Who took her?" Nikolai's voice sliced right through hers.

Rigel dropped the hand holding the gun to his side. "I don't know who they're bloody well working for, why do you think I'm here? It was werecain. A lot of them. They knocked her out, or she was...God, I don't know." Rigel's sallow face was dead white except for two fever-spots high on his cheeks, his dark hair matted down with blood. "I swear to God, Nikolai, I will pay you anything you want, *anything.*"

"Oh, Christos. So Grigori had a plan B." Selene tried to go past Nikolai, again found herself shoved back. *Oh, for God's sake.* "He's not going to shoot me, Nikolai, will you just *quit* it?"

"Put the gun down, Rigel." Nikolai's tone crackled through the foyer, dust skipping over the marble floor. The spilled water rilled out in a pattern of interlocking triangles, evaporating with a slight *phssht.* "Then we will bargain."

"Bargain?" Selene pushed at Nikolai's shoulders with both hands. Even with a Nichtvren's strength, she accomplished exactly nothing. "Nikolai!"

Rigel's hand holding the gun twitched. His gaze flicked over Nikolai, met Selene's. "I'll pay whatever you want." Rigel's accent made the words crisp and clear. "I swear it. Bring her back alive, and I'm yours."

"It is not like you to offer such a bargain, thrall," Nikolai said, and Rigel's chin dropped. He was breathing harshly, painfully. Blood dripped down from his nose, slid over his lip, pattered on the floor.

"For Christos's sake, Nikolai." Selene shoved at his shoulders again. "He loves her, goddammit, and she's a friend— *my* friend! Will you just *quit* it? Come on, let's go!"

"Rushing headlong after the healer will accomplish exactly nothing." Nikolai's voice could have frozen water. "*Verscht za?* For you, Rigel, you'll accept my service again, though the healer shall have the use of you. Accepted?"

Selene was possessed of the sudden irresistible urge to grab a handful of Nikolai's crow-black hair and yank it as hard as she could. "Nikolai, you bastard, quit playing the Nichtvren and get your ass in gear!"

"Accepted." Rigel yelled over her words. "Just get her back, Nikolai. Just bloody well get her back or I'll—"

His eyes fluttered up under his eyelids and he slumped.

A confused flurry of motion ended up with Selene catching him, his weight slight in her new Nichtvren-muscled arms and Nikolai subtracting the gun from Rigel's fingers. Selene eased him to the floor and heard footsteps. *Thralls. Summoned by Nikolai. Why didn't he before?*

"He must have fought them." Nikolai checked the gun absently, then laid it aside. His pale fingers felt Rigel's pulse. "Like a wolf, hmm?"

"What is he?" The floor was hard and far too cold under her knees. "He's too quiet to be human, but he doesn't smell paranormal."

Nikolai shrugged. "Ask him later." The footsteps drew closer. Voices rang—someone calling Nikolai's name, a panicked sound, high-pitched excitement. "You will need body-armor, Selene." He touched Rigel's forehead with two fingers. Blood marked his pale hand. His black silk T-shirt shifted as the muscle underneath moved. "We must be calm. The *sedayeenen* is valuable, Grigori will not harm her. Ease yourself." A curious look passed over his sharply handsome face. "What did you say of him?" He pointed at Rigel's bruised face.

Selene held Rigel's shoulders. *He's so light.* She pushed blood-crusted hair back from his forehead. *Christos, he's really messed up. Poor guy. Lucky Marina.* "What?"

He shook his head, dismissing it. "She is your friend, the *sedayeenen?*"

"Yeah," Selene said. *She was the only one who would help me, and he helped me because he loves her. I wish I...well, never mind. It's not like I'm not used to it.* "Is that a reason for you to rescue her?" The accusation in her tone tasted like sharp lemon.

Nikolai shrugged, holding the gun loosely. "Perhaps. I seem to be a fool for your pleasure, *nenaglyadnaya*. Besides, she is valuable." His voice was cold. He stood up, looming over her with the gun held loosely to one side, Selene twitched, pulling Rigel a little closer as if to protect him.

Nikolai's face closed with an almost audible snap as the slim blond thrall Selene had seen once before skidded into the foyer. "Master? News. The city, we've lost the clinic and two of your downtown holdings. Gutted, fire—"

"Call everyone," Nikolai snapped. "War on any paranormal who is not personally allied with me. Kill them all, God will know His own."

Selene gasped. The blond man glanced at her, then nodded, sharply. "Yes, Master. And him?" He meant Rigel.

"Send Eric. This thrall needs some care." Nikolai paused. "And be careful of my temper," he added, very softly. "I am not safe just now. Selene, leave him be, he will survive. Come."

The blond man nodded, spun on his heel, and was gone. There was an excited babble of voices.

Selene lay Rigel gently down on the marble, cradling his head. The thin man's pulse thudded strongly in his neck and temple, he would live. Nikolai wouldn't lie. "You'll take care of him?"

Nikolai rounded on her, his eyes completely black and sparking with green-gold shine. "Do you *doubt* my word?" That same cold soft voice that changed the air into black knives. "*Do you?*"

Selene's entire back rippled with gooseflesh. She opened her mouth, meaning to scream at him, but what came out instead was, "Don't talk to me like that. I only asked." Her tone was flat and she folded her arms so he wouldn't see her hands shaking.

Nikolai studied her for a long moment. All the air in the foyer drained away. The chandelier tinkled restlessly overhead. Then he nodded. "*Da,*" he murmured. "My apologies, dear one."

Selene's mouth dried out, her fangs aching and tender. She forced herself to take a step, another, and ended up facing him across barely a foot of space, her face tilted up to his and her fingers biting into her arms. *Miracles do happen.* She studied his face. *Did he just apologize to me? I think that's the first time I've ever heard him apologize to anyone.* "If you want me to stay with you for even a few minutes," she said, quietly, still in that new, calm voice she had just found, "you're going to have to treat me like a person instead of a fucking slave."

He stared at her, one muscle in his pale, smooth cheek twitching. *He never has to shave.* A flush spread up her cheeks. He watched her face as if he was trying to decode it. The same way she was watching his.

"Even for your own good?" The muscle twitched again.

*For Christos's sake.* "You can ask instead of ordering. I'm a reasonable person, Nikolai. Treat me like one."

A long pause, something new rising in the air between them. "You will need body-armor," he repeated. "Come with me." But some essential coldness had drained from his tone.

"Okay." She swallowed the human dryness from her mouth. *Is that all it takes?*

*Don't get cocky. It's like playing with a hand-grenade. He's old, and powerful, and he could just as easily turn on me.* "But don't talk to me that way, okay? It scares me."

Nikolai paused. Then, sharply, he nodded. It was a short sharp efficient movement. But when he spoke, his tone was infinitely gentle. "Then I will not speak so, *lyubimaya.*"

He held out his hand.

Rigel sighed behind her, a shapeless unconscious sound. Another set of footsteps sounded.

A tall man in a species of gray caftan, with an amazing shock of white-blond hair and a massive hooknose, paced out into the foyer. "Oh, look at this. Leaving a wounded man on the floor, Nikolai? *Really.*" He carried a first-aid kit in a blue metal box.

Selene's fingers closed over Nikolai's. He didn't look away from her face. "Take good care of him, Eric. There will be other wounded."

"Hrmph." The thrall made a sound halfway between a sniff and a grunt. He crossed the floor, his feet shushing over marble. "Go and break some bones or something. I think I've gone a whole week without pulling someone back from the brink of death, I was beginning to miss it." He dropped down next to Rigel and made a clucking sound. "Oh, look at this mess. Just *look* at this mess."

Selene's entire body flushed. Nikolai pulled on her hand, gently, and she followed him into the house.

# SEVENTEEN

HER HEART POUNDED in her throat. "This itches," she said, shifting uncomfortably.

He finished buckling his boot and glanced up at her. "Hm?"

"Why aren't you carrying any guns? And what about—"

He held up the sword in its sheath, shrugging so the long black leather coat fell correctly. "This is all I require. In my day, a nobleman carried nothing else, and counted it an honor." He glanced across the room.

The room was long and low, mirrors along one wall, windows along another, woven mats over some of the floor. Wooden walls held racks of weapons. A ballet barre was bolted to the mirrored wall.

People came and went, exchanging brief terse sentences. One woman with a ruff of sleek dark hair and a bandolier of knives strapped across her ample chest checked clips on a pair of nine-millimeters and slid them into holsters, her tanned face drawn into a thoughtful smile. The blond thrall Selene kept seeing—*Enrique*, she reminded herself—took an M-16 from the tall dreadlocked Bradley, who had a smear of white face paint on each cheek. *I had no idea he had so many thralls.* And they were all so competent, so thoroughly-prepared.

And they *trusted* Nikolai. They didn't seem afraid of him, but there was never a pause when he gave a command. They simply did what he told them, without any struggle but also without any sense of being forced. It was amazing, especially since Selene had heard all sorts of horror stories, here and there, about what a Master could inflict on his or her thralls.

Bradley, his dreadlocks bobbing, slipped between two small Asian men, one of whom wore what looked like a long black cassock with a Chinese collar. He crossed the huge expanse of floor, skirting a group of people buckling on gunbelts.

The prevailing fashion was black leather, with a sprinkling of camouflage. There was a small but definite proportion of women, who tended to dress very simply, without some of the flamboyant touches the men sported—Bradley's face-paint, the man who had what looked like dog-tags sewn onto the inside of his coat, the man with a bare Celtic-tattooed skull. One woman, tall and stick-thin with muscle rippling under her skin, shrugged into a leather harness and started making various weapons from the wall racks disappear into the harness and her clothes. Her short blonde hair slicked to her head with gel, she had the fair clear-skinned face of a Nordic princess.

Bradley reached the edge of what seemed to be Nikolai's personal space and stopped, bowing slightly. "We're ready." His dreadlocks bobbed. "The cars are waiting. Netley called. He's made the drop-off, Jorge is bringing him back."

Nikolai nodded. "Very well, then. Proceed as planned. Kill everything and everyone not explicitly allied to me. The Guard?"

"Ready and waiting." Bradley waited a beat. "It's been a pleasure, sir."

Nikolai inclined his head slightly. "On my part as well, Bradley. May our gods protect us."

"Amen to that," Selene muttered. Nikolai had found jeans, a tank top, a hip-length leather coat for her—black leather, of course—and a pair of combat boots that fit. *I'm dressed like I should know what I'm doing.* She swallowed against the sudden taste of copper in her mouth. Her wrists twinged, remembering Grigori's chains and the burning. *Give my regards to Nikolai.*

*Be careful, Selene.* Danny's voice whispered inside her head. The All-Dead Hit Parade just kept going.

Bradley made that slight bow again, and his face broke into a wide grin. He looked at Selene, his teeth very white in his dark face. He bounced back across the room, his own black leather trench coat shushing as he moved.

"You guys certainly have a weird fashion statement." Selene licked her lips. "Kind of like *kickass* mixed with *my mommy made me wear this.*" The guns were heavy, and the knife-sheath dug into her hip a little until she shifted. The Kevlar was uncomfortable, and if she'd been human she would have been sweating.

*If I was human I'd be a little puddle on the floor.* She bit her lower lip gently. The aura of fear, anticipation, and adrenaline in the air mixed with Power, hit the back of her throat like vodka and burned in her stomach like brandy going down.

Nikolai's gaze moved over the crowd of people at the far end of the room. His lips moved soundlessly. Was he praying?

Selene sighed, closed her eyes, and tipped her head back. *I wish we could just get this OVER with.* She took a deep breath. Another, and years of practice took over. The still quiet spot where magick lived folded around her.

Her shields were much thicker now, flexible stone instead of brittle glass. The glow of Power was much stronger, too, lining her entire body in a shimmer, Nikolai a red-tinged swirling at her side, little fingers of his awareness slipping around her, a thick pulsing rope of *connection* stretched between her foxfire glow and his spreading blur of Power. *That's a blood link.* She pulled back, opening her eyes.

So he *did* have a psychic connection to her. Sex, blood, and the Turn had cemented it; no wonder he'd always seemed to know where she was before. *You sneaky bastard.* And yet, after seeing how his thralls trusted him, and hearing him actually apologize to her, and seeing how bad Grigori was...

Well, Nikolai hardly seemed like the devil she'd known before.

Warring with that new perception was the fervent desire that he and Grigori would just hash something out that ended with everyone leaving her alone. And with Grigori dead as a doornail.

"Come," Nikolai finally said. "Leave everything to me, you must simply stay close."

She nodded. Her fangs pulsed in anticipation, she was slowly getting used to how sensitive they were. "Okay." *I wish I could stay here.* A shiver tightened the skin on her scalp. *How do I get into these things?*

Everyone was leaving. The tall Nordic-looking woman clapped Bradley on the back and paced out of the room, soundless. In the few moments it took Selene and Nikolai to cross the room, everyone, including Bradley, was gone. Power still echoed and boomed silently through the empty space.

*It's Nikolai. He's doing it. He was always so goddamn careful before, he treated me with kid gloves and I didn't even know it.*

"What if Grigori..." She swallowed the rest of the question. *What if he kills you? What if he kills both of us? What if—*

"He will not." Nikolai's voice was flat and matter-of-fact.

"What if we don't find Marina?" *I sound scared to death. What a coincidence, I am scared nearly to death. Go figure.* And now that the fear didn't send a spill of red-laced desire through her, she wasn't quite sure how to handle it. Was this what other people had felt instead of sex? How did they stand it?

How could she stand it, now?

*Stop your bitching, Selene. Just focus on the matter at hand.*

Nikolai's hand found hers, his fingers slipping through hers. The touch was warm, and oddly comforting. "Courage, *dorogaya moya.* Grigori wants us to find her. It would do him little good to take her otherwise."

# EIGHTEEN

*IT'S A GOOD thing I don't have to tell him he was right about the body-armor.* Selene gapped her mouth, so her breath eased soundlessly past her teeth. Her left arm ached fiercely; Nikolai had wrenched her out of the burning car on Sixth Street, glass crunching under his boots. The smell of the docks—seawater, a slight breeze coming from the salt expanse, petroleo and oil and the stench of ships and iron—didn't even begin to cover the reek of the werecain prowling around the tanker looming up before them, its bulk blocking out the night sky.

Sirens howled all through the city. Fire, police, ambulance. It was shaping up to be an interesting night for everyone.

The man on her left side let out a soundless sigh. He was Indigenous, wearing body-armor very similar to Selene's, his dark hair pulled back in a ponytail. He held an assault rifle, and there was a huge Bowie knife strapped to his leg.

*I don't even want to ask.* Selene touched Nikolai's shoulder. He didn't move, his attention on the tanker. It exhaled a cold breath of Power out into the night, and chill unease touched her nape. They were tucked out of sight, waiting, the rest of Nikolai's Guard—roughly a dozen men who appeared never to speak unless they absolutely *had* to—had peeled off and vanished into the night. All of them wore streaky black paint on their faces and hands except for the man next to her, who settled back into the wooden wall they were up against and closed his eyes.

Grigori had stayed on the docks, the only place where the interference of so much cold iron and ambient Power from the water would hide him from Nikolai's sense of the city as a living, breathing thing. Selene privately thought that it was stupid for Grigori to be where Nikolai would expect him to be, but...then again, they hadn't found the other Nichtvren yet.

She shivered. *You have no manners. I'd half like to teach you some,* Grigori's voice whispered in her memory.

*I hope we can just grab Marina and get out.* Selene set her teeth, heat bubbling under her breastbone, the medallion scorching as well. *He killed Danny.* The heat changed to a hard lump of ice against her heart. *Don't chicken out now, Selene. You've come this far.*

Nikolai was completely still. Selene had to look twice to see him, even though he stood close enough to touch, a deeper blot of shadow in the darkness. It was just past midnight. A fine mist drizzled over the city, night folding like a blanket over the streets.

The werecain had attacked on Sixth Street, and Selene could still taste copper adrenaline at the back of her tongue. *Me and my luck with cars.* Her mind jagged nervously from one thought to the next.

*I've never seen anyone move that fast.* She looked at the curve of Nikolai's cheek as he studied the jumble of wooden boxes on the pier, cargo stacked here and there, werecain prowling from shadow to shadow. He looked calm, and his pulse was unhurried. He held Selene's hand again, his thumb occasionally stroking over the inside of her wrist and sending a slight shiver down her back, heat sinking into her. *He tore the throats out of three werecain without even looking like it was work. He looked bored while he did it. God, I've really underestimated him.*

*That's a good thing now. The devil I know, instead of Grigori.* Selene shivered again. The cold fingers of unease walked up and down her spine, gooseflesh breaking out on her back, her nipples drawing up and tightening, muscles tensing.

*Something's very wrong here.*

She opened her mouth to whisper, but Nikolai squeezed her hand and moved forward soundlessly. She followed, trying to move quietly, shifted from foot to foot, eerily silent. It was a hunter's instinct, a predator's benefit to a Nichtvren.

Once he was sure she was following, Nikolai let go of her hand with one last gentle squeeze. *Now that I've seen how strong he is, I think I'm going to appreciate him being gentle a little more.*

Just a little.

A new thought struck. *How strong am I? How long would it take me to get as strong as he is?*

*And what would I do if I was?*

Selene slipped the gun out of her right holster. Behind her, the other man drifted, following. He was quiet too, for a human.

Nikolai edged around another corner and slid into the shadow of a stack of wooden crates. Selene's fingers lay on the outside of the trigger guard, and she held the gun low and ready, just like Jack had taught her.

The other man held his breath. A werecain in huntform— dropping down to all fours, its massive unlovely head swinging back and forth with its gait—prowled past them, its yellow-glowing eyes fixed straight ahead.

Nikolai was gone. A dark shape streaked soundlessly past the werecain, a single flicker of steel, and the huge furred body dropped with a barely audible thud, a thin wet sound bubbling up. He had slit its throat in one movement. Blood burst out along the pavement.

Then Nikolai was back, nodding at the other man, and they left the shelter of the stack of boxes.

The dock muttered under Selene's feet, wood creaking as water lapped at its underbelly. Her body automatically shifted weight with every slight movement, as if she was walking on the surface of a drum. Behind her, the man's pulse sped up slightly. Her nostrils flared. The smell of werecain was so deep and thick here she was grateful when her nose shut off and she could no longer smell it. Her hand shook slightly, a fine tremor she didn't like the feel of.

*Stay quiet. Just stay quiet. We've been lucky.*

Light seared her night-adapted eyes. Selene flung up her hand, a short cry escaping her. The sound was lost in the sudden roar of gunfire coming from onshore. *They've stopped being quiet.* Instinct threw her body into a crouch.

Nikolai snarled, a single syllable of focused Power. Glass cracked and tinkled, and the light died as suddenly as it had struck.

Running footsteps. Growls. The man behind her fired, one short burst, and something huge thudded to the dock's surface. "*Bogies!*" he yelled, in a surprisingly deep voice.

*No shit, you think?* Selene's eyes cleared enough to see Nikolai move forward again. She ran after him, doing her best to keep up, the narrow gangplank bent under their combined weight.

Something whistled past Selene; she let out a short sharp cry.

*You've got a predator's body,* Danny's voice whispered. *Just let it do the work for you.*

*Lovely. A ghost is giving me survival tips.* Selene's heart hammered. Copper flooded her mouth, her legs pumping. She swung over the side of the boat. Nikolai flashed through a pool of orange light from a deck lamp, the sword a bright length in his hands. Selene's fangs popped free, atavistic rage swelling under her ribs.

The deck was metal, and piled with ropes along one side, the wheelhouse to Selene's right—Nikolai was heading unerringly for it, probably forgetting he'd told her to stay close to him.

Another spate of gunfire, and something hit Selene in the side, driving her down. Her body tucked, rolled, she came up to her feet moving forward, moving, momentum slamming her from behind, sudden flash of light scoring her eyes.

Her left hand swept out, almost of its own volition, claws springing free. The werecain dropped, choking on its own blood. Its eyes were wide, surprised and very blue in the sudden flood of light.

*I did that?* she thought wonderingly, before she was driven behind another pile of wooden boxes by a spattering hail of bullets zinging off the deck.

She landed on hands and knees, the gun skittering away. *Shit!*

Screams. Werecain growls. More gunfire. *He's got thralls as well as werecain,* Danny said. *Selene, you're pinned. Get out, go along the rail side there.*

She obeyed, scrambling, her boots gripping the metal. Bullets pounded the deck behind her. *If I was as old as Nikolai I could ignore a few bullets.* She dove for another cover, a large metal box standing almost at the bow of the ship. Selene heard her own panting, quick and light, and a low thrumming sound that raised every hair on her body.

Over the smells of the ship—werecain, greasy petroleo, stink of iron, the dirty salt smell of the sea—came a breath of violets. And musk.

"*Marina!*" Her voice tore through the chaos of gunfire and snarls. Someone screamed, a long pitiful howling wail. "*Marina!*"

"Here!" A faint answering cry, almost lost under the cacophony. Selene gathered herself and was about to launch her body through the side of the metal box when her eyes snagged on a door.

*I hope it's not locked.* She gave herself a sharp mental slap for being a fool. *Of course it's locked, she'd be out here on deck if it wasn't.* Selene drew her left-hand gun. "Get back from the door!"

"Get me *out* of here!" Marina yelled.

Selene squeezed the trigger.

Her first shot ricocheted off the iron surface, digging a furrow in the red paint. *Goddammit, that always works for everyone else!* Selene swore viciously, and there was an incredible tearing sound from the other end of the ship.

A holocaust of light seared Selene's night-adapted eyes. The shock of the explosion knocked her sideways, skidding along the corner of the huge metal box. Her body twisted, hooking her claws into metal with a screech that would have ground her teeth down to shards if she'd been human. *Oh, Christos, I've lost the other gun, some hero I am.* She landed *hard* against the narrow strip of deck along the box, breath leaving her in a whoosh.

Her claws had torn the metal in six long jagged slices. Selene rolled to her feet, shaking her head, something warm dripping in her right eye. *Goddamn it. Am I going to lose all my hair in this mess?*

Smoke belched across the deck.

Selene made it back to the side of the box. "Marina!" she yelled, hooking her claws in the top slice. The rust-flecked metal was strangely warm. She inhaled—*why am I still breathing?*—and yanked down with one convulsive effort, a long *huuugh!* tearing its way out of her.

Metal groaned.

"I'm here." The healer's face appeared, pale in the lurid orange light exploding up from the ship. Crackling heat swept across Selene's cheek. "Selene? Oh, my God, you've *Turned!*"

*Well, you get fifteen points for stating the fucking obvious.* "Come *on!*" Selene snarled, and lunged in through the rough rectangular hole she'd torn. She grabbed the healer under the arms, just like picking up a little kid, and pulled.

Marina cried out hoarsely. Something clattered. "Rigel?" she gasped, as Selene hauled her bodily out of the box. "Rigel, is he—"

"He's back at the nest!" Selene had to yell over the incredible din. The noise was so huge it speared both eardrums, a painful weight. "Come *on!*"

*A hell of a time to have no weapons,* Danny's voice said snidely.

"If you can't say anything useful shut up!" Selene yelled. It was the crowning absurdity.

The entire ship shuddered. Thick black smoke belched up from the burning end. The bursts of gunfire were sporadic now, but something was snarling close by.

*Werecain.* She gave Marina a quick once-over, pulling her along the side of the ship. Something whined overhead and she pushed the healer down. Marina's long hair was tangled and she was dirty, smelling like werecain, her clothes torn and a stripe of blood on one hand. But she moved okay, and seemed to be otherwise unwounded.

*Great. Now I just have to get her off of here. Where's Nikolai? He said to stay close, but he ran right for the front of the ship, goddammit. Where is he, is he okay?*

They ended up crouching behind a stack of huge metal pipes. Bullets clanged and whined. "Are you okay?" Her throat burned from screaming over the smoke-laden noise.

"I've had better days," Marina called back. "You look *awful.*" Her blue eyes glowed, and her pretty mouth turned down at the corners under its mask of dirt.

*I screwed a Nichtvren this morning and got yanked out of a burning car tonight, and now I'm being shot at, again. No wonder I look like shit.*

"Come on!" She grabbed Marina's arm, careful not to squeeze too hard. "We've got to get you out of here!" *I don't want to disappoint Rigel, honey. You're so fucking lucky it makes my heart hurt.*

Marina nodded, tangled hair swinging down over her dirty face. Selene inhaled, shoved herself to her feet and began to run, carrying the other woman's slight weight with her.

They reached the gangplank. Two of Nikolai's Guard—the Indigenous man and a skinny Italian guy, both firing over the top of a hasty barricade of scrap metal—were holding the ship end of it. Four werecain were darting from the other side, their fur painted luridly by the fire, which sent up another quake of noise and massive fireball.

Selene fell flat. Marina recovered more quickly than she did, hauled her to her feet, and they made it to the shelter of the barricade.

Marina's ribs flared with deep gasping breaths.

*Smoke in the air. Shit. Hope she doesn't get poisoned.* "Is it safe?" Selene yelled, pointing down the gangplank. *Got to get her out of here.*

"They're firing from there!" the Indigenous man yelled back, pointing at a vicious firefight going on further down the deck.

Selene shoved the healer down. "Take care of her." She pivoted on the balls of her feet.

*What are you doing?* Danny's voice screeched at her.

*Something stupid,* Selene thought. *Nikolai went that way, and that's where I'm going, goddammit. Have to do it fast before I lost my nerve.* Her claws sprang free, and her heart gave another frantic burst. The heat was incredible, lying against her skin like oil. *Those werecain are between him and escaping from this hulk of metal, so I'm going to get rid of them.*

*Oh, no.* Danny sounded horrified. *I was afraid you were going to say that.*

Selene leapt.

THE BODY-ARMOR saved her again. The last werecain slammed into her, a furry hulk of rib-snapping force. She went down, claws skritching across her abdomen. Prickling cold hit her and she screamed, her claws fully extended, fangs glittering. She tore at the huge furred thing blindly, instinct tucking her chin down so its teeth couldn't find her throat.

Blood exploded, hot salt spraying up and drenching her face. Selene scrambled, twisting, her boots scraping across metal deck, the heat of the fire popping across her face. The werecain slumped, and she heard a victory yell from the other side of the barricade.

*I hope that's our side.* She didn't stop, her feet pounding the deck, up, *up*, she had to find Nikolai, where the hell was he?

Smoke billowed. The sound of clanging metal.

*What the...* Something seemed to punch her in the stomach, she lost most of her air. *Swords. Jesu.*

There was a sort of wheelhouse—at least, she guessed that's what it was, her maritime experience being nil—between her and the main fire. *Maybe the explosion was the engine. If this thing has a hold full of heavy petroleo we'll all be hashing this out in hell.*

The clanging was coming from the top. Selene spotted a ladder and leapt for it, unprepared for the speed and fluidity of her new body. She almost splatted face first into the ladder and saved herself only by a lunging effort, hitting her forehead on a metal rung that was dangerously warm. Stars flashed across her vision. She scrambled up, muscles beginning to burn, the thirst throbbing. *I'm going to need to feed.* The resultant shiver through her entire body almost tossed her from the ladder.

*Stop thinking with your groin and get up there! Nikolai needs you!*

"*Nikolai!*" The cry escaped her. She vaulted the top of the ladder and landed, amazingly, on her feet.

The fire's carnivorous heat, radiating directly now and not blocked by debris stacked on deck, smacked into her. She dropped to her knees, her eyes watering, and saw.

Nikolai paced back and forth, the sword balanced in his hands, his entire body focused on the other Nichtvren. His hair was scorched and half his face was terribly bruised, almost black, and shiny. *That's not a bruise, it's a burn.* Power pulsed out from them both.

Nikolai's shirt was in tatters. So was Grigori's.

Grigori, the beads in his hair clacking as he moved, circled as Nikolai did. His left arm flopped uselessly. He snarled, fangs extended and dripping with glittering saliva. He held a broadsword, handling the massive length with ease even though it looked dull and clumsy compared to Nikolai's slim shining blade.

*Oh, Christos. I don't have a gun.*

Nikolai moved forward, his burned face expressionless. Metal rang and flexed. The fire belched again, the deck heaved. Grigori closed with Nikolai—the older Nichtvren was bulkier, a few inches taller, and had the fire behind him. Nikolai gave ground, his blade ringing, slashing and feinting.

"Nikolai," Selene whispered. She drove her claws into the roof of the wheelhouse. Her wrists ached. *Nikolai, oh God, be careful. You've got to kill him. You've just GOT to.*

Grigori stumbled, his sword slipping aside, and Nikolai darted in with spooky, graceful speed.

The taller Nichtvren half-whirled, a flurry of movement—and Nikolai's sword flashed away in a high impossible arc. It landed on the wheelhouse roof, chiming, and skittered past Selene, who grabbed for it with unthinking reflexive speed. She had to wrench her claws out of the roofing, and her fingers closed only on air.

The ship heaved again, a fresh explosion rocking the entire massive structure of steel. The high tinkle of glass shattering only added to the booming tearing noise. *Oh, no, please, no—*

Grigori, his face a mask of utter rage, drove his sword into Nikolai's chest.

Nikolai fell backward.

Selene screamed. Some ceaseless spinning pulse inside her that she had never known existed....*stopped.*

Nikolai hit the roof of the wheelhouse and slid back, his limp body fetching up against an air-conditioning vent with a sickening crack. It knocked the housing sideways, the density of his body and the massive force he'd been flung with conspiring like thieves. Selene flinched, her jaw dropping. The medallion gave one scorching burst of heat against her chest.

Grigori tipped his head back and roared. The sound, and the wave of sheer Power accompanying it, would have flung Selene off the roof if her left-hand claws hadn't still been driven in.

She tore them free and leapt. "*Nikolai!*" she screamed, something ugly and hard pressing up behind her heart. It clawed free, this dark and horrible thing, and her palm slapped on the hilt of the broadsword. One twist and a yank, and it was in her hand, its tip black with Nikolai's blood.

"*SELENE!*" Danny's voice, not whispering in the middle of her skull but slicing through the confusion of oily black smoke and crawling flame.

The world slowed to a series of shutter-clicks.

*Click.* "You—" Selene, running, her entire body arched forward, her eyes bulging, her charred hair streaming.

*Click.* "Son—" Her breath jagged in after the word. Grigori's head snapped down. Power snaked for her, a missile of something dead and murderous.

*Click.* "Of a—" Selene leapt. Her chest cracked, her eyes split, her throat tore itself open. A blinding flash of blue-white light. The sharp sudden smell of ozone.

*Click.* "*Bitch!*" The sword curved down, an arc of solid silver.

Grigori flung up his arm. His claws raked for Selene's eyes—

And somehow, incredibly, *missed* as the deck heaved again.

The broadsword made a cracking sound as it clove through his arm and buried itself in Grigori's neck. Selene landed, her boots skidding, and the firecrack of her rage hit like thunder after lightning. *Hit with Power and physical force,* she thought dreamily. Everything was slow, caught in a bubble of stasis. *Anything else is useless.*

Like the glass globe of quiet closing around her when Danny died. A *killing* calm.

The sword drove down cleanly, splintering ribs. Selene heard a noise like the world grinding to a stop. A sheet of orange, oily flame billowed up, and she tossed the hilt away from her in a reflex action that saved her from being dragged into the inferno. Grigori fell backward into the wall of flame, burning like a fatty candle in a camp shack, the beads in his hair cracking and melting. She threw herself back, fighting momentum, the world slowing down, moving through syrup, her body struggling again without thought, claws digging into roofing with a rending sound lost under the bucking explosion of more heavy petroleo going up in flames. The blast actually helped, pushing her back, she rolled, her head smacking something metallic hard enough that her fangs clipped together and she lost a chunk of her lower lip.

*...where am I...*

"*GET UP YOU DUMB BITCH GET UP!*" Danny screamed, a delirium of terror.

*No wonder he's still talking. Maybe he was out of his body when he died.*

That broke her trance. She hauled herself half-upright, saw Nikolai's body, ten feet away. Shook her head, blood flying from her lip, the heat of the fire making her skin feel tight and shiny. Her hair was smoking, she could *smell* it, feel it crisping.

*Fire is every Nichtvren's enemy,* she heard her own voice in a lecture hall, long ago, in another life. *Open flame is the best defense against a Nichtvren gone bad. If any of them can be said to be good, that is.*

The whole class had laughed, and she'd felt gratified. *Leave him. Let him lie there.*

She finally reached him. Nikolai lay still, his burned face tilted back, eyes closed, strangely peaceful, his mouth slack.

Selene's claws dug into his shoulders. She pulled him up, hysterical strength nearly overbalancing both of them. "Don't you goddamn dare die on me!" she heard herself shout, a thin reedy sound, as the boat shuddered again and settled in the water.

Selene hefted Nikolai's limp body and looked around, wildly.

"To your left!" Danny's voice, reedy as a cricket's, almost physical amid the chaos. And the only voice that could have gotten through to her.

She immediately jagged to her left, dragging Nikolai, but her legs were limp noodles and he was so heavy, so heavy. The gunfire had stopped. Sirens were drawing closer. *The cavalry always comes late.* A kind of mad clarity settled over her. *There's a lesson in that, Selene.*

She was still running when the wheelhouse roof gave way underneath her. The speed she'd built up took her in a soaring leap, Nikolai dragged with her, his entire body limp and boneless. When they hit the water, she lost consciousness for a moment.

Blackness closed over her head. She surfaced, thrashing desperately in the water, great foaming chunks of it jetting up and splashing back down. *Am I doing that?* she wondered, and found she was arching for shore. The pier was burning too.

There was another massive ripping sound behind her, and the water steamed. Chunks of metal rained down, flaming bits of wreckage. Selene's arm locked around Nikolai's neck, dragging him.

*There is no comfort in alone,* Nikolai's voice whispered, faint and fading.

"Nikolai." She got a mouthful of seawater with a thick chaser of oil from the burning ship, choked, her lip stinging terribly. Her eyes smarted. Her entire body trembled, a thin fine shuddering made out of wire. "Don't you dare die on me, you bastard." She choked again, spat to clear her mouth. He was utterly limp. She swam for shore, churning at the water, Power bleeding out through her heavy arms and legs. *If I keep this up my heart will stop.*

She kept going.

The waves helped, and once she reached the side of another pier she found a ladder. She clung to it, wondering if she could carry him up.

"Selene!" Marina's voice. A rope, two, *three* ropes coiled down. One of them struck Selene's head, and she shook it away. "Tie him on!"

Selene nodded. Her fingers were cold and terribly numb. Still, she managed to get one rope tied around Nikolai's chest, under his arms. She almost lost him twice, his head falling limply back and his body slipping through her grasp.

When she had it knotted securely, she found herself treading water. "Haul him up," she said, harshly, and heard Nikolai's snap of command in her own voice. *Do I really sound like him?* She looked at the thin shingle ladder nailed together, and a sigh shook her heavy body in the water's cold arms. The medallion was a circle of ice against her chest, its life gone.

Sucking at her wounded lip, her eyes streaming tears, Selene began to climb.

# NINETEEN

THEY LAID HIM on the red-velvet bed, folding his hands on his chest. His face was charred up the left side, burned almost down to the bone, half his hair gone. The wound on his chest was still open and smoking, the ragged edges of muscle exposed, white broken spears of his ribs peeking out under peeled-back skin. All that was left of his clothes were a few scraps of the coat and his boots, and maybe a quarter of his jeans.

Selene coughed into her hand, engine oil coating the back of her throat. The smell of smoke twisted her stomach again. She dropped the pile of Kevlar by the door.

Jorge looked up from the bedside. "Selene?"

The red lace lamp glowed dimly. Selene shook her head, damp tendrils of her hair falling forward. Bradley, his dreadlocks wet with blood on one side, looked at her too. There were two others, she hadn't asked their names.

She didn't care.

They looked at her like she should know what to do.

"Get out." Her voice was an awful choked rasp.

She stood aside from the door as they passed. Then she swung the door closed, and dropped the iron bar from her side into the brackets.

With that done, she waited.

There was a whispered argument right outside the door. Jorge saying something about her being the Mistress now. Bradley hissing that Nikolai had to be alive, that he would rise, why else had she brought him back here?

Selene waited until they had gone away. Her arms and legs shook, waves of trembling spilling through liquid flesh. There was no desire in the shaking now. It was cold ash and exhaustion, nothing more.

Dawn wasn't far off.

She slid down the inside of the door, ending up sitting with her hands loose and limp to either side. "Nikolai," she whispered. "Nik?"

The ride back from the docks had been grimly silent, Selene cradling Nikolai's head in the back of the black van, Bradley stealing glances at them. Marina had been taken in a different car. The city howled with sirens, fires in different corners, chaos spilling out onto the streets.

If Nikolai didn't wake up, it would all be for nothing. The City would become a free territory, and Nichtvren would spill in to take it. The strong would fight, the weak would die, and a new Prime Power would eventually rise.

And Selene...what would happen to her? What would she do?

*Free. I'm free now.*

"Nikolai?" she whispered again.

Nothing. No tingle of Power in the air. No sound of his pulse.

*There is no comfort in alone.*

She scrubbed at her face. Soot crackled, fell off, drifted on the floor.

Her black bag lay forgotten by the side of the bed. Selene stared at it, fixedly, for a few long minutes, her jaw slack and her pupils dilated in the dim light. She closed her eyes and swallowed convulsively.

Finally she pitched forward, her palms meeting the wooden floor with a grating shock that clicked her teeth together again. Her lip stung. Her shoulders ached savagely. Her wrists were twin bracelets of agony, and her legs refused to fully obey her.

She crawled across the floor.

Finally, she reached the bedside. She flipped the bag open with trembling hands and slid the athame free. The blade glinted, sharp steel undimmed by blood. There was an echo, or did she imagine it? A faint breath of Danny's wards, lingering in the wood and steel.

*Oh, Danny.* Selene held up a fistful of her hair, set the knife close to her skull, and started sawing.

It took a while, but finally she finished. Each handful of hair she tossed over Nikolai.

*His body.* Grigori had stabbed him through the heart. And Nikolai had been burned and dangerously drained even before that fatal wound.

She stared at the knife's gleam, clasped in her hand.

The she jerked herself up onto her knees and flung the knife at the wall.

If it had cried out when it left her hand, she wouldn't have been surprised. Instead, it only made a thin whistling sound and buried itself, *tchuk!*, hilt-deep in the paneling.

Her tarot cards, in their hank of red silk, were next. She scattered them all over the bed. The Priestess landed on Nikolai's unmoving, bloody chest. The Four of Wands landed on his right hand. A thick drift of cards slid down to rest in the crevice between his body and the mattress on either side.

When she flipped over the Death card she hesitated only a little before she laid it gently on his forehead.

She tore the flannel shirt into strips and scattered them on the bed too.

*What the hell are you doing?*

*The only thing I know how to do now. I'm giving him the best sendoff I can.* In the camps they would just leave the bodies at pickup points for mass burial. The sendoff came afterward, with home-brewed hooch and filthy jokes, keening songs and fistfights.

But she was here, not in a camp. She would give what she had.

Finally, she dug out two quarter-credit coins—*emergency payphone, help, my brother called me...he's a shut-in, something's wrong*—and laid one on each eyelid. They glittered at her, winking.

Dawn's approach weighed her down with lead.

Selene's arms trembled. She braced them on the mattress and leaned over, pressed her lips to Nikolai's charred cheek. The skin was cold and leathery. There was none of the cold pulsing Power that had hung over him before.

"Nikolai," she said against his face.

*What are you going to do?* Danny's voice, awed and reedy. She found she didn't care if he was dead and really speaking to her, or if she was talking to herself. It didn't matter. *What are you going to do now, Lena?*

Selene hitched herself up to her feet. She stumbled to the door.

It took her two tries before she could get the iron bar down from the brackets. *They'll come to bury him, or burn him. He'll have planned something for this, of course he would.*

The thin edge of numbness between her and the huge crashing blackness grew a little thinner.

*I'm free.*

She dropped the bar with a clang. Then she dug under her ruined tank top and pulled the medallion over her head. The chain caught in a tuft of hair and she yanked. There was a moment of pain, the chain ripping free, then she turned the medallion over in her hand, tracing the lion's head with one soot-blackened, bloody finger.

Selene swayed on her feet. Her wet boots made little squeaking sounds.

She laid the medallion over his broken, laced hands. "I don't know what this is," she husked. "Isn't that ridiculous? All this time, and I don't even *know.*"

The bed shifted, just a little. Selene put her hands around one of the bedposts and pulled. *If the nest is attacked, you will find a safe passage out. It is hidden behind the bed, and will respond only to the medallion...I would ask that you stay.*

Sure enough, behind the headboard and a fall of red velvet was a small wooden door. It swung back when Selene squeezed behind the bed and pushed on it with tented fingers.

The "passage" was a tunnel carved out of solid rock. A soupy haze of exhaustion all over her, dragging her down. She slid into the tunnel; it was only four feet high. As soon as she was completely in, the door shut and the green glow of total darkness descended on the tunnel.

*I've got to get out of here, find a place to sleep for the day. Then, tomorrow night, I can find a bus, or even a transport. I've got enough money for that. Get out of here, go somewhere.*

*I'm free. He's dead and I'm free.*

*Why do I feel like crying?*

Selene hesitated for just a moment. She could stay here, take over Nikolai's thralls, keep the city under control. Except she had no idea of *how* to. She was tired and burned, there was a big gaping invisible hole in her chest, and going back into that room with a dead Nichtvren on the bed was the one thing she couldn't force herself to do.

She was free now. She'd worked and prayed and longed for freedom, and now that she had it, she didn't know what the hell to do.

*It doesn't matter. I'll find something. I always have.*

She didn't have a lot of time before dawn. Selene raised her chin, settled the bag strap more firmly, and began to climb toward the thing that had eluded her all her life.

She didn't bother wiping away the tears. They would stop when they were done. She couldn't do anything about it, she needed all her failing energy to find a safe bolthole. She would sleep through the inimical day and wake when the sun slid below the horizon. When she did, she would be a new person, a Selene who didn't have to beg or plead anymore. She would head to the bus station or the transport lodge, and get a ticket to anywhere.

And then, the world.

# EPILOGUE

THEY CAME BACK at midnight the following night, pulled by the force of the will they had sworn to serve. Jorge was first, carrying the cooler, Rigel paced behind him, his left arm in a sling, carrying the sword. Eric, his physician's bag bumping his thigh obediently, coughed. The sound fell dead into strained air.

Price Netley carried another cooler full of bloodpacks. "I hope she remembered to unbar the door," he said, nervously reaching over with his chin to scratch at his shoulder.

"He'll tell her," Jorge replied. "Or she did. Selene's not stupid."

"She killed Grigori." Bradley's tone was soft with wonder. The silence fell over them again, the silence of awe in the face of such an act.

The door to the sanctum was indeed unbarred, and Bradley set his shoulder to it. It swung open slowly, brushing the floor.

"Jesu Christos." Netley sounded like someone had punched him in the stomach.

"Get the packs." Jorge didn't hesitate.

They moved slowly into the sanctum.

Eric snapped his bag open. Hypos crackled in their plastic cartridges. "The sedayeenen wanted to be here," he said, and Jorge set the cooler down on the bed.

Nobody answered, though Rigel's eyes glittered. The healer was under orders to stay in bed and rest until they were sure of her recovery.

They worked together, Jorge snapping the hypos on the bloodpacks, Eric deftly pressing the hypos onto the transfer points. The bloodpacks began to drain.

It was Rigel finally who said what they were all thinking. "Where's Selene?"

"She can't have disappeared." Jorge handed the doctor another bloodpack. "Not during the day."

"Here come the others." Bradley accepted a full cooler of bloodpacks from Riverwolf. The tall man had spent shell casings tied in his long black hair.

"Tarot cards. And look at this." Eric pointed with his chin. His white-blond hair fell forward, hiding his expression.

Netley reached down and touched the tarnished, blackened surface of the medallion. It crumbled into fine-powder dust under his fingers. "At least she left this to keep him alive." His tone was flat, ironic, and terribly final.

The quarter-credits slid from Nikolai's eyes.

A chill wafted up, brushing the velvet of the bed.

They worked in silence. Six full coolers of bloodpacks came, were emptied, and left, passed out the door.

The flesh began to move on his bones. Ribs cracked, settling back into their accustomed places. There was a sharp crackling sound, and the black mask of burn on the pale, aquiline face slid aside.

"Search the house," Netley murmured at the door. "Find her. If she's on the grounds, find her."

A long, electric breath of silence descended on the sanctum. The men paused except for Eric, who jostled Jorge, reminding him to hand over another full bloodpack.

The nest began to pulse with Power again. A rushing breeze slid through the sanctum, blew tarot cards off the bed, fluttering to the floor. The Death card slid from Nikolai's forehead, fell behind the pillow. There was a faint soft sound as it slid, by some fluke, through empty space and finally touched the floor behind the headboard.

"Holy Christos." Jorge handed Eric another bloodpack. The chill plastic containers glowed like rubies. "The bed's moved. She's used the passage." He swore, vilely and passionlessly, in another tongue.

"You mean she—" Netley turned, the color draining from his cheeks.

Nikolai opened his eyes. The entire house sighed, and settled on its foundations.

He drew in a long endless waking breath, and his eyes settled on Jorge. "Jorge." His voice shivered the air. "Where is she?"

His first thought was of her. A ripple passed through the assembled men.

*Eric put the last hypo in. "Apparently she thought you were dead. She left you silver to pay the ferryman with." He sounded flat and unconcerned.*

*Nikolai's eyes were black from lid to lid. "Where is she?" he asked, very softly, and every man in the room—even Eric—took a step back.*

*"I saw her," Riverwolf said from the door. "She fought Grigori, when you fell. Cut him in half. Carried you back to the shore through the river of death." He nodded, the shell casings clicking in his hair.*

*Nikolai said nothing.*

*It couldn't be avoided. "It looks like she went out through the passage," Jorge said numbly.*

*A long, ticking silence.*

*"Leave me." Nikolai's tone was absolutely flat.*

*There was a momentary crowding by the door as they all hurried, Jorge and Eric carrying empty coolers, Eric's little black bag dangling from his big hands.*

*The door slammed shut almost on their heels, and the iron bars dropped, crashing.*

*Jorge stopped, as if tempted to look.*

*Rigel grabbed his arm. "Don't, Jorge. He'll kill you. Come on."*

*From behind the door, the deadly silence spread. There was a huge shivering impact, and dust pattered down from the roof.*

*"Was that the bed?" Netley's eyes were uncomfortably round.*

*Jorge turned away. "Let's go. Hurry."*

*The silence settled in again, and it wasn't until they reached the end of the hall, moving single file like a funeral cortege, that the scream rose behind them. It was a wrecked, massive noise that shook the entire house, echoing in every corridor, and rose into the swiftly-falling night beyond the manicured grounds to where the bleeding city licked its wounds, the fires finally put out, even to where the skeleton of a tanker ship settled low in the water, its ribs melted together and still sending up thin curls of smoke.*

'SELENE!"

finis

# JUST ASK

OF COURSE IT was raining.

The cold didn't bother Selene Thompson; Nichtvren were largely immune to temperature and in any case, it was much warmer than it had been half a world away. But stepping off the transport and onto the concrete of Santiago City's dock, she shivered. The chill radioactive heart of this felt was no different, even though she'd spent a century on the other side of the globe. Her body tingled, adjusting to the change in ambient Power, adapting in seconds instead of the day or so it would take if she were still human.

What a laugh. She'd be long dead by now. She bared her fangs at the thought, a swift flash of sharp white, then caught herself.

The rain didn't reach down here below ground level, but cold stray flirting breezes touched her long dark hair as the antigrav on the transports played havoc with air currents. She suppressed the urge to hunch her shoulders. In her coat pocket, the medallion gave a small fluttering pulse against her finger. She hadn't even been aware of touching it.

*Nikolai's hand polished the curve of her hip, something cool and metallic sliding against her skin. He drew it up over her ribs, under her breast, then the medallion lay where it used to, half the chain spilling down to pool on the sheet. He fastened it at the back of her neck, one-handed, and flattened his other palm against the silver lying between her breasts. "This is important, Selene. Without it, you're at risk. This gives you protection. You cannot throw it away. Understood?"*

She'd left it on his riven, bloodless chest as he lay on his deathbed, a hundred years ago. Two days ago it had arrived at her Nest in Freetown New Prague. A cedarwood box, the medallion on its tarnished chain, and a note on expensive linen paper. Two words in fantastical calligraphy:

*Come home.*

Her bootheels ground the concrete as she turned in a full circle. The flight had arrived after dark, but the new transport well was deep enough it didn't matter. A calculated risk, traveling by hover transport...but calculated risks were what she did best. Or at least, what she did now that she was a functionally immortal blood-drinker and very hard to kill.

There really wasn't that much difference, she reflected, between being a sexwitch whore and a Freetown mercenary. Both accepted money, but performed for a darker need. In Selene's case, it was all the cloned blood she could drink and the leeway to find the limits of her preternatural body and mind on the battlefield—because she hadn't had a Master to teach her about being a suckhead. The one who Turned her was dead. She'd seen as much, sent him to his afterworld with all the offerings she could manage.

*So who sent me this, then?* Her fingers touched the warm metal. *Oh, what the hell.*

She drew it out of her pocket. A hard silver gleam, the full moon rising. Spiked runic writing on one side, the figure of some odd animal scratched on the other. A lion, perhaps? Who knew? The fastening was tarnished shut, but she slid the chain over her head and dropped the medallion down her shirt. It felt like it belonged, cold metal warming and nestling against her breastbone. The Power in the medallion thrilled along her nerves, a small zing like biting tinfoil.

*Let's hope someone's noticed that.* The languor of dawn approaching weighted down her fingers, a warning.

There was another feeling. Anticipation. It ran along her veins, pooling in her lower belly. She hadn't felt the swimming weakness, the hunger, the *need* in so long. She didn't miss it— after a whole human life spent as a slave to a sexwitch's need, it was impossible to regret its disappearance.

And yet.

*Nikolai.*

There. She'd thought of him. Dark eyes, his fingers, the soft curl of dark hair that fell over his forehead. The sense of contained power and grace, the utterly frightening control he took of every situation she'd ever seen him in. Other memories crowded in, and the lump of cold iron in the bottom of her belly warmed. His blood in her veins, her curse in his; the *need* didn't rule her any longer but with no prospect of it ever being satisfied, it was best not to taunt it.

*I hated him,* she reminded herself. Then, judging she'd stayed on the transport dock long enough to be noticed by *someone,* she gathered herself and melted into the crowd of humanity. Up above the rain would blur her scent...but she would take care not to blur it too much.

THE GEOGRAPHY OF Saint City hadn't changed out of recognition. Spread, of course, and there were different peaks and valleys. Cities aged as slowly as Nichtvren, even in the New World.

How anachronistic of her, to call it the "new" world. By the time she'd been born, it was already old.

The International District was still rough-trade. She remembered hunting in these alleys to feed her human curse, sailors and soldiers while her brother stood guard. Time healed plenty, but it didn't ameliorate the sharp shame or disgust.

Even boomtowns had abandoned buildings, and she found what she was looking for after a half-hour's worth of wandering. The warehouse slumped against its bones, dispirited under the strengthening rain. Water falling from the sky bleached everything here, turned it gray.

Not really. Things had been gray since she left. She'd lost her curse, but also lost the hurtful color of the world.

In any case, it was child's play to break in past the maglocks and do some recon. She could have found a hostel downtown, one that catered to her kind...but why? *Make it difficult for whoever wants to trap you,* that was a rule of survival. She planned to make it just difficult enough.

She dug in her bag for the small rolls of tripwire, spent a precious twenty minutes laying surprises. A hard delighted smile lingered on her lips as she worked; spending fifty years as a mercenary was good training for booby traps. They had such delightful little toys nowadays, like the plasbursters and the new vaston explosive; light, easy to carry, wouldn't blow up unless you primed it but once you did, watch out!

Her fingers and toes were full of lead by the time she finished and settled in her chosen resting place. No chance of sunlight, even if they came after her; the explosives would take out support structure and bury her safely.

She was counting on whoever-it-was wanting to capture her alive. If that wasn't the case, well.

Selene curled into a corner, her back braced against concrete. The sun pressed against the horizon like a boil, she *felt* it with the queer inner clock every Nichtvren possessed. How long would it be before she could walk around by day but not in sun, like Nik—

Sunrise. The blackness took her. And as always, she dreamed.

Of *him*.

*AT LEAST THE space inside her head was her own.* "Go ahead and feed," *she whispered, and closed her eyes, shutting him out. Hot tears trickled down her temples, sank into her damp hair.* "Don't mind me." It doesn't matter to you, it never matters to any of them. Christos, just hurry up and take what you want, the sooner you do the sooner you'll leave me alone.

"You're weeping." *As if surprised.*

*Selene went limp under him, pliant.* Just get it over with, will you? Fuck me if you have to, but leave the rest of me alone. "Of *course I'm crying,*" *she said, her body gone hot and prickling with a sudden flush of Power.* "My b-b-brother—" Shut up, Selene. That's not his business. *The bed was soft underneath her, she sank down helplessly.*

"I did not want you to see..." *He sounded, of all things, uncertain.*

*Nikolai, uncertain?* No. I didn't hear him right. "I had to. He's my brother."

It's my fault, sucktooth. Someone else tore him into bits, but it's my fault. For once I'm not fucking blaming you, either. Even though I am, you got him involved in whatever killed him, but if I wasn't what I am you never would have been interested in me and—

*He freed his fingers from her hair long enough to stroke her cheek, a gentle and completely unexpected touch.* "A bargain is a bargain, dear one," *he whispered. But still he didn't move, though she could feel him pressing against her inner thigh, hot skin against slick dampness. She was wet and the low constant ache had started again. She wasn't drained, but her body wanted completion now.*

Again. My curse. *Selene's throat was blocked with unshed tears. "Just get it over with." It took work to force the whisper out.*

*"Do you still hate me?" He kissed along her throat. His teeth scraped above the pulse and Selene's heart slammed against her ribs.*

*"Don't," she began. "Nikolai—don't!"*

*"Too late," he whispered, and his hips came down. She was so slick and wet with need that he had no difficulty—and at the same moment, he drove his teeth into her throat.*

⁊∾

THERE WAS NO lying in bed half-awake for Nichtvren. When the sun sank, consciousness returned with a sound like metal breaking.

No. Metal clashing against itself. Chains, and fiery pain in her wrists.

Selene opened her eyes. Not quite a glare, but the light was painful. She disregarded it, stretched out her senses. Power swam in the air, a heavy weight against breath and heart and mind.

Another Nichtvren. She inhaled, tasted the air.

*That's not Nikolai. It's female. And old.*

The vaulted ceiling was stone. Softness under her, a type of padded platform. And the chains, clasped at wrist and ankle, pulled tight. Chill air against her bare skin. The medallion shifted against her breastbone.

*Well. This is interesting.*

"Don't bother testing the chains." A high tinkling voice, the Merican accented broadly. Something eastern-Europa, if Selene was any judge by now. "You'll just be damaged."

The burning at Selene's wrists intensified. She already had scars there, from Grigori's little mixture so long ago. He'd chained her too, but not for very long.

Selene blinked. The light scored her eyes, brought hot water out to trickle down into her hair. Her ankles began to prickle, too. Something was smeared on the insides of the restraints, an oily residue.

"You cost me eight thralls, with those little explosives." That high sweet voice smoked with contempt and absolute power. "But I caught you, nonetheless."

*You were supposed to, you idiot.* Well, at least this part had gone according to plan. Now she would find out who this was, and what they wanted.

A shadow in the light. It leaned over Selene, two blonde braids falling over her slim shoulders. A fair clear complexion, dainty fangs, half-lidded blue eyes, and naked skin dusted with golden freckles. She'd probably been Turned because of that fresh, freckle-faced look, like an Alpine milkmaid on an advertising holo.

*Jesu help me, I've been kidnapped by Heidi.* A rill of laughter rose in Selene's throat; she didn't even try to contain it. Her laugh came out as a harsh caw, bouncing off stone. The echoes gave her the dimensions of the room—large, a high vaulted ceiling, and it *felt* underground.

Blondie's face twisted itself up a little, smoothed out. She didn't like being laughed at.

That was the problem with so many Nichtvren Masters. So *touchy*. That prickly pride made them predictable, as far as Selene was concerned. It gave her an edge.

As a lone Nichtvren, she needed every edge she could get. Particularly since she was chained down and naked.

*Funny how things don't change. Spent a lot of my life naked at someone's whim.* Her lips peeled back from her teeth, exposing her own fangs. It was a show of aggression, and likely to madden this bitch, whoever she was.

It worked. The little nose wrinkled, and she slapped Selene hard enough to bounce her head off the padding. Selene didn't even strain against the chains. The Power in the air drew close and stifling, ice cubes against every exposed inch of her, and she calculated the little blonde girl was at least as old as Nikolai. But she didn't have Nikolai's sheer suffocating will, or his strength.

*Hmmm. Again, interesting.*

"Bitch." The woman climbed up on the platform, gracefully. She wore her nakedness like another woman would wear expensive silk; she'd been Turned right in her prime and she knew it. "Of course, this is what I expected from *his* inamorata."

Something in Selene stilled. The other Nichtvren must have felt her reaction. She leaned down, those blonde braids slithering down to brush against Selene. "He never spoke of me, I would hazard. I am Marya. *You* are Selene. His precious Selene. So easy to catch, and my vengeance is complete." Her lips brushed Selene's cheek, fangs scraping lightly. Instinct warred with will; Selene tensed.

Marya smelled of cloves and old rusted blood. Her breath was a little foul; she must have just fed because her skin was bloat-warm. Fed from something drugged, most likely, that would be the acridity in her mouth, her metabolism burning through whatever her victim or thrall had been high on. Loathing crawled through Selene, even as Marya's mouth met hers.

She *could* have bitten the bitch, she supposed. Her own teeth were just as sharp. But this woman had a script she was working from, and letting her play it out would get Selene further than violence at this point. Her fingertips played over the canvas cover of the padding, her hands twisting to feel at the cuffs. Whatever was smeared on the inside of the metal was beginning to hurt like hell, and the coppery-sweet scent of her own blood rose in the charged air.

Marya's tongue slid into Selene's mouth. Obviously nobody had taught her to kiss, she just shoved it in like Selene was supposed to be grateful for the privilege.

*Oh, Jesu. Nothing ever changes, does it.* Selene restrained the urge to roll her eyes and accepted it. She even went loose under the woman's dense weight, a Nichtvren's heavier muscle and bone pressing down. Her knees were on either side of Selene's hips, she settled like a dog crouched over a bone.

Marya broke away. "Once a whore, always a whore." A bitter little laugh, her young-old face contorting. You could have mistaken her for a teenager in certain very dim light, except for the mad, ancient thing peeking out through those bright, bright blue eyes. "Except I know you were *tantraiiken*, you filthy little..." A long rumble, the growl filling Marya's chest. She pushed herself up, settled her weight firmly on Selene's hips. She ground down, and Selene went utterly still.

*Her script's changing. Huh.*

Marya turned her head. "Bring him in," she snarled, the *command* unmistakable. There was a sound—ah, her thralls would be outside the door. Close enough to hear their Master, by flesh or mental call.

Selene tipped her head carefully to the side, a few millimeters. The other Nichtvren glanced back down, and she leaned forward. Her long, capable hands—they felt too broad and strong, rough as if chapped—closed around Selene's throat. But gently.

"What is the best revenge, *kallike?*" She smiled gently as a scraping sound filled the room. A door, opening. Selene didn't dare turn her head further to look. She kept her mouth shut, watching like she would have watched a client in her human days. When she would have been waiting for a cue, her curse throbbing through her flesh.

"The best revenge," Marya continued, her thumb stroking along the side of Selene's throat ever-so-gently, "is to kill the thing your enemy loves before him. While he is helpless."

*What the* hell *is this bitch talking about?*

"Look," Marya whispered, and tilted Selene's head to the side. "Look at him."

Selene did as she was told.

The scraping had been double doors, iron-bound and made of some dark wood. They were pushed open now, and the darkness behind them was absolute. A huge hideous creaking, and the shape became visible. Selene blinked again, fresh water trickling from her eyes. How did the other Nichtvren stand it so bright in here?

It was a low wooden cart on broad iron-rimmed wheels. The thralls—huge musclebound men with empty stares, their will erased by their Master's dominance—pushed it forward, straining. It barely cleared the opening, and threatened to tip over because a massive X of plasteel beams crouched on it.

There, spread-eagled and in rags, his face and body horribly mangled and seeping thick sluggish black blood, was Nikolai. A glitter of eyes under filthy hair showed he was conscious.

So he *was* alive.

THE SHOCK GRATED through Selene, her entire body frozen, pinned like a butterfly. Marya laughed and settled her hips more firmly. Her hands tightened just a little on Selene's throat.

*I don't* need *to breathe*, Selene reminded herself. *But if I don't, I'll burn through my cellular stores more rapidly and my body will start cannibalizing. Great. She's bound to have another means of killing me, this is just theater.*

"Demoskenos Kirai Nikolai." Marya's laugh was a chill little giggle, high-pitched. She sounded so *young*, it was the worst thing. "This is going to take a long, long time."

*So you think.* Selene gathered herself. Nikolai's eyes glittered. He hung there, and she could see the iron bolts driven through his wrists and ankles. The pain would have been excruciating.

But he was alive. *Alive.* All this time. How had he...he had been *dead*. She had been so certain.

There were more dragging sounds. One of the thralls was heaving another wheeled thing toward the platform. It was an iron frame, and the things stacked and hung neatly on it would have turned Selene's stomach if she hadn't spent so much time seeing the different ways a body—even a preternatural body—could be broken.

It had lost its power to shock. She wasn't sure if she should be grateful for that. The medallion flared with heat against her breastbone, a familiar old sensation.

Marya's fingers bit down. "This is just for beginnings," she chortled, and her hands turned into a crushing vice. "First I'll take your voice, so you cannot even scream. Then there will be the irons, and the rack, and the open flame—"

Selene pitched aside, every muscle tightening. The chains were strong and the cuffs were tight, but you don't spend your human life as a sexwitch without learning how to slip out of tight handcuffs. It would mean stripping flesh off the bone, but she'd heal.

If she escaped this.

She *yanked*, her skin ripping and the pain like a red bolt of fire up her arm, and her claws bit into the other Nichtvren's face, unloosing a gout of blood.

The pain was a spur, and she welcomed it. Her other hand ripped free, leaving a significant amount of flesh behind, and she *shoved*, getting good contact on the other Nichtvren's chest and heaving with every ounce of preternatural strength she owned.

Which was considerable, and battle-hardened as well. Marya went flying, a shattering wail of rage trailing behind her and threatening to pop Selene's eardrums. Selene curled up, her claws slicing through padding and closing on the chains holding her feet down. The metal parted with a screech and she was up in a flash, crouching on the platform and taking in the entire circular room with one sweep. *Know your ground*, another cardinal rule of survival.

*Another exit over there. And...Christos, that* is *an actual rack. She wasn't kidding.*

Selene threw herself aside, tucking and rolling. Stone grated against her naked back, bullets chewed the platform bed. Explosive ammo, meant to bleed her out. At least some of the thralls were free to act in an emergency. She gained her feet, moving smoothly through the roll, her legs bending and releasing as she *leapt*, twisting to avoid another spray of bullets. They were thralls, yes, but they were only human.

Selene...was not, now.

She landed behind the knot of thralls with submachine guns, her claws out and the growl filling her chest. Blood flew, bones splintering, and there was a shattering, ripping sound. Marya's howling changed pitch, and Selene bent backward like a gymnast, her foot flashing up and catching the last thrall under the chin with a sickening crack. She rolled aside again as the blonde bitch arrived out of thin air, her clawed face splattering blood, blue eyes rolling with mad hate.

*That's going to hurt as it heals.* The thought was a flash. Selene's body did the work for her, once she got out of the way and let training and instinct take over. *Goddamn, she's fast.* Her feet slapped the floor, cuffs and broken chains jingling musically, Selene's claws sank into the stone roof and she twisted, agonizing pain in her wrists, her hands spattering more candy-smelling blood. There was enough of the red stuff here to craze a newly-Turned; the thirst threatened to close a veil of red over Selene's vision. She landed on the floor, whirling and throwing her hands out in flat palm-strikes, Power burning through her as she connected.

*Hit me with flesh and Power both, Selene,* Nikolai whispered in the dim recesses of her memory. *Anything else is useless.*

The medallion burned, a sudden sharp spike of heat, a jolt of pure Power. Surprising, but Selene welcomed it. Any tool to do the job at hand.

That was, she thought briefly, the biggest difference between her human self and what she was now.

Marya flew back again, but not as far as Selene had hoped. The blonde hit the iron frame with its torture instruments, everything collapsing and flying with musical jangles. The noise was incredible—Selene's instinctive growl and the howling the blonde was doing, more gunfire somewhere outside the room.

A deep, powerful thrumming underlaid every other sound. It was coming from the plasteel beams where Nikolai hung. His head was up, the mad glitter of his eyes suddenly scorching, and Selene's heart gave an amazing leap.

*Stop staring at him and mo—*

It was too late. The blonde had gathered herself, and she collided with Selene. The sound was like a good hard break on a hoverpool table, and Selene *flew.* Claws tangled in her ribs, pulling—the bitch was trying to tear her heart out the hard way.

Selene punched her twice before they hit the stone wall, a shockwave jolting through her abused body. A life spent disassociating herself from the omnipresent swell of desire a sexwitch was prey to was good practice for learning to disregard pain, but she was losing blood fast now and hadn't fed in four days.

*Stupid, silly, goddammit, Selene, start thinking!*

It was too late. Marya's claws sliced further in, and the queer floating feeling of too much bloodloss began in Selene's flayed fingers and bare toes. She brought her knee up before they landed, her back scraping the stone wall. Another punch, blood flying from her knuckles as they fell. Hit the floor in a tangle, Marya's flesh feverish against hers, and Selene's chin snaked forward. Her teeth champed, a bare inch from the other woman's throat. Naked blood-greased skin slid, straining, and if she didn't end this fight soon, Selene knew she would lose.

Over Marya's bloodslick shoulder, Selene caught a flicker of motion. A familiar shape fell from the plasteel beams, the X toppling backward with a heavy clangor.

∽❧∾

CHAOS. SCREAMING. THE red haze of bloodshed. Selene's teeth clamped home, breaking through the hard crust of a Nichtvren's skin, just over the *carotid minora*. A hot flood of candy-spiced blood filled her mouth. She didn't precisely want to drink, just to bleed. If she could weaken the bitch enough—

More screaming, more gunfire. Selene's eyes rolled. She hugged Marya close, arms and legs pinning the other woman, disregarding her rapidly-weakening struggles. If she could just hold on long enough, swallowing what she could of the other woman's strength, it might be enough—

Marya howled. The sound battered Selene's damp hair back with clawed fingers, sharp spikes against her sensitive eardrums.

"Let *go!*" he yelled, and the *command* rang through her, a gong inside her head.

She fought, of course, the instinct of her own Mastery rising to deny him control. But he was older, and he had Turned her, and her arms and legs loosened of their own accord. Her teeth slid free of Marya's flesh, and the other Nichtvren hissed feebly as she was jerked back, her blonde braids looped around a bleeding, broken fist.

"You," Nikolai snarled, his gaunt dirty face contorted. He dragged her as she writhed, somehow avoiding the wild strikes of her claws. "*You.*" A sudden movement, preternatural bones crunching, and more blood flew. His fangs were out, and a cold prickling weight settled over the room.

How had this crazy blonde beast ever held him?

Selene blinked. She lay on her side against cold stone, her fingers twitching as the flesh repaired itself. Candy-sweet blood burned her tongue, sank into her parched throat. She'd always loved sugar—any child growing up in the camps learned to take as many calories in as possible, the sweeter the better—and this was so *good*. The best candy-spice burn was from the blood of another predator.

*How much did I take?* There was a lump of warmth behind her aching breastbone, another answering it from above.

Nikolai's chest swelled with the growl, a wall of subsonic vibration. His mangled hands tightened, swollen pale fingers, the ring and middle fingers terribly crunched and distorted, and he twisted sharply. There was a crack like well-seasoned wood, and Marya's body convulsed.

*Nichtvren don't throw up*, Selene told herself, swallowing hard. The habit of nausea was strong, even after all these years. One day, she supposed, she'd outgrow it. If she survived.

Nikolai straightened. He drew one wasted leg up, the knee a grotesque knob of bone and skin, and the fury twisting his face turned Selene's stomach even more. You wouldn't think it was the same maddeningly gentle, inflexible, always-controlled Nikolai she dream-remembered every time the sun rose and waking consciousness fled her.

He stamped down, *hard*. There was a sound like a stone watermelon breaking, and the screaming outside the room took on a frantic quality. Of course, every one of Marya's thralls would feel her skullspatter-death. They were condemned to an agonizing death of their own without her animating influence; unless Nikolai took them under his wing.

Or Selene. Or any other Master.

Marya's body twitched, her misshapen head lolling as Nikolai drew his foot away. Blood spread in scallops, a crimson lake. Selene swallowed again, hard, and flexed her fingers.

Nikolai stood, staring down at the body. The remaining rags of his clothing fluttered, but he was utterly motionless. The tension leaked out of him bit by bit, and Selene gathered herself.

He lifted his head. The mad twin gleams of his eyes, reflecting differently than a human's, were a flat catshine as he studied her in return.

*You were dead,* she wanted to say. Her lips twitched. In the end, she said nothing. There was no use in stating the obvious. She tensed, slowly, one muscle at a time, and when she was certain everything was more or less functional, she pushed herself upright.

A soft breeze touched her cheek. Selene flung up a hand, her claws extended, their razor edges a hairsbreadth from his *carotid minora*. The *majora* was more deeply buried under the changed structure of the throat, she didn't have the right angle for a strike.

There was no need. He simply watched her.

He was on his knees. Right next to her. The faint breeze died as the gunfire spattered to a halt. There were other sounds she recognized—the calls and short bursts of mopping-up instead of an actual battle.

*Nikolai's thralls*, she realized. Why had Marya left any alive? Or had they staged an assault?

Of *course* they had staged an assault, probably from outside. Once Nikolai, bleeding and bound on that iron X, had *told* them to.

*Well now, don't I feel silly.* She swallowed, roughly. Her hands were still raw, her ribs ached, but the worst of it had stopped. The wounds were closing over, and if she found a bar with a cloned-blood counter she would be right as rain in a few hours.

Another survival.

She eased away, along the wall. Twinges and vicious little nips of pain rang stitched through her. The trickles of blood slowed. Her exhaustion was a human habit, but still. Even a Nichtvren could get tired.

"Jesu Christos," she whispered. "That was entertaining."

Nikolai crouched, staring at her. His face didn't ease, and his eyes were now dark holes.

Selene sighed. So many things changed as the years passed, and so many didn't.

"You could have killed her at any time." She braced herself against the wall, leaving a long wide smear of blood as she pushed herself to her feet. "You were waiting. For me to show up, apparently. Whatever morality play you put together is concluded. I'll be on the next transport out. Nice seeing you again."

"Selene." Everything in the room rattled as he said it, from the wheeled carts to the scattered implements. Broken bodies lay everywhere. The blood seeping from Marya's broken body ruffled along its liquid surface. Someone was going to have a hell of a time cleaning that up.

She tested her legs. They would hold her up. The broken chains rattled as she took one step away from the wall. Another. Thirst prickled in her throat; it would rapidly become unbearable.

He likely wouldn't begrudge her hunting live prey here. But still.

"Master?" A thrall at the door—a tall bald man with a familiar voice, his submachine gun pointed at the floor and his well-cut suit spattered with fluids it was probably best not to think about. Selene almost shut her eyes. If she blinked every time something here reminded her of the past, she was going to look like a narcoleptic vox-sniffer.

"Jorge." Nikolai sounded like himself again. "Attend her."

Selene took another step. *Really doing well,* she congratulated herself. *Now let's find some clothes.*

Nikolai was suddenly there next to her, his mangled hand closing around her upper arm. "You need blood."

The first touch, after so many years—and her traitorous body lit up like a marquee. A different weakness spilled through her, and her breath caught. Selene tore her arm away. "I need a lot more than that, Nikolai." She could have sounded irritated, she supposed, but the only thing that came out was weariness. "Leave me alone."

"There is—" he began.

*No comfort in alone.* She could have finished the sentence in her sleep. "Shut. Up."

Miraculously, he did.

"Since you're so bent on being *helpful,* I'll need clothes. And cloned blood, preferably cut with cafetrol. Then I'll be on my merry." Her gaze fixed on the floor. She took another step, another. Did not sway.

"Very well." Chill and hurtful, now. "I owe you my thanks, after all."

Selene shrugged. "You could've killed her anytime you wanted to."

"Yes. But you came."

There was no answer to that. She put her head down, her naked skin prickling under the blood absorbing back into its surface tissues, and headed for the door.

A SHORT, SCORCH-HOT shower restored her. Her wrists would scar once more, from whatever Marya had painted the cuffs with. They flushed an angry red, traceries crawling down her hand and up her arm. She'd never tanned anyway, and now she was marble-pale; the crimson spiderwebs as her flesh reacted to the mixture was shocking contrast.

Selene took three long swallows of cloned blood, the sting of cafetrol hitting the back of her throat. She'd never drink espresso again, but the half-second jolt as her body burned through the artificial additive was good enough.

It made her feel almost human.

She would have preferred jeans and a T-shirt, but Jorge brought her midnight-blue silk, a long flowing skirt, low-cut, with spaghetti straps. It fit perfectly, which was...thought-provoking.

It also showed the medallion's gleam, and the mottling on her arms as the flush of nutrition from the cloned fought the allergic reaction. Her ankles weren't too bad, just a mild itching and a pinkish bloom on the skin.

Of course, the wrists were the most vulnerable. Her weakest point, the delicate structures of the claws and hand still not fully settled from her Turning.

She set the tankard down with a click. The table was a restrained ebonywood piece, and the room was done in oak, restful dark-blue velvet swathing the bed and hanging on the stone walls. Still underground, of course, and dust in the air. Had Nikolai changed his Nest, or was this Marya's doing? This looked like a female's room, with more delicate furniture and that massive, choked-velvet bed. The bookshelves ranked along one wall were mostly empty, except for some little tchotchkes. Two brass elephants, their trunks raised. An antique crucifix on a stand—it had to be pure gold, and the rubies dewing it were probably worth a pretty penny.

A gleam of blue caught her eye. Selene let out soft breath, brushing past the bed and its hangings. Silk rustled as she reached up, her aching fingers meeting cold glass.

It was the glass apple. It had fallen from her bag in the tunnel under Nikolai's Nest, the passage behind the bed she'd arranged his dead body on.

*Dead body. Well, he's looking pretty live to me.*

At least now she knew this was one of Nikolai's abodes, and Marya had invaded it.

Selene tapped the apple with a fingertip. She could still remember the panic at the bus station, the familiar weight missing from her canvas bag. It was, she reflected, the last time she'd had a wholly human reaction to something. Even though she had been Nichtvren then.

Afterward, simple survival had taken the place of human fear. She'd run as far and as fast as she could, as if something had been chasing her.

*Maybe something was.*

It would be ridiculous...except for the note. *Come home.* And this, waiting here for her.

The storm-tingle in the stillness warned her, so she didn't flinch when he spoke. His breath touched her hair.

"You look lovely."

Selene's fingers curled around the glass apple. The bracelet of pain around her wrist sent a sharp jolt up her arm.

"I did not think you would come. I told *her* you wouldn't. That you cared so little for me, and indeed believed me dead." Still the same voice, soft and inflected a little oddly. He spoke the Merican of her human life, as if he knew what a thorny pleasure it was to hear.

*No to the first. Yes to the last.* She shrugged, silk moving against her skin, her arm up and the glass apple cool against her fevered palm. She would run warm until she metabolized the blood. Then it would be time for more, possibly before she stepped on the transport to take her away from this goddamn town.

Anywhere in the world, now, you could walk into a bar and get a tankard of cloned. A Nichtvren always had money. The biggest change?

Saint City was no longer *home*. Now that she knew he was still alive.

"This has been...educational." She sounded steady enough, even to herself. Her fingers uncurled from the apple. It was the only thing she had left from Danny, but if she left it here, it would be safe. Nikolai would keep it until the dust drifted up over it. "But I've got a transport to catch."

"Unsafe." He stepped closer, and the heat from him told her he'd fed too. Cloned? Or from a willing thrall? Since this had all been a game anyway.

"They don't usually drop paying customers into the sunlight, Nik." It was just the right tone, she congratulated herself. Light, flippant, and with enough distance between them to need a transport to cross it.

She half-turned. He stood too close, and he was staring again. Yes, he had fed—and quite a lot, by the look of it. He was no longer filthy, the clothes were new: jeans and a black sweater, paper-thin but still palpably expensive. She didn't raise her gaze to his face, but the mottled bruising would be going down. His hands were still twisted into claws, but the fingers were crackling as they healed. The glaring wounds in his wrists were filling in, livid where the fresh blood was soaking through ageless tissues.

"Stay." Peremptory command. That, at least, was the same. He was never one to simply ask if he could demand.

She made a little clicking sound, like a mother with an overenthusiastic child. "I have a job to return to. Not to mention a life, Nikolai. Or unlife. Whatever."

"Mercenary." He made a restless movement, a simple flicker, and Selene almost flinched. "Must I pay you for your time?"

A few decades ago, it might have stung. Now, she laughed. "Why bother, when there are so many willing ones around?"

"You are not willing?" He said it like he didn't believe it for a moment.

Of course, he could hear her heart hammering, a Nichtvren's strong irresistible pulse faster than usual because every nerve in her body had tightened. The weakness was back, shortening her breath and turning her to liquid.

Well, if he could be hurtful, she could too. Or at least, she could *try* to hurt him. "When did that ever matter, to you?"

"Always." Another small movement, just a twitch before he restrained himself. "How could you think it would not?"

*Because I remember how you forced me, and how you didn't care if I cried as long as you got what you wanted. Here I am, a Nichtvren just like you wanted me. I even came to take part in this ridiculous little set-piece, whatever it is.* "Goodbye, Nikolai." A single step forward, her hip dropping in case he moved, and she was past him. He was fever-warm, a self-repairing furnace. "Next time, I won't answer."

His hand closed around her bare upper arm, the prickle of his claws a delicate reminder

"Selene." The dark tone that promised trouble.

A bolt of heat lightning crackled through her, each vein with its cargo of fresh cloned lighting up. She inhaled, sharply, the human habit of breathing too strong to break. There was that, of course—her response. A sexwitch's response, to only one man instead of everyone. Was it any better?

"What could I offer you?" His breath touched her cheek. Leaning in, his warmth against the surface of silk and the suddenly-more-responsive canvas of her skin. "The city. Blood. Spectacle. More, if you want it. What will it take?"

*Everything except the one thing I want.* Selene froze, the gnawing in her belly easing for the first time in years.

She had the chance now. She might as well use it. And perhaps, just perhaps, it would hurt him.

Selene turned her head, slowly, shower-damp hair sliding against her shoulders. He watched her from under his mask of bruising, dark eyes glittering. Like a hawk in a cage, perhaps.

Her fingers slid between his as she slid his bruising grip away from her arm. "Come here." And she led him, step by step, to the bed.

IT WAS A new thing, to push him down onto the dusty mattress and slide her hands under his sweater. Hard skin, muscle flickering under its stony surface, perfect and poreless. The shallow dish of his stomach, the angles of the ribs, responded under her fingers. He submitted, his eyes half-lidding and his bruised mouth, flushed with his own feeding, opening just slightly.

He didn't object when she slid her palms down his arms, the sweater's texture alive under her own skin, and pulled his hands up. Spread his arms, as if he was on the cross again. Pushed them down. "Don't move," she whispered. "Your hands stay here."

The slightest approximation of a nod—his chin dipping just a little, his mouth softening even more. There were swiftly-healing wounds all over his torso; she wondered what Marya had done to him.

"Why her?" She leaned down, touched a particularly vivid bruise. His entire body tensed, but he didn't move his arms.

"She was...Grigori's, too. She betrayed me to him, the first time I sought to escape." Nikolai swallowed, hard. "Selene..."

"Ah." Selene kissed the bruise, a butterfly-stroke of lips. Her tongue dipped, tasting; she could smell the blood under the surface and her fangs tingled.

It was actually pleasant. The swimming feedback of sensation echoing between them, the curse now a drug in her veins, her fingers working at his jeans.

*So many things change, but a pair of Levi's is forever.* She caught a laugh in the bottom of her throat; it turned into an inquisitive purr.

"I escaped Grigori." Nikolai's whisper touched the walls. "She did not. And she blamed me for it."

"Mh." She slid the zipper down, one small tooth at a time. "Lift up just a little...there. Good boy. I think that'll do." *Huh. Were you hopeful, Nik? Because I seem to remember you used to like boxer briefs instead of commando.* For a moment she wondered if a zipper would break if a Nichtvren male got something caught in it, and the laughter threatened to spill free.

"Selene—"

She decided to leave the jeans tangled around his knees. "Nikolai, unless I ask you a question, *shut up.*"

He did.

A tongue-touch, just a slight lap, like a kitten. Her tongue was rougher now, the barbs on the surface meant to help with the anticoagulant, meant to keep the blood flowing. Her fangs ached, sensitive razor points, and she toyed with the idea of distending her jaw and *biting*.

It would be a revenge, but not the type she wanted. So, instead, she set herself to learning him again.

He hadn't changed, of course. Still frozen in the same narrow-hipped body, a slim line of dark sparse curls from his bellybutton down, the same long legs and broad shoulders. The glaring welts and jagged lightning-shapes from cuts were flushed, but once she was close enough they weren't ugly. They were simply different, a roadmap of suffering. She played with them while the trembling pushed through him, his arms stretched out and his body making little betraying movements when she hit a sensitive spot.

Was this what it was like, to control someone? Had it been like this for him? Except she'd been truly helpless, and he...was not.

Selene's claws prickled. She ran them up the outside of his thigh, slowly scraping the skin. He actually shook, and a small sound escaped his throat.

Well, now. Wasn't that interesting.

"Your blood in my veins," she whispered. "My curse in yours. Is that what happens when you turn a sexwitch, Nik? I didn't get a chance to ask, before."

"Yessss—" The sibilant turned into a gasp as she moved, sliding snakelike up his body, her knees settling on either side of his hips. "It burns." His throat moved as he swallowed again. "I don't know how you stand it."

"It was worse when I was human. And now it's just...you." Selene considered his face. Eyes closed, mouth slightly open as he breathed in short gasps, the charcoal fans of his eyelashes laying obediently in their proper arc, his hair still damp from washing away the filth of confinement and torture. "It's not every man who wanders along," she whispered against his lips, sipping his breath.

Then she slid herself down, exquisitely slowly, and closed him in her flesh.

Still the same. There was nothing like the first thrust, her body closing itself against the invasion and yet accepting at the same moment. Nikolai's back arched slightly, but he stayed where she'd placed him.

Selene settled into a slow, rocking rhythm. The blood was burning through her, but it was the warm, slowly-rising aura of sex, like oil against her skin, that would feed her now.

Nikolai was actually sweating. It took hard effort to make a Nichtvren perspire; Selene's mouth turned up in a smile and she closed her eyes, her fangs touching her lower lip. His hands blurred up, but her reflexes were just a fraction faster and she caught his wrists, slamming them back down on the bed. Dust rose, and the change of angle made her gasp. His hips tilted up, Selene gasped again. Still-healing bones ground in his wrists as she squeezed, and Nikolai stiffened.

White fire raced through her veins as he bowed upward, his spine arching and a low throaty sound escaping. The bed shook, flesh and Power both quaking, and Selene rode the tide through, energy spilling through her skin as the curse, for the first time since she'd left, fed itself to completion.

It settled into a warm glow. Bones crackled, shifting, and new strength spilled through her entire body. She shuddered, half wishing he'd been able to hold off for longer. But almost a century was a long time, and she had the notion that perhaps he hadn't been using sex to feed for a while.

Her own completion didn't matter. This was about power, and about him.

"There." She opened her eyes, silk sliding as she moved. "You can say *you're welcome*."

"Don't leave." This time the rumble of Power was more definite, and the entire room resounded like the inside of a bell.

Selene sighed. She levered herself aside carefully, the skirt falling down with a whisper. She held his wrists until the last possible moment. It must have hurt, but they were whole and healed now. The rush of Power had restored him to himself, and eased her own hurts. "That's the trouble with you. You're too old. You don't learn a goddamn thing."

He had nothing to say to that. Selene slid off the bed, the silk draping soft and slick around her, and decided to look for some more reasonable clothes.

❧❧

THE TRANSPORT HOVE into sight like a gigantic gray bird, the whine of hover tech settling into Selene's back teeth. Her fangs itched a little, responding to the vibrations. The rain flashed, little jewels sparkling through streetlamp shine, and the wet breeze touched her tangled hair.

She'd found jeans and a T-shirt, and a jacket. The medallion was warm under her shirt, and she had thought of leaving it somewhere...but this way, it couldn't be used to lure her back. The glass apple, perhaps, but that was a different story.

There was another job waiting as soon as she stepped onto the dock in Freetown New Prague. It was a good place to work, especially since the paranormals were driving all the human mercs out. On the other hand, it meant nothing was as easy.

She suspected she didn't want an easy job for a while. Something complex would keep her occupied enough to forget.

Her entire body glowed, her skin fluorescing a little under her clothes. The feeling, she suspected, wouldn't last long. The wanting would settle back into her lower belly, and she would endure it.

Nikolai stepped up to the yellow line beside her. She'd chosen the most shadowed part of the dock, watching the endless flow of humanity as they filtered past.

*Christos, couldn't you leave it alone?* She spoke first, to forestall him. "You don't need to see me off."

"I am not willing to see you off." Quiet, but with an edge. "I have waited, and waited. If you will not stay, I have no choice but to follow."

*Well.* "Does it ever occur to you to just *ask*?"

He was silent for a few heartbeats, digesting this. "Would it matter if I did?"

"It would."

"If I asked you to stay, Selene..."

*How can you be so old and still not understand?* "I would say no, I have a job I'm contracted for. But after that, if you sent me a letter asking me to come back, I would. If you asked me to stay, I think I could manage it." *There. That's as far as I'm going.*

Another long pause. He was strung tight, a sharp hurtful readiness. "Is that all that is necessary?"

"Probably not. You're a petty dictator." She idly calculated the best angle of escape, wondering if she could move quickly enough.

"Do you ever tire of bringing me to my knees?" Lower now, and rough.

*Now there's an idea.* "Do you ever get tired of ordering me around?"

"You will come?" A pause. "If I *ask*?"

*Hallelujah. We've penetrated one of the thickest skulls on earth.* "Yes. If you ask. Not command, or demand, or manipulate. You're going to have to learn this skill. It's going to take you some time."

He obviously didn't think much of the idea. "Selene. Please."

She stepped out into the rain. Soft chill little pinpricks touched her cheeks, her chin. "You know what to do, Nikolai."

"Selene..." As if he'd run out of air. Finally, she'd reached him.

"Don't make me wait too long." She strode through the rain as the transport's upper doors opened. Another good thing about being Nichtvren—she didn't have to wait for boarding.

He was silent behind her. But the words came, laid softly in her brain like a gift, the blood-bond between them pulsing once, silently.

*I will ask.*

"Good," she whispered.

And kept walking.

# ABOUT THE AUTHOR

LILI LIVES IN Vancouver, Washington, with two dogs, two guinea pigs, two cats, two children, and a metric ton of books holding her house together. However, referring to her as "Noah" will likely get you a lecture.

# ALSO BY LILITH SAINTCROW

*The Dante Valentine Series*

*The Jill Kismet Series*

*The Bannon and Clare Series*

*The Strange Angels Series*

*Tales of Beauty and Madness*

*Romances of Arquitaine*

*SquirrelTerror*

*...and many more*